BARBARA TAYLOR BRADFORD

PLAYING THE GAME

St. Martin's Paperbacks

This is a work of fiction. All of the characters, organizations, and events portrayed in this novel are either products of the author's imagination or are used fictitiously.

PLAYING THE GAME

Copyright © 2010 by Beaji Enterprises, Inc.

Cover photograph of woman © Andrea Buso/Gallery Stock. Cover photograph of background wall and center frames © Todd Pearson/Getty Images; upper left frame © Daniel Allan; bottom frame © Viktor Fischer/Alamy.

All rights reserved.

For information address St. Martin's Press, 175 Fifth Avenue, New York, NY 10010.

Library of Congress Catalog Card Number: 2010029215

ISBN: 978-0-312-54686-1

Printed in the United States of America

St. Martin's Press hardcover edition / October 2010
St. Martin's Paperbacks International edition / March 2011

St. Martin's Paperbacks are published by St. Martin's Press, 175 Fifth Avenue, New York, NY 10010.

10 9 8 7 6 5 4 3 2 1

For Bob,
with my love

Contents

Prologue

✳

LONDON,
MARCH 2007

*

Annette Remmington sat at her desk staring across the room at the painting, or rather at the photographic blow-up of the painting. It was propped up on the credenza, leaning against the wall, and the ceiling light, carefully angled, brought it into focus.

Her marvelous painting. Her masterpiece. Her Rembrandt. Well, not exactly hers anymore, for it now belonged to someone else, the anonymous buyer who had bid for it over the phone, had won it for the staggering price of twenty million pounds. The highest price ever paid for a work by the famous Dutch artist.

What would *he* feel if he were alive? Would he have experienced the same thrill she had at the auction, as the price had risen and risen to that final staggering amount? Rembrandt had become something of a recluse when the painting had been finished in 1657, yet this *was* the period he had created some of his greatest masterpieces; he had been unfashionable then. She smiled inwardly. He was hardly unfashionable now.

It was gone, hanging on somebody else's wall, and all she had was the photographic blow-up of the Rembrandt. Anyway, it had never actually been hers. She had merely been custodian of it for a while. On the other hand, she had brought it back to life—by having it cleaned and restored. And singing about it; singing its praises to the world. That's what she thought she had done anyway. Others said, rather mean-spiritedly, that she had hyped it to death.

Annette laughed out loud at the thought. *No, not death. She had given it a new life.* The Rembrandt had not been seen in public for over fifty years, hidden away in the dusty art collection of a man who perhaps no longer appreciated it. And she had put it on view and then sold it for an incredible amount of money and at a time in the economy when art prices had dropped.

Rising, she walked across the room, stood admiring the photographic blow-up for several minutes. The portrait of the woman was so lifelike Annette felt that if she reached out to touch the woman's hand her fingers would alight not on canvas but on real flesh. That was part of Rembrandt's genius.

Walking back to her desk, Annette remembered what her sister had said the other day. Laurie called the Rembrandt the painting which had changed Annette's life, and there was a certain truth in this statement, in that she had suddenly become the new star in the art world. At least for the moment.

There had been so much publicity about her auction of the Rembrandt it had been extraordinary. Even her husband, Marius, had been taken aback at the fuss, the attention given to her. He, a seasoned hand in the business, regarded as one of the great art experts and dealers, had been startled by the acclaim she had received.

Marius had a fine reputation, as did so many other dealers. Yet it was to *her* that Christopher Delaware had come, seeking her out because he remembered her from a social occasion over a year ago now, when they had discussed art. That long chat had centered on her areas of expertise—Impressionist and Post-Impressionist paintings and, at the other end of the art spectrum, Old Masters. He had been keen to listen to her, to learn from her that evening.

And so he had arrived at this office one day, many months ago now, asking for her help. He had told her about his ancient uncle, a bachelor, who had recently died and left him everything, including an art collection with a Rembrandt in it. Could she, would she, take him on as a client? She had, and the rest was history. The auction had taken place a few nights ago and the art world had collectively gasped when the hammer had come down on the final bid of twenty million pounds. The audience was stunned. So was she.

Her sister had a favorite saying, which was "God protects you," and of course Laurie could not resist saying this when she heard about Christopher Delaware's first visit to her Bond Street office.

Recalling that now, Annette smiled faintly. In her mind, it was Marius who protected her. No, perhaps *guided her* was a better phrase to use. The faint smile flickered again. There were those who might say he controlled her, because that was what they believed.

Annette opened the folder on her desk and looked at the seating plans for the party tonight. It was her husband's sixtieth birthday and she had been planning the event for months; it had taken her weeks to seat their guests appropriately, with those she thought they would want to be with, and at the right table. Marius had called it a work of art the other day, when he had gone over it with her for the final check and a few last-minute changes.

The party was very meaningful to him, and she had done everything she could to make sure it would be special. He had taught her never to leave anything to chance, whatever it was she was planning. She had always listened to him, and learned; and she had left nothing to chance in this instance either. It was being held in the ballroom of the Dorchester Hotel on Park Lane, and anybody who was anybody had been invited, whether they were from the art world, society, or show business. It was an international crowd.

Because her Rembrandt auction had been such a stupendous success, Marius had insisted that they turn the party into what he called "a double-headed event." It would no longer celebrate only his birthday but the success of her auction as well. It didn't change anything. The overall plan for the party remained exactly the same, much to Annette's relief. Except that now he would get up and toast her and tell the world how clever she was.

Her sudden jump from relative obscurity in the art world to the big-time league was nothing short of miraculous, and no one was more surprised than she. Marius had taken it in his stride, and when she had said how startled she was by her success, after the auction was over, he had been swift to answer her, exclaiming, "But not I. I knew you would do something spectacular one day." And then he had suggested they give the party a new twist . . .

Her private line rang, and she reached out to pick up the red phone. "Hello?"

"Annette, it's Malcolm. Do you have a minute?"

"Of course I do. Is everything all right?"

"Absolutely. I just wondered if I could go over the birth-day toast I'll be making to Marius tonight. If you could listen now, it would be helpful."

"I can, and I'm sure anything you've prepared will be right on the mark." She laughed. "After all, you're one of Marius's favorite protégés, and you own his beloved Remmington Gallery. No one knows him better than you."

"Except for you," Malcolm Stevens shot back, chuckling, then swiftly went on, "so here goes." He began to read the words he had written about a man he admired, even revered. He had kept the accolades to a minimum, knowing Marius would squirm at an extravagance of hyperbole, but had included some hilarious stories and a few little digs which were amusing and made Annette laugh out loud.

When he finished he said, "And that's about it, unless I can come up with a few appropriate ad-libs at the last minute."

"You've done a great job, Malcolm! He's going to chuckle, be amused by some of it. You know he's got a fantastic sense of humor."

"If you approve, then that's it. I'm going to put it in my pocket until tonight. Listen, just one other thing. I had a rather strange phone call earlier today." Malcolm cleared his throat. "From a private detective looking for a woman called Hilda Crump, who he said used to work at the Remmington Gallery. About twenty years ago. He asked if we had an ad-dress for her. Apparently he has a client who wants to get in touch with her. Did *you* ever know someone called Hilda Crump?"

"No, I didn't," Annette responded, clutching the phone tighter.

"But if I recall correctly, you *did* work for Marius, didn't you? When he first opened the Remmington Gallery."

"Yes, that's true. But I didn't know anyone called Hilda Crump. Anyway, when Marius sold the gallery to you ten years ago I'm quite certain he put all of the files on the computer."

"Yes, he did, and there's no mention of a Hilda Crump anywhere. But this chap was so . . . well, so *insistent*, I just had to ask you."

"Sorry, Malcolm, I can't be of help."

"So be it then. No problem. Thanks for listening to the toast, and I'll see you this evening. With bells on. And I know we'll have the most marvelous time."

"That we will, Malcolm," she answered, and hung up.

For a moment Annette Remmington sat with her hand resting on the red phone, frowning. She was puzzled. Who was looking for Hilda? And why? What did they want? She had no answers for herself, but she did know one thing. She would never betray Hilda. Years ago she had promised not to divulge her whereabouts, and *she* never broke the promises she made.

Annette leaned back in the chair and closed her eyes, sinking down into the past, thinking of those early years, of all the terrible things she had buried deep because she did not want to remember them. She shivered, and goose flesh sprung up on her arms. She felt a trickle of fear run through her. So many secrets, so much to hide . . .

Part One

※

A REMARKABLE WOMAN

There is that law of life, so cruel
and so just—that one must grow,
or else pay more for remaining the same.

Norman Mailer, *The Deer Park* (1955)

Chapter One

Much later that same day, Annette Remmington stood in front of the long mirrored door in her dressing room, staring at her reflection but not seeing herself.

She was not focused on her image at this moment but on the small knot of anxiety which had settled in her stomach since she had returned home. She could visualize it quite easily. . . . It was the size of a pea but as heavy as a lead pellet.

Unexpectedly, she felt slightly dizzy and reached out a hand, steadied herself against the dressing table. After taking several deep breaths, she managed to get her suddenly swimming senses under control. Now she looked at her full image objectively, nodded approvingly at what she saw, and chided herself for being so ridiculous.

The mention of Hilda Crump had unsettled her earlier in the day, and the call from Malcolm had been nagging at her all afternoon. But her troubles with Hilda Crump had happened long ago, and Hilda had moved on, and out of her life. The past was the past and she mustn't let it come back to haunt her in this silly way.

I must put her out of my mind. And the past. It's gone. I must focus on now. The present. And the future. I've always pigeonholed things and I have to do that again. Immediately. Hilda must go back into her pigeonhole and remain there. She is no longer part of my life and therefore unimportant.

She can't hurt me. No one can hurt me. And I can't afford to waste time like this, reflecting on the past, a past I cannot change.

I've started a new phase of my life with the success of the auction. I pulled it off and I can pull it off again. Christopher Delaware doesn't have another Rembrandt, but he does have some fine paintings and I can auction them off the same way. Marius told me the sky's the limit, and he's right, but will he let me go to the limit? He always wants to be in control of everything. And me. I know how to handle him now after all these years. So I'll manage. I always have. I think I'll do my next auction in New York. It would be profitable. I've got good clients there—

"Are you ready, darling?"

She swung around. "Yes, I am," she answered at once, forcing a smile for her husband, who was walking across the dressing room. Surreptitiously, she glanced at the clock on the dressing table. It was just five-thirty. And of course he was ready on time, punctual as always.

"You're upset," he said, drawing to a standstill next to her, peering into her face.

"No, I'm not, not at all," she answered, and immediately wished she hadn't sounded so defensive.

"Yes, you are, Annette," he insisted in his usual firm manner. "Look at yourself in the mirror. You're only wearing one earring."

Startled, she immediately swung to the mirror. Surprise flickered. God, he was right! As usual. Where was the other one? She spotted it on the dressing table, snatched it up, quickly put it on. "I went to get my wedding ring from the bedside table, where I'd left it. I just became distracted, that's all, really." She felt flustered all of a sudden. He stood staring at her intently and she found his penetrating stare unnerving. Damn, she thought, he's going to pick on me all night, but she took hold of herself firmly, not wanting to be rattled.

Annette now offered him a warm smile. "You look very handsome tonight, Marius, and the new dinner jacket is fabulous." Stepping closer to him, she stood on tiptoe, kissed his cheek. "Happy birthday again, darling, and I do hope you're going to enjoy your party."

Relaxing his rigid stance, smiling in return, he said in a lighter tone, "I know I will, and let us not forget it's your party, too, my darling girl. We're celebrating your amazing success." His black eyes sparkled as they rested on her, and approvingly so.

Annette laughed.

Taking hold of her arm possessively, he brought her closer to him, wrapped his arms around her. "I love you very much, you know, darling," he said before releasing her. Holding her at arm's length, he added, as his eyes swept over her, "You look very beautiful, you really do."

"Well, thank you, but I think I've looked better," she murmured, meaning this.

Shaking his head, half smiling, he led her out into the corridor, wondering why she constantly found it hard to accept a compliment gracefully. He said, "We'd better go. I don't want any of our guests to arrive before we do. We can't be late."

Stay calm, she told herself. And keep cool.

"Wow!" Malcolm Stevens exclaimed, literally gaping at Annette, astonishment mingled with admiration flashing across his face. "*Oh, wow!*" he said again, more emphatically, in genuine awe. "You look fantastic, absolutely bloody marvelous." It was quite apparent he meant every word.

Her blue eyes sparkling, filling with laughter, Annette looked both pleased and amused by Malcolm's reaction to her appearance.

She stood with Marius in the long reception room which adjoined the Dorchester ballroom, and she leaned forward, kissed Malcolm on the cheek, and thanked him.

As she stepped back, his glance swept over her once more, taking in the stunning ice-blue strapless gown, worn with a matching satin stole lined with scarlet silk. That was the surprising touch, the brilliant red against the cool blue, plus the huge cabochon ruby earrings hanging from her ears, echoing the vibrant color of the silk.

Annette Remmington was elegance personified. Her blond hair, usually worn loose, was swept back from her face, wound up into a chignon at the back of her head. It suddenly struck him that her eyes looked bluer than ever tonight; perhaps it was the evening gown that heightened their color.

Gripping Marius's outstretched hand, Malcolm went on, "And you don't look half bad yourself! In fact, the two of you are so glamorous you'll put all your guests to shame."

Marius chuckled. "I'm afraid you haven't seen anything yet. Wait until the show business crowd arrive. They're much more glamorous than we are. But thanks for the compliments, Malcolm. And welcome. We're very glad you're here."

Now turning to his wife, Marius shook his head and chided lightly, "I told you how beautiful you looked, but you didn't believe me. Now that you've just witnessed Malcolm's stunned reaction, you must know I'm right."

"I did believe you," she protested, slipping her arm through his, leaning against him. "You're always right."

Clearing his throat, Malcolm interjected, "It's great to be here, and thanks for having me, but now I think I'd better move on, so you can greet your other guests. See you later."

Marius nodded, immediately turned around, and stretched out his hand to welcome some of the newly arriving guests streaming through the door.

Malcolm slipped away.

Moving down the room, he took a glass of champagne from a passing waiter and walked around, mingling with the crowd. He spoke to a few people he knew, then positioned himself near a pillar, leaning against it and watching the show unfold.

And quite a show it was. He spotted two beautiful American movie stars with their husbands, done up to the nines and dripping diamonds from every pore; a famous, recently knighted writer of literary fiction; a controversial politician with his busty wife; a duchess renowned for her young lovers;

and quite a few old friends and acquaintances, as well as a number of other art dealers.

The world and his wife, he thought. Everyone's here. And why not? When Marius gives a party on this scale, he usually pulls out all the stops. That is why everybody wants to be invited.

Actually it was Annette's party this evening. She had long planned it for Marius's sixtieth, and she had put a lot of time and effort into it. Just the way Marius had taught her. That was his way. He tended to be a teacher by nature.

Certainly Marius had been *his* teacher, and mentor, friend, and colleague as well. Their association had lasted a long time, and yet Marius didn't seem a day older than when they had met fifteen years ago. He stared down the length of the room, focused on him, thinking that he looked especially well this evening. Tall, slender, as immaculately dressed as ever, wearing an impeccably tailored dinner jacket no doubt from his favorite Savile Row tailor. His mane of silver hair gleamed above his lightly tanned face; Marius was forever popping off somewhere to catch the sun, and the tan gave him a youthful look. But it was his hair that Malcolm envied, and it was his hair, of course, that had inspired his nickname: the Silver Fox, they called him. Although he and a few others knew that it also referred to Marius's nature. He was considered to be decidedly foxy by some friends, so-called.

Malcolm had gone to work for Marius fifteen years ago, when he was twenty-seven, had been thrilled to be one of the team at the Remmington Gallery in St. James's. When Marius decided to sell the gallery ten years ago, Malcolm had borrowed the money from his father in order to buy it. He had kept up its fine reputation and garnered many new clients, and Marius said he was proud of him, was forever praising him for upholding the great tradition of the Remmington.

Wanting a less hectic life, Marius had taken offices in Mayfair and become an art consultant and private dealer with only a handful of steady and very rich clients. They had remained close, and Malcolm was an admirer of the older man.

Not everyone felt the same way he did. There were those who bad-mouthed Marius Remmington. They said he was arrogant, mercurial, temperamental, driven, and something of a manipulator. But there were lots of people in this world who loved to carp. Malcolm knew *that* only too well.

There had been gossip about the Remmingtons for as long as he could remember. In his opinion it was because they attracted attention, caused resentment and jealousy. Talented, socially acceptable, upwardly mobile, and highly successful, they were quite a remarkable couple. Reasons enough for tongues to wag. And wag they did.

Then there was the difference in their ages. Marius was twenty years older than Annette . . . sixty to her thirty-nine. But she would be forty in June, and the twenty-year gap between them didn't seem so startling now. But once it had, when she was eighteen and he was thirty-eight, and something of a man about town, considered a bit of a roué. Cradle-snatcher, he had been called, and worse.

There was mystery, so-called, surrounding Annette's background. No one really knew where she had sprung from. Except, of course, for the Marius Mafia, who bragged they knew. His mafia, so-called, was a cadre of young men who constantly surrounded him, whom he called his protégés, which is exactly what they were. Young men who'd been singled out for their talent, who had worked for Marius at some time, or still did, who were loyal, devoted, and forever at his beck and call. They enjoyed being around him because something was always happening. It seemed to Malcolm that there was a constant show going on. . . . Famous people, people in the know and in the news, gravitated to Marius. That was an essential part of his success as an art dealer, that charisma of his, the gregariousness, the bucketsful of charm and the clever way he had of pulling everyone into his orbit.

Malcolm was one of Marius's favorites and he had received special treatment from the very beginning. And he knew all about Annette, or at least he thought he did. The Marius Mafia had told him about Annette.

Seemingly she had come to London from some Northern city, he wasn't sure which, to study art. But there was not enough talent to lift her up into the stratosphere of genius which equaled eventual fame. Good-looking. But the looks were obscured by her hesitant manner, according to some of the Marius Mafia; it was a sort of diffidence, they said. Blond, blue-eyed, slender as a reed, and exceedingly bright. But ordinary. That was the way they had described her to him. He himself had not known her then.

Not so ordinary now, though, Malcolm thought, his eyes settling on her. It was an elegant creature who stood there. Not the most beautiful woman in the world, but good-looking, well put together whatever the occasion, and the current golden girl in the art world. Her auction of the Rembrandt had assured her a place in the front row, had given her art consultancy business a big boost. . . .

"What are you doing here all alone, Malcolm?" a familiar voice exclaimed.

Swinging around, Malcolm grinned. "Watching the show and having a bit of the old bubbly. How about you, David? And where's Meg?"

His old friend David Oldfield shook his head. "Still in New York. On business. I'm solo tonight." Reaching into his pocket, David pulled out a small envelope, looked inside, and said, "I'm at table ten. What about you?"

"The same. I have a feeling it's Marius's table. Come on, let's try and get to the bar. I'd like a vodka."

"Good idea," David responded, and together they struggled through the throng. Once they had each secured a Grey Goose on the rocks, they went off into a quiet corner. Clinking glasses, they both said cheers in unison, and David asked, "Is it true that Christopher Delaware inherited a lot of really great art from that uncle of his? And that Annette's going to be representing him?"

Malcolm said in an even tone, "I haven't heard about any great art, other than the Rembrandt. But I know he's Annette's client. Oh, look, there's Johnny Davenport. He's bound to know. Let's go and talk to him."

* * *

"Malcolm! Malcolm!"

He heard a woman's voice calling his name. Trying to be heard above the clamor. Swinging his head, he spotted her at once. An old friend. It was Margaret Mellor, the editor of the best art magazine in Europe called, very simply, *ART*. She was waving to him.

Catching hold of David's arm, he said, "Will you excuse me for a moment? Margaret Mellor's beckoning to me. Go ahead, chat with Johnny. I'll join you both shortly."

"No problem." David pushed ahead, moving adroitly between people, edging his way through.

Malcolm went in the opposite direction, toward his friend. When he finally reached her he grinned. "I almost didn't hear you above the din."

"It's bedlam. I was just with Annette. She wants us to go and see the ballroom before it fills up with guests. She says it's charming."

"Then let's go now, before we get trapped in this corner. The place is suddenly milling with old friends and colleagues. Plus loads of photographers, I notice." He frowned.

"Don't tell *me*! The press is swarming all over the place!"

Malcolm sighed. "That's Marius. He never does things by half and he does love the media. As far as he's concerned, the more the merrier."

"He's a glutton for punishment." She sounded sarcastic.

Malcolm laughed. That was Margaret. Spot on with her comments. He put an arm around her shoulders, guided her through the crush. Behind them, flashbulbs were already popping; it seemed to him that the crowd was swelling, getting bigger by the second. How many people had they invited? The whole world, he decided, and hoped the huge crowd wouldn't ultimately spoil the event. Why do I worry? *She* knows what she's doing, even if he doesn't, sometimes. *Marius*. Such an enigma.

Finally, Malcolm was pushing open the door into the ballroom. Instantly, a waiter confronted them. "I'm very sorry, but you can't come in. Mrs. Remmington doesn't want anyone in here for another half hour. She was very precise." Polite but determined.

"Yes, we know. Mrs. Remmington sent us to see the ballroom before it fills up. I'm Margaret Mellor of *ART* magazine, and this is Mr. Stevens, a colleague and friend of Mrs. Remmington's."

The waiter inclined his head but didn't budge, blocking their way. Still determined—to do his duty and keep them out.

"My chief photographer, Josh Brady, was here earlier," Margaret added. "Taking pictures for the magazine. You must be Frank Lancel. Mrs. Remmington told me to speak to you." Charm, a warm smile. Her tools.

"Yes, I'm Frank," the waiter answered, relaxing, but only slightly. "And I did help Mr. Brady a while ago, when he was taking his shots. So please come in, look around. I have to stay here at the door. Stand guard. Mrs. Remmington's instructions." He sounded droll.

"She explained that," Margaret answered. Taking hold of Malcolm's hand, she led him forward. The two of them finally stood at the edge of the ballroom floor near the orchestra stand, their eyes sweeping around the room with interest and anticipation.

They were both taken aback by the unique beauty and magical effect Annette had created. The room was a sea of pale green, that peculiar pale green with a hint of gray so often found in the interiors of French châteaux, which seems to create a misty look. This pale-green silk rippled down the walls from the ceiling to the floor, and was repeated for the tablecloths, napkins, and chair seats.

But what was so unusual and wonderful about the setting were the green dendrobium orchids with pink centers. These were massed in banks in front of mirrored folding screens and also stood on mirrored consoles, Venetian-style, placed against the green walls. There were literally hundreds of orchid plants in pale celadon-green pots, and those banked in front of the mirrored screens instantly appeared to be twice the quantity because of their reflections. Centerpieces on the tables were crystal bowls filled with stems of green orchids, surrounded by lots of votive lights. Tall crystal candlesticks holding tall white tapers were on either side of the bowls of orchids. Everything glistened and sparkled in the candlelight . . . the crystal wine goblets and silverware, the silver service plates.

The two of them stood there for a few minutes longer, endeavoring to take everything in. Then Margaret said slowly, "It's almost ethereal, dreamlike. What an effect Annette has created. . . . It's a garden . . . a garden of orchids. How clever."

Malcolm turned to her and exclaimed, "Yes, it is. And you can be sure of one thing. It's going to knock everybody's socks off."

Chapter Two

Marius was happy.

Annette could tell from the expression on his face. He was beaming, relaxed, leaning back in his chair at the head of the table positioned directly opposite hers. They faced each other, were in each other's line of vision, could communicate, at least visually, whenever they wanted.

The party was a success. She knew that even though it was only halfway through. There had been a feeling of excitement right from the beginning of the evening. During the cocktail period, a trio played low music in the background, champagne and wine flowed, there was an open bar for other drinks, and an array of delicious canapes was passed around, nonstop, by the busy waiters.

Now, in the ballroom, she was feeling an enormous surge of energy and vitality amongst the guests. They were getting up to dance to the popular music, and she glanced around, noted the hilarity, heard the laughter and the high-voltage babble of conversation. It seemed to her that everyone was enjoying themselves, having a great time.

Marius caught her eye and got up, walked over to her table. A moment later he was escorting her out onto the dance floor.

Taking her in his arms, he looked down at her and smiled, his black eyes warm, loving. "You've pulled it off again," he murmured. "It's a fabulous party. Everyone's enjoying it immensely. Are you?"

They began to move around the edge of the dance floor. She cocked her head and looked up at him, an amused smile in her eyes. "You've always told me that a hostess who enjoys her own party isn't being a good hostess."

Marius burst out laughing. "Touché, Mrs. Remmington. But in that instance, I was actually referring to parties given at one's home. Not in a public place. So *are* you?"

"As a matter of fact, I am. I was a bit uptight at first, when we came into the ballroom, but then I noticed that everyone quickly found their seats, looked happy where they were sitting. Also they'd enjoyed themselves during cocktails, so they were in the right frame of mind."

"Very true. Well oiled. I didn't see one glum face. But I must admit I did see a lot of astonished faces when they began to realize they were in the middle of an orchid garden." He squeezed her hand. "The setting is a triumph, darling. You were inspired."

"I'm glad you like it," was all she said as she moved closer to him, following him as he moved smoothly away from the edge, across the floor to the middle of the room. He was a good dancer, easy to follow, and she found herself relaxing even more, enjoying dancing with him. Eventually she became aware that all eyes were on them, and she smiled inwardly. She was proud of Marius, proud to be married to him, and also, deep down inside, proud of herself, proud of her hugely successful auction. The Rembrandt *had* changed her life. And she was glad of that.

She didn't stop dancing for the next half hour. When she was back at her table, Malcolm came and claimed her, then David Oldfield, followed by Johnny Davenport, all pals of long standing who had worked for Marius, were part of the Marius Mafia. And then unexpectedly Christopher Delaware was tapping Johnny on the shoulder, cutting in. This surprised her. Christopher was rather shy, reticent, and certainly not given to bold moves.

They glided around the floor in silence for a moment or

two, and then he said, "The room looks stunning. It reminds me of *A Midsummer Night's Dream*, or rather, I should say *a scene* from the play. It's all this grayish green, I suppose, the misty feeling it creates, and the orchids . . . a *forest* of orchids. . . . It's magical. You created something truly unique. Oh, and what about the tall mirrored screens? Brilliant. How did you think of those?"

"The Hall of Mirrors at Versailles sprang to mind, and thank you for your compliments. But tell me, if this is the play, where are Oberon and Titania, king and queen of the fairies? And Puck and Bottom? If this really were *A Midsummer Night's Dream*, they would definitely be here, you know."

He laughed. "They're around somewhere, although I haven't actually seen them yet. However, Lysander, Hermia, and Demetrius are here and—" Abruptly he stopped, cut himself off.

Annette stared at him, frowning, and then looked over his shoulder into the distance, wondering what he meant, although she believed she had a good idea.

Changing the subject swiftly, with a certain adroitness, Christopher said, "You are coming to Kent on Saturday, aren't you? To make the final selections for the next auction."

"Of course I am. I would have told you otherwise. I think we'll have the auction in New York, by the way. I'm certain a number of important collectors will be interested in some of the Impressionists, and several museums as well. Possibly the Metropolitan."

"I've never been to New York!" he exclaimed. He was suddenly excited. "I hope you'll show me around when we're there. When are you planning to do this? Have the auction, I mean? When would we go?"

"That depends on you to a certain extent, Christopher. I think we must analyze everything on Saturday. First, you have to tell me which paintings you would be willing to put up for auction, then we have to study their condition, to ascertain whether they need cleaning, restoring, or new frames, that sort of thing, and I have to really focus on what's happening in New York . . . other art auctions, gallery shows coming up, that kind of thing. I want this to be *big*. Bigger than the Rembrandt auction, actually."

"Oh, my God, that sounds fantastic." A pause. Then, "Will Marius be coming with us to New York?"

She stared at him again. Intently. She said, noncommittally, "I don't know. He has his own art business, as you're well aware, and I have mine. We're quite separate entities. However, he might be there because of his own work." She shrugged. "I can't say whether he'll be in New York or not. Why?"

"I just wondered," Christopher muttered, and held her a little more tightly, brought her closer, although she wasn't too surprised by this. Vaguely, she had sensed he had a crush on her for some time now. She wasn't troubled by it because she rarely saw him, and could handle it anyway. He was young, only twenty-three. But to bring up the love triangle among Lysander, Hermia, and Demetrius, characters in a Shakespearean comedy, was somewhat pointed. Still, it amused her. "We'll just play that by ear. If Marius does happen to be there, he'll be helpful."

"Yes, yes, I understand," he said quickly, having picked up on something, she wasn't exactly sure what. Her tone, perhaps?

Now it was her turn to change the subject. "What time do you want me to get there on Saturday?"

"That's up to you, Annette. Ten? Eleven? Whatever time you want to arrive is all right by me. I was hoping you would be able to stay to lunch." A blond brow lifted.

She smiled at him. "Lunch would be lovely, especially since I'm planning to be there all day. We've a lot of work to do."

His face instantly brightened. He gazed at her. "Oh good, very good, and I'll try to be as helpful as possible with the collection, decisive."

She merely smiled at him again, made no further comment.

* * *

Annette had just returned to her seat at the table when Marius caught her eye. He glanced in the direction of the podium and nodded.

She understood what he meant immediately. He was going to go up there within a few minutes, say nice things about her, and congratulate her. Once he was finished she would thank him and invite Malcolm to join them, to come up and make the birthday toast.

After this the birthday cake would be wheeled in, the orchestra would play "Happy Birthday," and Marius would cut the cake. The plan had been made yesterday and it was all very straightforward.

But she was taken aback when Marius rose almost immediately and headed in the direction of the band. A moment later Malcolm was at her side along with David Oldfield, and the three of them followed Marius, stood with him to one side of the band.

When the last song finished, there was a loud drumroll, and everyone left the dance floor and went back to their tables. Another drumroll echoed as David walked over to the podium and picked up the mike. "Good evening, everyone, and welcome. Now, please don't get worried. This is not going to be an hour of speeches. No, not at all. Neither Annette nor Marius wanted that. However, there will be a few words from Marius before he cuts his birthday cake."

There was a round of applause when Marius stepped forward. He went to the podium to join David, who handed him the mike.

"I want to thank you all for coming," Marius began. "I'm thrilled and flattered to see you all here tonight at my sixtieth . . . so many good friends and colleagues. But this is not simply a birthday party for me, but a celebration of Annette as well. The other day I decided it must be a double-headed event; I felt my wife should share it with me. Because I believe she deserves to be honored . . . for conducting one of the greatest art auctions ever held. Her sale of the lost Rembrandt was extraordinary, and *she* is extraordinary. In every way . . . a wonderfully talented painter, an art consultant of enormous expertise, a dealer par excellence, and for a number of years my right hand when I still owned the Remmington Gallery. Altogether a unique woman."

Marius paused, looked across at Annette, and said, "Come and join me, darling."

She did so. Putting an arm around her, he said, "Congratulations, Annette. You really pulled off a big one, and have now entered the big league of art dealers." He laughed. "I suppose I could say you're now one of my competitors. But why not? I love it, and I love you."

A waiter brought glasses of champagne. "Here's to you, Mrs. Remmington," Marius toasted.

There was a burst of applause and Annette kissed him on his cheek, and then just stood there holding her glass, smiling, enjoying for a moment being in the limelight. And then unexpectedly she felt that small knot inside her stomach, and the lead pellet of anxiety lodged there once again. She managed to keep the smile on her face as she thanked the guests, thanked Marius once more for his lovely words, and then introduced Malcolm Stevens.

Taking hold of Marius's hand, she led him to one side so that Malcolm could take over. He was witty, clever, insightful, serious, and cheeky by turn. He had everyone laughing within seconds as he drew a verbal portrait of a man he obviously admired and cared about, and whom he truly understood, and who would not be troubled by his irreverence.

The audience loved Malcolm and his words, and there was much laughter and applause, and at times a few whistles, hoots, and cat calls. Hilarity prevailed, as Malcolm had intended.

Marius loved Malcolm's speech as much as everyone else, and he came over with Annette to stand with him when a waiter rolled in a table. Standing in the middle was a giant birthday cake, and sixty candle flames fluttered on top of it as the waiter pushed the table across the ballroom.

Stepping forward, Marius picked up the cake knife and stared out at their guests, his face creased with laughter. He blew out all the candles and plunged the knife into the cake.

At this moment the orchestra began to play; the entire ballroom began to sing "Happy Birthday." And everyone raised their glasses to Marius.

Annette joined in, but she suddenly felt her throat constricting. Thoughts of that phone call about Hilda Crump intruded. What *was* that about? That name from her youth was linked to trouble in Annette's mind, and she shivered as her past loomed large. You never escaped your past, did you? Inevitably, it came back to haunt you. The past was immutable.

Chapter Three

✳

She went to see her sister on Friday morning. She usually spent part of Saturday with her, but this week she was going to Kent to make decisions about Christopher Delaware's paintings and the auction of them.

Laurie was waiting for her, full of smiles and eagerness, happy to see her. As she usually was. There wasn't a day when Laurie hadn't welcomed her with a loving, wide-open heart and open arms, her pleasure to be with Annette reflected on her face. *Laurie.* The real beauty in the family, with her green eyes and golden-red hair. Laurie, who had wanted to be an actress when she was a child and had been cheated of the chance.

The two of them sat together in front of the fire, in Laurie's den in her flat in Chesham Place, just around the corner from their home in Eaton Square. It pleased Laurie that she and Marius lived nearby, because it gave her a sense of security; Annette felt the same. If ever Laurie needed her urgently or in any kind of emergency, she could be there within minutes on foot.

Almost immediately she told her sister about the phone call from Malcolm Stevens earlier that week, and how he had brought up the name of Hilda Crump.

Laurie was focused on her, listening, her face calm, the expression in her intelligent eyes changing ever so slightly by the time Annette finished.

There was a small silence, and Annette realized Laurie was running everything through her mind in that analytical way she had. Finally Laurie said softly, "I hope you're not worrying about this."

"I have been. Well, a little bit. It was such a jolt, hearing that name, out of the blue, and I couldn't help wondering who could possibly be looking for Hilda Crump."

"Yes. *Who?* Yes, indeed, *who*? And also *why*? But listen, it doesn't really matter. Hilda went away years ago, she'll never be found, not unless you break the promise you made. You're not going to do that, are you?"

"No, I'm not. Obviously."

"*We'll* never know who's looking for her anyway, not unless the private detective informs Malcolm, and he then tells us. But whoever it is doesn't matter. Hilda's not available and we can't give anybody any information."

"But we were so involved with her, we were privy to so much."

"Only you and I know that, and it happened long ago. Over twenty years, Annette. Believe me, it doesn't matter."

Annette leaned back in the chair, staring at her younger sister. "If that's the case, all right."

"There's no question in my mind. Just please stop worrying, because if you don't I'll start worrying about you." Laurie laughed. "Now, please tell me more about the party. On the phone you've been awfully sketchy. I'm longing to hear everything." She meant this, eagerness reflected in her eyes.

Annette said, "I wish you'd been there, enjoyed it with us, Laurie. I can't understand why you were so adamant about not coming, and neither can Marius. He wanted you to be with us as much as I did."

"In this? In this wheelchair? Don't be silly. I'd have been a useless encumbrance. *An inconvenience.*"

"Don't say that! You're none of those things. We really did hope you'd change your mind, that you would join us, and you know I never lie to you."

"I'm sorry, don't get upset. And I do know how sincere you were about my coming. But I see things differently than you at times, Annette. I didn't want to be a burden. And look, I didn't want you to have questions to answer later. About me. People asking you why I was in a wheelchair, et cetera, et cetera. All that nonsense. I've told you before, you don't need a cripple hanging on to your apron strings—"

"Don't say that, you know how I hate you to say that!" Annette exclaimed, her voice rising.

"But I *am* a cripple, no two ways about it. I was in a bad car crash and now I'm a paraplegic."

"You've lost the use of your legs, yes, but you survived. The others died, and you're still a beautiful woman. Intelligent, charming, and clever, and you are *not* an embarrassment to me. Nor to Marius. Besides, you've been with us on many occasions with friends and—"

"Very close friends," Laurie interjected.

Annette continued, "And there's never been any problem."

"That's quite true. The birthday party was different, though. You'd invited two hundred people, and they'd all accepted. I knew it would be a heavy-duty evening for you."

"I would have put you at my table, or with Marius, and you know so many of our close friends, like Malcolm and David, Johnny Davenport. You'd have been perfectly fine."

Laurie smiled. "I know. Don't go on about it. Please. Look, I preferred not to come." Laurie made a face. "It would have been quite an effort for me, actually."

"Are you all right? You're not feeling ill, are you?"

"No, I'm not ill. Listen, it would have been a bit tough for me, that's all, the crowds, lots of people I don't know." She gave her sister another loving smile, her eyes reassuring. Laurie had not gone because she had not wanted to be a reminder of the bad days, not on this particularly special night in Annette's life. But then a name from the past had done that. Unfortunately. Taking a deep breath, Laurie said, "Please tell me about the party. And don't you dare miss out one detail."

There were not many people about as Annette walked next to Laurie in the motorized wheelchair, crossing Eaton

Square, making for her flat on the far corner. But then it was cold, breezy, a typical early March day, with a hint of rain in the air. People stayed home on days like this.

They were moving along at a fairly quick pace, both wanting to get inside, into the warmth. She glanced up at one moment and was startled to see that the sky had changed in the last hour she had been at her sister's flat. It had become a deeper, brighter blue.

"We've suddenly got a Renoir sky," she exclaimed, glancing at her sister. "It was pale, almost gray, earlier."

Laurie lifted her eyes and nodded. "Yes, it is that lovely blue he used for his own skies and bodies of water, and frequently for the dresses he painted on his incomparable women." Swiveling her head, she looked up at Annette and smiled. "Only you would call it a Renoir sky."

"I know. But then he is my favorite Impressionist."

"And mine. And of course Rembrandt's a favorite now! Let's face it, he's a painter who has been lucky for you. Does Christopher Delaware have any more tucked away in his house?"

"If only." Annette laughed.

"He might find some other treasure put away, you know," Laurie ventured. "Collectors like his *peculiar* uncle often bought paintings and simply stashed them away, hid them actually. Because they didn't want anyone else to look at them."

"That sometimes did happen, and it still does. However, I imagine that by now Christopher has scoured that house from top to bottom."

"You bet he has." Laurie suddenly shivered, turned up the collar of her coat, brought her scarf to her chin, and, continuing to shiver, fumbled with the scarf through her cashmere gloves.

Annette, who missed nothing when it came to her sister's well-being, asked swiftly, "Are you feeling the cold?"

"No, not too much. And I'm glad to be out and about with you. Thank you for taking the day off to spend it with me."

"I'm happy to be with you. A whole day with you is one of my real luxuries."

Her sister smiled at this comment, snuggled into her coat, and let her gaze wander around Eaton Square. "The trees are sad today, bereft, lifeless. Twigs in the wind. This is such a beautiful square, but I must admit I like it best in the summer, when the gardens are filled with leafy branches. They make such a lovely cool green tent over our heads when we picnic there." Laurie let out a long sigh. "I'll be glad when spring comes. It's been a dreary, weary winter."

"We'll go somewhere warm soon. In the spring. We'll make plans," Annette assured her, love echoing in her voice for her only relative. Well, there was their brother, Anthony, but he was long gone from their lives. Who knew where he was, and their parents were dead. They only had each other. She's enough, Annette thought. She has such a big heart and so much to give. She's strong and determined and filled with compassion for others, and then there's her bravery and courage, and her selflessness. Yes, she's enough. She might be petite and delicate, but she packs a wallop. Also, Laurie was her good right hand, a brilliant researcher and an integral part of her art business.

"Here we are," Annette exclaimed a moment or two later.

Annette now came to a stop in front of a dark-green front door, turned the wheelchair around, and backed up the two steps, pulling the wheelchair after her. Once she was on the top step, she rang the intercom bell which had the brass nameplate engraved with the name REMMINGTON next to it.

"It's us," she answered when Marius's disembodied voice echoed down to them.

There was a loud buzz and a click; Annette pushed the door open, and Laurie took control of her chair again once they were in the hall of the building. She headed straight for the lift. A few seconds later they were on the landing, where Marius was standing at the open door of the flat.

Beaming at Laurie, he leaned over her, kissed her cheek. "Hello, sweetheart," he said warmly. "Let's get you in front of the fire. Your face looks pinched."

"It's lovely to see you, Marius," Laurie responded, removing her gloves and scarf, shrugging herself out of her coat.

After pulling the coat out from under her sister, Annette went to hang it up in the coat closet, and took off her own, put it away.

Marius said, "We'll go into the living room, darling."

"Good idea. I'll be with you in a moment."

Laurie loved this large, beautifully proportioned room, which overlooked Eaton Square, with its tall windows and a white marble fireplace at one end. The color scheme was a mixture of yellows, which gave it a sunny feeling whatever the weather outside, and the accent colors were blue and white. A fire was burning brightly in the hearth and the scent of flowers was fragrant on the air. There were bowls filled with blooms scattered about, but Laurie knew Annette always used Kenneth Turner's scented candles throughout the flat to get the proper effect she wanted.

Once she had positioned herself near the fire, Marius went to the drinks table nearby and took a bottle of Dom Pérignon out of the silver ice bucket. As he popped the cork, he looked at Laurie and said, "You're a naughty girl, not coming to my sixtieth, you know. I was very disappointed."

Before she could answer, Annette came hurrying in with a plate of canapes. "Marius, don't chastise her! I've done that already!"

"Well, of course you have," he remarked with a cheerful laugh, then asked, "So, who wants a glass of bubbly? Both of you, I hope. Certainly I'm going to have one."

"Can't wait," Laurie answered, beginning to thaw out in front of the blazing fire. She was filled with happiness to be with them; she adored Annette and loved Marius, who had never been anything but nice to her, and very kind.

"I'll have one, too," Annette said, and went and sat on the sofa. As Marius poured the champagne, she asked, "What time's your plane this afternoon?"

He glanced across at her, still pouring the wine. "I had a bit of luck a short while ago. Jimmy Musgrave has offered me a lift on his private jet."

"Who's Jimmy Musgrave?" Annette asked, a brow lifting. "Do I know him?"

"No, you haven't met him yet because he's been in Los Angeles. He's a new client of mine, came to me through one of my Hollywood contacts. He called to tell me he was flying to Barcelona later today and couldn't see me next week. I said, What a coincidence, so am I. And he was quick to invite me to fly with him. He said he'd like my company; that we could talk art was the way he put it. To answer your question, I have to be at the airport at five."

"That *was* a lucky break." Annette accepted the flute of champagne from him and smiled. "It should be nice in Barcelona this weekend. You'll be able to get a bit of sun."

Walking over to Laurie, he handed her the glass, then sat down in the chair next to her. "I doubt it," he murmured, addressing Annette. "I really do need to spend some time with the director of the Picasso Museum, and I want to do a good long walk-through, to refresh my memory."

"How's the book coming along?" Laurie asked, referring to the one Marius was writing about the painter.

"Rather better than I expected. It's odd, Laurie, it just started to take off in the last six months or so. I've done more work in that time than I did the whole of the previous year. I think Picasso really comes alive on the page at last. And by the way, ladies, I've decided to dedicate this book to the two of you . . . my very special muses."

"How lovely," Laurie cried, and raising her glass she said, "Here's to your new book, Marius, and thank you for the dedication to us."

Annette said, "That's nice of you, darling, yes, thank you, thank you very much."

A small silence fell among them; the three of them sat back, sipping their champagne, relaxing, enjoying being together in this beautiful room in front of the blazing fire on this cold day.

It was Marius who broke the silence when he asked, "Are you still planning to drive down to Kent tomorrow? To review Christopher's paintings?"

"Yes. I must make some decisions. In fact, he must, too. I've got to start making my plans for the next auction."

"You've never actually said what else there is in his late uncle's collection." Marius gave her a very direct, penetrating look. "Either there's something really special or absolutely nothing at all. Come on, sweetheart, spill the beans."

Annette shook her head. "No, no, I'm not keeping secrets from you, if that's what you're suggesting," she instantly shot back, a frown knotting her brow. "And actually, I *did* tell you there were a couple of Impressionists, and also an important piece of sculpture. As for paintings, there's a Cassatt and a Degas, and I *did* tell you."

Catching the nuance of irritation in her voice, he said, in a placating tone, "Come to think of it, that you did, I'd just forgotten. In fact, didn't you say there was a Giacometti sculpture in the collection also?"

"I did, and I know it's valuable. Oh, and there's a Cézanne. I admire his work, you know. For some reason it's really dirty, and therefore it must be cleaned. I can't imagine what that uncle of Christopher's was like. A careless man, I suppose, at least when it came to taking care of his art collection. Imagine neglecting a Rembrandt and a Cézanne. He didn't even have the collection catalogued, at least as far as I know. And Christopher doesn't know very much more than I do. Apparently he wasn't close to his uncle, hardly knew him, but since there was no other heir, he inherited the collection."

"Everything else as well," Laurie murmured. "I read about it in the papers. There was some sort of really sad incident in his life, and he became a recluse, as well as being something of an eccentric anyway, the uncle I mean."

Marius, thoughtful, said slowly, "I believe it was a broken engagement, or a divorce. There was a woman involved, some tragedy, if I remember correctly. I think you and I read the same newspaper stories, Laurie." He glanced at his wife. "Don't you know any of the family background?"

"Not much. Christopher has never told me anything. He's rather shy, reticent."

"Ho, ho, that's what you think, is it! Well, he's certainly not too shy to ogle you. He's got big eyes for you, Annette." Marius laughed. It sounded a little hollow.

"That's not true. And he's only twenty-three, for heaven's sake!"

"What's age got to do with anything? Age is merely a number, that's all. And he *does* have eyes for you. I saw it myself at the party on Tuesday night. Come on, admit it."

"Oh pooh," Annette exclaimed in a dismissive voice, not wishing to acknowledge the truth in what Marius was saying. That would only give him ammunition to tease her, or taunt her, as he was sometimes prone to do. It was another way to control her.

Laurie sat back, watching them, not daring to enter into this conversation. She knew it was wise to remain silent. She was only too well aware that Marius had always been extremely possessive of Annette, and jealous. There were times when Laurie had seen him watching her sister like a hawk, his face a mask of anger, if there was another man showing interest. Whenever she had mentioned his dreadful possessiveness, which seemed pathological to her, Annette had dismissed it vehemently. Nonetheless, there *was* a certain problem there, whatever Annette believed.

Marius stood up, went to fetch the bottle of champagne, refilled their glasses, and then took it back to the silver bucket. He stood there for a moment, his hand on the bottle, looking from his wife to his sister-in-law. Finally he said, "Listen, the two of you, I've just had an inspired idea. I think you should *both* go down to Kent tomorrow to that house of Christopher's, his uncle's huge pile. You'd enjoy the outing, Laurie, wouldn't you? And Laurie would be company for you, Annette. I'll tell you what, I'll talk to Paddy on my way to the airport. I know he'll be happy to drive you to Kent, wait, and bring you back. Now what do you say about that, the two of you?"

Laurie was absolutely silent, frightened to speak.

Annette looked across at her sister and smiled. She said, in the most loving of voices, "Marius has just had a brilliant idea, Laurie, I'd love it if you would come with me. I wish I'd thought of it myself."

"Oh, honestly, I don't know," Laurie answered quickly,

staring at Annette. "Look, I don't want to be in the way, you're going there to work." She bit her lip. "I'll just be a nuisance, under your feet."

"No, you won't, you'd be lovely company for me on the drive there and back, just as Marius said. Please say you'll come." Annette sat back on the sofa, smiling at her sister, genuinely wanting her to make the trip. She had felt badly about canceling their usual Saturday rendezvous, and it had never occurred to her to ask Laurie to drive to Kent with her. Now that Marius had suggested it, she thought it was a great idea. She laughed inwardly. Two can play this game. You think you pull the wool over my eyes, but you don't. I've been married to you for twenty-one years and I know you well. Better than anybody.

Laurie said softly, "If you *really* want me to drive down with you, I'll come. Of course I will." A smile touched her generous, pretty mouth. "For me it would be a great treat. . . ."

"Then it's settled!" Marius declared. He glanced over his shoulder when their housekeeper appeared in the doorway. "There you are, Elaine. I suppose lunch is ready?"

"It is. A cheese soufflé. You've got to come. Before it drops."

"I've got my orders," he murmured.

And seemingly so have I. Annette took a deep breath, and then experienced a little frisson of annoyance. He could be so manipulative.

Chapter Four

The house was called Knowle Court and it was located not far from Aldington in Kent. A long gravel drive led up to the house, skirted on either side by lines of tall, stately poplars, and it was the trees which gave the property a sense of dignity. They reminded Annette of France, where there was many a driveway just like this, standing sentinel in front of some grand château.

As if picking up on this thought, Laurie turned to her and said, "Have we crossed the Channel without me noticing and entered France? That's what the trees are telling me."

"I know what you mean, but no, we're still here in hop-growing country, and not very far from Noël Coward's old home. Though I'm afraid Knowle Court doesn't have the charm of Goldenhurst. Unfortunately."

"What a pity. I like that lovely Elizabethan house. So, what *exactly* did Christopher inherit from his uncle?"

"A Jacobean pile of stone, turreted and moated, no less. More like a small castle, actually. Not my kind of place. I came here several times last summer and even then, on a sunny day, it seemed a bit . . . *daunting*. Oh, look, Laurie, there it is!"

Leaning forward, she said to Paddy, "There's a circular drive up ahead, and Mr. Delaware told me you should park near the drawbridge that leads to a big door."

"Righto, Mrs. Remmington."

"He also explained that you're welcome to relax in the back parlor, to read or watch television. And that the housekeeper will give you lunch later. It's up to you."

"Thanks, Mrs. R. I think I'll drive around the area a bit, take a dekko, and come back later for a spot of lunch. Mr. R. said you'd be working here all day."

"That's right. I hope we can leave about four or five, not later than that. So, you can please yourself, do what you want. Oh, and Mr. Delaware said you're to make yourself at home if you do decide to relax in the back parlor."

Paddy nodded. "That's very kind of him." As he brought the car to a standstill and pulled on the brake, he added, "And here we are, ladies." Opening the door, he jumped out, then poked his head back inside. "I'll get the wheelchair, Miss Laurie, and then I'll lift you out. Won't be a tick."

At this moment the huge iron-studded oak door opened, and Christopher appeared on the drawbridge with a young man Annette recognized as his friend James Pollard. Before she could open the car door, Christopher was hurrying forward, doing it for her and saying hello to Paddy at the same time.

Helping her to get out, he grinned and exclaimed, "You've made it in good time! Welcome to the old homestead." He then muttered, "If one can call it that. It's more like a stronghold."

Once Annette was out of the car, he glanced inside again. "Hi, Laurie. I asked my friend Jim to come down for the weekend. He'll keep you company while we work. I'm sure you remember him from the auction."

"Yes, I do, and that was thoughtful of you, Christopher." She gave him a wide smile, and then turned to Paddy, who had appeared at her side of the car.

The driver had worked for Marius for eighteen years and knew her well, and it was with great care that he lifted her out of the car and carried her to the wheelchair. And as usual he thought the same thing he always thought as he held her gently, like a baby, in his arms: *What a gorgeous girl, what a shame.* In his own way he loved her, but then everybody loved her. You couldn't help yourself. She was of the sweetest nature and he'd never heard her complain once. A shame. A bloody shame.

"Thank you, Paddy," Laurie said, looking up at the big warm-hearted man, with mischievous obsidian-black eyes and a shock of dark, wavy hair. If anyone was a genuine black Irishman, it was Paddy.

"My pleasure," he murmured. He put her into the chair and she went across the drawbridge.

"I've never seen anything quite like this place ever before, have you, Miss Laurie?" he asked, walking next to her.

This was said in such a droll way she couldn't help laughing. "No, I haven't." As she spoke she glanced up at the castle, which is what it really was, and took a deep breath. An involuntary shiver ran through her. Annette had used the wrong word. It wasn't merely *daunting*, it was forbidding. And she shivered again as a strange sense of foreboding took hold of her and she shrank inside.

A moment later, Jim Pollard was hurrying alongside her, greeting her. "It's so nice to see you again, Laurie. I was delighted when Chris asked me to spend the weekend, and especially chuffed when I knew that you were coming for lunch today. We can keep each other company and laugh like we did at the auction. I haven't had as much fun since then."

"Me neither," she answered, and realized how glad she was that Jim was here. She would have hated to sit alone waiting for Annette in this gloomy place. It was so dark and unwelcoming.

There was a bit of fuss and lots of bustle as Christopher led everyone into the house. He insisted on showing Paddy to the back parlor, where he introduced him to Mrs. Joules, his housekeeper, as she came hurrying out of the adjoining kitchen. Immediately, she took charge of Paddy. Christopher then asked Jim to escort Laurie to the blue sitting room. Linking his arm through Annette's, he led her down a corridor, across the vaulted hall, and into the library.

She remembered this room very well. It was gargantuan, paneled in light oak, and had a huge fireplace at one end and soaring mullioned windows at the other. Filled though it was with books, there was some free wall space where two exceptional horse paintings by George Stubbs were hanging on either side of the fireplace. She was quite certain they had been painted about 1769, or around that time. She loved the formality of the composition, the glossy coats of the horses, their elegant stance, the traditional landscaped park in the background, which was so very English. They were incomparable. And at least they were in excellent condition. Sir Alec Delaware, Christopher's uncle, had looked after these two beauties very well indeed. This pleased her. If Christopher wanted to sell them, she could get a fabulous price for the pair.

"You looked at those horse paintings last summer, and long and hard, just as you're doing today," Christopher remarked, coming to a standstill next to her. "You said they were valuable."

"They are. Paintings by George Stubbs are hard to come by. I haven't seen any on the market in a long time. But of course they wouldn't sell anywhere in the same range as your Rembrandt did, although they would bring an excellent price if you were to put them up for auction."

"I'm going to keep them. They look very handsome and fit this room extremely well. They genuinely belong in here, and they enhance it."

"Your uncle most probably purchased them specially for this library."

"No, actually he didn't, Annette. My mother told me that the horse paintings were inherited from my grandfather, Percy Delaware, and that he'd inherited them from *his* father. They've been in the family for many years."

"How long has this house been in your family, Christopher?"

"Hundreds of years, since the Stuart period, the 1660s, and it's entailed, you know, it can't be sold. It must always pass to a direct descendant."

Annette nodded. "The family is not titled, though, is it?"

"No. Uncle Alec was knighted for services to British industry, but the knighthood ended when he died. That's how he made his money, through big business, I mean."

"Yes, I know. I did a bit of research."

He gave her a faint smile, and walked over to the coffee table in front of a leather chesterfield. "How about a cup of coffee before we get to work?"

"Thanks, Christopher, I'd like that." She sat down on the sofa and accepted the cup when he handed it to her. She needed this after the long drive from London. Yet she was anxious to get to work. *I must make this coffee break quick,* she decided.

Christopher remained standing in front of the fireplace, his back to it, sipping his coffee. After a moment, he remarked, "I've really searched the house, almost ransacked it you could say, and I've found a few interesting things."

Her head came up alertly. "That sounds promising. What did you find?"

"A notebook of my uncle's. It was in an old briefcase, and I must tell you this. His father did buy the Rembrandt in the 1930s. There's mention of it in the notebook. So the bill of sale is incorrect because his mother's name is on it."

"That's interesting, but it doesn't matter. It came into this family at that time, so the provenance is valid. But may I see it?"

"At once." Christopher leaned forward, put his own cup down, and walked around the chesterfield to the desk which was backed up against it. He opened a drawer, brought out a black notebook, and took it over to her.

Annette saw that it was shabby, worn at the edges, and had been obviously much handled. "What's in it? Not a catalogue?" A blond brow lifted hopefully; she stared up at him. "Oh, that would be just wonderful!"

"Not quite a catalogue, but references to some of the paintings and a list."

She flipped through the pages, glancing at them, finding the small, precise writing difficult, and handed the notebook back to him. "You know where the interesting bits are, so please find them. It will be much faster. I would be searching blindly."

He took the book from her, and found one of the pages he wanted. "Let me read this to you . . . 'In your arms was still delight, quiet as a street at night; and thoughts of you, I do remember, were green leaves in a darkened chamber, were dark clouds in a moonless sky.'" He paused, then murmured, "Beautiful, isn't it?"

"Yes, it is, and it's part of a Rupert Brooke poem called 'Retrospect.' But it doesn't refer to a painting."

"It does, actually. Below those lines he wrote this . . . 'Oh my poor Cézanne. Lost to me. My lovely darkened chamber. Ruined. Gone forever. Damn that bloody soot. I should have had the chimneys cleaned.' . . . Could it be soot on the Cézanne, Annette?"

"Most probably." She sat up straighter. "You know, I thought it was years of *grime* on it, but it is *soot*." She grimaced. "I hope it can be cleaned off . . ." Her voice trailed away; worry clouded her light-blue eyes.

"So do I. We can go and look at it. I have it in one of the sitting rooms I emptied of furniture. I turned it into a storage room."

"When did you find the notebook, Chris?"

"About a week or two ago. Why?"

He should have told her before. Careless not to. Didn't the art matter to him? Clearing her throat, she said, with a shrug, "I just wondered. That's all. I'd like to see the Cézanne again, and I want you to bring it up to London early next week. I'll ring you on Monday and give you the address of the restorer to whom you must take it. I hope he's available. He's the most brilliant restorer in the business. His name is Carlton Fraser."

"I'll do that. Annette?"

"Yes?"

"Are you upset about something?"

"No, why do you ask?"

"You've got an odd look on your face."

"Have I?" Another shrug of her shoulders. "I was thinking about your uncle, and how eloquently he described the Cézanne, at least the way *he* saw it . . . all those dark greens that Cézanne favored. Most appropriate."

"He was an interesting man. Here's something else he wrote." Christopher flipped the pages again, and went on. "Just a few words, which baffled me at first. So listen to this. . . . 'My poor little girl, gone from me. The beautiful girl, beautiful no more. I must bury her.' That's all there is. But I found her."

"Oh, my God! Is he referring to a child?" Her hand came up to her mouth and she shook her head. "Did he bury a child?" She shuddered involuntarily, aghast.

"No, no. Don't look so alarmed. It's not a human child. What I found was a rather disreputable-looking statue. Do you want to see it?"

"Immediately." She stood up. Her face was white.

"I'm sorry I frightened you," he apologized, lightly touching her arm.

No, not you, she thought. There's something about this house that chills me to the bone, and for a reason I don't understand. Taking a deep breath, Annette said, "I'm fine, I was just startled. The way you presented it to me was . . . well, I thought he'd buried a dead child."

Annette followed Christopher across the enormous hall, with its high-flung vaulted ceiling, polished oak floor, and huge chandelier. She glanced around, shivered. There was something creepy about this place. Why had she not noticed it last year? It had been summer. Warm weather and sunshine, of course. On this cold March day it had acquired bleak aspects.

She was glad she had worn a gray flannel trouser suit and cashmere sweater, and that she had told Laurie to do the same. Even though Knowle Court was centrally heated and fires burned in almost every room, a damp coldness seemed to permeate the whole place.

As they walked toward the sitting room where he was storing pieces of art, Annette asked, "How did you manage to find the statue?"

"There are quite a lot of trunks and boxes stored in the attics, and I went through them all. It was fortunate that my uncle had scrawled *my beautiful girl* on one side of a large cardboard box, and when I opened it I discovered the sculpture."

"That *was* lucky. The box is in the room where the Cézanne is stored?"

He nodded. "I've put some other artworks in there, since you said you might want to have more than one piece in the next auction."

"I'm glad you did."

"Here we are." Christopher opened a door, ushered Annette inside. "Do you want to look at the Cézanne first? It's over there on the trestle table."

She hurried across the floor, anxious to view the painting again, apprehension trickling through her as she thought of the damage the soot could have caused to the canvas.

Christopher, moving ahead, whipped the cotton sheet off the trestle table and stood waiting for her, the painting revealed.

When she looked down at the Cézanne, she saw immediately that the painting looked a bit darker in parts than it had last August, when she had first seen it. But that day was sunny. Perhaps it was something to do with the dreary light today. Soot didn't run or spread. It was composed of carbon deposits from burning coal, and she was certain it was difficult to remove from anything.

Oh, God, she thought, leaning closer, peering at the canvas. However will Carlton bring this back to life? He was most probably the only man who could, if that was at all possible.

Christopher, hovering next to her, was suddenly nervous. "You seem worried."

"I am," Annette responded. "However, Carlton Fraser is a genius, and I'm not going to give in to anticipatory despair.

The painting *is* full of those wonderful dark, dark greens Cézanne loved to use, and so perhaps it looks worse than it really is. Now, where's the statue?"

"It's here." As he spoke, Christopher pulled a large cardboard box across the floor and opened the top flaps.

Annette looked inside. What she saw gave her quite a start; instantly, she pulled back, the breath knocked out of her, then knelt down, opening the flaps wider for a better view. She stared for a long time at the object lying on the bottom of the box, hardly able to accept what she genuinely believed she was seeing. A little surge of excitement ran through her, and she prayed she was correct about the statue. Putting her hand in the box, she touched it tentatively and closed her eyes.

After a moment she stared at Christopher. "Do you know what this is?"

"No, I don't."

"You have had it out of the box, haven't you?"

"Yes, I have, but I wasn't very impressed with it, so I put it back."

"Would you lift it out, so that I can look at it properly, please, Chris?"

"Of course I will." He did as she asked. "Where do you want me to put it?"

"I think over there, on the round table near the window, please." To think she could have seen this two weeks ago if only he had had the sense to phone her. She was beginning to have her doubts about him.

Once it was on the table, Annette walked in a circle, viewing the piece from every angle. Her heart was pounding. She could hardly contain herself, her excitement growing. Suddenly she experienced that wonderful surge of joyousness that came over her when she looked at a great Impressionist painting, most especially a Renoir. It was a kind of momentary ecstasy, and thrilling.

He said, "It looks so grubby. Surely it's not anything of any importance. Why are you so interested in it?"

For a moment Annette could not bear to answer him, and

she certainly couldn't look at him. She was afraid he would see the irritation on her face.

Finally, she said, "The last time I saw something very similar to this at auction, the hammer came down on it for eleven million dollars. And that was ten years ago."

Chapter Five

I f I'm correct, and I'm fairly certain I am, this is *The Little Fourteen-Year-Old Dancer* by Degas," Annette said, turning around. She noticed that Christopher looked stunned and understood why. The thought of another art windfall in the millions must have dazzled him. In fact, she herself was somewhat stunned by his find, unexpected as it was.

"A Degas! I can't believe it. I thought it wasn't very important. Uncle Alec discarded it, put it away in an old cardboard box, shoved it in the attic. I wonder why? Because it's so grubby-looking? Do you think that's the reason?" Christopher asked.

"I've no idea. However, this little bronze dancer is not something anyone discards. Rather, it is to be treasured. Just because the net tutu is torn, also worn and dirty, is of no consequence. It's a Degas. And I believe this is one from a special unnumbered edition of about twenty-five examples which were cast in the 1920s. I'm very excited about this, Christopher."

"You said it was sold for eleven million dollars about ten years ago. Was it my uncle who bought it? Is this *that* statue?"

"No, no, you misunderstood me. I told you that a sculpture *similar* to this, another Degas ballet dancer, was auctioned around 1997. By Sotheby's in New York."

"Why would a copy be so valuable?"

"It is not a *copy*, not in the way you mean it," Annette said. "Let me try and explain this to you. A posthumous second-generation cast of the *original wax sculpture* by Degas was made at the Hébrard Foundry by perhaps one of the greatest casters ever, Albino Palazzolo, and it was supervised by the sculptor Albert Bartholomé, who was an intimate friend of Degas. I don't think I'm wrong in believing *this* is one of those which were cast in the 1920s from that original wax sculpture by Degas." Annette added, "Laurie is an expert on Degas, and I frequently use her for research. She's full of knowledge. Would you ask her to come and look at this, Christopher?"

"Right away!" he exclaimed, and hurried out of the room.

Once she was alone, Annette turned to look at the bronze dancer again. She was absolutely convinced that this really was a Degas, and another rare find at Knowle Court, just as the painting by Rembrandt had been.

Stepping closer to the little dancer, she reached out, touched her head, caressed it lovingly, and then touched the torn and dirty tutu, very old now. Unexpectedly, her eyes filled with tears, so moved was she. This little dancer had always been a favorite of hers, and she often went to see the one on display at the Louvre when she was in Paris.

Imagine. Who would have ever thought that I might be auctioning this. It will be mine. For a short while. I will be its custodian. How thrilling that is. Her thoughts suddenly swung to Alec Delaware, and she wondered, When had he bought the little dancer and where? I need the provenance. Oh, my God, where *is* the provenance? Her chest tightened and sudden anxiety took hold of her. There were not many papers here. How could a man like Alec Delaware, a highly successful businessman, have been so careless? Christopher didn't seem to know too much about his uncle's affairs, and there were only a few metal filing cabinets containing a handful of papers referring to some of the art. But not to all of it.

At this moment Laurie came rolling into the room in the chair, her face lighting up when she saw the bronze dancer on the table.

"Oh, Annette, how wonderful! It's *The Little Fourteen-Year-Old Dancer*, the famous Degas bronze. Oh, God, I must touch it." As she spoke, Laurie, stopping in front of the sculpture, stretched out her hand and stroked the statue. Turning her head, she focused on Christopher. "Aren't you the luckiest man alive! This is a famous masterpiece. Any serious collector would kill for it."

"Are you sure it *is* what we both think?" Annette interjected.

"Yes, I am," Laurie answered, very positive.

Annette's voice was as serious as her face when she said to Christopher, "I need the provenance, proof of previous ownership. Is there such a thing?"

"Not that I know of."

Annette glanced over at the cardboard box. "Was there anything else in that box when you opened it? An envelope maybe?"

"No, it was full of crumpled paper. What I mean is, my uncle had lined the box with balls of newspaper and tissue paper. That made a cushion for the statue, and there was a lot more paper on top, covering the bronze."

Annette stared at him. "So where is all this paper now?" She prayed he hadn't thrown it away.

"I put it in a plastic bag and left it in the attic. I know what you're thinking, Annette . . . that the provenance might be in amongst the paper."

"You're right."

"I'll go and get the plastic bag," Christopher announced and left the room.

Jim Pollard, his friend, watched him go, shaking his head. He then looked over at Annette. "I vaguely knew Sir Alec, though not through Christopher. It was my father who introduced us. He had dealings with Sir Alec in business. Apparently he was an eccentric, in some ways rather like the proverbial absentminded professor. And yet he was sharp, a superb businessman. Odd dichotomy there. Look, this is what I wanted to say. I don't think he would be careless about documentation for his art. He was a serious collector, as you know, since you're now well acquainted with the art collection here."

"Do you think there are some files somewhere in this house which refer to the art?" she asked.

"Yes, I do. Hidden. You see, Sir Alec did undergo a change when his fiancée died. . . . He became weird, secretive, difficult to deal with. That's also when he suddenly became a recluse."

"When was that?"

"About fifteen years ago. I'm sure it was the shock, actually. Finding her like that."

"What do you mean?" Laurie asked, staring at him intently, detecting something odd in his voice.

Jim looked from Laurie to Annette and said quietly, "Didn't you know she committed suicide?"

Both women shook their heads; Annette asked, "How did she . . ." She couldn't finish the question and her voice trailed off on a slight waver.

"She hanged herself," Jim murmured. "In their bedroom. Here. A few days before the marriage." He hesitated, then muttered, "She was wearing her wedding gown."

"Oh, my God!" Laurie looked at Jim aghast.

Annette, speechless, shook her head several times, as if denying this. "That *must* have been a terrible shock for him. What a horrible thing to have to live with."

Jim said, "My father thought her suicide sent him raving mad, and perhaps Dad was right. I think Sir Alec did go off his rocker, after Clarissa killed herself."

"That was her name?" Laurie asked.

"Yes, Clarissa Normandy. She was an artist."

"I knew her work, but not much about her," Annette remarked, recalling an art show she had been to some twenty years ago.

Christopher came in with the plastic bag and immediately started pulling out pieces of newspaper. Jim went to help him, and after a few seconds it was Jim who cried, "Eureka!" and waved a crumpled envelope in the air. He strode over and gave it to Annette, a smile on his face.

"It *is* the provenance, thank God," she exclaimed a second later as she took several pieces of paper out of the envelope and glanced at them. "We're lucky to have found this envelope," she added, sounding relieved. "Otherwise I would have had to have Laurie track this little darling's travels over the years, in order to have some sort of provenance for it, to prove it is really what it actually is."

It was referred to as the morning room, and as far as Annette was concerned it was the warmest and most welcoming spot in this vast mausoleum. Octagonal in shape, it was of medium size, with three arched windows which looked out onto the park at the back of Knowle Court. The ceiling was coffered, and there was a fireplace with a carved oak mantelpiece.

"We've made a space for you here," Christopher said, indicating where Laurie's chair would fit comfortably at the table.

"Thank you," she answered, and rolled herself into the empty space, thinking how cozy this room was with its pink silk lampshades and a fire blazing up the chimney.

As she glanced around, taking everything in, Laurie suddenly realized there were no paintings hanging here. How odd. Settling herself comfortably, she had the sudden startling thought that Christopher didn't care about art very much. Just its monetary worth. Was that why Annette had seemed irritated earlier? Undoubtedly she had realized that. Long ago perhaps?

Jim pulled out a chair for Annette and sat down at the round table between her and Laurie; looking from one to the other, he said, "Mrs. Joules is a great cook. Lunch will be marvelous. We're in for a culinary treat."

As if on cue, the door opened and Mrs. Joules came in carrying a tray laden with bowls of steaming soup. A young maid followed. After placing the tray on a sideboard, she and the maid passed a bowl to each of them. Mrs. Joules said, "I hope you enjoy it . . . my special pea soup with coconut."

They all thanked her, and when she and the maid disappeared, Christopher announced, "You'll love it. I've never had soup quite as delicious."

Annette was pleasantly surprised when she tasted the soup. It had a hint of mint along with the coconut, and was indeed special.

Her thoughts strayed away from the conversation Christopher and Jim were now having about a horse Jim had recently bought. Instead she was thinking about the art in this house, and what Christopher would put up for auction. Probably all of it in the end, but right now he was going slowly. Still, he had indicated he would sell five pieces, and he would make a decision about which ones to auction after lunch.

There was no question in her mind that he was a nice young man, pleasant, a little shy, and reticent, although he had seemed more open, less diffident today. And yet she had been slightly turned off earlier; she knew the reason why. She had a reverence for art, and for artists, and she had been annoyed when he had been so offhand. He was not interested in the bronze dancer for its beauty, nor did it matter to him that it had been created by such a master as Degas. He didn't care that it was a renowned piece. His only concern was how much she could get for it.

Annette sighed under her breath. Perhaps that was only normal. He had told her he knew nothing about art right from the beginning, when he had first come to see her. And later on he had even said he relied on Jim Pollard for help when making decisions about the collection. That was probably the real reason Jim was here for the weekend, not to keep Laurie company today. But that didn't matter; she found Jim compatible, and he seemed genuine, sincere. Not only that, he did have a knowledge of art, and at times today he himself had appeared impatient with Christopher.

Annette settled back in her chair and joined in the conversation the others were having about a new play in the West End, not wishing to appear rude. But her interest kept straying.

She started to think about Hilda Crump and the awful things that had happened. What if someone found out? If those early years caught up with her, then her world would be shattered. And therefore so would Laurie's. This last thought struck terror in her. Who would look after her sister if she was in jail?

The lunch progressed at a smooth pace. After the soup Mrs. Joules brought in lamb chops, new potatoes, and baby carrots, and afterward dessert, which was peach pie. When she presented this the housekeeper told them that coffee was awaiting them in the library whenever they were ready.

Relieved that lunch was finally over and out of the way, Annette got straight to the point when they were settled in the library sipping their coffee.

Within minutes she brought a card out of her handbag and addressed Christopher. "I know you wish to sell the Giacometti sculpture, you already told me that, so what about *The Little Fourteen-Year-Old Dancer*? Do you want to keep the Degas or have me put it up for auction?"

"I want you to sell it, and also the Degas painting of horses . . . I'd like to get rid of the Mary Cassatt of the mother and the child, and the Cézanne, if it can be restored."

"Let's hope Carlton can work a miracle," she responded noncommittally. "So, that makes three paintings and two sculptures." Annette leaned forward and handed him the card. "As you can see, those are the pieces I thought you *would* sell. Not the Degas bronze, because I didn't know you had such a thing."

A huge smile spread across his face. "You second-guessed me very well."

"I'm glad we brought the statue back with us," Laurie said, staring across at Annette. "It's safe here, and perhaps Carlton Fraser will agree to come over and look at it."

"I know he will," Annette responded, leaning back on

the sofa in the yellow drawing room of her flat. "Aside from anything else, his curiosity will get the better of him. Who wouldn't want to come and see the most famous of Degas's sculptures?" Leaning forward slightly, she focused her eyes on the dancer, and in particular on the tutu. "The net is awfully dirty and worn, isn't it?" She glanced at Laurie and made a face. "But then perhaps that's part of its great appeal."

"You weren't thinking of asking Carlton to do anything with it, were you?" Laurie asked, her voice suddenly an octave higher.

Annette shook her head. "No, no, of course not. For one thing, the tutu might disintegrate, and secondly, its age and griminess add to its value."

"*The Little Fourteen-Year-Old Dancer* was the only one of all of his sculptures that he exhibited, if you remember all of my research. Degas actually showed it at the 1881 Impressionist exhibition in Paris. This statue isn't *that* one, though, but one of those cast in the 1920s."

"Almost a hundred years ago." Annette shook her head. "*Unbelievable.*"

Laurie gave her sister a careful look and, changing the subject, said, "You don't really like Christopher Delaware anymore, do you?"

"No, no, that's not true, I do still like him, Laurie. But I have to admit I did become irritated with him yesterday at Knowle Court. He is so offhand about the art in his possession, which he now owns, and I know he's itching for the money, can't wait to sell it."

"Only too true," Laurie agreed, and then laughed. "I don't suppose we should complain about that, since you will be the one to auction it. And you will reap the benefits, in more ways than one: you'll make money and enhance your reputation. When will you have the auction?"

"I'm not sure. I need to know what Carlton thinks about the cleaning and restoring of the Cézanne."

"Oh, Annette, honestly, that's going to be a *big* job, don't you think?"

"I do. And I might have to auction off just the two sculptures and the two other paintings, and put the Cézanne on the block at a later date, in six months to a year." Annette rose, crossed the sitting room, dropped another log onto the fire, and continued, "Going back to Chris, I do like him, Laurie, but you must remember I don't know him very well. And anyway, I mustn't be judgmental. After all, he hasn't been immersed in art as we have, and his uncle's collection does belong to him, so he can do whatever he wants with it. And I'm glad he chose me to be his dealer."

"It's just that he's so . . . *careless*. Casual about it. Even Jim Pollard said something like that to me, and by the way, he's very bright."

"I like Jim," Annette answered, and returned to the sofa. She asked, "Are you hungry, Laurie? Shall I make some lunch?"

"A bit later, I don't think I could eat just yet . . ." Laurie left her sentence unfinished, and her mouth began to twitch with laughter.

"What's so funny? What is it?" Annette raised a brow, puzzled.

"Chris does have a crush on you, you know. Marius was right about that."

"Don't be so silly!" Annette exclaimed, shaking her head. "You and Marius are far too imaginative, and—" The ringing phone interrupted her and she got up to answer it, then stood talking for a moment to Malcolm Stevens, who had called to invite them out to dinner that evening.

Chapter Six

In the interior recesses of her mind, in those small, well-hidden places, old memories lay dormant, lived in quietude. Until one of them unexpectedly crept out, became vividly alive, swamped her entire being.

And thus it was on Sunday night. Annette lay wide awake in bed, endeavoring to sleep without success and then it suddenly happened. . . . She was engulfed in a memory of long ago, a memory from the buried past. Clear, precise in every detail.

There it was, a replay. Accurate. Disturbing. Looming over her . . . that forbidding, frightening house, silent and dark, where evil lurked in shadows, and little girls, young, innocent, and beautiful, roamed the solitary rooms, taking the only joy they ever knew from each other.

She heard singing . . . a child's high, light voice . . . It washed over her, soothing her, and she strained to hear it better, needing to be close to her, close to that little girl with golden curls . . .

"My name is Marie Antoinette, and I'm the Queen of France. Please won't you come and join me in my dance. I'm the Queen of France. Come and waltz around the room, around and around we'll go, playing your favorite tune. Look at my beautiful golden gown, it comes from the very best shop in town. Isn't it grand, and here I stand. My name is Marie Antoinette and I'm the Queen of France."

The girls held hands and danced around the room, laughing and happy to be with each other, their eyes sparkling brightly, the tapping of their little shoes echoing on the bare wood floor.

Now another voice, lilting and sweet, came floating on the air. "I am Josephine, Empress of France. Come and dance. My husband's name is Bonaparte, and he's definitely stolen my heart. He's a general, strong and bold, and we're a legend, so I'm told. I have a crown, it shines very bright, and I wear it every night. I'm married to Napoleon. He's my man, so come to see us as fast as you can. And we'll dance the whole night through, until the dawn breaks softly blue. My name is Josephine, an empress new and true. Come and dance and dance and dance, with an empress of la belle France."

There was the sound of feet running up the stairs and a loving voice calling, "Girls, girls, come on, let's go out to play, let's have some fun." And she was there then, the tall, sweet cousin they loved with devotion, who looked after them, protected them. They ran to her and they left together, racing outside into the golden sunlight of this summer day.

They ran through meadows filled with wildflowers, the tall grass undulating under the light breeze blowing down from the hills. Their long hair flew out behind them and their summer frocks billowed around their legs. It was a clear bright afternoon and they ran together holding hands and laughing . . . golden girls on a golden day . . .

The memory stopped as abruptly as it had started. Annette sat up, got out of bed, and went into the bathroom. Turning on the light, she saw that her face was damp with tears, and she was filled with a terrible longing, a yearning really, for that tall, willowy girl who had loved them so much, and whom they had loved in return.

Will the yearning for her never go away? she wondered, and then she splashed her face with cold water, patted it dry. A few minutes later, back in bed, her thoughts were jumbled, sorrowful, and as she struggled to sort them out she fell into a deep sleep that was dreamless.

* * *

Although Marius had phoned twice over the weekend, Annette had not told him about the extraordinary find at Knowle Court. It had proved difficult for her to hold back, to not share with him her delight about the discovery of the bronze, but her desire to surprise him had won out in the end. She wanted to witness the expression on his face when he saw the famous Degas sculpture standing on the glass coffee table in the sitting room of their flat in Eaton Square.

As she sat at her desk in her Bond Street office on Monday morning, she began to make plans for her next big auction, which she fully intended to hold in New York. She was setting her sights high, but that was the way she was.

Because of her extensive knowledge of art, she knew that the Cézanne could not be cleaned as quickly as she would like. She also knew the job had to be done by a great restorer. And the only *really* great one was Carlton Fraser. He had been abroad and not available to clean the Rembrandt for her, but hopefully he would be able to take on the job of restoring the Cézanne.

Having always been a pragmatist, quick to make decisions, and expedient by nature, Annette was not one to waste time now. She picked up the phone and dialed Carlton Fraser's studio in Hampstead.

His phone rang and rang, and the voice mail did not come on. Growing impatient, she was about to hang up when he finally answered with a faint "Hello?" sounding far away.

"Carlton, it's Annette Remmington. How are you?"

"Hello, darling!" he exclaimed, his voice instantly stronger, convivial. "Lovely to hear you. And I'm grand. So sorry to have missed your gorgeous big bash. I hear it was spectacular, and look, I couldn't come because I was in Rome. But you knew that."

"Doing some work for the Vatican, I suspect."

He chuckled. "No flies on you, are there, my dear? And yes, I am."

"Congratulations. Listen, Carlton, I have a job for you, a

painting to clean and restore, and I do hope you're free to do it, at least to start it. You see, in my opinion, you're the only one who can bring it back to life."

"Thank you for the compliment. I can only say I do the best I can, and I am free. The new Vatican job is planned for the autumn, I'll be in Rome for a month. Cleaning some ancient frescoes. So what's the painting you want me to work on?"

"It's a Cézanne, and I'm fairly certain it was covered in soot which fell from a chimney, and also that somebody did attempt to clean it, or, let's say, dust it."

"Good God, no!" He let out a long groan and cursed.

"I'm afraid so," Annette responded quietly, alarmed by the intensity of the groan, his expletives. He had just underscored the feeling she had had about the painting right from the beginning. It was a mess, and it would need meticulous work.

There was a silence, and then Carlton muttered, "It could take me months. Soot's the worst."

"I know. But *can* you take it on? *Now*? Or are you fulfilling other commitments?"

"I'm working on an Old Master for a client, but I've just about finished it. I can start on yours this weekend, if that's all right."

"It's not all right, it's fantastic! What a relief. I wouldn't trust anyone but *you* with this job. I'll have the owner deliver it to you tomorrow, if you can accept it then?"

"I can, but in any case, Marguerite is always here. And who's the owner?"

"Christopher Delaware, my Rembrandt client. His uncle left him quite a collection, some really good paintings and a couple of fantastic sculptures. A Giacometti and a Degas. A bronze. A little dancer."

"Lucky blighter! And if I remember correctly from the massive publicity you so shrewdly engineered, his uncle was Sir Alec Delaware."

"Yes, that's right. Did you know him?"

"No, but I vaguely remember he was engaged to a painter I was acquainted with many years ago, when she was still a student at the Royal College of Art. . . . Wait a minute. . . . Now what was her name? Oh, yes, I recall it now. It was Clarissa Normandy. I think there was something rather strange about that engagement, though. Or was it the marriage?"

"Not the latter." Annette cleared her throat and plunged in. "She killed herself. I think it was only a few days before the wedding. Actually she was wearing her wedding dress. Just imagine that. It was something quite awful, wouldn't you say?"

"Oh, God, yes! I heard about it through the grapevine. But actually, Annette, there was a weird aspect to their relationship, a scandal of some kind. Unfortunately, it just slips my mind right now. Not unusual. Getting old, I suppose."

"The only thing I found out the other day was about the suicide," Annette remarked. "I don't know anything else."

"Mmmm. However, there *was* another element. Something not quite right, or, as my darling wife would say, not quite kosher. I think it was about stolen paintings . . . paintings going missing. And I do believe it was Marguerite who told me that at the time. Clarissa's not quite kosher, she said to me. And there was the suggestion of some impending scandal."

Always quick on the draw, Annette exclaimed, "Are you suggesting that by killing herself Clarissa Normandy averted a scandal?"

"I think *avoided* might be a better word."

"I see. Well, I didn't know her, nor does any of that matter now. But I admit I am riddled with curiosity and I'd love to know more, just out of interest, if Marguerite can shed any light on it."

"So would I." There was a pause, before he added, "As I recall, Clarissa was controversial, and prone to drag trouble in her wake."

Annette sat at her desk for a few minutes after hanging up the phone. She was thinking about Clarissa Normandy. She had heard about her some years ago . . . about her being a painter of promise, one of those young artists everyone predicted would become famous but who never did. Nothing much had happened to Clarissa's career, and she had fallen by the wayside eventually. And yet now, after the conversation with Carlton, she, too, recalled gossip about a scandal. What kind of scandal it was she couldn't remember. A flicker of a thought hovered at the back of her mind and was instantly gone. And she realized that the discussion had made her forget to invite Carlton to come over to see the dancer.

Sighing under her breath, and moving on in her head, Annette stood up, walked over to the cardboard blow-up of the Rembrandt, lifted it down.

Tonight she would take a picture of the Degas bronze, have a blow-up made, and within days her new piece of art would be propped up against the far wall.

A big, brilliant campaign, she said under her breath, and her eyes sparkled. She was about to start promoting *The Little Fourteen-Year-Old Dancer*, and within days the whole world would know about the Degas sculpture again.

She glanced at her watch. It was only ten o'clock; too early to call her New York office, but she would be in touch with them later this morning, would share her thoughts with them about the impending auction.

Bigger and better. I must make it bigger and better. And there was no doubt in her mind that she would succeed. She sat staring into space, her mind racing, and after a while she began to make notes, jotting down the ideas that had begun to flow so freely. The thought of the auction, of holding it in New York, excited her, made the adrenaline rush through her. Quite aside from the Degas bronze and his horse painting, there was the Giacometti, and the Mary Cassatt painting of a mother and child. It was beautiful, but she had known from the start that Christopher would surely put this up for auction. It did not appeal to him, nor did he understand about Mary Cassatt and what an important Impressionist painter she had been, one of the original group working in Paris in the 1800s, a close friend of Degas, as well as his colleague, rival, and benefactor.

After an hour, Annette stood up and walked across her

office, stretching. Her eyes fell on the blow-up of the Rembrandt, and she went over to it, picked it up, carried it to the back of her office, and put it in the large closet where she kept such things. Closing the door, she turned around, her eyes sweeping over the room, liking what she saw: a huge space with two large windows, cream walls, a dark blue carpet, and a paucity of furniture. The only pieces were her desk, an antique French *bureau plat*, resembling a large table with drawers; two chairs, one on each side of it; and the credenza along the end wall facing the desk.

She smiled to herself as she sat down at the desk, thinking of the clients who took one look around when they first came here, and asked where the art was. Her answer was always the same. "I'm waiting for it," she would say. "The art you are going to sell. Or buy."

There was a knock on the door, and her assistant, Esther Oliver, came in, carrying a folder. "You asked for this the other day, Annette," she said, indicating the folder, and then handing it to her. "Requests for interviews from every newspaper and magazine you can think of." She grinned at Annette as she took the chair on the other side of the desk and finished, "You'll be busy for months if you decide to do them all."

"Marius said he would go through them with me when he gets back from Barcelona later this week. I think he intends to pick out only a couple. We know I can't do them all."

"There are quite a few top-notch journalists asking to meet with you," Esther pointed out.

"Marius will make the decision," Annette murmured.

Doesn't he always, Esther thought, but said, "In the meantime, you haven't forgotten your appointment at noon with Mrs. Clarke-Collingwood, have you? About her two Landseers."

"Oh, bother, I had." She glanced at her watch. "But I'm all right, she won't be here for half an hour." Shaking her head, Annette explained, "I just got carried away with thoughts of the new auction I'm planning."

"It's going to be exciting. You can certainly generate a

great deal of publicity in the next few months. Where will you hold it? Sotheby's or Christie's?"

"Sotheby's. In New York."

Esther stared at her, for a moment lost for words. "Fantastic," she responded finally, and wondered what the controlling Marius Remmington would have to say about that.

Chapter Seven

The Degas bronze was standing exactly where she had left it that morning . . . in the middle of the glass coffee table in the living room of their Eaton Square apartment.

Annette stood gazing at it, admiring it, almost gloating over it, before she went to the storage room and got out two spotlights and various cameras.

Carrying the equipment back to the other room, she quickly set up and was soon shooting the statue from various angles. She was an excellent photographer, especially when it came to inanimate objects, and after two hours she was satisfied she had a series of great photographs. Amongst them would be the one that would make a perfect blow-up, she was quite certain of that.

Leaving everything where it was, in case she decided to take a series of pictures the following morning in daylight, Annette went into the kitchen. She found a note from Elaine telling her there was a cottage pie in the refrigerator that only needed heating up. Not feeling hungry, she poured herself a glass of sparkling water and carried it to her small office at the back of the apartment. She sat down on the sofa and dialed her sister.

"It's me, darling," she said when the phone was picked up.

"Hi!" Laurie exclaimed. "How did it go today?"

"Really very well," Annette answered, and went on to

explain, "I had several conversations with my New York office, and Penelope and Bryan were instantly geared up. Within minutes."

"I can well imagine. It's your enthusiasm. It ignites everyone else's."

Annette laughed. "I hope so. Anyway, they're one thousand percent behind me and my plan to hold the auction in New York. They were bubbling over with ideas, quickly pulling up lists of their clients who might be potential buyers, suggesting various dates, and even focusing on the design of the invitation."

"When do they want you to have the auction?"

"September. After Labor Day weekend, obviously, and we finally did settle on a tentative date in the middle of the month. Tuesday the eighteenth of September. Or the next day, Wednesday, but not any later that week. I think I will settle on the Tuesday, since they seemed to think this was best. But they will have to check that out with Sotheby's, to be certain that this date is still available."

"What thoughts did they have about the invitation?" Laurie now asked, very curious, because she herself had been working on ideas for the invitation and a theme for the auction all day.

"To be honest, they didn't actually have anything special, or specific. I was a bit startled that they would even try to come up with something. They only just heard about the new art to be auctioned. Still, I didn't want to discourage them."

"I have several thoughts," Laurie volunteered, "but only one idea works, in my opinion."

"And what's that?" Annette asked eagerly, knowing full well that her sister was immersed in Degas and had a superior knowledge of Mary Cassatt's work and her life in Paris. If anyone could come up with a theme for these two artists, it was Laurie. "So come on, tell me. You're not saying anything."

"I went back to my research on Degas, just to refresh my memory, and I rechecked Cassatt again. As you know, they were great friends but not romantically involved. They fought. He was a difficult man, had a bad habit of slapping people down, mostly artists like himself. She stood up to him, stood her ground. She'd learned to do that with her difficult father, good practice, I suppose. Also, she was extremely independent. Anyway, to get to the point, you have two pieces of art by Degas, the great painting of the horses and carriage at the races and the bronze dancer. But only *one* Cassatt. I wish you had another. Then we could build a theme on Degas and Cassatt, friends, rivals, and admirers of each other's work. Or master and pupil, since Cassatt learned so much from him."

"It had occurred to me that we could link them, but you're correct, we do need another Cassatt. Incidentally, where does that leave the Giacometti? He was a Modernist and the sculpture we have was executed in the nineteen-sixties."

"I realize you wouldn't want to keep that back for another auction at another time, but it might be the wisest thing to do."

"Oh," Annette said, and fell silent, thinking.

Laurie waited for a moment before asking, "Are you there, Annette? I've shocked you, haven't I?"

"Yes, you have, and in a way it's not exactly my decision, is it? There's Christopher Delaware to consider."

"That's true," her sister agreed. "But he *will* take your advice. I mean, after all, that's what you're there for. *To advise him.*" When Annette did not answer, Laurie decided to press on, and said in a quiet tone, "Listen, whatever *you* think, he does have a crush on you, and he'll want to please you. God knows he doesn't need money anymore. He doesn't have to sell the Giacometti now, not after the twenty million quid you got him with the sale of the Rembrandt."

"Yes, you're right on all points."

"So you *do* know he has a crush on you?"

Annette sighed. "It's not such a big crush, and I have been very cool with him, not risen to the bait, or even addressed it. I've ignored it, and actually I think the crush is beginning to subside, if that's the right word to use. I know how to be indifferent, show a total lack of interest without hurting feelings."

"*I* know that. But does Marius?"

"Laurie, don't be so silly!" Annette was both startled and shocked by this comment, and added in a firm voice, "Marius was only teasing me the other day. Surely you of all people know that. Perhaps Christopher had ogled me a little at the party, but he's very *young*, and I'm absolutely sure he's getting the message."

"If you say so," Laurie murmured, and continued swiftly, "Why don't you pick another Impressionist painting from his collection? I did notice a Morisot. Perhaps Christopher would agree to sell that."

"But Berthe Morisot was influenced by Manet, and later Renoir, not Degas."

"I know, but don't forget she and Mary Cassatt were friends, used to paint together. And here's another point: they were the two most important women who were involved in the Impressionist movement in the eighteen-hundreds."

"My God, you're right! How could I have forgotten that!" Annette's mind began to race as she went on. "That would do it, don't you think? If we could link the three of them, rather than Degas and Cassatt only. I shall phone him tomorrow."

"I know he'll agree." Laurie sounded confident. She was, because James Pollard had let something slip, inadvertently, on Saturday at Knowle Court. Christopher Delaware did not intend to keep any of the art which had been left to him by his uncle, for a very simple reason: he wasn't interested in art. But he had to go slowly because of taxes. Taking a deep breath, Laurie confided this to Annette, as well as other comments Jim had made to her.

"Very enlightening," Annette responded before they both hung up.

Sleep was elusive. She began to doze off and then something would awaken her with a start. The ticking of the clock, the patter of rain against the window, the rustle of the bedroom curtains as a gust of wind blew in. She had always been a light sleeper and tonight she seemed unable to settle down. Turning on her side, she shut her eyes and endeavored to visualize the Morisot painting at Knowle Court. It was one of the artist's earlier works, and not her greatest. On the other hand, Morisot had acquired something of a following in recent years. The painting hanging in the gallery at Knowle Court was of a woman sitting at a mirror doing her hair. Annette had liked it when she first saw it, and now, given the idea Laurie had presented to her, perhaps it would work if shown with the Cassatt. It was worth a call to Christopher, to ask him to put it in the auction. She would phone him tomorrow.

Throwing back the bedclothes, Annette got up, went to the kitchen, and poured herself a glass of milk, then hurried down the corridor to her small office. Turning on the light, she sat down at her desk, began making notes to herself regarding the auction. Marius had teased her for years, calling her a workaholic, and she was, but she couldn't help that. It was the way she was made. Her nature. She enjoyed work, was well organized and adept at what she did, and she had a lot of stamina, could sit at a desk for hours.

After half an hour she put down her pen and sat back in her chair, thinking about her younger sister, Laurie, who was now thirty-six.

Because of the horrific car crash, she had never been able to fulfill her desire to become an actress. Or perhaps she lost the desire and the drive. But, encouraged by Marius and herself, she had studied to be an art expert, focusing on certain Impressionist painters, mainly Degas and Cassatt. Laurie had worked for them for a number of years now, as a research assistant, and was brilliant at it. Once Marius had agreed that Annette could start her own business, Annette Remmington Fine Art, she had made Laurie the only other director of her company, and her sole heir. She wanted to protect her sister's future, give her security.

It pleased Annette that Laurie was as interested in art as she was, and that she had a job she loved, and which gave her a life. Also, she was proud of her little sister, who had made a career for herself with courage and determination. I'll take her to New York, she decided all of a sudden. I'll take her to the auction. We'll go by ship, that would be a nice way to travel for a change, a little holiday. When they went to Europe, they used a private plane, so flying was easy, but she was not sure Marius would let her charter a plane to take Laurie to the States. Seven and a half hours was a long flight for her sister. Yes, a sea voyage would do her good.

This sudden decision to include Laurie brought a smile, a sudden feeling of happiness, and Annette finally left her desk and went back to bed, knowing she would soon fall asleep. But she did not. . . . The past intruded. . . . Another memory slid out from one of its dark hiding places, and she heard them again, those innocent little girls, heard their voices in her head . . . and floating all around her. . . .

"My name is Marie Antoinette and I am Queen of France. Come and dance." Another lilting voice echoed in the air. "I am Empress Josephine, favorite of the French, and there's my husband Napoleon sitting on the bench. Emperor of France. Come and dance. . . ."

Their voices fell away in receding echoes, and the light changed in the cold and silent house where evil lurked in the shadows . . . and as night came down the girls lay trembling in their beds, always afraid now that he had come back. The monster, they called him.

"He's coming," Josephine whispered, her voice trembling. "I can hear him outside the room."

"Stay quiet, stay still," Marie Antoinette whispered back. "Slide down, pull the blankets over your head. Don't make a sound."

The door opened. He came creeping in, knelt down next to Marie Antoinette's bed. He slid his hand under the bedclothes, touching her legs, lifting her nightgown, pushing his fingers into her, harder and harder, pushing them higher, hurting her. Pain shot through her. His head came down on her mouth; she tasted stale beer, averted her face, and began to shake all over. "Please, please don't do this," she begged. But he did not stop, pushed harder. She cried out again in pain. His head came down next to hers on the pillow. He harshly snarled, "If you make another sound, I'll kill her. Understand?" Terrified, she took a deep breath, pleaded with him: "Don't hurt her. Please don't hurt her." He did not answer. His response was to pull off the bedclothes, drop his trousers, and climb on top of her. He was more intoxicated than usual and could not do it tonight. He fell against her, breathing hard, his weight heavy on her. She tried to push him off, tried to slither out from under him, found she could not. Suddenly, in a rush, the door was flung open and bright light from the hall flooded the room. Alison was flying in, shouting angrily. Their cousin pulled her drunken brother off Marie Antoinette, dragged him out of the room. He was like a limp rag at first. Unexpectedly, he came to life. He jumped up, pushing Alison away, but she grabbed him, struggled with him, fought him. She was tall, strong, and sober. Even though she was more terrified than ever, Marie Antoinette peeped around the door again. Her grandfather appeared, hurrying out of his room, shouting at Gregory. He was fighting Alison, beating up on her. They had moved across the landing, were struggling hard, were too close to the top of the stairs. It happened in a flash. Marie Antoinette brought a hand to her mouth to stifle a scream as they both fell down the stairs. They landed in a heap in the hallway at the bottom. They lay still. Neither moved.

A cacophony of sounds. Grandfather shouting. Gregory shouting back. Not a sound from Alison. She went back to Josephine, crept into bed with her, put her arms around her, and held her close . . . protectively, lovingly. The six-year-old girl was sobbing; she endeavored to comfort her, stroking her red-gold hair, holding her close, promising to look after her always. And she did.

They had been sent away from that dangerous house after that. . . . Those sweet, innocent girls . . . sent to live with their mother, and things got worse. . . .

The scene was so vivid, so real, Annette wept into her pillow, filled with hurt for those tender little girls. She wept herself to sleep. And the memories of that fateful night of long ago stayed with her for days.

"And I had this fantastic idea. I'm going to take you to New York with me in September. We'll sail on the *Queen Elizabeth* and you'll be at the auction and we'll have fun. You would come, wouldn't you?"

Laurie could hardly believe it. Annette was inviting her to go with her to New York, where she'd never been, for the auction! Excitement rushed through her. "Of course I'd come. I'd love it, being there with you."

"Then it's a done deal, darling."

"Wonderful! I'm thrilled." There was a moment of hesitation before Laurie said, now haltingly, "But what about Marius? Will it be all right with him?"

"It really doesn't have anything to do with him, does it?" Annette answered swiftly, almost sharply. "Anyway, he'll be pleased, I'm sure. He likes you to participate in things. And, more than likely, he'll be there himself."

"That's great. I can't wait until September." Laurie had a huge smile on her face as she said goodbye to her sister and put the phone down.

As she sat at her desk in her flat, her happiness knew no bounds. The trip was going to be a fantastic experience, and her head was reeling. Slowly she settled down, peering at her computer, but within minutes her mind was far away from her work; she pushed her wheelchair back, rolled out of the office, across the foyer, and into the kitchen. Angie, her caregiver and live-in companion, was talking to Mrs. Groome, the housekeeper who came every day to clean and cook.

They both glanced around as she paused in the kitchen doorway, and saw Laurie. Her face was flushed, her expression reflecting her enormous happiness.

"Annette's going to take me to New York in September!" she exclaimed. "When she has the next auction."

"Isn't that wonderful!" Angie cried, beaming at her.

Mrs. Groome looked surprised, but sounded pleased

when she interjected, "It'll be a really special trip, going there with your sister. And isn't she the one, a proper darling, she is, always thinking about you, caring about you. She's an angel."

"That's true, and there's nobody quite like her in this whole world," Laurie agreed. "But I'd better get back to work, I just wanted you both to hear my exciting news." The two women smiled at her, and Laurie turned the wheelchair around and went back to her office.

It took Laurie a few minutes to settle down, to calm herself. Then she finally returned to her desk and her computer, to tackle the last three pages she had to write. She was completing an in-depth study on Manet for Malcolm Stevens, and he was coming to collect it later in the day. In the past six months she had done a great deal of research for him, and they worked well together. She liked Malcolm; he was a lovely man, and part of the business "family," in a certain sense. Ever since Malcolm had bought the renowned Remmington Gallery, Marius's great creation, he consulted with Marius, and frequently with Annette. Laurie knew he was one of her sister's admirers, in a platonic way, and a good friend, forever reminding them all that he watched Annette's back at all times.

An unexpected cold shiver trickled through Laurie, and she sat back in her chair, stared blindly out the window in front of her desk. Her thoughts went to the phone call Annette had received from Malcolm, who had told her sister that someone was looking for Hilda Crump, was asking questions about her. This had alarmed Annette and she understood the reason why. They did not need someone delving into their past. Their past spelled trouble for them.

Laurie closed her eyes, focusing on her sister. Annette had been everything to her. Mother, father, protector, savior, guardian angel. And also chief caregiver after the car crash. Her sister had given her a full life through her devotion and unconditional love, and by imbuing in her a sense of security. And finally she had helped her to create a career in the art world, a career she loved.

Suddenly, a shiver ran through Laurie again, and goose-flesh spreckled the back of her neck. "*I want you to have a career in art.*" That sentence often replayed itself in her head, the words uttered in the voice of Aunt Sylvia, who had always promised, "*And I am going to get it for you.*"

It was Sylvia, their mother's older sister, who had taken them in at the time of their trouble, after they had left that dark and silent house, left the little town of Ilkley forever. They had been sent to live with their mother, who was residing in London with an actor called Timothy Findas, the two of them holed up in his ramshackle flat in Islington.

Findas was a failure, not a very good actor, and a drunk and a drug addict; and by this time their mother wasn't much better. An actor herself, she had led a rackety life after their father died. Their life with their mother and Findas had been one of deprivation, suffering, and pain. He beat their mother and he beat them, especially Annette. There was never any food or love or kindness. And no communication between them and their mother, who was always high on drugs, or out cold. It was Annette who had taken her hand, and her mother's bit of jewelry hidden under the floorboards in their room, and led her out of that awful flat. Together they had run away, gone to Aunt Sylvia's home in Twicken-ham. A good woman, she had taken them in, and with loving kindness. A widow, with some private means, she had been able to support them financially.

Thank God Annette kept me safe; thank God Aunt Sylvia took us in without a second thought and sent my sister to art school, where she belonged. Laurie swallowed, fighting back the incipient and unexpected tears.

They had never gone back to their grandfather's house in Ilkley, nor did they ever see that ineffectual man again. He died alone in that silent house of gloom.

Laurie sat bolt upright in her wheelchair, recalling Knowle Court and their trip there last Saturday. She had taken a dislike to the place at once, and now she knew why. It reminded her of Craggs End, where their grandparents had lived all of

their married life, where their mother had dumped them after their father's death.

Architecturally, they were totally different, and Craggs
End was much smaller, not like a castle at all. Yet curiously
the atmosphere in both places was the same. An icy coldness and a sense of evil pervaded them.

Dragging her thoughts away from that dark and silent
house in the north of England, she focused on the paintings
of Manet, one of the founders of the Impressionist movement. And she was able to lose herself in his genius, the
enormous beauty of his art.

Chapter Eight

It had been worth waiting for, this astonished look on Marius's face, which instantly changed to total disbelief and then unadulterated pleasure. He stood staring down at *The Little Fourteen-Year-Old Dancer*, and it was quite obvious to Annette that he had been taken by surprise . . . by the statue . . . by her. The latter was something of a novelty in itself, since he could usually second-guess her.

When he finally looked up, stared at her, a silver brow lifting, and asked, "Where on earth did this little beauty spring from?" she simply smiled enigmatically.

Walking over to stand opposite him, the glass coffee table and the Degas bronze between them, she said, "I'll give you three guesses."

He seemed puzzled, pondered for a moment, then responded in a doubtful tone, "It couldn't possibly have come from Sir Alec Delaware's art collection, could it?"

"Aren't you the clever one! However did you guess, darling?"

"Because I usually have my nose to the ground, sniffing out art, as you well know, and there have been no strange whispers about a Degas dancer on the float. And since you represent Christopher Delaware, I simply made a quick assumption. But why didn't you know about it before?"

"Even *he* didn't know he had it, because it wasn't on view in the house. However, he'd begun to poke around in boxes stacked in the attics several weeks ago, and came up with this, and thought it was nothing of importance. Actually, he didn't tell me about it until last Saturday, when we went to Knowle Court. And even then he was awfully dismissive. He didn't think it was worth anything, because it was old and dirty . . . that was the way he put it."

"Silly bugger, but, as my mother used to say, it takes all sorts to make a world." Marius strode around the table, stopped next to Annette, took hold of her, and hugged her to him. Then, a split second later, he held her away, as he so often did, his dark eyes roaming over her face. Gazing at her, his face suddenly filled with adoration, he murmured, "You look very beautiful tonight, my sweet. *Stunning.*"

"You don't look half bad yourself, either," she answered, gazing back at him. He had caught the sun in Barcelona, had acquired a light tan that showed up well against his silver hair, gave him a youthful look. Also, he appeared to be slimmer. "Have you lost weight? You're extremely trim," she announced in an approving tone.

"A little bit, and you would've, too, if you'd been scampering around the Picasso Museum, up and down stairs and through large exhibition halls." He released his grip on her shoulders and confided, "But I'm pleased I went, because it refreshed my memory about Picasso's earlier works now lodged there permanently. I'll tell you something else. I thought it was rather useful to meander through the city where he lived for so many years, and where his family remained after he went to Paris. I got a good sense of the place. It was truly a good trip, and totally necessary for the book."

"So it's full speed ahead now, right?"

Marius nodded, his eyes still focused on her, his expression warm. "So continue with your tale about Christopher's find."

"You know everything. There's not much else to tell. Except that I did ask for the provenance, which he didn't have. Fortunately we found it in the cardboard box where the bronze had been stored."

"Good to have, obviously, but there wouldn't be much

doubt about its authenticity. This is too famous as a piece of sculpture. I'm assuming Laurie has examined it?"

"She did, and she says it's the genuine thing."

"So you're going to put it on auction fairly soon, are you?" he asked, his curiosity aroused.

Annette nodded, walked over to the drinks table, and poured two glasses of champagne from the bottle she had opened a few moments ago. She carried them over, handed him one.

Marius said, touching his glass to hers, "Congratulations, my darling girl. Here's to you."

She smiled at him lovingly. "And to you, Marius, you who taught me everything I know."

He laughed a little dismissively. "Well, not quite, let's say *almost* everything." As he spoke he sat down on the sofa and focused on the sculpture again. "What an amazing life this little dancer has had. . . . Let's hope you can sell her to a collector who will keep her and keep her safe." There was a pause, then he asked, "When do you plan to hold the auction?"

"I'll tell you over dinner, Marius," Annette answered, and continued rather swiftly, "I've booked a table at Mark's Club, because it's quiet and we can talk. I know you prefer more jazzy places, but I've lots to tell you."

"I like Mark's well enough, and it's a good choice for this evening. By the way, I saw the folder of requests for interviews with you on my desk in the den. You've caused quite a sensation, haven't you?" He grinned at her, his delight in her sudden fame apparent, and shook his head. "Over one hundred and fifty requests for interviews. Talk about the new movie star in town . . ." He chuckled.

"I suppose some people would find it flattering. However, I don't. It worries me. Even agreeing to do a few of them would take up too much of my valuable time. I'm very busy at the moment. And anyway, you know I don't like talking about myself. I'm rather a boring person."

"Come, come, Annette, don't be so modest!" he exclaimed, eyeing her oddly. "You're not boring. . . . You're a talented woman, gifted, in fact, and you can hold your own with anyone in business and socially, and in any conversation."

"As long as it's about art," she countered quietly.

"No, no, that's not true. You can talk about a lot of things. Books, the theater, music, and politics, so don't be so silly, and don't put yourself down. There are too many people ready, willing, and able to do that."

"I don't want to talk about myself to the press, Marius, honestly I don't. It frightens me."

Leaning closer to her, fixing those mesmeric eyes of his on her, he said authoritatively, "There is no reason for you to be afraid. The past is the past, Annette, and nobody's going to bring that up, or start digging. Who you are today, what you've become, is all that matters."

She stared into his face, trusting his judgment as she had for as long as she'd known him, yet thinking about the phone call someone had made to Malcolm Stevens about Hilda Crump. *Marius didn't know about that phone call and the mention of Hilda's name after all this time. Should she tell him? No, it didn't matter. It didn't. She had to believe that.*

Slowly, she said, "I think it would be better if I turned everyone down. There was a lot of publicity when I sold the Rembrandt. So why does another interview matter now?"

"Another doesn't. However, a really important interview in a major national newspaper *does*. The Rembrandt auction wasn't your last; in fact, you've got another one coming up, which has now become even more newsworthy because of the discovery of *The Little Fourteen-Year-Old Dancer*. Let's put it this way, darling, you're doing the *selling*, not the buying. You're always going to need a big splashy feature about yourself; every renowned art dealer does, whatever you think. I'll tell you what, as I promised we'll go over the requests tomorrow morning, and I'll select a few journalists with you. I will then ask around about the ones we choose, get the dope on them. How's that?"

"All right," she agreed; nonetheless, she sounded reluctant.

Changing the subject, Marius said, "You told me you'd

had the Cézanne sent to Carlton Fraser. What did he have to say?"

"It's not great news. Carlton is troubled about it. He's not sure he can get the soot off parts of the canvas." She paused, and sounded genuinely worried when she murmured, "He said something really peculiar—" She cut herself off, shook her head, her expression dismal all of a sudden.

"What did he say?" Marius asked. "Come on, tell me, Annette."

"That a fall of soot from a chimney would definitely float in the air and could easily settle onto a painting hanging in the room. Then he muttered something about deliberate damage, that it looked to him as if someone had *deliberately* rubbed the soot into some areas of the painting."

"Good God! Who on earth would do such an horrendous thing? It's verging on the criminal! To destroy a painting by the great Cézanne, or any other artist for that matter, is wicked." Marius sounded angry, and there was a look of genuine pain in his eyes. He sat rigid on the sofa, staring at her.

Annette recognized his fury at once. He could not bear to see anything of great beauty desecrated, and neither could she. Wanting to soothe him, she said, "I'm not sure Carlton is right about the deliberate damage part. I myself thought that someone had attempted to clean one side of it, not an expert but an amateur, and that they made a mess. Accidentally."

Marius sat back on the sofa and closed his eyes. After a moment he snapped them open and exclaimed, "Whoever did that is an idiot. And that person should be stood up against a wall and shot!"

Chapter Nine

Mark's Club on Charles Street in Mayfair was quiet tonight, but then it usually was on Friday, since many of its members had already gone off to their country homes for the weekend. Although his preference was for jazzier places to dine, Marius was suddenly glad Annette had booked a table for them here. He'd had a hectic week in Barcelona and Mark's was always a haven of calm tranquillity.

They climbed the stairs to the bar, which years ago Mark Birley, the founder of the club, had decorated in the manner of an English country house parlor. A fire blazed in the hearth, and since the room was only partially occupied by fellow diners, they had a choice of comfortable chairs and sofas on which to sit.

"I'm always a sucker for a fire, as you well know," Marius remarked as they entered the room, and he guided her to the sofa near the hearth. A moment later he was ordering two glasses of champagne as they settled back and made themselves comfortable.

After a small silence, Annette said, "Going back to Cézanne, and our conversation earlier, even if Carlton does manage to clean and restore the painting, it presents a problem because there's no provenance."

His eyes narrowed, and he pursed his lips. "It beggars belief that a man like Alec Delaware, who made a huge fortune in business, didn't protect his investment in art." Marius shook his head and looked off into the distance, his mind turning rapidly. Bringing his intense gaze back to his wife, he asked in a low voice, "How *good* is the provenance on the Degas dancer?"

"It's perfect. The lineage is a straight line of ownership. It was one of those cast in bronze at Hébrard's, and it was eventually sold by the Hébrard Gallery to a French art dealer, who eventually auctioned it off to a wealthy collector in Paris. The bronze passed through a few hands after that . . . several art dealers, private collectors in New York and Beverly Hills, and eventually it was bought at auction in New York by Alec Delaware in 1989. It was *not* the one sold in New York by Sotheby's in 1997, by the way. The papers are at home and you can look at them later, and you'll see they establish provenance beyond any doubt."

"Sounds like it. Does the bronze itself have any identifying mark, by the way?"

"Yes, Laurie thoroughly checked it, and the bronze is marked with a G. The bronzes which were cast in the 1920s were marked with a letter from A to T, and those were intended for sale to the public. Others were reserved for the Degas family, and for Hébrard. They were marked differently."

He gave her the benefit of a wide approving smile. "You two are the very best," he murmured, and asked, "What about the other art from the Delaware collection? Where do you stand with those pieces?"

"There are documents which establish provenance, I'm relieved to tell you."

"So what's going on the block, Annette? As well as the Degas dancer?"

"A Degas painting. It's a carriage with passengers, parked at the races. There's a Mary Cassatt of a mother and child, and also a Morisot, of a woman facing a mirror. Laurie thought these three Impressionist paintings worked well together, and the artists were contemporaries, friends. It makes a theme."

Marius nodded, sat back, looking thoughtful. After a moment he said, "Laurie could help establish provenance for the Cézanne, perhaps. It's a tough job, but she has the talent and patience to trace its history through old books, old catalogues, archives, bills of sale, if there are any. What do you think?"

"She can give it a try. Perhaps she'll enjoy the challenges," Annette answered, and wondered if her sister would. She also wondered if it was worth the effort. Carlton Fraser had sounded extremely glum about the outcome of his cleaning and restoration work. But she did not mention this to Marius. She had learned long ago to be careful, to edit what she said to him. He had a short fuse and easily became annoyed and upset. This was the reason she had not mentioned the phone call Malcolm Stevens had received about Hilda Crump. Better that he didn't know. And Malcolm would never say anything either. He knew her husband almost as well as she did. Marius didn't deal in trivia. It was the big picture which counted.

The dining room at Mark's was a favorite of Annette's because of the art hanging on the walls. All of the paintings were of dogs and had been painted in the nineteenth and early twentieth centuries. Beautifully framed, they had been cleverly arranged and hung by Mark Birley himself many years before.

The two of them sat on a banquette facing the longest wall in the room, at the table Annette considered to be the best. From where they were sitting they had a perfect view of the oil paintings, all of which were beautiful as well as charming, amusing, often poignant, and which never failed to bring a smile to her face, or touch her heart.

"Oh, good, they've got bangers and mash on the menu tonight," Marius exclaimed as he eyed the menu. "Yes, it's nursery food for me, sausages and spuds. Takes me back to my childhood. What would you like, Annette?"

"You know I always have the potted shrimp when we

come here, they're the best in London, and I think I'll have the grilled sole."

"A bit of a fishy dinner, darling, isn't it?" he teased. "But I'll order a good Pouilly-Fuissé. How's that?"

"Lovely, Marius, and what are you going to have first?"

"Like you, the potted shrimp." He indicated to the maître d' standing near the doorway that they were ready to order, and he came over at once, smiling, his pad in hand.

Once they had ordered their dinner, Annette swiveled slightly on the banquette and put her hand on Marius's arm. She said in a light voice, not wanting to be overly dramatic, "I really don't want to do any interviews. *Not even one.* Can't I just skip it?"

Turning to her, studying her for a moment, Marius took hold of her hand, held it in his. He said, finally, in a low voice, "No, you *can't* skip it, Annette. And for a variety of reasons, which I'll get to in a moment. I want to say something else first, and it's this. Don't be afraid, darling. The past is dead and buried, and nothing's going to come out about your early years. Trust me on this. I do interviews all the time, and the press these days is mostly interested in the art, and only the art. How much is the painting worth? What will you get for it? Who owned it before? Art is now equated with big money, huge money, and that's what they love to write about. Money, provenance, who's competing with each other to buy the latest and most important symbol of power and wealth. Please believe me, I'm right about this, and then there's the sudden discovery of *The Little Fourteen-Year-Old Dancer. Your* new prize piece. It's vital to get tongues wagging about it, and what better way than in an important interview?"

A sigh escaped, and she said quietly, hesitantly, "I suppose so . . ." She broke off, shrugged, looked directly at him. "I can't tell you how much I hate the idea of doing even one interview, whoever the journalist might be," she added, her tone suddenly stronger.

"I know that. But listen to me—you really do have to do *one*, at least. And it must be a big one. Art is a bit of a cut-throat business, *you* know that, and everyone is scrambling to be at the top. The competition is fierce, you've lived through it for years. Suddenly, and unexpectedly, you became a star overnight. Partially because Christopher Delaware remembered you were nice to him at a dinner, and he brought the Rembrandt to you. *Luck.* Sheer bloody *luck,* sweetheart! So you must keep your name up there. You can't simply turn away and hope to go on making big deals without promoting yourself."

He paused, took a sip of the wine the sommelier brought for him to taste, and nodded. "Very good. Nice and cold, too. Thank you."

He gave the waiter a faint smile, and turned back to his wife. "You've done well with Annette Remmington Fine Art because of the route you went, setting yourself up as an art consultant and art expert, rather than opening your own gallery. You know only too well what that costs. But *your* overhead is in the medium range because you have a small office and a small staff. It all works in your favor. But you've got to keep making the big deals, the superlative deals, and publicity is mandatory. Your clients, the right clients for you, *must* be the wealthiest in the world. The tycoons, titans of industry, lawyers, bankers, the billionaire bunch who can afford those much-desired famous paintings and sculptures by the world's greatest artists. Because expensive art is *the* status symbol today."

Silent, she sipped her white wine, made no comment. She was taut inside.

In a much firmer voice he continued, "You've got to keep your eye on your ultimate goal. Okay? *Focus. Determination. Drive. Ambition. Taste. Knowledge of art.* Those are *your* special attributes and you must not lose sight of them. And there's another thing: I won't be here to protect you for the rest of your life. Let's not forget, I'm much older than you. I want you to stay at the top, to stay where you are today. A star in the art world. And you *can* do that. If you manage your career properly. That is an imperative."

"You're right," she admitted at last, knowing that he really was speaking the truth. "All right, I'll do it," she agreed. "On one condition."

"And what's that?" he asked, a brow lifting, wondering what she was about to say now.

"That you stop talking about being older than me, intimating that you won't be around to protect me as you have in the past."

"I have, haven't I? Because I love you. And I've protected Laurie as well," he pointed out.

"Yes, that's true, darling, and I'm grateful. Please don't think I don't know you have my best interests at heart, because I do." She forced a laugh. "I'm just being silly about the past, aren't I?"

"*Absolutely*. Nobody cares what you did when you were eighteen."

I wish that were true, she thought. I wish the law didn't have different ideas. She merely smiled and said nothing. A still tongue and a wise head. She started to eat the potted shrimp, which had just been placed in front of her. After a few seconds had elapsed, she remarked casually, "I think I'd prefer to do an interview for one of the Sunday papers, and you can make the decision which one it should be."

"Good girl," he responded, and took a long swallow of the wine, pleased that she had come around, saw things his way. He believed he did know what was best, but he was aware she felt the need to fight him sometimes.

They talked about a number of other things during dinner, and it was when they had finished the main course that Marius suddenly said, "By the way, you haven't told me when you plan to have the next auction. Have you given it any thought?"

"Of course I have, Marius! I've planned everything," she exclaimed, a ring of excitement in her voice. "I'm going to have it in September. In New York. The office there has already sent me client lists and ideas, and Laurie has been working on it—" She stopped abruptly when she noticed the look on her husband's face. It was a combination of surprise and anger. She sat quite still, waiting for the explosion.

"*New York!*" His voice was low but vehement. "Why *there*, not here in London? And why have you gone ahead with everything without even discussing it with me?"

She took a deep breath and answered as evenly as possible. "Because I usually make these decisions myself. I chose London for the Rembrandt sale because it felt right to hold it here. I had the same visceral feeling that the Degas ballet dancer and the Impressionist paintings would do better if auctioned in New York. At Sotheby's."

"I certainly don't think the auction would do better in the States! You'd be better off doing it at Sotheby's here," he said.

She noticed that he was holding his temper in check, now spoke in a lighter voice, erasing the anger from it as best he could. She knew he didn't want to quarrel with her, not in public and not when he had been away for a week. She never knew what he did on those many trips he took alone, nor had she ever asked. But he was always slightly different when he came back, more considerate, less bossy, not as controlling.

But deep inside herself she knew he was going to manipulate her tonight, as he so frequently did. He had to have his own way. He had to win. She thought about mentioning her idea of taking Laurie to New York, and decided against it. What would be the point? He wouldn't care about that. For his own reasons, he wanted the auction to be held in London, and what *she* thought didn't matter. It never had. That was the way it had always been and always would be.

Annette sank down into herself, filled with disappointment, annoyance, and a strange sadness. He had given her a degree of independence when he had agreed that she could open her own office, but he was still the boss. As far as he was concerned. Don't argue with him, let it go, she told herself. And so she did.

The silence that fell between them was long and somewhat awkward. Annette was determined not to be the first one to speak, and she was strong-willed when she wanted to be.

Eventually, Marius was forced to say something. "What would you like for dessert, sweetheart?" he asked, his manner mild.

"Nothing, thanks," she responded swiftly, then added, "Chamomile tea will be enough."

"Not hungry?" he asked, peering at her, taking hold of her hand, holding it in his. "You know you like the puddings here."

"Not tonight, Marius. Honestly, I'm not hungry anymore."

"Don't be angry with me, darling. I want what's best for you. I know you must concentrate on doing important things in London at the moment. This is where you live, where you're based, and where your career is. Where you had your first huge auction, your great success. I don't think things would work in your favor in New York. Just as they wouldn't if you chose to do it in Paris."

"Whatever you say. After all, you've been playing this game longer than I have. Anyway, I trust your judgment." A smile wavered on her mouth and was instantly gone. "London, Paris, and New York, the biggest art cities in the world. So then, let's pick London this time around, and why not? You've made some good points, Marius."

A sense of relief rippled through him, and he felt himself relaxing against the banquette. He did not like to quarrel with her, and rarely did he have to, because she was usually acquiescent. But he had noticed of late that her inbred independent streak had grown stronger, and this rattled him occasionally. He needed her to be in step with him, not bucking his decisions. Thankfully she had fallen into line once more.

Looking at her, he said softly, "I promise you this will be the biggest auction London has seen in decades. And it will be far more important than your Rembrandt sale."

"And obviously bigger than it would be in New York? Is that what you mean?"

"Yes, if you put it that way. London *is* better in this instance."

"All right, I'll cancel the plans I made, and concentrate on making everything work here."

He couldn't help thinking how beautiful she was tonight. She was wearing a delphinium-blue silk suit and aquamarine earrings, and the two blues emphasized the color of her eyes. Her blond hair was well cut and styled, shining in the candlelight, and she had the air of an accomplished, successful, and sophisticated woman about her.

In a flash, in his mind's eye, he saw that starveling girl he had first met when she was eighteen, so thin she was like a wafer, a look of poverty and deprivation clinging to her. She had come to him for a job at the Remmington Gallery in the early days, when it was first located in Cork Street, and he had taken her on to do weekend work out of pity.

She was neat and clean and nicely spoken, and she had tugged at his heart. And how clever she had been, so talented, a top student at the Royal Academy of Art. Her sense of color, perspective, and composition was extraordinary, and he was impressed with her paintings, which she had shown him so proudly. Yet with his innate taste, his extraordinary understanding of art, his superior knowledge and experience, he had realized that although she was good, even brilliant in certain ways, she would never be a great artist. She would be one of many good painters, never a star.

He had given her a receptionist job at the gallery, taken her under his wing, looked after her. Within only a few days he had recognized the inherent beauty of her face; the high cheekbones, the delicate, perfect features, and those heart-stopping eyes, huge, bright blue, filled with intelligence. He had seen her potential as a woman, started to take an interest in her, instilling a sense of personal style in her, grooming her, teaching her about art, sharing his knowledge. And then one day she had let him down. It was only then that he understood about himself, his feelings for her. And he was shocked at his emotional entanglement. He had fallen in love with the starveling girl who had been stolen from him. *Briefly.*

She had come running back when serious trouble wrapped its tentacles around her. Frightened, panic-stricken, afraid of the police and what might happen to her, she had come to him and he had done the only thing he could do to make her feel safe, secure. He had married her. A few days after her nineteenth birthday in early June. Twenty-one years ago this summer.

Slowly, painstakingly, with love and skill, he had created the woman he thought she could be and was today. She was entirely of his making. His creation. There were those vicious, jealous gossips who said she was Trilby to his Svengali. That wasn't so, not in his opinion. He truly loved her, had from the moment he had first seen her.

His best friend at the time had accused him of cradle snatching, and he had laughed in his face. He had been thirty-eight, she a mere eighteen, so perhaps there was some truth in that, as he looked back now.

"Marius, darling, what is it?" Annette asked, touching his hand, staring at him. "Are you all right?"

She had roused him from his memories, and as he turned to her, he pulled himself together. "I'm fine. I was lost in my thoughts, that's all." He cleared his throat, took a sip of wine.

"What were you thinking about?" she probed.

"Something dragged me back into the past, to when I first met you, and I was thinking how beautiful you were."

Annette stared at him, her brows puckering, and she shook her head. "I was such a funny thin little thing," she countered. "Half starved, half demented, and hardly beautiful."

"Don't say that. . . . You were beautiful to me then and you still are now."

Chapter Ten

There is something quite splendid about Marius this morning, Annette decided, as she sat opposite him in the breakfast room, drinking her coffee.

Showered, shaved, and with his mane of silver hair brushed back sleekly, he looked the epitome of good health and well-being. Dressed in a blue-and-white-checked shirt, open at the neck, and gray trousers, he had a youthful look about him, due in no small measure to the tan he had acquired in Spain and his remarkably unlined face. He wears well, she thought. He looks so much younger than he is.

He was genial and affectionate with her as he ate his toast and marmalade, and between sips of coffee chatted to her about the book he was writing on Picasso.

From experience, she knew he was in a good mood because he had won hands down last night. But then he always does win, doesn't he? Whenever he manipulated her into doing what *he* wanted, he was like this. Warm and purring. And then, of course, she had assuaged his anxiety about *her* mood, because she had succumbed to his overtures in bed. As she always did, although sex was not a big part of her life. If she never had sex again, she wouldn't miss it.

He had been a passionate yet tender lover since their first sexual encounter when she was eighteen. Nothing had changed; he still was. Marius knew how to arouse a woman, and she had learned long ago to accept his overtures grace-fully. He could not tolerate any kind of rejection, in bed or out of it. Also, that addictive charm of his was in place most of the time, and it could be irresistible even to her.

"Whatever's wrong, darling?" he asked, interrupting her thoughts, aware she wasn't paying attention to him.

"Nothing," she answered, sitting up straighter, offering him a warm smile. "Just lost in my thoughts for a moment. Sorry."

"You look as if you have the troubles of the world on your shoulders." He gave her a penetrating look and went on in a knowing voice, "You're worrying about the Giacometti sculpture, aren't you?"

She wasn't, but she seized on this immediately and ex-claimed, "Yes, I am, actually. I just don't know whether to put it in the next auction or wait for my third. I'm not sure that it quite fits into the theme Laurie and I developed. . . . You know, the three Impressionist painters being the link."

"I wonder if that really matters," Marius responded, en-gaged instantly and looking thoughtful. "Giacometti sculp-tures are going for high prices these days, so why hold it back? Perhaps there's a way to change the theme, or expand it. Or not have a theme for the art at all."

"All are options," she agreed. "Christopher has a few modern paintings which would fit into a Modernist theme, but he doesn't want to put them on sale right now. Otherwise I suppose we could create a second theme."

"Which painters?"

"Ben Nicholson and Lowry."

"Hats off to Sir Alec! My God, he certainly knew what he was doing when he chose his art, if not when it came to cataloguing it. And why doesn't Christopher want to put those on the block? Did he tell you?"

She nodded. "He wants to go slowly because of taxes. As you know, he did inherit everything from his uncle, so there have been huge death-duty taxes." She noticed the sudden gleam flashing in his dark eyes, and said, "And if you're thinking I can make him change his mind, you're absolutely wrong."

Marius was no fool, and he knew his wife extremely well, and so he said, "I believe you. Therefore, I suggest you start the auction with the Degas and the Giacometti sculptures *first*, and then bring on the three paintings. You might tag them great sculptures from two centuries and let them stand alone. Then you could tie the three paintings into the Impressionist theme. But don't hold the Giacometti back, sell it while the going's good."

"Not bad for quick thinking! And thank you, Marius, you've solved my problem."

"My pleasure. And how about solving another one? Together?"

"You want to go through the requests for interviews, is that it?"

"It is," he answered, and pushed back his chair. "Let's go and sit in my den, and scan them. It won't take long."

Annette was glad to escape the flat after several hours had been spent on deciding about the journalist who would do the interview with her. Marius had finally settled on the one he wanted, who he thought would draw the best portrait of her in words.

The man's name was Jack Chalmers, and Marius knew a little about him already. But in order to check him out properly, glean a few more facts, he had phoned Malcolm Stevens a short while ago, "just to get the lowdown," was the way he put it to Malcolm.

According to Malcolm, who was a fund of information about all sorts of people and things, Chalmers was a young hotshot reporter who had swiftly risen up through the ranks of British journalism to make a name for himself. He had also written two brilliant histories of World War II, and was highly respected by editors and colleagues alike. According to Malcolm, Chalmers was under contract to *The Sunday Times* and wrote profiles of people in the news for the paper.

Apparently he was considered to be a nice chap, never needed to go for the jugular or felt it necessary to stick a knife into the heart of an interviewee. Yet he managed to write riveting copy everybody lapped up. "Without resorting to invective or bitchiness," Malcolm had finished, adding, "That's a formidable talent."

After repeating the rest of Malcolm's conversation to her, Marius had made the final decision, although he had said, "If that's all right with you, darling." He always said that and had for years, but it meant nothing.

Of course it was all right with her. She had never had any choice, actually. About anything. Marius was the law.

As she walked down Eaton Square, heading for her sister's flat in Chesham Place, Annette suddenly filled up with anger. It rose like bile in her throat, choking her. But it was not anger at Marius; rather it was anger with herself.

Why was she so weak-kneed? Why did she accept whatever he said as gospel? She had done that last night, had allowed him to manipulate her out of having the auction in New York.

She had sat back this morning as Marius had chatted away to Malcolm, and again had nodded in agreement when he had settled on Jack Chalmers.

She was a fool, and she knew it. She could be, and had been in the last twenty-one years, very strong about a lot of things, and yet when it came to herself and what she wanted, she just gave in without a protest.

Oh, to hell with it, she thought, trying to push all these worrisome thoughts away. Who the hell cares about Jack Chalmers! Robin Hood or Tom Thumb can come and interview me for all I care. The interview was a nuisance anyway. She couldn't wait to do it, get it over with, and move on to more important things.

Her main concern at the moment was Laurie, and the disappointment her sister would experience when she found out they were not going to New York after all. Annette suffered when she could not follow up on something she had promised Laurie, even though this only occasionally happened. The car crash had ruined Laurie's life; Annette forever endeavored to give her sister joy and a little fun, and make living less boring for her.

She'll guess straightaway, Annette thought, as she stepped into the foyer of the flat and greeted Angie, Laurie's caregiver. She'll read my face, she decided as she shed her coat. In order to forestall this, Annette pushed a smile onto her face and went into the living room, exclaiming, "Here I am! Sorry I'm late."

"That's all right, Annette," Laurie answered, smiling. "I was busy talking to Malcolm anyway. We had a few things to discuss. I just finished another pile of research for him and he's going to take me to dinner tonight. As a special treat."

"That's great. He's always been so nice with you," Annette murmured. She bent over and kissed her sister, sat down in the chair next to her. "Where do you want to go to lunch?"

Laurie shook her head. "We're not going out. Mrs. Groome is making lunch for us today, and so we're going to have it here. I hope that's all right?"

"It's fine, whatever you want." Annette reached out, touched her arm, and said, "Listen, before we get lost in our usual chitchat, I've something to tell you."

Laurie stared at her, frowned. "You sound very serious all of a sudden. What's wrong?"

"Nothing's wrong, not in the sense you mean. But I'm afraid we won't be sailing off to New York on the *Queen Elizabeth*. I hate to disappoint you, but Marius thinks we should have the auction in London, not New York."

Laurie's face dropped, but in an instant a smile spread across her face. "Oh, don't worry. Malcolm had wanted to come with us on the trip, so perhaps the three of us could still go, after the auction in London, I mean."

"Malcolm wanted to come with us!" Annette sounded startled. "I didn't know you were . . . *so friendly.*"

"Oh, yes, we are. Very, very good friends. He often comes over for dinner, and he takes me out quite a lot."

For a moment Annette didn't quite know what to say, so

surprised was she, but she finally found her voice. "Well, he's always been one of my favorites, and I know he'll look after you properly when you're out together."

Laurie burst out laughing. "I can look after myself, you know that. And we're good friends," she added again. "We enjoy each other's company, we've a great deal in common."

"I know you do." Annette sat very still for a moment, staring into the fire, watching the flames shoot up the chimney. She wondered if Marius would approve of this growing friendship, and then pushed the thought away. One thing was certain. She would never permit him to interfere in Laurie's life.

As if Laurie were seeing into her head, she said, "I know you're angry with Marius. Inside, Annette. You're not showing it, but I can feel it. You're angry because he always manages to manipulate you, control you. And listen, why does he think London's better for the auction?"

"Because I had my first big auction here with the Rembrandt. My first big success. He wants me to repeat it . . . wants it to be bigger and better."

"But you could have done that in New York, couldn't you? Made it bigger and better?"

"*I* think so. But perhaps he knows something I don't."

"I suppose it doesn't matter really," Laurie murmured, giving her sister a hard stare. "When there's a newly discovered Degas sculpture, and especially when it's *The Little Fourteen-Year-Old Dancer*, you know the auction is going to be a smash hit wherever it is held."

Annette stared back. "How right you are," she responded, thinking how smart her sister was. She also realized that Marius had known exactly the same thing. They *could* easily have had the auction in New York; it would have worked just as well there as here, because of the fame and quality of the artworks. But for a reason she had no inkling of, he had been determined to make her have the auction in London.

Laurie swung her chair slightly, faced Annette, and smiled at her sister. "Listen, I know it annoys you, this controlling of his, the manipulation that's gone on for years. But you do get your own way in so many other things. Because you're very clever, and he has always looked after us, hasn't he?"

"Yes, and I've always played the game, been loyal to him."

There was a pause before Laurie said, "Whatever would we have done without him?"

"I don't know," Annette answered, thinking that she might have gone to jail and Laurie would have been dependent on the kindness of their aunt. Not very great prospects, to say the least. Taking a deep breath, she remarked in a very positive voice, "The main thing is to make the auction a big success. So I guess where it's held doesn't really matter. Now, on to something else. You're an avid newspaper reader. . . . Have you ever heard of a journalist called Jack Chalmers?"

"He's fantastic. I think he writes like a dream, beautifully, and he's incisive. I read every profile of his in *The Sunday Times*. Oh, my goodness, is *he* going to interview you?"

"He is . . . that's who Marius has chosen."

Laurie exclaimed, "I think he'll do well by you." She grinned. "Marius made a good choice."

Part Two

THE HOTSHOT
JOURNALIST

There is no god higher than truth.
                    Mahatma Gandhi (1939)

Chapter Eleven

J ack Chalmers liked all things familiar, be it a particular home, city, country locale, ski resort, beach, bar, restaurant, or pub. His desire for the familiar also included people.

He had his preferred bartenders, maître d's, waiters, and, most important, publishers and editors who understood him and who he believed could turn dross into pure gold. All of the above made him feel comfortable, relaxed, and at ease, whilst giving him a great deal of pleasure; he thought of them as the simple things in life, which not all of them were, of course.

This particular week, the last in March, was extra special for Jack. . . . He was in Beaulieu-sur-Mer, his favorite town in the south of France, where he had a beautiful villa overlooking the Mediterranean.

The Villa Saint-Honoré was his permanent home, filled with yet another collection of old familiar things which made up his life, and which, to him, made sense: his IBM Personal Wheelwriter 2 by Lexmark, a wonderful typewriter on which he wrote his books; his computer for research and writing his newspaper and magazine pieces; thousands of books; a plethora of framed photographs from his childhood and his older years, plus pictures of his mother, his father, his brother, and the rest of the family.

Other polished wood surfaces were covered with unique

mementos collected on his world travels, as well as stacks of prestigious awards for his work, somewhat carelessly displayed, and, in a corner near the window, there was a huge antique world globe on a stand which he had loved to spin and gaze at when he was a child.

There were also chests, cupboards, and closets full of extremely expensive but understated casual clothes, the kind he favored, and a collection of worn trenchcoats that he loved and couldn't bring himself to throw away.

Now he stood in front of one of these closets in his huge upstairs office on this Tuesday morning, looking through his jackets. Finally selecting a lightweight beige linen, he slipped it on over his navy V-necked sweater and jeans and left his office.

Here in his charming house on the sea he was in seventh heaven. . . . The familiar piled up on top of the familiar . . . what could be better? He smiled inwardly, his spirits lifting as he ran down the stairs, crossed the terra-cotta-tiled hall, and went along a corridor to the kitchen.

Opening the door, he stuck his head around it. "*Bonjour*, Hortense!"

His housekeeper swung her head and gave him a huge smile. "*Bonjour*, Monsieur Jacques."

"I'm going out for a while, but I'll be back for lunch around one. Where's Amaury?"

"He went to Nice. For magazines, newspapers you want. They didn't have here. Do you need him, monsieur?" she asked in her almost perfect English.

"No, no, Hortense, it's nothing important. See you later." He flashed her a smile and was gone.

Jack went out of the front door and down the path, glanced around, sniffing the air, catching the scent of mimosa and, underlying this, the fresh smell of the leaves on the trees, the newly mown lawns on each side of the path.

He loved this time of year in the south of France, relished being back after a month working in Beverly Hills and New York, doing three important interviews and drafting them.

He had flown directly here from the States four days ago,

and already he felt refreshed, ready to tackle the last chapter of his third book, which his publishers were expecting in a week. It would go in on time. He had never missed a deadline in his life, and he prided himself on that achievement.

Walking up the Boulevard Maréchal Leclerc, he lifted his eyes at one moment and looked up. It was a periwinkle-blue sky this morning, filled with pale sunlight filtering through a few wispy white clouds; it was a sparkling day, not cold at all, and although there was a light breeze blowing in from the sea, it carried a hint of warmth.

Jack was heading in the direction of La Réserve, one of the loveliest hotels in the world, in his opinion, and one which he had been going to since he was five. That was when his mother had first taken him there. *The summer of 1982.* My God, twenty-five years ago, he suddenly thought, I've been living in this town on and off for most of my life. No wonder it feels like home turf in so many different ways.

After waiting several minutes for the traffic on this main road to slow, he made a quick dash across the boulevard when there was a gap and went through the open gates of the hotel. He paused for a moment, taking everything in, before strolling through the front gardens and down the short driveway leading to the entrance.

A moment later he was entering the lobby, warmly greeting the concierge, then striding toward the long bar. Traversing this, he went through the empty dining room and out onto the terrace overlooking the Mediterranean, where breakfast was usually served.

The terrace was empty, and there were no waiters in sight; he sat down at a small table with an umbrella positioned close to the balustrade. Taking off his dark glasses, he shaded his light-gray eyes with his hand and looked out across the sea. How calm it was this morning, not a ripple, almost like a pond. Slipping his glasses back on, he pulled out his cell phone as it rang, put it to his ear, and said, "It's Jack."

"Morning. It's Kyle. How're you doing?"

"Great. Just got back a few days ago. Guess where I'm sitting right now?"

"You're back in Beaulieu, aren't you?" his stepbrother asserted, always knowing where Jack was.

"I am. But guess where I'm about to have breakfast?"

Kyle's amused chuckle came down the line. "La Réserve, I've no doubt, you spoiled bugger. It's always the best places for you, Jacko. So where else would you be? Especially since you just got back. You can't resist the old haunts when you've been away, my lad."

"Full of memories, Kyle. And you know that only too well. You're the same about certain places. Anyway, what's up?"

"I'll cut to the chase. I was at Dad's solicitors yesterday. We can now put the house on the market, everything's sorted. Or if you don't want to do that, you still have the right to buy my share of it and own it yourself."

"I don't want a big house in Hampstead, Kyle! And neither do you. The two of us are always on the move, and you indicated you'll be directing a film in Hollywood in a few months. Let's do what we've always said we'd do. Let's sell the house. Okay?"

"Okay, it's a done deal! And I *did* get the movie. I'll be going to Jordan to direct it, though, not Hollywood."

"*Jordan*. Jesus, Kyle, that's too close to Iraq and Afghanistan, too close to the battlefronts for my liking."

"It's safe, though, isn't it?" Kyle asked swiftly.

"Yep, it is, and they're pro-West, but don't go straying off. Don't go anywhere I wouldn't go. Okay, buddy-boy?"

"You got it. Are you going to be there for long?"

"A couple of weeks. I have to edit my interviews, which I drafted after I'd done them, to save time. And I've one chapter to go on the new book, *Dunkerque*. The manuscript has to be in next week."

"You've got your hands full, but you like that, Jack. By the way, I've been meaning to ask you something. When you sent me a copy of the jacket, I noticed the French spelling of *Dunkerque*, and not *Dunkirk*. Why?"

"I don't know, to be honest, except that I've always liked the French spelling. Also, everyone understands what it means, even non-French-speaking people. The publishers like it as well. They think it has a certain flair."

"It does, actually, now that you mention it. So listen, when will I see you, buddy-boy?" Kyle asked.

"I'm thinking of bringing the manuscript to London. I need to check up on a few things in the flat, and also see my agent. I'll let you know. In the meantime, I've got my work cut out for me in the next week."

"You love to be overloaded with writing assignments and to have piles of work surrounding you. It gives you a thrill."

Jack began to laugh. "It sure as hell gets my adrenaline flowing, that I do know."

"How's Lucy?"

"I guess she's fine, Kyle. To tell you the truth, I haven't been up to see her yet. We've spoken on the phone and she sounds great. I'll be seeing her tomorrow, to catch up."

"That's an odd way of putting it," Kyle said, and quickly added, "Sorry. None of my business. See ya, Jacko."

"See ya, Kyle."

Jack clicked off the phone, put it in his pocket, and instantly noticed the jug of orange juice which had miraculously appeared on the table, along with a tall glass. Glancing around, he spotted one of the waiters he knew, and beckoned for him to come over. After they greeted each other in a friendly manner, Jack said, "The usual, please."

The waiter nodded and hurried off.

Before he had even finished the glass of orange juice, the café au lait and basket of croissants arrived, along with butter and a dish of apricot jam.

Sipping the juice slowly, Jack's mind focused on Kyle's last comment, and he knew his brother was right. It was an odd thing to say . . . that he and Lucy would *catch up* tomorrow. *Lucy Jameson.* The woman in his life at this moment. But was she really? He wasn't quite sure what to do about her. Or what he felt about her.

Jack was suddenly surrounded by a bustle of activity, which sent all thoughts of Lucy flying right out of his head. The waiter who had served the juice was pouring the coffee and milk, deftly removing the empty glass and jug, while the headwaiter, Pierre, who managed the breakfast hours, was hurrying over to greet him. Following behind were several hotel guests obviously wondering where to sit. After showing them to different tables, Pierre continued down the terrace, finally stopped at his table, a smile on his face.

"Bonjour. And welcome back, Mr. Chalmers. It's nice to see you."

"And you, Pierre. How're things? Is the hotel busy?"

"It was at the weekend. It's slackened off. We'll be full at Easter. As usual. Can I bring you something else? Eggs? Fruit?"

Jack shook his head. "No, thanks, this is perfect."

With another smile and a nod, the headwaiter went over to speak to the newly arrived guests, and Jack sat back, enjoying his café au lait, the croissant, the pleasant weather, and the spectacular view across the bay. Lucy had gone out of his head only momentarily. As he thought of her now, he realized he did not want to focus on the problem of her today. *Problem? Was she a problem? More than likely, yes. Another day. I'll think about her another day.* He laughed to himself. *Margaret Mitchell got it right. Tomorrow is another day.* He laughed to himself again.

Jack ran his brother's phone call through his head, thinking of that rambling old house in Hampstead where they had grown up.

It *was* big, no two ways about that, but it was a great home for a family. A growing family. He doubted they would have trouble selling it.

A surge of unexpected memories filled his head with sudden nostalgia, thoughts of the past . . . the picnics under the big apple tree on hot summer afternoons, the swings which carried them high into the sky, the mock battles with wooden swords and rubber breastplates when they played soldiers, and those fabulous garden parties their parents had given, and which he and Kyle had attended when they were young . . . actors surrounding their father, who was a theatrical agent; producers; writers and directors; journalists and celebrities.

Kyle was two years older than he was, and they had always been close, ever since his mother had married Kyle's father; they were still close today. Bonded forever. His big brother. His protector. But now sometimes he felt more like the protector of Kyle. *Role reversals*, he thought. *It sometimes happens.*

He hated the idea of Kyle going to Jordan. It *was* a safe country, and the king was pro-Western and smart, but part of the Middle East was a war zone and Kyle was inquisitive, trusting, and fearless. Also, he was prone to taking side trips when he was working on a film abroad. *I'll have to talk to him before he flies off. I need him to get his ducks in a row, need him to understand exactly what's going on, the inherent dangers he faces. I've got to make him promise he'll stay put, not wander off into one of the nearby countries when he's finished the movie.*

It struck him then that he hadn't asked about the movie Kyle was about to direct, and he was annoyed with himself. Kyle was always interested in his work, his life, and concerned for him.

He pulled out his phone, dialed his brother, and when he answered, Jack said, "Hey, Kyle, I didn't ask what film you're about to direct."

"It's about a woman called Lesley Blanch, who was a writer—"

"She wrote *The Wilder Shores of Love*, among other books," Jack interrupted. "And she was married to a French author called Romain Gary."

"Correct. I might've guessed you'd know who she was. Anyway, it's about their marriage. As I told you, I'm mostly shooting in Jordan, then later in your neck of the woods, as well as in Paris," Kyle explained. "So I hope you'll be around when I'm in Nice."

"I sure will," Jack answered. "And you'll stay here with me." He wondered if he should now give his brother advice about taking care of himself on location, and instantly decided against it. Instead, he added, "Talk to you later," and they both clicked off.

* * *

The sprinklers were whirling and spraying the lawns as Jack walked through the big gate which led into the grounds of the villa. In the distance he could see Amaury bending over one of the large glazed-pottery flower tubs at the end of the terrace.

"*Bonjour!*" he called. "I'm back, Amaury."

Amaury looked up and waved, then made his way along the terrace. Drawing nearer to Jack, he said, "The newspapers are in your office, Monsieur Jacques. I found them."

"Thanks. I was just on the phone with my brother. He's going to be staying with us in a couple of months. That should please you. He'll be shooting part of his new film around Nice."

"*Ah, très bien,*" Amaury exclaimed, his walnut-brown face lighting up. He suddenly chuckled, shook his head. "Hortense, she remind me the other day. . . . She say we know you for twenty years. *C'est pas possible, eh?*"

Jack grinned. "I know what you mean, but it *is* true. Remember, I was only ten and my brother twelve when our parents rented this place from Madame Arnaud for the first time. We all fell in love with it, and came back every summer for years. And aren't I lucky, Amaury, that Madame Arnaud wanted me to have the chance to buy it when she died five years ago?"

"Only you must live here, Monsieur Jacques. Madame Arnaud she tell me this . . . tell me to make the phone call when she die. She say you must have the villa, you love it. . . . And so I call you, like she say."

Jack put his arm around the older man's shoulders, full of affection for him. "Madame Arnaud spoke the truth, you know, I do love it and I consider the Villa Saint-Honoré my home. My *only* home."

"It is, it is," Amaury responded swiftly, emphatically.

When they reached the front door, the two men talked for a few minutes about the gardening and the grounds, and then Jack went inside. He let Hortense know he had returned and climbed the stairs to his office.

The housekeeper had turned on the two ceiling fans and closed the wooden shutters. The room was shady and cool. He went over to his desk, sat down, enjoying the sense of peace he felt here; it was the perfect place for him to write. And he owned this villa thanks to Colette Arnaud.

Some things had gone wrong in his life, but, for the most part, he had been fairly lucky. Widowed and childless, Colette Arnaud had taken a shine to them all, and to him in particular. In the summer months, when his parents rented the villa, she moved into the small guest house at the far end of the garden, behind a cluster of tall poplars. Although she remained on her property for the duration of their stay, she never intruded on them.

He went to see her every day; she had marvelous stories to tell, and they got on very well, the old woman and the little boy. He loved her, and she reciprocated his feelings. They were the best of friends, understood each other.

He had been stunned when Amaury had phoned him in London to tell him she had died. She hadn't been ill at all, and had passed away in her sleep. Peacefully, which was the best way to go. She had been eighty-seven. Jack had been so filled with sorrow and grief about her death when Amaury called, he hadn't properly understood what the caretaker was saying about her wanting him to buy the villa.

Her solicitors in Nice had made it clear a week later when they wrote to him. In the letter they explained that Madame Arnaud had wanted him to be offered the villa for a reasonable amount, because she knew how much he cared about her home. If he did not wish to buy the villa, then it would go on sale at the current market value, obviously at a much higher price. The money would go to her only heir, a niece who lived in Paris, had a seaside home in Deauville, and had not needed the villa in Beaulieu.

Of course Jack wanted it. But how to pay for it? He only had half the amount in savings. His devoted mother and stepfather had come to the rescue and loaned him the rest of the money. Luckily, he had done well with his writing and had managed to pay them back within two years.

There were a few stipulations regarding the villa in Madame Arnaud's will, and Jack had to agree to them in writing before he could buy the Villa Saint-Honoré, at what the solicitors called "a ridiculous bargain price." He had to live in it part of the year; he could not sell it for ten years, though he could rent it out; and if he eventually sold it and made a profit, this had to be shared fifty-fifty with her niece, Florence Chaillot. Jack had willingly signed the contract and so had Florence Chaillot.

Jack knew that he had done the right thing in buying the house. It had proved to be the ideal place for him to live on a permanent basis, and he had done great work here. He kept a small flat in London, which he used when he plied his trade as a journalist, but this was home to him. He knew it always would be.

Rising, he walked across to the closet, hung up his linen jacket, and remembered to retrieve his cell phone. He was opening some of the slatted wooden shutters when the landline on his desk began to ring. Striding over, he picked up the receiver. "Jack Chalmers," he said, walking around to the other side of the desk and sitting down in his chair. His agent, Tommy Redding, said, "Hi, Jack, you got it."

"Got what?"

"The interview."

"Which interview?" he asked, frowning, squinting in the sunlight. He swiveled his chair to look at the wall, trying to focus his eyes.

"Don't tell me you've forgotten already? You were mad for it. The interview, I mean."

"With whom?"

"Look, have you really forgotten, or are you having me on, kidding me?"

"No, I'm not kidding. Listen, Tommy, I'm up to my eyeballs in *stuff*. I've the three American interviews to finish writing, and I've the last chapter of the book. I'm sorry, but whom am I supposed to interview?"

"The woman who sold the Rembrandt. Annette Remmington."

"Oh, hell, you're right! It went out of my mind momentarily. I was keen, and I am keen. So what's up?"

"*The Sunday Times* wants it, of course. A one-on-one interview. The usual profile piece you do for them. I know you thought of doing something different, but they won't go that route. However, *The New York Times* would like a longer interview for *their* Sunday magazine. How do you feel about *that*?"

"I feel okay, but can you get permission?"

"I already have. *The New York Times* won't be running it for some months, maybe four months hence. No problem at all with the London *Sunday Times*, since the profile will run first, and will be forgotten by the time the Yanks come out with your longer piece."

"You've hurt my feelings, Tommy. Nobody forgets my pieces," Jack chided in mock indignation.

Tommy laughed. "Okay, so do you want the dope?"

"Yep, I've got a pen in my hand and a yellow pad."

"Okay, here's the deal."

Chapter Twelve

"So what you're telling me is that I'm going to interview a woman who doesn't want to be interviewed, is that it?" Jack said, leaning back in the chair, propping his feet up on his desk. "Thanks a lot." Then he began to laugh at the absurdity of the situation.

Tommy laughed with him, then explained, "It's like this. . . . She hasn't done any interviews. *Ever.* Because she's shy, according to her husband, who says she doesn't like talking about herself."

"That's a change. Most people who have leapt into sudden prominence can't shut up about their favorite subject. *Themselves.*" He groaned unexpectedly, muttered, "It's going to be like pulling teeth. She'll give me a hard time, and I won't get what I want in order to make it a good piece."

"Don't underestimate yourself, Jack. You're a good-looking man with loads of charm and the smoothest tongue in the business. In other words, cast your usual spell. And I know she'll find you irresistible. You'll get her to open up, and then some."

"I doubt that," Jack muttered.

"Don't. I know what I'm talking about. If you use that clever brain of yours you'll meander through this interview with the greatest of ease. Her husband, Marius Remmington, told me that she's extremely intelligent, has enormous knowledge about art, and is articulate. He thinks she'll make a good interview, although he also said she has a tendency to hide her light under a bushel."

"I bet! Oh, what a cliché *that* is. She's probably got an ego the size of the Eiffel Tower. . . . Hide her light under a bushel indeed!"

"I believed him, and so should you. It was Marius who chose you to do the interview, and incidentally there were over a hundred requests."

Jack was silent for a moment, thinking. Then he sat up in the chair and said, "Okay, let's get down to details. The interview is *on*. When is the lady available?"

"This is where you're in luck, Jack. She can't do it until after Easter. On April the eleventh, to be precise. That's about two weeks from now. Time for you to finish up those three interviews you did in the States, and to write the last chapter of *Dunkerque*."

"Thanks a lot! Hire the elves immediately and ship 'em over here. They can help me write on all the night shifts I'll be doing for the next ten days."

"*Very funny.*" Tommy did actually chuckle before saying, "Seriously, though, you can get everything finished if you pace yourself properly. And you work best under pressure."

Jack groaned. "That's what you always say. Well . . . let's see . . . I did draft the interviews after I'd done each one, so I'm ahead of the game in one sense." There was a pause; he said slowly, "I must have really been intrigued by Annette Remmington a couple of weeks ago to even think of doing an interview with her when I had so much on my plate at that time. And still do."

"Don't sound so surprised, Jack, you were. You called me from New York and asked me to set it up. And so we rang her office, then e-mailed the request. And my God, we got it! 'Gee, thanks, Tommy, thanks for being such a great agent.'"

Laughter suddenly bubbled up in Jack and exploded down the phone. A moment later he managed to control himself enough to say, "You are, Tommy, the best in the world, and don't I sound like an ungrateful SOB. But I'm not. I *am* eternally grateful to you, and you are *absolutely* the greatest in the business. If I sound a bit sour it's just that I loathe doing interviews with people who feel as if they're under duress to talk to me."

"Annette Remmington won't feel that way. Her husband explained she's just a little shy. Marius did assure me she genuinely understands the importance of the interview with you. Apparently she's planning a new auction, which he indicated would be as sensational as the sale of the Rembrandt. What he was saying is that she'll cooperate because she needs the publicity for her next show."

Bringing his feet to the floor, rolling the chair forward to his desk, Jack hunched over the phone and asked, "And what is the prize piece of art this time? Did he say?"

"No, of course not. Get her to tell you."

"That might prove to be tougher than you think. She might want to save that bit of information for a press conference at a later date."

"Give it a try. And it'll most likely make a helluva story."

"Probably it will. If I can get it out of her. Did Marius Remmington name a venue and a time for the interview?"

"Yes. Her office at ten o'clock. I'll e-mail the address and a few other details."

"Okay. So, go ahead, Tommy, confirm the interview. Now, can we move on and talk about a couple of other things before we hang up?"

"I'm all ears," Tommy answered.

After hanging up on his agent, Jack spent a couple of hours reading the interviews he had drafted and made a few notes about each one. He was pleased with the drafts; they were better than he'd thought, didn't need quite as much additional work as he had believed.

At one o'clock he went downstairs and hurried out to the terrace, where Hortense was setting the table. She glanced up when she heard his steps, and smiled warmly. The housekeeper had known him since he was a little boy, and she had always fussed over him, spoiled him. Now she said, "I made a salad Niçoise, the way you like it," and hurried back to the kitchen before he got a chance to thank her.

He was holding his cell phone and when it rang he brought it to his ear. "Jack Chalmers."

"Jack! Hi! It's Lucy."

"Hello, Luce," he responded, and sat down at the table. "I was just going to phone. You beat me to it."

"I thought you'd forgotten me," she shot back swiftly, sounding accusatory. "I've been expecting a call for the last hour or two."

"Sorry. I was on with my agent for ages," he explained. "We'd a lot to go over." Why was he apologizing? They'd agreed to meet tomorrow; he hadn't even promised to call her today. He asked, "What time do you want me to come over tomorrow night?"

"Around seven, or is that too early?"

"Let's make it half an hour later. Seven-thirty. I want to get a bit of writing under my belt in the next few days."

"That's fine. You sound funny. Did I phone at a bad time?"

"I'm starting my last chapter, and it's tough," he improvised. "Can I call you back a bit later, Luce?"

"Sure, that's okay," she answered in a pleasanter voice, and was gone before he could utter another word.

He stared at the cell phone, placed it on the table, and leaned back in the chair, his mind focused on Lucy Jameson. Why was she so strange with him when he had been away? Didn't she trust him? Did she think he messed around with other women? What was it that brought out this accusatory attitude in her? That almost belligerent tone of voice? He sighed. He didn't know. And, quite unexpectedly, he wondered if he cared.

Hortense interrupted these thoughts when she appeared with the salad bowl, placed it on the table, smiled, disappeared, and came back with a breadbasket and a butter dish a moment later. "*Bon appetit,* Monsieur Jacques," she murmured.

"*Merci,* Hortense," he replied, and gave her the benefit of his best smile.

* * *

After his light lunch, Jack spent the rest of the day at his desk, finishing the two different interviews he had done with a director and a screenwriter in Beverly Hills. Both men were English and they had worked on several movies together, had become a renowned team. They had just finished a new film about a very famous and extremely bloody war. Not anything recent from the present, but from the past. It was named for the place where it happened. *Agincourt*.

Jack pushed his chair away and stood up, stretching, then walking across the office.

He stood for a few minutes staring out at the Mediterranean, then opened the window and took a few deep breaths of air. In one afternoon he had managed to tie up the few loose ends which had been worrying him. He was relieved. Now all he had to do was polish the third interview with the star of the film and write the last chapter of his book and his current commitments would be completed.

After that he would do his research on Annette Remmington. Whatever Tommy said, he knew it was going to be a challenging interview.

On this March afternoon in France, Jack Chalmers had no way of knowing just how challenging it would prove to be. Or that his first meeting with Annette Remmington would change his life irrevocably, and that he himself would never be the same again.

Chapter Thirteen

※

Lucy Jameson considered herself a hybrid. And an exotic one at that. She was half American and half French, and had been brought up in both countries. Mostly raised in New York, she had spent every summer in the south of France since she was a small child.

Her father, Luke Jameson, was an American architect, and her mother, Camille, now deceased, had been French. A talented artist, she had been born in Nice, in this very house where Lucy now lived with her two small daughters.

La Ferme des Iris, as it was called, was a very old farm which had been in her mother's family for over a hundred years. It was now hers, given to her by her aunt, her mother's older sister Claudine Villiers. As the firstborn of three daughters, Claudine had inherited it, and had then passed it on to her niece four years ago. Some years earlier Claudine had renovated the farm and turned it into a more villalike structure without loss of its original character. To Lucy's way of thinking, the most important renovation had been the enlargement of the rustic kitchen where she was now sitting at the huge oak table, twenty-two feet long. It was at this table that she prepared food, wrote her books, and entertained her friends, because this unique kitchen was the center of the house.

Lucy ran her cooking school at the farm from September to the beginning of December, and during that time she allowed four of her students to rent rooms in the farm if they so wished. The rest of the year she worked on new and innovative dishes and wrote her cookbooks. The first two, *Simple French Cooking* and *Simple French Menus*, had been very successful, and she was now working on her third, entitled *French Cooking à la Carte*.

Lucy was jotting down chapter headings and making notes when the door opened and her aunt came hurrying in with two bottles of wine.

"I thought Jack would enjoy this," Claudine announced, walking over to the big table and placing the two bottles in front of her niece.

Lucy looked at the label and exclaimed, "Oh, my God! Château Duhart-Milon Domaines Barons de Rothschild (Lafite) 2000! Aren't you splashing out, Tante Claudine! It's not a special occasion. He's just coming to dinner tonight."

"It *is* special, Lucy, and you must make *him* believe this. You have not seen Jack for some weeks. Flatter him, make a fuss over him, spoil him. It's the only way to treat a man. . . . Listen to a very romantic old Frenchwoman, and follow her advice."

"Not so old, Claudine, you're only sixty-five. That's the new fifty-five today."

"*Mon Dieu*, is it so? And who decreed this?" Claudine smiled, obviously amused.

Lucy smiled back. "I don't know, but it sounds good, don't you think?"

Claudine laughed, took a seat opposite her niece, studied her for a split second. "Has something . . . gone wrong between you and Jack?"

Lucy stared at her aunt, hesitated uncertainly, wondering how to explain, and finally murmured, "I wouldn't say that, but, well, it's not exactly *right*. I think this is because of the pressure and stress we're both under at times, mostly with our work, and traveling. *He* travels a lot."

"*Mais oui*, I understand. But when he is here with you, at the farm, you can make it . . . *work*. Can you not?" Claudine's brow furrowed as she stared at Lucy.

"*Sometimes.* However, there are two problems, and they're not mine, Claudine. They're Jack's problems," Lucy announced, suddenly sounding irritated, a troubled look in her eyes.

Claudine raised a brow questioningly, but decided to say nothing, hoping Lucy would confide.

After a moment or two Lucy volunteered, "Basically Jack has trouble committing himself. To a woman. He has been engaged twice in the past, has broken it off each time just before the wedding. We've talked about it, but he can't really explain his behavior to me. It puzzles him, and it sure puzzles me."

"Perhaps he is afraid of marriage?"

"It could be that. But there's something else, and this worries me even more. . . ." Lucy shrugged. "There's no real point talking about it, because you and I won't have the answers."

"Ah, a mystery. What is it?"

"Not really a mystery. You don't know this, Claudine, but Peter Chalmers was not Jack's biological father. He was his stepfather, although, from what I understand, he loved Jack as much as his own son, Kyle, and was a devoted father to both boys. Despite this, Jack is haunted by thoughts of his biological father. From what I gather, *he* was a cheat, an inveterate womanizer, and a no-good kind of guy who was hardly ever around. Jack's mother left him when Jack was six. She married Peter, who was a widower, when Jack was—" Lucy lifted her hands in Gallic fashion. "Eight? Nine? Something like that."

"That often occurs. A curiosity about a biological parent a child has not properly known."

"I suppose that's what it is, actually. You're right. Once Jack told me he worried about his inability to make a commitment to a woman, and muttered something about him probably being like his biological father, a no-good guy who flitted from woman to woman and couldn't be true."

"Is he like that, *cherie*?" Claudine's brow lifted again.

"I don't think he is. But how do I know? I mean, he comes

and goes, flies around, from here to London to New York and
recently to Beverly Hills. And now he's back in Beaulieu.
Obviously I don't know what he does, and with whom, when
I'm sitting here at the farm."

"I doubt he has much time for liaisons," Claudine murmured, meaning this. "He works hard. So I would put such
disturbing thoughts out of your head. Take Jack at . . . how
do you say? Face value. Yes, that is what I would do. Trust
him, Lucy. Men are quickly aware of lack of trust in a
woman. And it annoys them."

"I do trust him, actually, it's just that he can be so irritable
at times, and snotty, and often this makes me . . . *nervous*."

"Don't be. Be tranquil, be yourself. Stay calm. And I will
not join you for an aperitif this evening. You must be alone."

"No, no, Claudine," Lucy protested. "I need you to be
here for a drink. You can leave after that, but please, I want
you to be here. To give me an opinion about Jack. I want you
to observe him, surreptitiously, of course, and then tell me
how you find him."

Claudine nodded. "All right, but then I will leave you
alone for dinner *à deux*." Claudine suddenly sniffed, her nose
wrinkling, and exclaimed, "*Ah, Lucy, parfait! Tu prépare
boeuf bourguignon*. It smells delicious. The red wine I chose
is ideal."

"Won't you stay for dinner?" Lucy said, carefully eyeing
her aunt. "Jack wouldn't mind. He likes you a lot. And I
wouldn't mind either."

"But I would mind. I would feel like the third shoe, as
they say."

"I've never heard that expression. What does it mean?"

"*Redundant*."

Lucy couldn't help grinning. "I think you just invented
that."

"No, I did not," Claudine answered, and asked, "Where
are Chloé and Clémence?"

"Marie took them with her to Nice. She went to see her
mother, to deliver a birthday present for her sister. They
should be back soon." Lucy glanced at her watch. "It's just

four o'clock, so they shouldn't be long. Don't go rushing off to the house; wait for a bit and you can give them a hug at least."

"I will."

"How's the decorating coming along?" Lucy asked, closing her notebook.

"Slowly. But that is because I must get the *exact* color for certain rooms. The painter, well, he has much repainting. He does not have a good eye for the colors."

Lucy nodded, suppressing her laughter. Her aunt was a perfectionist, and Lucy knew she was currently driving the workmen crazy with her constant changes and demands. Claudine had spent two years building a smaller house across the courtyard, and now that it was finished she was in the midst of the interior decoration.

Rising, Lucy went over to the oven, put on insulated oven gloves, and took out the casserole. She placed it on top of the stove, lifted the lid, and looked inside. As she did so delicious aromas of beef, vegetables, and wine wafted into the air.

"*C'est bon*, Lucy!" Claudine beamed at her niece, whom she had encouraged to follow her dream to become a chef.

"I hope Jack thinks so," she answered, and put the lid back on the casserole, which she returned to the oven. "I have to admit, I did use the Julia Child recipe today, because that's the one Jack prefers."

"It's the one I use, Lucy." Claudine glanced at her. "I do believe you've always used it, too." She frowned.

"I have. But he doesn't need to know that, does he?" There was a hint of mischief in Lucy's sparkling brown eyes as she returned to the table and sat down on the stool. "I'm supposed to spoil him, aren't I?"

Claudine merely smiled.

Claudine Villiers loved children, and most especially her two great-nieces, Lucy's beautiful four-year-old twins. Because they were identical, Claudine had trouble knowing which one was which, but then so did their mother. Lucy had long ago confessed that sometimes even she couldn't quite tell them apart from each other.

They were the spitting image of Lucy, and Villiers through and through. There wasn't an ounce of Alexandre Rosset in them, at least not an ounce that was visible.

Claudine had never understood why Lucy and Alexandre had divorced; nor had she ever understood why her niece had married him in the first place. Alexandre had gone back to Paris, where he lived with someone these days; Claudine, for all of her understanding of the vagaries of life, found it hard to believe that he could give up those two little girls so easily and rarely ever came to see them. It all seemed so cold-blooded to her, not normal.

Lucy, when she questioned her, just shrugged in that very French way she had, and called him a bad name, before adding, in an extremely cold voice, "There's no love lost there, Tante. I'm glad he doesn't come to see them. They don't miss him either. They hardly know him." That was the truth, Claudine was well aware.

Now, as she stood watching the two little girls clutching at their mother affectionately, chattering to her rapidly, excitedly, Claudine wished she had a camera close at hand to capture this idyllic little scene.

The girls were dark-haired like their mother, and also had the huge black eyes of the Villiers family. Lucy had taken them to her hairdresser in Monte Carlo recently and had her own stylist cut their hair in bangs; today they looked adorable in their neat navy blazers, pleated gray skirts, and white T-shirts. They were big for four, and had long legs. Claudine smiled to herself. They would grow up to be as tall as Lucy's mother, her sister Camille, who had been five foot eleven. Darling Camille, her beloved sister, who had died so suddenly of breast cancer eight years ago and had never seen her grandchildren.

Claudine swallowed, blinked, turned away, then suddenly began to laugh as four hands were clutching at her skirt and two high-pitched voices were shouting, *"Tante Claudine! Tante Claudine! Chocolat! Chocolat pour tout!"*

"Don't give them any of that chocolate of yours," Lucy warned in a sharp tone, and shooed them to the fireplace at the far end of the kitchen, where a sofa and chairs were grouped in front of the hearth.

"Aunt Claudine is making mint tea. But the two of you can have a glass of milk and some of my warm raisin cookies." Lucy glanced at Marie, who had been hovering in the doorway, and asked, "Would you like mint tea, Marie? Or something else?"

"Mint tea would be fine, thank you."

Lucy, settling the twins on the sofa, said to them, "Now if you're very good you can stay up a bit later tonight. To say hello to Jack."

"Oh, Jack is coming!" Chloé squealed, obviously pleased at this news, and Clémence, the quieter of the two, murmured, "I hope he has brought me my cat."

"A cat? What's all this about a cat?" Lucy demanded, her face changing.

"He promised me a cat," Clémence explained.

"He said he hoped he'd find one," Chloé corrected. "He didn't promise."

I hope to God he didn't forget, Lucy thought, as she went over to the refrigerator and took out the bottle of milk. Just in case he had forgotten all about it, which wouldn't be unusual, she would have to have a story ready.

Her aunt, holding a tray of glasses filled with tea and fresh mint, gave her a knowing look and whispered, "If he's not brought her a cat, you must say it's something to do with shots from the vet. That she will perhaps understand. N'est pas?"

Lucy simply nodded.

Chapter Fourteen

The two little girls, dressed in their nightgowns and robes, were in the kitchen and spotted him first. Chloé ran to him, exclaiming, "Jack! Jack!" followed a little more sedately by her twin, Clémence.

Lucy and Claudine, who were at the other end of the kitchen, swung around on hearing Chloé's voice. Claudine lifted her hand in greeting, and Lucy smiled, immediately came toward him, moving gracefully across the floor.

He grinned at the two women and waved, then put the shopping bag and flowers on the floor, knelt down, and opened his arms to the twins. As usual, Chloé made it into them first, Clémence holding back a little shyly, her face turning bright pink.

After hugging them tightly in his arms, he stood up and said, "That was the best welcome I've had in the longest time. Thank you, girls, and I'm so happy to see you both."

Chloé, as always blunt and impatient, said in a loud whisper, "Did you bring the cat? You didn't forget, did you?" As she spoke she glanced around eagerly, then frowned. "No cat! I don't see a cat."

"Now, now, Chloé," Lucy said, her tone stern. "You're being rude—"

"No, I didn't forget the cat," Jack said, swiftly cutting across Lucy. "But I must say hello to your mother first, and Tante Claudine." As he spoke, Jack reached for Lucy, grabbed her tightly, held her close to him, whispered against her ear, "You look fantastic."

Breaking away from him, she smiled into his face, thinking, *So do you*, but said softly, "Thank you, Jack, and listen, I must apologize for Chloé—"

"Oh, don't be daft," he interjected, and picking up the bunch of flowers, he took them over to Claudine. "These are for you," he murmured, and leaning toward her he kissed her on both cheeks. "I noticed when I crossed the yard that your house is finally finished," he added.

"It is indeed. And *merci*, Jack, the flowers are beautiful. Excuse me, I must find a vase."

"But about the cat," Chloé began, running to him. "Clémence was expecting the cat."

"Really, Chloé, stop this!" Lucy was shaking her head in annoyance. "Otherwise I shall send you straight upstairs to bed. You mustn't ask for gifts in this way. You are being very naughty."

"But—"

"Stop right there!" Lucy cried. "Not another word about the cat."

Jack walked back to Clémence, who was still standing near the door, and when he reached her he said, in an apologetic voice, "I'm afraid I couldn't bring you a *real* cat. Not without your mother's permission. However, I have a substitute." Reaching into the shopping bag, he pulled out a beautiful furry black cat with big eyes and a long tail. "This is for you, Clémence," he said, putting the toy into her hands. "What are you going to call it?"

Clémence had turned an even brighter pink and her eyes were huge in her face. She looked at the cat and then at Jack, said, "Oh! Oh! Is it really *mine*?"

"Yes. I found her for you, Clémence. So come on, think of a name."

"Say thank you, darling," Lucy whispered, touching her daughter's shoulder gently.

"Thank you, Jack," Clémence said obediently, and gave him her biggest smile. "I love this cat."

"What are you going to call it?" Chloé cried, coming to join them. "Call it Spot."

"Spot is a dog's name," Jack pointed out. "Oh, and by the way, Chloé, I know you like dogs, and want one badly. So it occurred to me that I should get *you* a substitute, too. Here it is." He took a fluffy white puppy out of the shopping bag, and handed it to her. "This is yours, Chloé."

"Oh! Oh! Oh! Jack, a puppy! Thank you. Is it to keep?"

Jack couldn't help laughing; Lucy laughed as well. Jack said, "Of course it's to keep. And you should think of a name, too."

"I will," Chloé answered, and frowned. "Is it a boy or a girl?"

Lucy suppressed the sudden laughter rising in her throat. Only her precocious little Chloé would think of asking that kind of question. She said in the steadiest voice she could muster, "It's a girl. And so is the cat. Right, Jack?"

He was swallowing his laughter as well, and he could only nod.

Chloé stood thinking hard, staring down at the toy dog.

Her sister was stroking the cat, and she suddenly announced, "I shall call this cat Hector."

"But it's a girl!" Chloé cried.

"Perhaps Hectorine would be better," Claudine suggested, coming to stand with them near the fireplace.

"That's a very nice name," Jack said. "Do you like that, Clémence?"

The child nodded and patted the cat. "You're Hectorine."

"And what about your puppy, Chloé?" Lucy asked.

"I don't know. . . . I like Spot. . . ." Her voice trailed off.

Lucy said, "But she's such a pretty little puppy, and very white, so why not call her Snowy?"

"I will!" Chloé nodded, and went and sat next to her sister on the sofa. The girls were both enchanted by their new toys.

"Well, that's all settled," Jack murmured, and took a last package out of the shopping bag. "This is for you, Lucy."

"Why, Jack, how nice!" She ripped off the paper and exclaimed, "Oh my goodness, Chanel No. 5. Jack, you're so extravagant. Thank you so much. It's my favorite."

"I know."

Claudine said, "Shall we have an aperitif? What would you like, Jack?"

"A glass of white wine would be nice, thanks."

"Lucy?"

"The same, Claudine."

"Is there such a name as *Hectorine*?" Lucy asked, looking over the top of her glass at Jack, her dark eyes sparkling with laughter.

He took a long swallow of the cold white wine, savoring it, and then said, "How would I know?"

"But you're the writer. . . . You *should* know."

He gave her an amused look and countered, "It sounds French, so *you* ought to know."

"I'm only half French. The other half is American, in case you'd forgotten."

"It was Claudine who came up with it. Let's ask her when she comes back," Jack suggested.

"I am back," Claudine announced from a few feet away, walking over to the huge fireplace where Lucy and Jack were perched on the wide hearth.

Claudine was carrying a plate of small toast points on which there was caviar, paté, and smoked salmon. She offered the plate to them, and went on, "Hectorine *might* be a French name. Or it could have come from my imagination. But Clémence accepted it—"

"And so did Chloé," Lucy interjected. "And she's always the one who argues and questions things in the most interminable way."

"Possibly, no, most *probably*, she'll want to be a lawyer when she grows up," Jack pointed out, and gave them a knowing look.

The two women laughed, and Lucy remarked, "The main thing is, you didn't forget about the cat, and you were thoughtful and brought something for Chloé as well. She's thrilled with the puppy."

"Yes, it was kind of you, Jack," Claudine agreed, her voice approving. Placing the plate of canapés on the coffee table, she sat down on the sofa, sipping her wine. After a moment, she said, "If either of the twins asks me, I shall answer that it is indeed a French name from long ago . . . an ancient name."

"That's a great answer." Jack, smiling at her, now asked, "Any chance of a tour of the house? I've watched it slowly grow into the finished thing, and I'd love to see it."

"*Mais oui*." Claudine immediately stood, picked up her glass, and walked toward the door, saying, as she did, "We can just go at once before the light fades."

"Don't you have the electricity in yet?" Jack asked.

"*Oui, oui*, but not every room has a lamp. I shall take the flashlight, however."

The house across the large courtyard was built in the same style as the farm, with pale-pink stucco walls and a red-tiled roof, but it was much smaller.

Inside it was beautiful. It had been very well designed by Claudine herself, and Jack couldn't stop admiring it as she led him through the main rooms downstairs, with Lucy trailing behind.

Lucy knew it well by now, but every time her aunt brought her over to see something newly finished, she couldn't help but exclaim about the quality of the work.

"It is not a big house, Jack," Claudine said as she showed him into the living room. "There is not one room that I do not need. I made sure I created only spaces I would use. And enough walls for my art."

"So I see," Jack responded. "And I think this room is my favorite. Not just because of the many windows, the fantastic views, and the fireplace, but because of its proportions. And I love the kitchen."

"So do I," Lucy said. "It's a perfect replica of the farm kitchen but scaled down, and I can't wait to cook the first meal in it."

Chapter Fifteen

Jack poured himself another glass of white wine and sat down on one of the stools at the big kitchen table, his eyes and his thoughts focused on Lucy.

She was busy taking the casserole out of the oven and putting it on top of the stove; she lifted the lid and looked inside, stirring the stew gently, concentrating on the dish.

He sniffed. The fragrant smells emanating from the big pot were making his mouth water. "Oh boy, does that tantalize me!" he exclaimed. "I can't wait to taste it, Luce."

"I'm glad," Lucy said without turning around. "I made it especially for you."

"I know, and thank you. I also know you much prefer to stick to your *cuisine du soleil*, which is much lighter."

"Not my *cuisine du soleil* but Roger Vergé's," Lucy answered. She put the lid back on the pot and turned her attention to the bowl of potatoes which she had boiled earlier.

Glancing around, Jack noticed that Claudine was not with them, and, frowning, he asked, "Where's your aunt?"

"She's probably still over at the little house, as she calls it, but she won't be joining us for supper, Jack. She says she'd feel like the third shoe. *Redundant.* But she did bring up two bottles of marvelous red wine from the cellar, and knowing her she probably opened one of them already. To let it breathe."

Jack strolled across to the plate-glass window which

overlooked Nice on the right and Beaulieu to the left, and in the far distance he could see the glittering lights of Monte Carlo. What a fabulous panoramic view it was, and it never failed to impress him.

As he picked up the wine bottle and read the label, he noticed that Claudine had poured half of the bottle into a decanter, which stood on the table. He called across to Lucy, "She opened the bottle, decanted some of the wine."

"Oh good," Lucy muttered, concentrating on what she was doing.

As he walked back to the big table, Jack studied her again, thinking how lovely she looked tonight. Lucy had long black hair, which she normally wore in a plait, especially when she was cooking, but tonight her hair fell down her back, looked like flowing black silk. She was wearing tight black trousers and a loose red cotton tunic, Moroccan in design, the kind she favored.

She was a fabulous cook, and he knew that with her it was a true vocation. She had started cooking as a little girl when she came to stay with her mother's family here at the farm; eventually she had gone to Roger Vergé's cooking school in Mougins. Later she had trained under the famous Vergé himself, working in the kitchens of his renowned restaurant Moulin de Mougins, and her style of cooking was based on his own creation, "cuisine of the sun," which accented the fresh, light flavors of Provence.

Swinging around, interrupting his thoughts about her, she said, "Come over here, Jack, I want to serve you some of the *boeuf bourguignon.*"

"Immediately," he answered, and hurried over to the stove where she was standing, filling a plate for him. "It looks wonderful," he said.

"I'll bring the bowl of potatoes," she murmured, and shooed him over to the table near the glass window.

Picking up the decanter, Jack poured the red wine, and sat waiting for her. She arrived a moment later with her own plate and the bowl of buttered parsley potatoes. "The perfect addition to the beef stew," she announced, and sat down opposite him.

"Oh, it's delicious, Luce," he sighed after the first few bites. "Absolutely fantastic. I don't know how you get it to taste like this."

"I follow Julia Child's recipe," she said, laughing, deciding to tell him the truth, and picked up her fork, taking a bite herself. "Oh, yes, it *is* good tonight," she muttered almost to herself.

He raised his glass. "Here's to you, Luce, my favorite chef."

"And to you, Jack, my favorite writer."

They were both hungry and enjoyed the beef stew, and when Jack's plate was empty Lucy suggested he go for a second helping.

"I think I will," he said, and got up, took his plate, and served himself.

Once he was back at the table, and had eaten a few forkfuls, they finally began to have a conversation. It was Jack who spoke first, apologizing. "I'm sorry I didn't talk much when we first sat down," he said. "I'm afraid I was very busy with this most perfect stew. So it's your fault I was silent, actually."

Lucy looked across at him and nodded. "I didn't say much either because, like you, I really did need to eat." She had finished her own food and did not want any more; she leaned across the table and said quietly, in an even voice, "Thanks, Jack, for bringing the gifts for us all, and especially for the twins. It was so sweet of you, very caring."

"Well, I did promise her the cat, you know. And I didn't want to disappoint her. And I couldn't come without anything for Chloé, that wouldn't have been nice. Or for Claudine, or you."

"You spoil us."

"My pleasure."

Lucy sat back, falling silent, endeavoring to relax at last after a busy day.

In the last thirty minutes or so they had made only desultory conversation about the success of her second cookbook, the new one she was writing, and Jack's magazine pieces, and yet Jack fully understood that much more was going to be said. Very shortly. On the surface everything was calm, easygoing, friendly, but Jack knew that Lucy was not pleased with him. Yes, she was being nice, and especially about the gifts, but there was an undercurrent of irritation running through her, although she wasn't being obvious about it.

He was very intuitive, could pick up on things quickly, and he also *knew* her. She was somewhat possessive by nature, and he had long ago realized that she wanted a steady and continuing relationship with him, one which was meaningful and which would eventually lead to marriage.

He was uneasy with himself when it came to thoughts of marriage, of settling down and making a proper commitment. He enjoyed his travels, his journalistic career, and all the places it took him. He really wasn't prepared to give that up. Not yet. Within himself he knew that Lucy would prefer it if he were in Beaulieu all the time, writing his books and being with her, being a permanent fixture in her life.

Quite suddenly she stood up, startling him, and picked up their plates, carried them over to the work area of the kitchen.

Sitting up straighter, he called, "Do you need help, Luce?" Not waiting for her to respond, he pushed back the chair, rose, and picked up the bowl of potatoes. He carried it over, put it on the countertop, touched her shoulder lightly.

"Thanks." She gave him a quick smile, went over to the island counter, and said, "I hope you have room for dessert."

"You know I can't resist anything you make," he answered, and asked, "What is it? My favorite blood-orange tart, I bet."

"Exactly."

He laughed. "They say a way to a man's heart is through his stomach, so you have my heart, Luce."

She glanced at him, gave him a hard stare, and said nothing.

Suddenly he felt like an idiot, stood there waiting as she cut two portions of the blood-orange tart, put them on plates, poured a trickle of vanilla cream sauce on them, and handed him one.

"Thank you," he said as he took it from her.

Together they walked across to the table without saying a word to each other. They remained silent as they ate dessert, and Jack wished he had kept his mouth shut a few minutes before. The look she had given him confirmed what he had been thinking. She *was* upset with him, probably even angry. He decided to be quiet, believing it was better to let her open up to him if she had something on her mind. Why seek out trouble?

"I want us to talk, Jack," Lucy suddenly said, putting down her wineglass. Without saying another word, she rose, went to the fireplace, and threw on another log, poked it into place.

Jack sat back on the sofa, watching her, admiring her dark beauty, the streaming jet-black hair almost waist length, the dark intense eyes, the lightly tanned skin, the lovely face, totally without makeup. She was a natural beauty, slender but shapely, and she had a unique physical grace when she moved. He could kick himself for neglecting her, for being so ambivalent. Lucy was a prize and in so many ways, and he had been very stupid.

As she walked back to the sofa and sat down at the far end it, she exclaimed, "You were staring at me awfully hard just now."

He nodded. "I was, because you're gorgeous." Sitting up straighter, he said, "You want to talk and so do I. Look, I know you're angry with me—"

"No, I'm not angry," she cut in. "I think *hurt* might be a better way of putting it." When he said nothing, she hurried on, "Listen to me, Jack, you and I are supposed to be in a relationship, but you didn't even come up to see me when you first got back. I just don't understand that."

He said swiftly, "I was wrong, Lucy, I realize that now. But I was suffering from a combination of things . . . jet lag, genuine fatigue from that very busy New York–L.A. trip, and the pressure of having to finish my magazine pieces. But I did call you twice."

"Not the same thing," she shot back, staring at him. "I was longing to see you, but obviously you didn't feel the same."

"I did, but I became focused on my work. Selfish. I was being selfish. And you know I have to keep at it and at a good pace. I do have to earn a living, you know."

"I understand. And so do I. I need money, too." Lucy now spoke in a lower voice, steadying herself, squashing the sudden flare of anger. "When my aunt gave me the farmhouse, she didn't give me the money to run it. That's my responsibility, although she does share the cost of the two gardeners. And yes, she's good about paying rent for her apartment in the farmhouse. But that's about to stop, since she's going to move into her little house. And Alexandre's a shit. He's supposed to pay child support, but it's always late, and sometimes it doesn't come at all." She shook her head and sighed. "That's why I have to do the cookbooks as well as run the school. Like you, I need the money."

"I know, and I realize you're under pressure, just as I am. And that makes us awfully stressed. . . ." He stopped, gave her a long loving look. "I'm sorry I didn't come up for a quick meal or a quick kiss. I really am, Lucy darling. I was *wrong*. Will you accept my apology?"

"Yes, but I do want to ask you where we actually stand. Are we going to continue together, have a relationship? Or do you want out? I need to know and you must be honest." She took a swallow of the red wine and finished, "Whatever you say, I'll accept, and I won't make a big scene."

Since he had been thinking hard about their involvement for the last twenty-four hours and had come to certain conclusions, Jack had his answer ready. "No, I don't want out,

Luce. I truly don't. I want to be in this relationship with you. Let's see where it takes us, shall we?"

"Yes, I'd like that, too."

"However, I can't just stop traveling. I have to move around for my work. I love being a journo, you know that. I get a kick out of it. I've built a fairly good career for myself, and I do have to be in London for part of the time. That's where most of my work comes from."

"So what you're saying is that things will be the same," Lucy answered in a steady voice.

"No, I'm not . . . not really. I'll pace myself better. I'll spend more time with you when I'm here. And look, I will be starting another book soon, so I'll stay put in Beaulieu for long periods."

She nodded, but he noticed the worried look in her eyes, the sudden tautness of her shoulders.

"Let's not be rigid . . . about a routine, I mean. I can't live that way. My life has to be much more fluid. Also, you'll be busy with your new cookbook, and with the cooking school in a few months. Surely we can work it out. It's got to be give-and-take between us, that's the only way it's going to work. Because of who we are and what we do."

Lucy did not respond. She sat quite still, staring off into the distance, her mind racing.

Jack moved closer to her, put his arms around her shoulders, and said, "Let's have a new beginning, Lucy. I'll try harder not to get carried away with my work all the time, to be there for you more."

She turned finally and looked at him thoughtfully. She knew he was ambivalent about her at times, just as she was about him. And yet they did have something special together; she understood he was being sincere, that he didn't want to break up. And that was good enough for her. At this moment in time.

Leaning into him, she kissed him on the mouth. He responded at once, kissing her back, and ardently so. After a moment, he pulled away, said, "And we're good at this, good together like this, I mean."

Lucy smiled. "Perhaps we *can* make it work, Jack."

"I'm sure of it." He touched her cheek lightly. "Can I stay the night?"

"I should hope so. And I wouldn't let you leave, the state you're in, Jack, and—"

"Yes, I am a bit hot and bothered," he interrupted. "And ready to jump on you."

"I meant you've had too much to drink. I'm not sure you'd make it down the mountain safely. I can't take that chance."

He laughed and stood, pulled her to her feet. "I think we'd better go and find a bed. There are small children in this house and I wouldn't want them catching us on this sofa doing all sorts of things."

Part Three

✳

A DANGEROUS ENCOUNTER

The angels keep their ancient places—
Turn but a stone and start a wing!
'Tis ye, 'tis your estrangéd faces,
That miss the many-splendored thing.

Francis Thompson,
"The Kingdom of God" (1908)

Chapter Sixteen

Annette Remmington stood at one of the windows in her office in Bond Street, staring out but seeing nothing. She was filled with anxiety, and it dominated her at this moment.

"Do you want me to make coffee or tea, boss?" Esther Oliver asked.

Startled at the sound of her assistant's voice, Annette swung around and exclaimed, "You made me jump! I didn't hear you come in!"

"Sorry," Esther apologized. "But I thought it might be a good idea to get ahead of the game, and have something ready when Jack Chalmers arrives."

"Let's get the interview going first," Annette murmured. "You can always make beverages later, or he might prefer water."

Esther was studying Annette. Her eyes were narrowed when she announced, "You're taut. *Tense*. You're not still worrying about the interview, are you?"

"I guess I am, and I'm probably being neurotic about it. You know I hate any kind of interview. Talking about myself seems, well, so boastful, show-offy. . . ." She let the words fall away, grimaced.

"You're not boastful or a show-off. Nothing of the sort. But look, you've no choice now. He'll be here soon, so it's definitely too late to cancel, boss."

"I realize that, Esther. I'm stuck with it." She let out a long sigh. "Marius told him he could do the three sessions he'd asked for, and you know very well I'd no option but to go along with it."

"Listen, he's doing a big piece for the *New York Times* Sunday magazine, and that's great for you and the New York office. Just because you're not doing the next auction in New York now doesn't mean you won't do one another year. It's great publicity for you, Annette."

"Yes, I know."

"Don't sound so mournful. He's only a journalist, after all, and you'll see, everything'll be fine." Esther gave her an encouraging smile. "I hear he's a nice guy."

"*Oh.* Who told you that? Marius?"

"No, Laurie."

Annette shook her head and exclaimed, "Now how would she know what he's like? She's never met him."

"Malcolm Stevens told her. Apparently Malcolm has run into him several times at various functions in the past, and once with Margaret Mellor. He's done a couple of pieces for *ART* magazine, so that means he's not coming cold to the subject of your job, boss."

"I do wish you wouldn't call me that, Esther, it drives me crazy."

"I really like it, and it's a good name for you. I tell everyone you're my boss lady. I think it sounds great."

Annette sighed to herself a little impatiently and walked across the room, glancing around. Suddenly she paused and said to Esther, "I'm glad I had those two French chairs brought in last week, and the coffee table. That corner near the credenza now makes the perfect spot to do the interview."

Her eyes fell on the photographic blow-up of the Degas dancer, which she'd photographed several weeks ago, and she hurried over, began to lift it down.

"Oh, let me help you, Annette!" Esther cried, going to join her.

"I've done it, but thanks."

"Why are you removing it?" Esther asked, her curiosity aroused.

"Because I don't know whether I'm going to talk about *The Little Fourteen-Year-Old Dancer*. I want to see what he's like, test the waters, so to speak." Carrying the large photograph mounted on board across the room, she opened the cupboard door and put it inside, next to the photographic blow-up of the Rembrandt.

"Malcolm told Laurie that Jack Chalmers is good-looking, movie-star good-looking," Esther now volunteered, smiling at her.

"Oh, God, save me from that! He's probably got an ego the size of a house and is full of himself, loves being known as the hotshot reporter."

Esther began to laugh, as always enjoying Annette's slightly acerbic comments, especially about people whom she didn't know. "Apparently Malcolm mentioned that he's got a look of the young William Holden," she explained.

Annette groaned. "Oh, God, that's enough to get her going! She loves that old movie he was in . . . *Love Is a Many-Splendored Thing*. As you well know." Annette sat down in her chair at the desk and continued, "You've had to watch it with her almost as many times as I have."

"She's very romantic," Esther said, and before she could stop herself she added, "I think she's very keen on Malcolm."

This unexpected comment took Annette by surprise, and she sat up straighter. "It's odd that you should say that, but I've thought the same thing lately. They seem to be spending a lot of time together, and it's not always about work."

"I know, and I'd go as far as to say she's very emotionally involved with him," Esther confided.

"Do you mean in love with him?" Annette asked, her voice rising, astonishment in her eyes.

Esther nodded, ran a hand through her short curly brown hair, and pursed her lips. After a moment, she said quietly, "Don't look so worried. If anyone knows Malcolm, it's you. He's a decent man, isn't he?"

"He is, yes. What else have you picked up, Esther? Is Malcolm in love with *her*?"

"Laurie hasn't confided anything about that, and I've not seen them together, so I can't say." Esther bit her lip, and murmured in a low voice, "Laurie once told me she could . . . you know, have sex. Is that true?"

"Yes, she can. Some women suffering from spinal cord injury are often able to have a sexual relationship, and there are different degrees of injury, you know. Laurie did have some nerve healing over the years, as it happens, and she did regain a bit of movement."

Annette stood up, walked over to the window once more, glanced out, and then looked across at her assistant. "She is very beautiful. Aunt Sylvia always said she was the real beauty in the family. . . . I do hope Malcolm won't . . . hurt her. I couldn't bear it if he caused her any pain."

"He wouldn't. He's not a shithead like some men I've come across. Besides, I don't know how far the relationship has gone, boss. Laurie's not actually come out and said, 'Oh, Esther, I'm in love with Malcolm,' or anything like that. Still, I know her so well, and I've just kind of picked things up . . . you know, the way she speaks about him, about going out with him." Esther moved toward the door, asking as she did, "What's your feeling about it?"

Annette shrugged. "About the same as yours, I guess. He has been spending a great deal of time with her, and they do have a lot in common. I suppose she'll tell me. *Eventually*."

"I'm sure of that, boss," Esther muttered, and wondered what Marius would say when *he* found out. He certainly wouldn't be happy about Malcolm and Laurie. She was absolutely positive of that. He didn't like to lose control of anybody close to him, and what they did was always his business. He was a megalomaniac, in her opinion. Sighing to herself, Esther closed the door.

Feeling restless and anxious, Annette got up, walked around her office, ended up at the window again. She leaned her forehead against the glass, considered Laurie and Mal-

colm for a few moments. And then her thoughts went to
Carlton Fraser.

The restorer had been taken to hospital with a bad case of
pneumonia two weeks ago, on the first day he had started to
work on the Cézanne, of all things. He was getting better,
according to Marguerite, and his wife had also reassured
her he would be back at work soon.

She wasn't going to worry about the restoration of the
painting today. She had other things on her mind, better fish
to fry. She also put aside her concerns about Laurie. Jack
Chalmers would be arriving in a few minutes, and she knew
she must be calm, cool, and collected for the interview. And
on her guard.

Accompanied by Esther, Jack Chalmers walked into Annette's office at five minutes past ten, and she was taken
aback when she experienced a jolt of recognition. Although
she was absolutely certain she had never met Jack Chalmers
before, she felt she knew him.

His eyes remained fixed on her, and as she stared back at
him with interest his step faltered, but only momentarily.
Then he swiftly walked over to her, hand outstretched. Before Esther could say a word, he introduced himself. "Jack
Chalmers, Mrs. Remmington, good morning."

"Good morning," Annette replied, and took a step forward. She put her hand in his, and unexpectedly felt goose-
flesh spreckling the nape of her neck. "I'm pleased to meet
you, Mr. Chalmers," was all she could manage to say, so
startled was she by her reaction to him.

"Thanks so much for seeing me today," he murmured.
"And for agreeing to this interview . . ." Jack hesitated,
appeared to be suddenly at a loss for words, and simply
stood there, gazing into her face. He discovered he could
not look away. Nor could he let go of her hand, much to his
amazement.

It was the click of the door closing as Esther left the room
that caused Annette to blink. Since his arrival, only a few

seconds had passed in actuality, yet it seemed so much longer to her, as if time had stood still.

Pulling herself together, and very gently slipping her hand out of his, Annette attempted to be businesslike. She gestured to the French chairs near the credenza. "Let's sit over there, shall we? And would you like something to drink? Coffee, tea, or water?"

"Coffee with milk would be great, thank you," Jack answered, and, moving toward the two chairs, he glanced around the office, taking everything in.

Annette sat down at her desk, picked up the phone, and pressed the intercom button. When Esther answered, she said, "Mr. Chalmers would like coffee with milk, and so would I, please, Esther. Thanks."

Replacing the receiver, Annette rose, walked slowly around the desk, and headed over to the chairs. She had not expected Jack Chalmers to be like this, so very handsome, and yes, it was true, he did bear a strong resemblance to the young William Holden.

He was slender, with fair hair and light-gray eyes, but there was something else about him, other than his superb good looks, that caught and held her attention. Suddenly she understood exactly what it was, a calmness, a stillness in him, and he had an air of refinement and breeding. He was classy.

His clothes were equally as quiet. Dark gray slacks, a light-gray cashmere sports jacket, a crisp white shirt, and a dove-gray silk tie. The clothes were subdued in color but beautifully made, and obviously expensive. The other thing she noticed were his shoes. He was wearing her favorite American-style penny loafers made of brown leather, and they were highly polished. She wondered then if he'd lived in America, because there was something American about him. The clothes? The disarming friendliness?

He did not sit down until she did, and then he looked across at her and said, "Your office is somewhat minimalistic, isn't it? And what's so surprising to me is there isn't one painting hanging here." His extraordinary translucent gray eyes were focused on her again, and his smile was warm.

"The walls are empty because they are waiting for paintings. One I might be selling, or one I might be buying. I don't want anything of my own which I love competing with them. I like to be totally objective about art I'm buying or selling."

"How very clever," he exclaimed. "And of course I realize you don't own a gallery, that you're an art consultant with private clients."

"Yes," was all she said.

There was a sudden knock on the door, and Esther came hurrying in carrying a tray, which she brought over to the table between the two chairs. "Here we are," she said. "There's milk, sugar, sweeteners, and a few shortbread biscuits." With a quick nod and a smile she was gone, disappearing as Annette called, "Thank you."

"I did a little research on you, in readiness for our interview," Jack volunteered. "But there wasn't very much to Google. I think that perhaps you don't really like doing interviews." A brow lifted as he spoke, and he smiled at her again.

The smile was just as disarming as his easygoing, casual manner, and she immediately responded to this. Her anxiety about the interview was already much diminished because of the calm, the stillness, that surrounded him, plus his gentle demeanor.

She said, "There's nothing to Google because I haven't done any big interviews, just small things after I sold the Rembrandt. There's nothing much on the Internet about me. You see, I hadn't done anything special until I held that auction. Only then was I sought out by the press."

"Thanks, by the way, for selecting me. I must admit I was very flattered when my agent told me I was your choice. Anyway, I must admit something to you. I'm terribly curious about the Rembrandt, and how it came to you. I read that it belonged to Christopher Delaware, that he had inherited it from his uncle, Sir Alec Delaware. However, there hasn't been anything written about how he came to be your client."

"It was a fluke. Or luck. Whichever you prefer."

"Or a bit of both?" he suggested. "So tell me."

"About eight or nine months before Christopher came to

see me about the Rembrandt, he had been seated next to me at a dinner given by a mutual friend. When he inherited his uncle's art collection, he suddenly remembered me, made an appointment, and arrived here with the Rembrandt." She began to laugh. "In a shopping bag, of all things."

"Good God! Wasn't that a bit dangerous? Couldn't it have been damaged?" Jack's surprise was evident.

"Absolutely. But he had enough sense to wrap it in a thick blanket before putting it in the shopping bag. He showed me the painting, told me he wanted to sell it, and asked if I would do this for him."

"And you said yes."

"Wouldn't you?"

Jack nodded and laughed, enjoying being with her. He opened a packet of sweetener, shook it into the coffee, stirred it, added milk. He took a quick sip, then went on, "I know you are an expert on Old Masters but you're also an expert on Impressionist paintings. I found that rather curious since there's such a big difference in the two schools of art."

"That's true, yes, there is a huge difference. I started out studying Impressionists, and then later I moved on and studied Old Masters because I wanted to be well rounded in my knowledge of art and art history. But to be very honest, I have always been drawn to Impressionist painters, most especially Renoir, Manet, and Degas, and these are very personal choices on my part, I must explain. But my sister pointed out a long time ago that I must have what she called a second string to my bow, and I always listen to her." This was a downright lie. It was Marius who had led her toward Old Masters and not Laurie at all. For some reason, she didn't want to mention her husband. Well, she knew the reason. . . .

Jack said, "I have to tell you, I'm a fan of Renoir, too. I love the color, the vividness of life he portrays in his paintings."

"Anyway, going back to *my* Rembrandt, as I call it. Obviously when Christopher came to see me I was excited, thrilled, and very flattered."

"I bet you were. I can understand that very well. The Rembrandt you auctioned was a portrait of a woman, wasn't it?"

Annette jumped up. "Would you like to see it? I have a photographic blow-up."

"I certainly would. Oh, yes, please."

Jack's eyes followed Annette as she walked down the room, his attention riveted on her. She was tall, willowy, and had the greatest legs he'd seen in a long time. But it was her blondness, the clear, light blue of her eyes, the delicacy of her features, that had instantly captivated him. She had knocked him for a loop when he had walked in a short while before. The odd thing was, he felt as if he already knew her. There was a strange familiarity about her that made his chest tighten. He had recognized her as a kindred spirit.

Jack had truly not bargained for a woman like this, a woman who had so stunned him that his step had actually faltered when he walked into her office. Dangerous, he thought. Dangerous for me . . .

"Here it is," Annette announced from the other end of the room, and took hold of the photographic blow-up, pulling it out of the cupboard.

Jack was on his feet, hurrying over to her, and he immediately took hold of the blow-up. Their hands touched, and she pulled hers away so rapidly he stared at her, frowning.

Annette looked at him, swallowing, saying nothing. His touch was like an electric shock. Slowly, a pale-pink blush spread up from her neck and flooded her face.

The bloom is on the rose, Jack thought. Or on the peach. My God, what a complexion she has. It was utter perfection. A typical English rose, he thought, then asked, "Where shall I put this?"

"I usually prop my blow-ups on the credenza," Annette replied, walking down the room, furious with herself for blushing the way she had. But the look in his eyes was so penetrating, so intense, she felt as if he could see right through her clothes, see her naked. She realized he wondered why she had pulled her hand away so quickly. Scorched, she thought, he scorched me. But there was no way she could tell him that. . . .

The ringing phone brought her up short, and as she went

to answer it, she said, "Sorry about this, and perhaps you can prop the blow-up over there."

"I will."

"Yes, Esther? Is this important?" Annette asked.

"It's Carlton Fraser. He says he must speak to you."

"Oh, my goodness! Yes, put him through." Covering the receiver with her hand, she called out, "Mr. Chalmers, I'm so sorry, but I must take this. I'll only be a couple of minutes. Would you please excuse me?"

"No problem. Look, would you like privacy? I can step outside."

"No, no, it's all right, honestly." She smiled at him, sat down at the desk. "*Hello!* I'm so relieved to hear your voice. I've been very worried about you. How are you?"

"Almost better, Annette, my darling. They let me out on Good Friday, so I've had a few splendid days here at home with Marguerite, and her presence and her unique cooking have done wonders for me, restored me no end. I hope to be able to get back to work in another week to ten days."

"Oh, please, don't worry about your work for me. Your health is so much more important."

"Yes, I must take care of myself, I know that, I'm not getting any younger." He chuckled down the phone and added, "But look here, I have a *warden* for a wife, so rest assured she'll watch me like a hawk. Now, Annette, I must see you. *Today.* Is that possible?"

"Of course," she said at once. "But it will have to be this afternoon."

"Splendid. Thank you, my darling girl. Can you come here to the house? For tea? Say about four o'clock?"

"Well, yes, I can." She frowned and asked, "Is there something the matter? Is there a problem?"

"I need you to see something."

"What?"

"The Cézanne."

"*Oh.* Why? Why do you want me to see it? Is it about the soot?"

"I have to show you something interesting."

"What?"

"Annette, it's hard to explain over the phone. *Will you come at four?*"

"I will, yes. I'll see you later." She stood with her hand on the receiver, wondering what this was all about. Carlton was usually so open, straightforward, even blunt, she couldn't imagine why he was being so mysterious. Shaking off thoughts of the odd conversation, she walked over to join Jack Chalmers.

"I'm sorry about that," she apologized.

"Oh, please don't worry. I've been busy studying the painting . . . the famous Rembrandt."

"And?" she asked, looking at him, seeing the puzzlement in his eyes.

"Twenty million pounds was a lot of money for someone to pay for it, wasn't it?"

"It was indeed," she answered. "Shall we continue the interview?"

"Absolutely!" Jack said, and much to her consternation he took hold of her elbow and escorted her to the French chair. She could smell his cologne, he was so close. What was it? Guerlain, of course. Impériale. How odd. She often wore that herself, even though it was a man's cologne. Taut inside from his close proximity, she was relieved when she sat down in the chair, and he took the other one.

Chapter Seventeen

Swinging his head to look once more at the Rembrandt photographic blow-up on the credenza, then turning back to Annette, Jack said, "So how did it feel when the hammer came down at twenty million pounds? It was your first auction, after all, so you must have been thrilled, excited, astonished, stunned? Pick one of those, tell me how it felt."

Annette shook her head. "I can't. It's *impossible* to choose *one*, because I experienced all of those feelings. It was a very emotional moment for me. I suppose I was astonished at first, thrilled, even disbelieving for a moment, and a little stunned, yes. And I was certainly excited for my client. Naturally, Christopher was ecstatic. And just a bit gobsmacked."

"I bet he was." Jack now took a small recorder out of his pocket, placed it on the coffee table, then looked across at her. "I'd like to tape our conversation, if you don't mind. I prefer that to taking lots of notes, which always seems somewhat obtrusive to me, off-putting for the person being interviewed."

"It's fine, and I agree with you. I think a pad and pencil would probably make me a bit self-conscious, even tongue-tied."

He glanced at her swiftly and then chuckled. "I'll be honest, Mrs. Remmington, my agent told me you don't like doing interviews. So I want to make this as easy as possible for you. Listen, I'm just doing a story about a successful woman in the art world, I'm not out to get you."

Annette was silent, and then staring at him intently, she said softly, "I didn't think you were."

"I'm glad of that." Leaning back in the chair, he crossed his legs. "Tell me a little bit about the day Christopher Delaware brought the Rembrandt to you. What you thought, how you felt when you first saw it, Mrs. Remmington."

"I will, and I'd prefer you to call me Annette."

"Of course, happy to, and call me Jack. So, tell me about that day." As he spoke he turned on the digital recorder and sat back in the chair, his eyes and all of his attention focused on her.

She began to speak, a little slowly, and carefully. "Looking back, I realize I was totally flabbergasted. I could hardly believe my eyes. *A Rembrandt in my office.* It just seemed to be impossible. A dream. I remember I began to shake, but with excitement, not fear. At first glance I could see it needed cleaning, and required a bit of restoration, which is quite normal for a very old painting. But to sum it all up, I was . . . well, over the moon."

"Why do you think it went for so much money?" Jack asked, giving her a long stare, his eyes narrowed.

Annette, suddenly aware of a certain skepticism in him, looked thoughtful for a few moments. Finally she answered him, "Firstly, Rembrandt is considered to be one of the greatest painters of all time. In my opinion, he is also and most definitely the greatest of the Dutch masters. Secondly, that particular painting hadn't been seen for fifty years by the public. It had been hidden away in the collection of Sir Alec Delaware, where it had simply gathered dust. Also, paintings by Rembrandt are not often on the market. They're not two a penny, you know."

He smiled at her last comment, finding it amusing, checked the recorder, then said, "I know Margaret Mellor. I've written several pieces for *ART* magazine. I spoke to her about you in the course of my research. She's a big fan, by the way."

Annette seemed pleased when she said, "As I am of her. She's a good friend and very talented. So, what did she say about me?"

A blond brow lifted questioningly, and Jack noticed the quickening of interest in her eyes. He said, "I didn't really ask her about you in a personal way. I just wanted to know if she'd been at the auction, and she said she had. She also indicated you did a fabulous campaign beforehand, really made the Rembrandt incredibly famous before it went to auction."

Annette couldn't help laughing, and, through her laughter, she managed to say, "I just sang its praises. However, a lot of people were critical of me, and said I'd hyped it to death. Frankly, I believe I brought it to life. And, incidentally, it was the highest price *ever* paid for a Rembrandt."

"I read that in one of the pieces written about you, and, by the way, Margaret told me you were very masterful in your promotion of the auction, confided it was a brilliant campaign."

Leaning forward slightly, Jack continued, "I'm not all that familiar with Rembrandt, and his work, and although I can research him, I wonder if you'd mind giving me a few insights into him, your thoughts about him. I believe that would make it more personal, more accessible to the reader."

"Rembrandt was a genius," Annette began. "Aside from being such an extraordinary painter, he had a profound humanity. I think that's why his portraits are so . . . *so alive, so real*. When I first looked at that woman in that blow-up over there, I felt that if I reached out I would touch human flesh, not paint and canvas."

Annette rose, went over to the credenza, pointed to the dress in the painting, and, looking at Jack, she murmured, "This taffeta looks so real I can almost hear it crackle. I think what Rembrandt did was see inside the people he painted. Let me put it another way. I'm sure he had enormous psychological insight into his models, knew what made them tick, and managed to bring out their inner lives, shown in the expressions on their faces."

Returning to her chair, Annette explained, "He finished

that painting in 1657. For me it is a marvelous symbol of his triumph over enormous adversity. He had a lot of personal problems at that time. He was widowed, broke, had many debts, had withdrawn to the country to escape his creditors. And he was depressed at times. Unfortunately, he had become reclusive. But worst of all, he was considered to be unfashionable as a painter."

Annette shifted slightly in the chair and let out a sigh. "Just imagine coping with all those things. Yet he painted his greatest masterpieces during those years." She shook her head. "*Unbelievable.* And *my* Rembrandt, as I still call it, is one of Rembrandt's great triumphs, an example of his immense talent, and of sheer willpower. He obviously never let anything get in the way of his work."

Jack exclaimed, "How wonderfully articulate you are! And I'm right. . . . I couldn't get anything like that just from Googling him. By the way, another question for you, but you probably won't answer it."

"Oh. And why not?" Again a blond brow lifted.

"Because I don't think you can, inasmuch as you probably aren't allowed to do so. However, *I* can't help asking you. Who was the buyer who paid twenty million pounds?"

"I can't answer that, but only because I simply don't know. It was an *anonymous* buyer bidding over the phone, and I'm perfectly certain it was an agent making the bids, and not the actual buyer."

"I understand. Well, look here, my congratulations! You conducted a fabulous auction by all accounts, and you've become a star. I want to say overnight, but I guess that's not quite correct, is it?"

"Not really. I've worked for many years in the art business."

"How did you get into it? How did you start?" Jack asked. It was his first personal question about her background, and he was curious.

For a moment Annette was silent, and then she took a deep breath and plunged in, well prepared with her story. "I was always interested in art as a child, forever painting pictures.

Eventually, when I was older, I was able to attend the Royal College of Art, and I learned a great deal over the few years I was studying there. However, I was born with a critical eye, and I began to understand that I wasn't going to be another Mary Cassatt, Berthe Morisot, or Dame Laura Knight. And so I decided to become an art historian instead. I've always believed that was a wise decision, a good move on my part."

"You said earlier that it was your sister who told you you should have two strings to your bow, and that's why you studied the Old Masters as well as Impressionist painters. Did she, was she, very influential in your career?"

"Only by encouraging me," Annette replied. "She's always been a big booster of mine."

"Is she in the art business as well?"

"Sort of. She's an art historian as I am, and she does a lot of research for art dealers. She's an expert on Degas and his work, actually."

"What's her name?"

"Laurie. She's several years younger than me, and actually she's a paraplegic. She was injured in a car crash some years ago."

"Oh, I'm sorry to hear that. . . ." His voice trailed off.

Annette now confided, "She's a marvel, an inspiration to everybody. Never a complaint, cheerful by nature, and she enjoys her busy life as well as her work." As an afterthought she added, "She's very beautiful."

"What's her last name? It can't be Remmington, that's your married name."

"Watson, she's Laurie Watson."

"Is she married?"

"No, she's not." Annette gave him the benefit of a warm smile. "You can talk to her if you wish. I've no objections."

"Thank you," he said, smiling back. "I might want to do that. Later. Now, I've just a few more questions about your work, and then I'll get out of your hair. Until Friday, that is."

"Yes, of course." She glanced at her watch. "Goodness, it's almost twelve-thirty. How the time has flown."

"Hasn't it just," he responded, eyeing her speculatively. He wanted to ask her to have lunch with him, but he was wary of doing so. He didn't want her to get the wrong idea, and he did have two more interviews with her before writing his piece for the London *Sunday Times*. No, better keep this all business, he told himself. Safer by far.

He had finally left.

She sat there staring into space. And she felt alone. *Really alone.* Jack Chalmers had filled the room with his presence, his laughter, his geniality, and his charisma. There was no doubt about it, he was a man who had been born with enormous natural charm, and he certainly knew how to use it to his advantage.

Yet Annette realized he was genuinely sincere, caring, and considerate. He had been determined to put her at ease, and certainly he had done that.

It was obvious to her that Marius had told Jack's agent she was reluctant to do interviews; Jack had alluded to this once, then made a point of it to her. It had disarmed her, as he had intended, but she trusted him.

What surprised her was that his questions had not been at all probing, at least not about her background or her early life. Perhaps they would come later, but she was no longer apprehensive about him.

Before he left he had asked her if he really could talk to her sister, and she had acquiesced, promised to arrange it. Her reward had been a dazzling smile and profuse thank-yous.

Leaning over her desk, she stared at the report in front of her. It had come in from the New York office, and was about a couple of available paintings. Two different owners wanted to sell; one a Monet, the other an early Picasso. She began to read, but within seconds found it impossible to concentrate.

Swiftly she put the papers back inside the folder, slid it into a drawer. Closing her eyes, she let her mind empty, pushed aside thoughts of work, and all the things she had to do today. Instead she focused on herself, and her extraordinary reaction to Jack Chalmers.

She had been thrown off balance by him, truly shaken up. She had never felt like this before. . . . No, not true. She had *once*, a very long time ago, and she had succumbed to those feelings only to find herself in trouble. Her reaction to that other man had, in the end, changed her life, and in the most profound way.

Decades suddenly dropped away.

She fell down into the past, remembering so much. . . . There was no one to help her in her trouble. Laurie in a wheelchair, their older brother, Anthony, gone away God knows where, Aunt Sylvia working and coping with Laurie, as best she could. And so she had had no alternative but to go back to Marius. He had rescued her, married her, and had never once uttered a word of criticism.

A long sigh rippled through her. . . . For a moment in time she had had an amazing brief encounter. She had known true ecstasy . . . pure, joyous, exciting, fulfilling, and she had been head over heels in love with that man. And then he was gone, and she was alone, and it had never happened to her again. No one else had ever filled her with those feelings of intense sexual passion, of raging desire, of total bonding.

Quite simply, she had never met anyone else like him. Ever. Until today.

Jack Chalmers had affected her in exactly the same way. She had almost fallen apart when he had walked into the office, although she had endeavored not to show it.

He had managed to make her feel at ease about the interview; nonetheless she was shaking inside, drawn to him, aware of a deep physical attraction, sexual desire, and an indescribable yearning she couldn't explain to herself. Was it the need to touch him, to be close to him, to be intimate, to truly know him?

The shrill of the phone brought her upright in the chair. "Yes, Esther?"

"It's Laurie, boss."

"Thanks, put her through." Annette swallowed. Her voice sounded odd to her, thick, hoarse.

"Hi," Laurie exclaimed, and went on in her cheerful way, "I know I'm not disturbing you because the interview is over."

"It is, yes."

"How did it go?"

"Very well. It's the first of three, as you know, and I'm seeing him again on Friday, then early next week. After that he would like to talk to you."

"What about?"

"I suppose *me*." Annette suddenly laughed. "I said he could, so I hope you don't mind. Maybe he can meet with you sometime next week?"

"That's fine, as long as it has your approval."

"It does, and he's very nice, you'll like him."

"See, I told you so."

"No, Malcolm told me so, via you," Annette answered, teasing her.

"Only too true. Could we get together later today? There's something I'd like to talk to you about, Annette."

"Can't we discuss it on the phone?"

"No, not really."

"I have a busy afternoon, but how about six, thereabouts?"

"That's good, and thanks, Annette."

Putting the receiver back in the cradle, Annette couldn't help wondering if her sister wanted to talk to her about Malcolm Stevens. *Was* their relationship serious? She had no objection to it, if it was, but what would Marius's attitude be? Malcolm was a favorite of his, a protégé. Would Marius approve of Malcolm and Laurie? Maybe. *Maybe not.* One thing she was sure of, though: she would not allow him to interfere. He might well run her life in that controlling way of his, but she was damned if she was going to let him manipulate Malcolm and Laurie. Over my dead body, she thought.

* * *

Paddy drove her up to Hampstead for tea with Carlton and Marguerite Fraser at their rather lovely old house near the heath. Once she was settled in the back of the car, Annette closed her eyes, let herself drift with her thoughts. Inevitably, they settled on Jack Chalmers.

How old was he? Was he married? If so, did he have children? Or was he involved with someone? Of course there was a woman in his life, he was too attractive, too eligible, not to be surrounded by gorgeous girls. Where did he live? Did he have parents still alive? Siblings? What did he do in his spare time? What restaurants did he favor? Why had his step faltered when he came into her office? Did he have the same feelings as her? No, not possible. Besides, he was forbidden fruit, wasn't he? She was, after all, a married woman. Marius. Oh, my God! Marius was infuriated if another man even looked at her.

"Here we are, Mrs. Remmington," Paddy was saying, and Annette sat up swiftly, pulling herself together.

"Thanks, Paddy," she said. "I'll leave my briefcase on the backseat."

"Righto, Mrs. R.," he responded. He jumped out of the car and went to open the door for her.

As she mounted the steps to the elegant Georgian house, the front door opened and Carlton was standing there with a big smile on his face.

It was obvious he had been ill. A tall man, he now appeared to be a little stooped. He had lost weight and his face was gaunt, paler than usual, but perhaps that was because he was wearing a black corduroy jacket over a black sweater, and black drained color from anybody's face.

"There you are, my darling girl," he said, smiling hugely.

She saw that his hazel eyes were clear and bright, and there was strength in his voice, and she was pleased about this.

"You look better than I expected," Annette said, going into his open arms, embracing him on the top step.

Closing the door behind them, he led her into the front

hall, explaining, "I had the best doctors, and you know I'm a tough old coot. I spring back pretty quickly. In another week I'll be my old self."

"Where's Marguerite?" she asked, glancing around.

The words were hardly out of her mouth when Carlton's wife appeared in the arched doorway of the sitting room, a smile on her face.

"Here I am, and it's wonderful to see you, Annette. And by the way, you must always wear pale blue. You've made it your own color."

Annette said, "Why, thank you, and it's lovely to see you." She went over to greet her with a kiss on the cheek. They were old friends, and Annette had always had a soft spot for this lovely woman who took such great care of Carlton, ran his business, cooked gourmet meals, and managed to always look chic.

Slipping off her wool topcoat, which matched her pale-blue suit, Annette handed it to Marguerite, who took it over to the coat cupboard and hung it up.

Carlton said, "I would like you to come to the studio before we have tea. To look at the Cézanne."

"Is it the soot that's the problem?"

"No."

"What is it then?"

"It's the painting, Annette."

"What do you mean?" She frowned, looked puzzled.

"It's *wrong*."

She gaped at him. "It's a *fake*? Are you telling me it's not a real Cézanne? *That it's a fake?*"

"I am."

Chapter Eighteen

✳

T he studio where Carlton worked was a large room filled with natural daylight, which came in through three tall windows overlooking the garden.

Two huge klieg lamps, which Carlton had bought at a sale held by a defunct film studio, spread additional light across the whole area. He also had four tall standing lamps, two on either side of the easel where the Cézanne was propped.

Leading Annette over to the easel, Carlton switched on the four lamps and angled the heads to focus directly on the painting.

Annette cringed as she stood staring at the painting, so badly scarred by the patches of black soot. "The intensity of the lamps really brings the soot into focus," she murmured, glancing at the restorer, grimacing.

Carlton said, "Look up at the right-hand corner. You can see where I started to clean it. Very cautiously. In tiny sections. As I *slowly* moved down the painting that first morning, I knew I was facing a dilemma. . . . I needed to remove the black patches, but in doing so I was afraid I might ruin the painting. You see, the soot is deeply embedded. Marguerite made me stop for hot soup at lunch time, I had such a bad cough, and I never made it back to the studio. I collapsed, and she had to send for an ambulance to get me to Emergency as fast as possible, and you know the rest."

"When did you discover the painting was wrong?"

"Several days ago, when I came in here for the first time since that first day." He moved closer to the easel and touched the canvas. "Come and look at this," he said, pointing to a corner of the painting. "The paint underneath the soot had obviously run a little the morning I started working on it, but I didn't come back in here, I went to the hospital instead. So I never saw it. As you well know, old paint doesn't normally run. It suddenly struck me that it was *new paint*. How could that be? I was baffled. I took the painting down and examined the back of the canvas. It looked old, but I was still concerned about that paint."

Annette nodded. "Cézanne was working in the mid to late eighteen-hundreds. . . . When I first saw this, I thought it had been painted around 1879, or thereabouts, when he was prolific."

"At first glance, yes, you would think that. But I believe it was done only about *eighteen* years ago." Carlton pursed his lips, shook his head. "I didn't want to say anything to you until I was certain, so I brought in Ted Underwood, with whom I've frequently collaborated in the past. He's a bloody good restorer, as you well know, and extremely knowledgeable. He agreed with me about the paint, and, in fact, he tested it himself and within short order he got the same results. So we decided to remove a few nails to look at the canvas yesterday. As you can see, the painting is out of the frame, which I'd removed when you first sent it to me, so it was a relatively easy task to pull the canvas away from the stretcher. Ted and I knew at once the canvas was not old, even though it looked it, by the way."

"The canvas was doctored?"

Carlton nodded.

"Forgers have their special tricks, tricks of the trade," Annette asserted. "Soaking new canvases in tea to stain them, to give them an aged look, using rusty old nails, and buying old pictures, cleaning them, and then painting over the old canvas. There was a very famous forger called Elmyr de Hory, a Hungarian, who was extremely successful in the late fifties and early sixties. Actually, there was a book written about him by Clifford Irving. Apparently the world had not seen anything like de Hory. He fooled hundreds."

"Well, they certainly heard of a couple of similar chaps ten years ago!" Carlton exclaimed.

"Oh, God, yes! The art world will never be the same again in certain ways," Annette said. "You're talking about John Myatt, that forger who had such a long run, and his puppet master, John Drewe, aren't you?"

"I am indeed. John Drewe was a manipulator of the first order and a brilliant con artist. A villain, actually, who used everyone to suit his own ends. Myatt, struggling artist though he was, happened to be a brilliant painter, and fell into his clutches. Drewe got away with it for years. What a scam."

"Are you suggesting that this painting might be a forgery by Myatt?" Annette asked, staring at Carlton intently.

"I don't think so. Although I wouldn't swear to it, of course. Looking back, remembering the trial as best I can— it ended in 1999 if you recall—Myatt did not paint any Cézannes."

"So who forged this one?" she asked, pointing at the canvas on the easel.

"God only knows, and He won't split," Carlton muttered, using an old saying. "But somebody did attempt to destroy it. I suspected that the soot had been rubbed into the canvas the first time I saw the painting and told you so. Now we know why. But not *who*."

"I think I know who rubbed the soot into it," Annette said. "Sir Alec Delaware. I bet he discovered it was a forgery and decided to ruin it, so that it couldn't be sold later as the real thing, by an heir, for example."

Carlton gave her a swift glance, nodding his head. "You have a point there. It might have indeed been Sir Alec. I can't imagine who else could have done it. But why didn't he just destroy the painting?"

"I have no idea. And here's another thing. There's no provenance for this, you know, and that has always presented a problem to me, Carlton."

"What about the other art in the collection?"

"The Degas, Cassatt, and Morisot paintings all have pristine provenances, and so does the Giacometti sculpture. And, thank God, *The Little Fourteen-Year-Old Dancer*, the Degas masterpiece, has a perfect lineage. There are some modern paintings by Nicholson and Sutherland, and they each have provenance. But there's a lot of unimportant paintings by not very well-known artists hanging at Knowle Court. I wasn't interested, so I didn't ask about those."

"Mmmmm, so why did I think the collection was much larger?" Carlton asked, frowning at her.

"I don't know, but I do have some thoughts about Sir Alec Delaware."

"What kind of thoughts?" he asked, peering at her intently.

"I think there are other paintings somewhere at Knowle Court, probably hidden away. It's not unusual for people to buy paintings and store them; some of my clients do that all the time. They put them in attics or warehouses and bring them out later. They change paintings around. Or they buy them as an investment, and store them, until prices rise."

"Yes, I know that happens a lot. However, what brings you to the conclusion that there is art hidden in that old house? Did someone tell you?"

"Not really, but I've picked up bits and pieces from Christopher Delaware, and a friend of his, James Pollard. Look, Sir Alec apparently became weird, secretive, difficult, reclusive, fifteen years ago. After his fiancée committed suicide—"

"Clarissa Normandy," Carlton cut in. "You told me about that, how she died. Awful business."

Annette nodded. "Sir Alec was a very well-known collector, rumored to have a lot more paintings than are showing up at this moment. Who knows where he put them, since he was behaving strangely. I think I'm going to ask Christopher to do a bit of investigating again, and I might even go down to Knowle Court to take a look around. But in the meantime, what do we do about that?" She gestured to the canvas on the easel.

"Once you've told your client that it's a fake, I think you

ought to destroy it. Mind you, no one would ever try to sell it, not with all that soot on it and also because it has no provenance."

"That *is* the only thing to do, destroy it," she immediately agreed. Walking over to Carlton, she took hold of his arm. "Come on, let's go and have a cup of tea. I could certainly use it."

"I'm so glad you're early," Laurie exclaimed, her face filling with happiness when Annette walked into her office in her apartment in Chesham Place. "Would you like Angie to make you a cup of tea?"

Annette kissed her sister on the cheek, and shook her head. "No, thanks. I drank endless cups of it with Carlton and Marguerite. I'll float away if I have any more."

"How are they? And how's the Cézanne coming along?"

Sitting down in a chair next to Laurie's desk, Annette said, "I've got some bad news about the Cézanne."

"Don't tell me that Carlton can't clean it, that it's ruined?"

"It *is* ruined. By the soot. But that's not the point."

"What do you mean?"

"Carlton says it's wrong."

"A forgery?" Laurie cried, her voice rising an octave. "How can that be?"

"I don't know. In fact, as of this moment, I suppose nobody knows. And I don't think we'll ever find out. Carlton told me it's a relatively new canvas, no more than eighteen years old, and where he originally started to clean off the soot two weeks ago, the paint has run. He brought in Ted Underwood, another fantastic restorer, as you know, and together they took out a few nails in order to examine the other side of the canvas. No doubt about it, the Cézanne is not right, therefore *wrong*, and very much a bloody fake."

"Oh, my God!" Laurie stared at her sister. "Have you told Christopher Delaware?"

"No, not yet, I haven't had a chance. I came straight here from Carlton's house."

"He'll be surprised when he hears that a painting from his illustrious uncle's art collection is a forgery, and that it can't go into the auction."

"I believe he's become aware it can't be sold, Laurie, since I've warned him the soot might never come off. I also pointed out several times that there's no provenance, and without that we have a problem."

"Now we know why, don't we? It's hard to *fake* provenance."

"Too true." Annette shook her head. "Carlton thought someone had attempted to damage the painting by rubbing soot in rather than cleaning it off, and he said that when he first saw it. I now believe he's right."

"Who would do that?" Laurie stared at her sister, looking baffled.

"How can I possibly know? But to hazard a guess, I'd say perhaps it was Sir Alec himself. He must have bought the painting in good faith, believing it to be a Cézanne, and when he found out otherwise he may have wanted to make it impossible for an heir to sell it at a later date."

"Why not simply destroy it?" Laurie's eyes were questioning; she was puzzled.

Annette shrugged. "I don't know. It's a bit of a mystery, isn't it? Anyway, I'll phone Christopher tomorrow and explain everything. I am going to insist the painting be destroyed, Laurie."

"You should." There was a pause. Laurie went on, "It's a good thing the other paintings you're planning to auction have the proper provenance."

"It is indeed."

Laurie began to roll her chair out of the room, saying as she did, "Let's go into the sitting room, Annette, you'll be more comfortable in there."

Once they were settled in the other room, Annette said, "You told me you wanted to talk to me about something, when you phoned me this morning. Are you all right? There's nothing wrong, is there?"

As she spoke Annette's eyes searched her sister's face,

and she couldn't help thinking she had just asked two rather stupid questions. Laurie looked as if she was in the best of health. In fact, she was blooming. She was more beautiful than ever, her abundant red-gold hair shimmering around her face, her peaches-and-cream complexion flawless, her eyes sparkling, full of life.

Leaning forward a little, Laurie said, "I'm pregnant."

Thunderstruck by this announcement, Annette gaped at her, at a loss for words.

Laurie began to laugh. "Don't look so upset. Malcolm and I are having a baby and we're both thrilled."

"I'm not upset, just . . . *startled*. You've taken my breath away."

"I thought I would, but I did think you might have guessed Malcolm and I were . . . *involved*."

"It had crossed my mind, yes, but you never confided in me, so I wasn't exactly sure whether you two were just extremely friendly, great pals, or having an affair. When did you become so involved?"

"Oh yes, it's an affair all right, and we're in love and, to answer your question, we've been serious for six months. And we're planning to get married. Which is what I wanted to talk to you about."

Annette was silent as she absorbed her sister's words.

"You are upset!" Laurie exclaimed, staring at Annette, her eyes clouding. Her expression changed; she suddenly looked apprehensive.

"No, no, I'm not, honestly, darling. And if you're happy then I'm happy, too, and I know Malcolm's a decent man, very reliable. It's just that—"

"You're afraid for me, aren't you, Annette?" Laurie interjected. "About the baby, I mean. But I'm fine, really I am. And I will be fine."

"Are you sure it's *safe*? I know how practical and sensible you are, but you have seen your gynecologist, haven't you?"

"Yes, I have, and she says everything's going to be all right. Paraplegic women can come to full term, and deliver a healthy baby, you know. My doctor also pointed out that if it should be necessary the baby could be delivered by Caesarean section. You mustn't worry. *Please*."

Annette stood up, went to her sister, and wrapped her arms around her, gave her a warm and loving embrace. "I suppose I will worry a bit, Laurie darling, but you look and sound so happy I'm thrilled for you. And there's nobody like Malcolm, he's very genuine, true-blue."

"That he is, and he loves me and I love him. We wanted you to be the first to know that we're getting married and about the baby, of course."

"How many months are you along?"

"Not months," Laurie corrected. "Just weeks. Six weeks exactly."

Annette nodded, gave her a reassuring smile. "So, we have a wedding to plan, don't we? Have you and Malcolm picked a date?"

"Not exactly. I wanted to talk to you. Also, there's another thing. . . ." Laurie paused, and a concerned expression settled on her face. "What do you think Marius will say about this?"

"He'll be very happy, I'm certain of that," Annette responded, although she wasn't sure that he would be. "Is Malcolm going to tell him?"

"I don't know. Perhaps I should. What do you think?" Laurie bit her lip, sudden nervousness getting the better of her.

"I think this. We're going to have dinner next week, just the four of us, and you and Malcolm can tell him then," Annette announced, her voice positive and very firm. She was determined that Laurie was going to have a happy life with Malcolm Stevens. Whatever she had to do to ensure this, she would do, and she would not allow Marius to interfere in any way. Laurie's life must be her own; Laurie must be free.

She walked home.

She needed air; she needed to breathe; she needed to be alone, to steady herself. To take control of her being. *Calm.*

Peace. Solitude. Privacy. She craved these things at this moment in time. *This moment in time,* she thought again. These few minutes, this *now* would never come back, never be hers again. That was the truth. Time fled, went on, running away and with speed. Tomorrow would come. And go. And never come back.

Today had been a day of surprises.

First, the arrival of Jack Chalmers and her overwhelming reaction to him. Second, Carlton's news that the Cézanne was a fake. Third, Laurie's announcement that she was pregnant. She wouldn't forget today.

Now, focusing on the events of earlier, Annette understood that Jack Chalmers had been the biggest surprise of all. She suddenly remembered something Penelope Sloane had said to her, when she had been with her at the New York office last year. Penny had described her feelings when she had first met the man who was about to become her husband that summer.

"I felt as if I'd been hit by a Mack truck," Penny had confided. "*Wham!* I was a goner. I've never really recovered from the impact of Matt. He knocked me off my feet, knocked me for a loop, as they say."

She had understood what Penny meant. Because of that one experience long ago. She could draw on those memories, easily envision it again. She shivered, even though it was a warm night.

Someone walked over my grave, she thought, recalling an old saying. No, it was not that. *It was fear.* He frightened her. She must be brave.

Jack Chalmers, she thought. And pushed his name to the back of her mind.

Laurie's pregnancy frightened her. She could do nothing about it, only wait and see, and in the meantime pray all went well. What she could do, of course, was talk to her own gynecologist, seek proper information, which would undoubtedly help her to feel less uneasy. And there was Marius's reaction to this new situation. What would it be? Later. I'll think about these ramifications later.

Suddenly she was at the far end of Eaton Square. Home. She took her time as she went into the building and up in the lift to the flat. Marius was having dinner with an American client; she would eat whatever dish Elaine had cooked and left in the kitchen for her. Food was never a priority, and she wasn't hungry.

In her dressing room she shed her blue wool coat, slipped off the matching suit jacket, and went down the corridor to her office. Within minutes she had Christopher Delaware on the phone and was explaining about the Cézanne.

She finished the conversation by saying, "So, Chris, what I would like you to do is to meet me at Carlton Fraser's tomorrow morning around ten, if that's convenient. Carlton will explain exactly how and why he came to his conclusions."

"I'll be there, Annette, and thank you for all the time and care you put into handling my art collection. I'm very appreciative. See you tomorrow. Good night."

"Good night," she answered, and hung up. That had been relatively easy. The good thing about Christopher was that he was bright, usually got it, and went along with her advice.

Her next call was to Margaret Mellor, who she knew would still be at *ART* magazine. She was, and she picked up her direct line after only two rings.

"It's Annette. I wanted to say hello, and thank you for saying nice things about me to Jack Chalmers."

"Annette, hi! It was my pleasure, and my God, isn't *he* dishy? I could eat him up with a lovely big spoon. Yummy."

Annette burst out laughing. "Margaret, you're a hoot. I've never heard you wax poetic about a man, at least not like this."

"Wax poetic, eh? That's a nice way of putting it. But I've got to tell you, I've always had a sort of yen for him. However, he wouldn't be interested in a short, plumpish woman like me. More like a tall, blond, gorgeous babe . . . why, somebody just like you!"

"Don't be so ridiculous, Margaret. Anyway, you're not short and plumpish at all. You're very good-looking and chic."

"Thanks for that. I know I'm not his type, though."

"He did an interview with me this morning," Annette went on in her fast, businesslike way. "He's doing a piece, a profile of me actually, for *The Sunday Times*, and he mentioned he'd chatted to you. So again, my thanks for being kind."

"He asked a few innocuous questions, and I told him the truth." Margaret chuckled. "Hearing his voice made my day, to be honest. He's the sort of man who incites women to fight each other, commit adultery, or cry gallons of tears when he dumps them. He's a real heartbreaker, in my opinion. Or has that potential, don't you think?"

Annette could hardly breathe; nor could she speak for a moment. But at last she managed to say, "He is good-looking and charming, I've got to agree with you there. But surely he's married. I mean, a man like that . . ." Her voice petered out; she didn't want Margaret to think she was on a fishing trip. Which she was.

Margaret exclaimed, "Oh no, he's not married, that I know for a fact! I'll say this for him, he's a workaholic. He's almost remorseless with himself at times, and relentless. A real pro. One of the best journalists I've had the pleasure to work with, all joking apart. And by the way, he'll do a good piece on you, I'm sure of that."

"I have a feeling he doesn't go for the jugular."

"Now why on earth would anybody go for *your* jugular, Annette? Good heavens, everybody loves you in this town."

"I doubt that," she answered swiftly, "but thanks for the compliment."

They talked for a few more minutes and then hung up. Annette leaned back in the chair and discovered much to her astonishment that she was shaking. Why? Because of the things Margaret had said, of course. He was single. And therefore had nothing to lose. This thought terrified her even more.

She and Marius sat in the yellow living room, his eyes fixed on her as she told him about her meeting with Carlton, and his harsh opinion about the Cézanne.

When she had finished, he said, "But why didn't *you* spot this? You've got a keen eye, and you know Cézanne, he's one of your favorites, for God's sake."

She stared back at her husband, his words rankling. He had sounded critical and accusatory. She exclaimed, "I told you all along that the black patches completely disfigured the painting, altered its appearance. I defy anyone to have spotted something *wrong* with the painting, because it looked *right*. Except for those patches of black soot. Carlton only found out because the paint had run whilst he was in hospital."

"I understand. You don't have to sound so shirty. I suspect it's a mistake I would have made, too." He frowned. "I wonder who the forger was. Or is?"

"How could anybody know? According to Carlton and Ted Underwood, it was painted about eighteen years ago, or thereabouts."

Marius nodded. "That was around the time John Drewe was setting up his art-forging operation, along with John Myatt."

"We discussed that, but Carlton seemed to think it was *not* theirs. Anyway, one thing seems certain: it must have been Sir Alec who threw soot on the painting in order to do plenty of damage."

"Why do you say that?"

"Because he must have discovered he'd bought a fake. Who else would damage a painting but the owner—" Annette broke off, sat up straighter in the chair. "Oh, there was the fiancée, she might have realized it was a fake. Certainly she could have thrown the soot on it."

"The fiancée?" Marius frowned. "Wasn't there something about a scandal? I vaguely remember some odd story."

"Yes. She committed suicide. She hanged herself in the master bedroom. A few days before their wedding. She was wearing her wedding gown."

Marius winced and gaped at her. He began to shake his head. "Why would a woman do such an horrific thing?"

"To wound him, hurt him? Alec Delaware, I mean."

"I see." His eyes narrowed slightly when he asked, "Who was the fiancée? I really have forgotten the details."

"Her name was Clarissa Normandy."

"Oh yes, I vaguely recall. . . ." Marius picked up his brandy and took a sip, then leaned back against the sofa.

Moving slightly on the chair opposite, Annette glanced across at her husband and wondered why he was suddenly looking so pale. She asked, "Don't you feel well, Marius?"

"I'm perfectly fine. Why do you ask?"

"You've gone a little pale."

"I think perhaps it's a combination of too much wine at dinner, a rich meal, and this ghastly tale of suicide, that's all."

"You know something, Marius, I've just had the strangest thought. What if it was his fiancée who'd forged the Cézanne . . . this Clarissa Normandy? She was an artist, you know."

"No, I didn't," he answered. He took another sip of the Napoleon and changed the subject.

Chapter Nineteen

He wanted to write about her.

Writing about her would bring her closer. But he hadn't finished the interviews; he still had two more to go. Nonetheless, he had sat at his computer, staring at the screen all afternoon since leaving her office, and he was still in the same place, although it was now nine o'clock at night.

It wouldn't come. The words wouldn't flow, even though he had such vivid images of her in his head. Annette Remmington. Blond, beautiful, elegant. And also intelligent and articulate. She was oddly enigmatic, Mrs. Remmington. Mysterious. Yes, that was the perfect word to describe her. She was different, certainly unlike anybody he had ever met in his life. And he couldn't get her out of his head.

Jack sat back in his chair, endeavoring to relax, and slowly he read his last version of his profile on her. It didn't work for him, so it wouldn't work for anybody else. Of course it didn't work. He didn't have enough personal material yet in order to get inside her skin, to truly understand her and what made her tick. He needed more. Frustrated, he deleted everything he had written, every version, got up, walked into the kitchen, took a bottle of water out of the fridge, and returned to his desk.

He sat down at the computer, about to start all over again. And changed his mind. What was the point? He had to finish the next two interviews to make sense of her, to understand fully *who* and *what* she was. Endeavoring to construct something now was utterly futile. He was wasting his time and his energy.

Jack understood why he was doing this, knew what this was all about. He believed that writing about her would bring her closer to him tonight, and it would in a certain way. But that wasn't going to happen. It would only happen when he had so much material he would be discarding parts of it.

Jack blew out air, stretched his shoulders, picked up the bottle, and took several swigs of the water. He glanced at the phone on his desk and then looked at his watch, suddenly remembering Lucy. He'd forgotten to call her earlier, and now it was too late. It was ten o'clock in France. He'd call tomorrow.

Filling with relief at this decision, he rose, went over to the sofa, sat down, turned on the television, turned it off, walked over to the window, looked out, and gave up. He was frustrated, restless, and ill at ease with himself.

Back at the desk, he lolled back in the chair, his thoughts churning around in his head. *Women.* Why am I always in a mess with women? he asked himself.

Suddenly, unexpectedly, he thought of his father. A man who had loved women, who was always in a mess with women, and apparently lots of them. A journalist. He had inherited his father's talent for writing, just as he'd inherited his father's penchant for womanizing, no two ways about that. He was a chip off the old block.

"Always running off, chasing wars or chasing women, both dangerous. He lived for danger," was the way his mother had put it once, when he was old enough to understand what she was saying, around fifteen by then. At the time he had imagined that his father's life must have been very romantic. But now, as a grown man, he accepted that it had more than likely been a big mess.

His father had died at the age of thirty-eight, far too young to get blown to smithereens. He'd stepped on a land mine in some God-forsaken country. . . . "Chasing another war, addicted to war," his mother had muttered to him on that day when she had finally been able to talk about his father. She had sounded angry, and always would when it came to her first husband.

The things he remembered best about his childhood were from the years after his mother had married Peter Chalmers. What had gone before was sort of foggy in his head. Except that his mother's words about his biological father had, quite oddly, remained clear. She had been bitter, he realized that now. And still in love with his father?

He'd once asked her sister Helen, his aunt, about that, and Helen had laughed. "No way. Eleanor was far too pragmatic to cling to a man who was never around. She loved Peter and the security he gave her."

Yes, she *had* loved his stepfather, and so had he. Peter had been a *real* father to him, had adopted him, brought him up as his own. Unlike his mother, Peter had never bad-mouthed his biological father; in fact, he had rarely ever mentioned him at all. Such was the way of men, Jack suddenly thought. We're so bloody different from women. No wonder we don't understand them.

Thinking about Peter had reminded him that he had to return Kyle's call of earlier, and he dialed him immediately.

His brother answered on the sixth ring, just before the voice mail picked up. "I'm here, Jacko. What's up, kid?"

"Hi. About that trunk you've been nagging me about. How big is it?"

"It's huge, Jack. I think you might have to hire a van in order to move it, and you'll need help to carry it, as well."

"How big is it, for God's sake? And do I really need it? Couldn't I just go and empty it, put the stuff inside a suitcase?"

"You could do that, yes," Kyle responded. "You'd probably need two suitcases, though, and you might want to keep the trunk. It's a great piece of Louis Vuitton. Mum must've spent a fortune on it even back when she bought it."

Jack laughed. "Well, you know our mum, she loved expensive *stuff*, especially expensive *French* stuff. Actually, it might be a good idea to use suitcases anyway, easier to handle. What's in the trunk, anyway?"

"I haven't really gone through it, to be honest, but it's mostly things to do with *your* early childhood, mementos, photographs, her own early life, that kind of thing."

"Do I really want all that?" Jack sounded suddenly doubtful.

There was a short silence. Finally Kyle said quietly, "Yes, I think you do, kid. It has a luggage label tied on the side handle with your name written on it, and very clearly. You should have it, Jack, because Mum wanted it to go to you, and Dad mentioned it to me just after she died. Listen, you're a sentimental bugger, even if you pretend not to be at times. So go and get it, within the next week or so. Okay?"

"Sure. I'll go for it. And just out of curiosity, what else is left in the house?"

"Some furniture. Antiques for the most part. I thought we could send them to a dealer to be auctioned off, along with china, and some other things. The young couple who made an offer for the house haven't come back to the estate agent yet. So who knows what's going to happen."

"I might go and get the trunk tomorrow, actually."

"I thought you were in the middle of a profile for *The Sunday Times*."

"I am. But I have two more interviews with the subject. The next one is on Friday. So I'm at a loose end tomorrow."

"Fine, then do it, get it out of the way. Shall we get together tonight? Have dinner? Before I go off to Jordan?"

"Sure, great idea. I'll come over around seven-thirty."

"See ya," Kyle answered, and hung up.

"I don't know about destroying the Cézanne, Annette. I might want to keep it," Christopher Delaware said, looking across at her, biting his lip, shifting slightly on his feet.

It was Thursday morning, and they were at Carlton's studio. Annette was taken aback for a split second and quickly glanced at Carlton, and saw a sudden look of astonishment crossing his face. He seemed baffled as he returned her gaze.

Addressing her client, she said, "Well, of course that's up to you, Chris, but I think it would be much wiser to be rid of it. It's of no value to you, or anyone else for that matter. Why do you even want a fake?"

"How do you destroy a painting?" Christopher asked, ignoring her question, giving her a long, hard stare.

"Cut it up, or burn it, I guess. I've never done it before, you know, so I'm only guessing."

Carlton said in a firm voice, "You should destroy the painting, Christopher. If you lived in France, you'd be forced to do so, because there that is the *law*. You cannot keep a forgery, once it's proven to be one, even if you've paid millions for it."

"But what's the harm in keeping it?" Christopher asked, edging closer to Carlton, who stood near the Cézanne on the easel.

Annette's mobile began to ring; she pulled it out of her jacket pocket and walked away from them, heading for the window. "Hello?"

"Boss, is that you?"

"It is, Esther, yes. What's up?"

"Nothing special. I wanted you to know I just gave your mobile number to Jack Chalmers. He said it was urgent he speak to you. I hope that was okay. It was, wasn't it?"

"Yes, of course. What does he want?"

"He didn't explain. He said it was about your Friday appointment. The interview."

"Okay. No problem, thanks for alerting me. I'll deal with it. Talk to you later." She clicked off, and, holding the phone in her hand, she absentmindedly looked out the French window at the garden. Spring was definitely early this year. Bluebells were already in flower.

She walked back to Carlton and Christopher, and stood listening to them talking about the Cézanne. Suddenly, she decided she was getting bored with this continuing discussion, wanted to get it over with, and get on, and she couldn't help wondering what Jack Chalmers wanted. She hoped he wasn't canceling tomorrow's meeting.

The phone rang, and she stepped away again. "Hello? It's Annette."

"Hi! It's Jack Chalmers."

"I know."

"I hope I'm not interrupting anything important, but I do need to talk to you for a moment."

"It's fine. I'm with a client and a restorer. Would you give me a moment? I want to excuse myself, go outside for better reception." Walking back, drawing closer to the two men, she said, "Carlton, Chris, please excuse me for a moment, I have a business call."

Carlton nodded, smiled, waved her away, and exclaimed, "No problem, Annette, take your time."

Hurrying back to the French window, she opened it and stepped out into the garden. "Here I am," she said into the mobile phone. "Esther said there's a problem about tomorrow."

"No, not a problem. I was just wondering if we could change the time, meet at noon tomorrow, and then I thought we could go to lunch around one-thirty."

"Lunch," she repeated and realized how startled she sounded. She went on in a more even tone, "Well, I suppose so, yes."

"Good. I thought it would be nice to talk in different surroundings. Not always in your office. Hence the idea about lunch. Listen, I'm going to interrupt myself, to ask you a question. I heard you mention the name Carlton. You don't happen to be with Carlton Fraser, do you?"

"Why, yes, I do, Jack. Do you know him?" she asked, surprise echoing.

"He was a friend of my parents. In fact, they were neighbors. In Hampstead. Hey, wait a minute. You're not there now, are you, by any chance? At his studio?"

"Actually, I am. Why?"

Jack laughed. "How weird this is. Guess what? I'm just a few houses away from you. My father died recently, and I came up to the house to collect some things of mine. Well, well, what a coincidence."

Annette was filled with a swirl of emotions. Fear, anticipation, excitement, and dread . . . Because she knew what he was going to suggest, what he was about to do.

She said slowly, "Isn't that extraordinary, Jack, that you're just next door."

"A *few* doors away. Stay there, don't leave. Tell Carlton and Marguerite I'm coming up, just to say a quick hello. Please."

"Yes, I will." She clicked off the phone, reached for the door handle, and noticed that her hand was shaking. In fact, she was shaking all over. Standing near the door for a moment, trying to calm herself, she couldn't help wondering if the gods were at play up there in the heavens. And what mischief they were making.

What had brought Jack Chalmers up here to Hampstead this morning? And why had she suggested to Christopher that he should meet her here?

She had no idea, no answer. The only thing she knew was that she was filled with sudden panic.

Annette took a moment to pull herself together, and after pushing a bright smile onto her face she walked back to the other side of the studio, where Carlton and Christopher were still standing near the easel.

She took a deep breath, and, focusing on Carlton, she said in a light voice, "What a coincidence! I just took a call from a journalist who's doing a piece on me and it seems you knew his father, who was your neighbor, lived a few doors away."

"Good Lord!" Carlton exclaimed, his expression changing into one of genuine pleasure, his eyes full of sudden sparkle. "You must be talking about Jack Chalmers. How is he?"

"You're about to find out. He's only a couple of doors away, at his father's house, and he's popping up to see you and Marguerite, just to say hello."

"How nice of him. Marguerite will be thrilled. Jack was always a favorite of hers, and mine, as well. We watched Jack and his brother Kyle growing up."

Carlton seemed to have regained his equilibrium, and Christopher was suddenly looking more relaxed, much to her relief.

Turning to her, Christopher now said, "I know it's probably silly, wanting to keep the painting that's damaged and a fake, but I do."

"I think you ought to destroy it," Carlton murmured.

Christopher glanced at Annette, a quizzical look in his eyes.

She said, "You are the owner of the painting, and as long as you don't sell it as a *damaged* Cézanne, because it's *not* a Cézanne, that's fine. It is a forgery. And let's get it out of here now. Before Jack Chalmers arrives. He's the journalist writing about me, and you, Chris, are the client whose Rembrandt I sold for twenty million pounds. He's bound to be curious, and he'll probably want to talk to you."

Christopher nodded. "Is that all right with you?"

"Yes, as long as you don't refer to the fake Cézanne. You can only discuss the auction and the Rembrandt."

"I understand," Chris said.

"Now, Carlton, let's get the fake off that easel and out of here," Annette said.

"Immediately!" Carlton took the canvas down off the easel. He said to Christopher, "I'll put the painting back in the frame. Can you come and pick it up later today?"

"No problem," Chris answered. "Thanks."

Annette followed Carlton, saying as she did, "I'd better let Marguerite know that Jack Chalmers is stopping by for a moment." She was heading into the kitchen when the doorbell rang.

Chapter Twenty

Suddenly he was in the middle of her life, and she was still breathless, startled by the way it had happened. So accidentally, so unexpectedly, and so very fast. A quick phone call about changing the time of the interview, and her day had changed.

Marguerite Fraser had created a flurry of excitement when he'd arrived a few minutes ago, had drawn him into the large hall, displaying great affection toward him, clucking like a fond mother hen. Carlton had rushed out from the studio to embrace him in a bear hug, and even Christopher was obviously itching to meet him.

And there *he* was. Jack Chalmers. Looking for all the world like the golden boy, with the Frasers fussing, Christopher gaping in awe, and she lurking almost furtively in the background. To her, Jack appeared somewhat embarrassed as he stood there helplessly, staring across the hall at her.

Annette realized that she had lost control of the situation when Marguerite appeared on the scene, and now she took it back. Smiling at Jack, gliding forward, she said in a steady voice, "Isn't it a small world after all, Jack?" Coming to a standstill next to him, she thrust out her hand.

He took it in his, holding on to it tightly for a split second, then let it go. He returned her smile and explained, "I spent a lot of time in this house, when I was a kid growing up."

Marguerite took his comment as a signal to be the hostess. "Let's go into the kitchen, shall we? Where we can all have coffee."

"Oh no, really, I don't want to interrupt business." Jack did not take his eyes off Annette as he spoke. "I just wanted to say hello, that's all." He moved slightly closer to Annette. "And firm up *our* date for the interview tomorrow," he added, touching her arm.

She simply nodded.

Marguerite said, "Please stay and have coffee, Jack. We haven't seen you since your father's funeral, and it would be lovely to catch up."

"Yes, do stay," Carlton insisted.

"I feel I'm intruding," Jack murmured, continuing to gaze at Annette as if he were mesmerized.

Wondering if he might be seeking her permission to stay, she said, "You're not intruding at all, Jack. In fact, we have just concluded our business. And it just occurred to me that you might like to chat with Chris. Let me introduce you. . . . This is my client Christopher Delaware. Chris, meet Jack Chalmers. And Jack, you could talk to him about the Rembrandt if you like, and the auction. That is all right, Chris, isn't it?"

"Of course," Chris said, shaking Jack's hand.

"Hey, this is great," Jack said. "I'd like to get your view of the auction, and perhaps you'd give me a few words about Annette."

"She's the greatest." Chris grinned at him, then looked at Marguerite. "Where should we go and sit, Mrs. Fraser?"

"Please call me Marguerite, and why don't you pop into the living room. Jack knows where it is."

"That I do," Jack exclaimed, leading the way.

Marguerite turned to Carlton and said, "This is a wonderful surprise, seeing Jack, and so unexpectedly. If you'll excuse me, Annette, I'll go and make the coffee. I'm sure you and Carlton have plenty to talk about."

Left alone in the hall, Carlton said, in a low tone, "I hope he doesn't mention the Cézanne. He seems awfully young and inexperienced, Annette."

"I know he does, and he is in many ways, and yet he's smart about certain things. He won't mention the Cézanne, that I feel confident about. He'll just waffle on about the lost Rembrandt, his surprise when I got so much money for it. Don't worry, he won't make any waves."

"I trust your judgment, my darling girl." Carlton took hold of her arm and led her back to the studio. "I do wish he would let us destroy the fake. It worries me that it's floating out there."

"It's not really floating. Now is it? And it does belong to him. Frankly, I think he'll stick it back in the room he's using for storage and forget about it. I got the impression he thought we were bullying him a while ago. But if it makes you feel better, I'll talk to him again later. And by the way, he's twenty-three."

Carlton laughed. "When you're in your sixties, twenty-three seems awfully young."

Annette just laughed and took a seat near the window. "Chris might mention the next auction to Jack, but it doesn't matter if he does. I was going to tell him about it anyway, to get the ball rolling for my publicity campaign."

"And your biggest item is the Degas sculpture, isn't it?"

"Correct. And don't forget the Giacometti. I'd like you to come over and look at them next week, Carlton, if you would. I think they both need cleaning, but you can't touch the net tutu on the Degas. I believe it would fall apart."

"You're correct. I wouldn't dream of it, and I'd be thrilled to get the two sculptures up to snuff for you. . . . It would be an honor, my dear."

As they walked down the street to the house where he had grown up, Jack said, "It was great to see the Frasers. They're both terrific. But I must admit I was glad when Chris said he had to leave."

"So was I," Annette replied. "I'd been itching to break it up, and somehow didn't know how to do it without Marguerite taking offense. She's such a lovely woman and I adore her, but the coffee break was starting to get too long."

"Well, here we are. This is where I grew up," Jack announced, and taking her arm he led her up the short path to the front door.

When he drew close to her like this, she began to shake inside, conscious of his physical presence, and the effect he had on her. She wanted to step away from him; she realized it would look awkward if she did, so she stayed where she was.

As he unlocked the door, her mobile began to ring, and she stared at him, grimaced, and muttered, "Excuse me, Jack."

Nodding, he went inside, leaving her standing on the top step, obviously wishing to give her privacy. Flipping open the phone, she said, "It's Annette."

"Hello, it's Malcolm. Do you have a minute?"

"Of course. And by the way, congratulations."

"Thanks, Annette. That's why I'm calling you. Are you and Marius free for dinner tonight? With Laurie and me."

"As far as I know, we have nothing. I'd have to ask him. Or better still, why don't you do that? Tell him you've talked to me, and that we have no prior engagement. He might, though. You know he often sees clients for dinner."

"Yes, I'll do that. Listen. I'm thinking of going to see him this afternoon. I've lunch with a client, and I thought I'd slip over to his office around four. What do you think?"

"To talk about you and Laurie getting married?"

"Yes . . ."

There was a silence and static. Annette said, "Malcolm, are you there? Or have I lost you?"

"I'm here," Malcolm said. "I'm worried about how he'll react when he hears our plans. He's very possessive of her."

"I know that. But you don't need his permission, you know. She *is* thirty-six. Neither do you need mine, or anyone else's for that matter." She laughed. "Just go and tell him. *Okay?*"

"Yep. Thanks, Annette, and I'm so glad *you* approve."

"You knew I would. You're the best. See you tonight."

Closing the phone, she slipped it into the pocket of her black knitted jacket and stood for a split second, thinking about Malcolm.

She, too, was somewhat concerned, a trifle worried about how Marius would react to the news. He couldn't help being controlling, it was part of his nature, but it was a very troubling characteristic, most especially when he became overbearing. However, in the long run, her money was on Malcolm Stevens in this matter of Laurie and their marriage. He would handle Marius with kid gloves, diplomatically, but she was well aware her old friend wouldn't take any nonsense from anyone, not even his famous mentor.

Annette stood in the doorway looking into the house. The entrance hall was small, she noticed, but several doors were open, and the windows in three empty rooms filled it with shimmering sunlight. Dust motes rose up like a myriad of tiny delicate insects, sparkling in the air, and the hall was absolutely quiet, very still.

Her eyes settled finally on Jack. He was unaware she was there as he knelt on the floor, looking into a trunk. She could see his shoulder blades through the thin cotton of his white shirt, and unexpectedly her throat tightened. How defenseless, vulnerable, he looked at this moment; she wanted to reach out, touch him, as one might affectionately touch a small child. What a dangerous man he was, the way he got to her, affected her on so many levels. If she had any sense, she would turn around and run as fast as she could.

Instead, she stepped over the threshold and went into the hall.

He heard her step, straightened, and stood up. Swinging around, he smiled at her. It was that huge generous smile of his that showed his perfect, very white teeth and was a reflection of his geniality and that fatal charm.

"It'll just take me a minute," he explained. "I've done all I can with this at the moment. I'll get my things together and call for a radio cab. I can drop you off at your office, or wherever you want."

"Thanks." She eyed the trunk. "That's a beautiful piece of old Louis Vuitton," she said, wanting to be friendly, and was amazed she sounded so normal.

"Isn't it just! It was my mother's. She died before Dad, going on four years now. She left it to me, along with everything in it. My brother's been on my back to remove it since Dad died, because we've put the house on the market. So I've been emptying everything into these two suitcases, which are much easier to carry."

Annette nodded her understanding. "Don't get rid of the trunk, though. It's a collector's item and worth a lot, I should think."

"I know. I'm definitely keeping it. My mother had a little shop in Primrose Hill, a sort of hole-in-the-wall. But she loved it. Her junk shop, she called it, and there *was* a lot of junk there. But also some really good stuff, including the trunk. And she did occasionally deal in superior antiques, some of which ended up here. Kyle's going to send those to be auctioned."

Glancing around, endeavoring to relax, Annette said, "This looks like a really nice family house. It must have been lovely growing up here."

"It was, and Kyle would tell you the same thing." He threw her a very direct look and asserted, "You grew up in Ilkley, didn't you?"

"Yes," she answered, wondering how he knew this. What else did he know? She held herself perfectly still, suddenly anxious, a little panicky. Be careful what you say, she warned herself. Be wary. Her guard went up.

Jack exclaimed, "So, you're a Yorkshire girl from the moors! Do you miss them? I bet you do. They're staggeringly beautiful."

She could not respond. After a moment, she managed to say, "No, I don't miss them."

"My father was a theatrical agent," Jack told her. "Every year he gave a big party. Here in the summer. And he invited everyone."

Now Jack began to walk into the center room, beckoning

her to follow him, saying, "Come on! Come and look at the garden where he had the party. Mum always referred to it as THE GARDEN PARTY in capital letters. It was Dad's special event of the year. He reveled in it. He got such a great kick out of it."

Annette had the impulse to flee, to get away from him. How cleverly he disarmed her with his effortless charm, his easygoing manner, his way of confiding in her all of a sudden, telling her about himself. She wondered how to tell him to order the cab; she discovered she couldn't say the words. Because . . . she wanted to be here, didn't she? Finding her voice at last, she asked, "And were you and your brother allowed to attend the party?"

"Yes, when I was about eight and Kyle was ten. It always started at six o'clock and went on until God knows when. Everyone wanted to be invited and they were, because Dad didn't want to disappoint anybody. Or hurt anybody's feelings. He was just the greatest guy. He gave Kyle and me so much. Chase your dream, he would tell us both, go for it, catch it, keep it, live it. He was behind us all the way, encouraged whatever ambitions we had."

Turning suddenly, grabbing her hand and startling her as he did so, he led her into the middle of the lawn. "This was tented, just in case of rain, you know our bloody weather as well as I do. And there was a band and an open bar set up, and tables groaning with food. It was just the best place to be."

"I wish I'd been here," she said without thinking, and swallowed, feeling foolish.

"So do I," he murmured, giving her a pointed look.

Annette glanced away, and extricated her hand from his.

He said softly, "Dad dealt in dreams, you know, since he represented actors, writers, directors, producers. . . . I used to call him the dream catcher sometimes, or the dream maker, and it made him smile. What did your father do?"

"He was a teacher," she answered, caught unawares.

"In Ilkley?"

"No, Harrogate," she corrected, and could've bitten her tongue off.

"Oh. I thought you lived in Ilkley."

"Yes, after Daddy died. We went to live with our grandparents."

"And your mother, too?"

"Yes." She took a deep breath. "Jack, I'm sorry, but I think I ought to be getting back to the office."

"Oh sure! God, I'm so sorry, wasting your time with all this chatter about Dad and growing up here. Let's go inside."

Chapter Twenty-one

Annette stood with Esther in her office, staring at the photographic blow-up of the three-foot Giacometti sculpture of a walking man. It had arrived earlier this morning, while she was at Carlton's, and Esther had unwrapped it and put it in place on the credenza.

"It really looks *great*," Annette said at last. "I just have a good feeling about this sculpture. I think the price is going to soar. Marius told me to keep it in the September auction, not to hold it back for a later date, because Giacometti's pieces have been doing very well. And I believe he was right in his advice."

"When you say *soar*, what exactly do you mean?" Esther asked, looking at Annette, ready to believe anything she said, because her boss lady was the most brilliant woman she had ever met. She trusted her judgment about art—and most other things—and implicitly so.

"I'm thinking in the range of about twenty million to twenty-five million."

"*Pounds*?" Esther gasped.

"Well, of course *pounds*, the auction is going to be held here in London, at Sotheby's, because Marius thought it would be wiser. Had you forgotten that?"

"No, I hadn't, and if it goes for twenty-five million pounds then it will have outdone the Rembrandt, won't it?"

Annette grinned. "I told you I wanted to top myself this time around. I fully intend to beat my own record."

Laughing, Esther exclaimed, "You'll get just as much for *The Little Fourteen-Year-Old Dancer*, don't you think?"

"Yes, maybe even more, because it's one of the few sculptures Degas ever did. On the other hand, Giacometti has grown awfully popular in the last few years."

"What about the recession that's supposedly looking us in the face? And is it about to hit us next year?"

"It well might, but I don't think it will have any effect on the megarich, and especially on the art they buy. The super-rich are always looking for *trophy* art to show off to their friends."

"From your mouth to God's ears," Esther said. She spun around and walked across the office. Turning when she reached the door, she said, "There're a few phone messages, and Marius called to say you're having dinner with Malcolm tonight. Malcolm also called, and Laurie."

"Thanks, Esther."

Smiling at her, Esther opened the door, paused, and, looking back at Annette, she said, "Is the interview with Jack Chalmers still on for tomorrow?"

"Oh yes, it is. Sorry, I forgot to mention that he's coming at noon, though, and then he wants to take me out to lunch, to continue the interview in a different environment."

"I understand that. He wants to see different sides of you, different aspects, and it is a bit, well, sort of *clinical* in the office."

Annette began to laugh. "Oh, Esther, you have such a unique way of putting things. Clinical indeed."

"Well, it's true, boss, take it from me," she muttered, and closed the door behind her.

Staring at the door, Annette focused for a moment on Jack. He had been casual, chatty, in the cab, and had not asked her any more questions, which she was glad about.

The one thing he *had* said, during the long cab ride from Hampstead to Bond Street, was that he did not usually do interviews for a newspaper profile. The reason he needed the extra material, he had continued, was because he was going to write a rather long article about her for the Sunday *New York Times Magazine*. She appreciated that quality in him, his thoughtfulness, his desire to make her feel at ease.

He certainly did that when it came to the interviews. It was his physical presence, his charismatic personality, and his magnetism that threw her off balance, made her feel, and ridiculously so, like a silly teenager. For that reason she must keep everything on a businesslike footing, not become overly friendly with him, not too chummy, and, most important, she must not be confiding at all.

Glancing at the phone message on her desk, she first called Agnes Dunne, Marius's assistant. There was no answer, so she left a message saying she had received Marius's message to her, and understood about the dinner arrangement. Her next call was to Malcolm, whom she caught on his mobile just as he was leaving the Remmington Gallery for a lunch date.

"I got a message we're all having dinner," she said when he answered.

"Yes. Eight o'clock at Mark's Club. I chose it because of Laurie. It's such an easy place for a wheelchair."

"I like Mark's anyway. How was he, Malcolm? Did he agree to a meeting at four?"

"He did, yes, but later, at five. He doesn't know why I want to see him. Actually, I asked him for dinner first."

"Don't sound so worried. It's going to be fine. Just tell him, be confident, firm, and don't stand for any nonsense."

Malcolm chuckled. "You keep saying that, but who better than you knows what a bloody tough customer he can be, and argumentative."

"Forget that. Forget it's Marius, your mentor. He is after all just another man. Tell him straight to his face that you're marrying Laurie, and that's that."

"Yes, sir, by your command, sir. And for now, goodbye, sir."

"Goodbye, Malcolm," she said, laughter in her voice, and hung up the phone.

Eyeing her sister's message, she thought about her for a few seconds and then called her back. "Hi, little one, how are you?"

"I'm great. Fine, Annette. And very happy. I'm glad we're having dinner tonight, and that Marius was able to join us, that he'll be back from Cirencester in time."

"He's gone to Cirencester?" Annette couldn't keep the surprise out of her voice.

"Yes, he told Malcolm, who called him on his mobile. Apparently Marius was on the way to Gloucestershire to see a client."

"Well, he does have several there. Anyway, I just wanted to tell you that Chris understood everything Carlton was saying about the Cézanne, and he's taking it back to Knowle Court this afternoon. It seems he doesn't want to destroy it, but instead he's going to keep it. His prerogative of course. It *does* belong to him."

"That doesn't matter, does it? He can't very well sell it, not the way it's so badly smudged with black soot, and there's no provenance."

"That's everything I pointed out to him, and to Carlton, who seemed a bit put out. He wants that painting dead and gone."

"But he's like that, Annette, a bit of a stickler for . . . law and order and all that jazz."

"I know. So I'll see you tonight, darling."

"You will, and you'll also see my engagement ring. It's an emerald. Malcolm gave it to me last night."

"I'm so happy for you, Laurie, really and truly happy. You deserve a good man like Malcolm, someone to look after you."

"I can look after myself, thank you very much, that's how you brought me up . . . to be my own woman and a strong one at that."

After dropping Annette at her office, Jack had returned to his apartment in Primrose Hill. He was very hungry, and the first thing he did was make himself a smoked salmon sandwich and a cup of coffee. As he sat eating it, watching the news on CNN, he thought about the woman he had just left.

He had longed to ask her to have lunch with him, but had suddenly decided against doing so. She had been a bit stand-offish in the cab, so he had retreated into himself a little, chatting to her intermittently, not saying too much, keep it strictly business.

No, not standoffish, he now thought. Wrong terminology. She was . . . *cool*. Very cool indeed. And calm. And collected. Absolutely in control of herself. Very self-possessed.

He sighed under his breath. He felt just the opposite; his emotions were running amok. Imagine, he had only met her twice in his life, and yet she was dominating his thoughts. He wanted to be with her, to spend time with her, to get to know her better. And to possess her. His physical attraction to her yesterday had so startled him he had been thrown off balance, although he had endeavored not to show it.

He felt like a schoolboy with an overwhelming crush. But he wasn't a schoolboy. He was almost thirty years old and experienced, had been with enough women to know that the first rush of heat, that overwhelming feeling of sexual desire and passion, gradually began to lessen, and sometimes rather swiftly.

Not this time, he thought. No, not this time. Not at all. Because I've never actually felt exactly like this before. Not ever. Not with the two fiancées. Not with Lucy.

Oh, God. *Lucy*. He hadn't called her. He'd forgotten again. That ought to tell him something about himself, his feelings for Lucy. And also for Annette. His preoccupation with *her* over the last twenty-four hours had truly fouled up his head, hadn't it?

Turning off the television, he took the plate and mug to the kitchen and went back to his desk, sat staring at his laptop screen for a few minutes.

Finally, he sent Lucy an e-mail explaining how busy he was, and promising to phone her at the end of the afternoon, and then he clicked onto Google to gather some information about Laurie Watson, Annette's sister.

She popped up immediately, and he looked harder at the screen, doing a double take, leaning forward when her photograph suddenly appeared. My God, she was a real knockout. Incredibly beautiful, with shining red-gold hair, an exquisite face, and large green eyes. She had a slight look of Annette, but that was all, and they were very different types altogether.

The caption told him the photograph had been taken at Sotheby's, on the night of the auction. Annette was standing next to Laurie, who was seated in a wheelchair and fashionably dressed in a beautiful gown, well turned out.

As he gazed at Annette's image, he noticed she was more simply put together than her younger sibling, wore a suit and a minimum of jewelry, just a single string of pearls and pearl earrings. Conservative, understated, elegant, and a little reminiscent of . . . *who*? Now who did Annette remind him of in this photograph taken in March?

Her blond hair was swept back in a chignon, and her blue eyes looked even more vivid under her dark brows. Her expression was . . . enigmatic. The wheat-colored suit and pearls spelled class to him. Of course. Now he had it. She had a look of Grace Kelly . . . in *To Catch a Thief.* His favorite old movie, all sea and sky and the south of France. Witty, sophisticated Cary Grant and lovely Grace in that masterpiece by Hitchcock, which was as viable today as it had been in the fifties.

After a few seconds, he clicked off Google and went to other search engines, looking for information about Annette Remmington and Laurie Watson. He could not find anything other than those interviews given on the evening of the Rembrandt auction, and a few lead-up stories which had been carried earlier in the year.

Well, she had told him that, hadn't she? Had explained that she didn't do interviews because there had never been anything to interview her about. "The Rembrandt auction is my sole claim to fame," she had muttered the other day in her office. And he realized this was the truth. Until Christopher Delaware had fortuitously brought the painting to her, she had merely been a successful private art dealer, not a star in the art world.

Clearing the screen, he began to type up the bits and pieces of information he had gathered earlier that day at Carlton Fraser's house, and in the time they had spent alone afterward. Once he had done this, he began to formulate his ideas about the profile he had to write over the weekend, in order to meet his deadline for the London *Sunday Times*. Once this was completed, he began to work on the outline for his much longer piece for the Sunday *New York Times Magazine*.

When the telephone suddenly shrilled, he jerked his head toward it, momentarily startled, so concentrated was he.

"Hullo? Jack Chalmers."

"Jack, it's Annette."

"Oh," he said, startled. He quickly recouped and asked, "Is everything all right?" And immediately felt like kicking himself. What a stupid thing to say to her.

"Yes, everything's fine. But I've just had a thought about the interview tomorrow. I was wondering if you would like to see the two pieces which will be the 'star' items in the new auction I'm planning?"

"Well, yes! My God, I certainly would!"

"In that case, could you come to the flat? That's where I have the sculptures."

"*Sculptures.* Who are they by?"

"You'll see." She hesitated, then murmured, "I want to surprise you. Let me give you my address in Eaton Square."

"Go ahead, I'm at my desk."

Once she had given him the address, she said, "The same time we arranged. At noon tomorrow. Is that all right?"

"Yes, yes. And lunch afterward. Okay?"

"That would be very nice. See you tomorrow. Bye."

She had hung up before he could respond. He sat back in his chair, realizing he was going to get the news before anyone else. Just as Tommy had said he would. He was pleased about this. It would make a wonderful lead-in, and now he must rearrange his thoughts about the first part of his profile.

And select a nice restaurant near Eaton Square for their lunch. That was easy, no problem at all.

The phone rang again, and he grabbed it. "Jack Chalmers."

"Hi, Jack," his brother said. "About tonight, do you mind if my producer Tony Lund comes to dinner with us?"

"Does he have to?"

"Sort of. He just flew in from the Coast the other day, and although I've had a couple of meetings with him, I keep promising him dinner. He picked tonight. He's off to Paris tomorrow."

"It's all right, I don't mind. Anyway Tony Lund's a talented guy. I'd like to meet him."

"Great. Eight o'clock. At Harry's Bar."

"Harry's Bar! We are getting fancy, aren't we?"

"That's where *he* wants to go. Good thing Dad made me a member two years ago."

"Let's face it, the food's great and it's sort of jazzy, and I promise I'll wear a tie."

Kyle laughed. "Listen, how did the moving go? Did you get the trunk out?"

"No, I'll be taking everything away this weekend. I got interrupted this morning, I'm afraid."

"Okay. I've gotta go. See you later."

"Great, Kyle." Jack hung up and dialed his agent's number. He had the urge to tell Tommy how right he had been, and that Annette was showing him the prize pieces of her next auction tomorrow. He was not merely getting the information but also a preview.

Chapter Twenty-two

✳

"W hy didn't you tell me?" Marius bellowed from the doorway of her dressing room. She was sitting at the dressing table wearing a robe, and she jumped in surprise, immediately swung around, and stared at him. She had not heard him come into the flat, and she was startled by his sudden arrival and angry tone.

"Because Malcolm wanted to tell you himself," she shot back swiftly, "and that's why he came to see you today. I'm presuming he did so, that he didn't announce his engagement to Laurie over the phone."

"I saw him a short while ago. And to say I was stunned by the news would be the understatement of the year. I was bloody flabbergasted, actually *stupefied*, for a moment or two. I just couldn't believe I was hearing correctly. And—"

"Why are you so upset?"

"What a question to ask me! *You*, of all people!" he exclaimed, anger still echoing in his voice. "It's so ridiculous, these two getting married. What sort of life are they going to have together? Not a very good one, if you want my opinion. Laurie's in a wheelchair, a paraplegic, and Malcolm's a normal, heterosexual man with quite a taste for women, and the owner of a highly successful business, where high-powered entertaining is essential. No, it's not going to work, I'm certain of that," he asserted, leaning against the door jamb, staring at her balefully. "They're ill suited."

Annette gazed back, her face cold. "So what you're saying is that Laurie is inadequate as a woman, because she's a paraplegic, and that she won't make him a good wife."

When he did not immediately reply, Annette went on, "Actually, what you're saying is that she's not good enough for Malcolm Stevens, your protégé, who owns the Remmington Gallery, which you started, and which he has made even more famous than it ever was under your aegis, if the truth be known."

Marius gaped at her, taken aback, suddenly aware of the steel in her tone, her icy blue eyes, recognizing that he was treading on dangerous ground. Instantly tempering his voice, he responded in a quieter tone, "You've taken offense, when I didn't mean any. I love Laurie, you know that, and I've always looked after her, been conscious of my responsibilities. But let's be honest about this situation, Annette. She has her limitations. As a wife."

Inside Annette was enraged, furious with Marius, but she kept her expression neutral, her voice even when she answered him. "Are you referring to their sex life?" she asked, a brow lifting sardonically.

"Of course I am. Malcolm's forty-two, healthy, virile, attractive, something of a man about town, in a quiet sort of way. I don't want to see Laurie get hurt, also I—"

"Malcolm's not going to hurt her," she cut in peremptorily. "He loves her, is *in love* with her. And in any case, Laurie is quite capable of having intercourse, and has been for years. In fact, she had a relationship three years ago with Douglas Brentwood, and he also wanted to marry her. She broke up with him because she wasn't in love with him. But she is in love with Malcolm."

Marius was suddenly looking utterly bewildered, and he straightened up against the door, a quizzical look entering his eyes. "Laurie can have sex?" Still puzzled, he frowned, shook his head in apparent disbelief.

"Yes, she can, and she enjoys it, too." Annette suppressed a smile; she had been unable to resist making that last comment.

"I never knew that," he muttered almost to himself. "I never equated Laurie with sex."

"I didn't think it necessary to tell you, or to discuss it with you, or anyone else. And Laurie wanted her privacy. Insisted on it. Furthermore, she's a bit shy, as you well know. I can hardly see her discussing her sex life with you. You're a man."

"I see." Recovering slightly, he went on, "But look here, Annette, let's be sensible, practical. Sex isn't enough to make a marriage work. What about children, bringing up a family? Then there's the entertaining and traveling. It can all be very stressful, and it can wear anyone out, never mind a woman in a . . . I mean a woman who is handicapped."

Annette did not speak for a moment. She gave Marius a thoughtful look, and finally said in an acerbic tone, "Obviously Malcolm didn't tell you that Laurie is six weeks pregnant."

"Pregnant," Marius repeated and sat down heavily in the chair near the door. "*Laurie's pregnant?*"

"Very much so, and they are planning to have the wedding in July. Furthermore, they are both thrilled."

Marius didn't respond. He closed his eyes for a moment and began muttering to himself.

"I didn't hear you, Marius," Annette exclaimed. "What did you say?"

Opening his eyes, he glared at her. "I said she could have an abortion."

Holding herself very still, drawing on every ounce of her bred-in-the-bone self-possession, Annette said slowly, very precisely, in a steady voice, "No, Marius. Laurie is not going to get an abortion. She and Malcolm want this baby, and they are going to have it. And they are going to be married this summer . . . before the baby is born. Because Malcolm, in particular, wants that."

Marius went on gaping at her, seemed befuddled, at a loss for words, and then he leaned back in the chair and closed his eyes.

After a moment or two, Annette stood up, went over to him, shook his arm. "Marius, sit up and listen to me."

He was unresponsive. She shook him harder and cried, "I will not permit you to interfere in their lives! And they won't allow it either. Malcolm came to speak to you out of good manners. It was a courtesy. Because very frankly, they don't give a damn what you think or what you want. Nor are they interested in anyone else's opinion. They're grown-ups, Marius."

"Yes, I know that," he murmured as he opened his eyes. "Not that they are behaving like adults."

Walking back to the chair in front of her dressing table, Annette sat down, studying him as she looked across the room. At last she said in a voice dripping ice, "You have always run my life, manipulated me, and controlled me as much as you could. For years people have said you're my Svengali, but I've ignored that, dismissed it, paid no attention. After all, I chose to remain with you, to share your life. But if you interfere in any way with Malcolm and Laurie's marriage, I promise you now that I will leave you."

He threw back his head and roared with laughter. "Leave me," he spluttered a second later. "You know damn well you'll never leave me." His voice was full of self-assurance.

Annette was silent, knowing he spoke the truth. He knew far too much about her painful past, the trouble she had been in, what she had done. She was caught in a trap of her own making. She had confessed to him.

Marius finally said, "Come on, darling, let's not fight about these two ridiculous people. They're idiots, and you and I—"

"They're *not* idiots!" she snapped. "They are two people I care about, who are madly in love, having a child and planning a wedding. They are fully in charge of themselves and their lives, and that's the way it's going to be. And you're going to accept that, or otherwise you and I will no longer have the same kind of relationship. I promise you *that*."

"You can never leave me," he said in a threatening tone.

"I know. We can share a flat but we don't necessarily have to share a life."

Although Marius knew that his hold over her was unbreakable, and that she would not, in fact, ever leave him, he was also aware that over the years she had developed a will of iron. She was not only intelligent, ambitious, and a relentless workaholic, but also determined, strong, and decisive. And often made many decisions he did not always agree with. However, he had not fought her. Long ago he had recognized that he must give her space if their marriage was to remain loving, sexual, and intrinsically warm. Now, at this moment, he understood that she would fight to the death to give Laurie what she most desired. He could not compete with her baby sister when it came to an issue such as this.

Standing up, he walked over to Annette, reached down, took her hands in his, and pulled her to her feet. Looking into her face, smiling at her, he said quietly, "You're right. I am wrong. I promise you I won't interfere. After all, Laurie's thirty-six and Malcolm's forty-two, and they have to live their own lives."

Annette nodded. "I'm glad you've come around to my way of thinking."

"I was taken by surprise, it was the shock, you know," Marius said.

"I understand. But I think we'd better hurry, if we're going to get to Mark's Club on time. We don't want to be late."

"Oh, it's been changed," Marius said, letting go of her hands. "Malcolm decided Harry's Bar would be a better place to have a celebration. It's also an easy place to take a wheelchair, like Mark's."

"In that case, I think I'll wear something different." Annette walked over to the closet, looked inside, decided on a black dress.

"And I'd better go and change my suit." Marius hurried off without another word.

Annette sat perfectly still for a few seconds, staring at herself in the mirror on the dressing table. Her face was calm, serene actually, and it belied her inner turmoil. She had been seething during the discussion with Marius, infuriated by his obdurate attitude. It was only through sheer willpower that she had been able to speak to him with civility when he had finally capitulated.

She sighed as she picked up the cosmetic brush, dipped it in powder, and stroked it over her face. She had instinctively known he would object to this union between Laurie and Malcolm, but she had not bargained for his anger and vehemence. Fortunately, she had won. Not only the battle but the war. Her threat had been powerful enough to stop him in his tracks, make him retreat, and then surrender.

They both understood that she was unable to leave him, leave the marriage, but now *he* understood she could and would change the emotional content of it. She had made it perfectly clear she would lead her own life without him whilst still remaining his wife—in name only. And she had meant what she said.

Annette was fully aware that he would never be able to face that, let alone accept it. He needed her on every emotional level.

Her hands were steady as she swept her blond hair into a chignon and fastened it in place with pins. After applying lipstick and spraying herself with perfume, she rose, took off her silk robe, and walked over to the mirrored clothes closets on the other side of the dressing room.

She suddenly knew exactly what she was going to wear. Having selected a black dress a short while before, she put it away, took out a cream wool dress with a V neckline and long sleeves, partnered with a matching jacket. Once she was dressed, she selected a triple-strand necklace of pearls and pearl earrings, then stepped into a pair of black patent high-heeled shoes.

She was putting a few things in a black patent bag when Marius appeared in her dressing room. He was smiling and his expression was pleasant. Having given in to her, he had now adopted a demeanor of geniality and exuded warmth. She knew he had fully accepted the situation with Laurie and Malcolm and that there would be no further objections from him. Ever again.

* * *

Annette made only one reference to her sister when they were in the taxi on the way to the restaurant. Glancing at Marius, touching his arm lightly, she said in a quiet voice, "You know, Marius, you and I suffer from the same thing."

"And what's that?" he asked, returning her gaze, a smile playing around his mouth again; he was relieved that she was sounding like her normal self and not a warrior on the warpath.

"We're overexposed to Laurie, and because of that we get accustomed to her, and we forget how truly beautiful she is. You'll see, tonight every man in the restaurant will be staring at her, ogling her."

"Yes, what you say is true," he concurred. Marius meant what he said; he was not trying to placate or please her, and he accepted that there was an element of truth in her words.

There was more traffic than usual tonight; Annette knew they would be late after all, and so she was relieved when the taxi finally pulled up outside Harry's Bar in South Audley Street. She got out and went ahead of Marius, pushing open the door and hurrying inside.

As soon as he saw her, the maître d' came forward to greet her, and they stood talking for a moment as she waited for Marius. When the maître d' turned away from her for a split second to speak to a waiter, she glanced around, looking for Laurie and Malcolm. She spotted them immediately, and lifted her hand, gave a small wave.

Then she saw him.

Jack Chalmers.

He was sitting with two other men on the left side of the room, diagonally across from Malcolm's table. Her stomach lurched. She wondered how on earth she would get through the evening.

Chapter Twenty-three

The radiance reflected on Laurie's face, the happiness in her eyes, touched Annette's heart. She sat down at the table next to her sister, reached out, and clasped her hand in hers. "I'm so glad for you, Laurie darling, and you, too, Malcolm. This is the most wonderful news."

Annette was sincere, meant every word. Her sister's well-being and security were the most important things in her life. Already she was feeling a sense of ease about Laurie's future. She forever worried about that, about Laurie being alone if anything happened to her. Now that worry was erased. With Malcolm in the picture, Laurie's future looked very bright. He was such an old friend; she trusted him implicitly, and she knew that he was reliable and responsible, as well as a kind and caring man.

Malcolm leaned across the table, and, as if zeroing in on her thoughts, he said, "I love Laurie very much, Annette, and you can trust me to look after her. She'll always come first with me, you know."

"I do know that, and I'd like to say welcome to the family, Malcolm." Shifting her gaze to Laurie, she smiled and said, "Come on then, let me see the ring."

Laurie put out her left hand to show her sister Malcolm's engagement ring. It was a square-cut emerald surrounded by diamonds. "Isn't it beautiful?" she murmured, looking at the ring and then at Annette.

"Yes, it really is," Annette agreed. "Gorgeous."

"Only emeralds from now on, you know, to match the color of her eyes," Malcolm announced.

"Aren't you the romantic one!" Annette exclaimed, and then looked up at Marius as he arrived at the table.

"Sorry. Someone stopped me at the bar," he explained. He sat down and immediately said, "Congratulations, you two!" Leaning closer to Malcolm and Laurie, he went on, "And it's thrilling news about the baby. I feel as if I'm about to become a grandfather."

"Now, now, you're not *that* old," Annette protested. "More like an *uncle*, don't you think?"

He laughed. "*Uncle Marius.* Yes, jolly good. I like the sound of that. And I must be godfather, you know. I'll be hurt if you choose anyone else but me." He stared at Malcolm.

"Godfather it is," Malcolm replied, and motioned to a waiter, who came over and poured champagne. Laurie asked for only a drop, just enough for the toast.

Instantly, the champagne was sipped, toasts were made, and for the first ten minutes there was much hilarity at the table. The activity kept Annette totally involved and so she was able to avoid looking across the room at Jack. She was acutely conscious of his presence, though, and felt his eyes on her from time to time, yet managed to stay cool, calm inside.

What genuinely pleased her was that Marius was gazing at Laurie with admiration, as if he were suddenly seeing her in a new and different light. Her sister looked especially beautiful tonight. She was wearing a silk dress that was an unusual moss-green color with a slight hint of iridescence in the weave of the fabric, and it emphasized her green eyes and was perfect with her porcelain skin and shimmering red-gold hair. Glancing surreptitiously at Marius, Annette knew that he was suddenly captivated by Laurie's stunning beauty, for the first time in years.

Marius turned to Annette, gave her a pointed look, then said, "Laurie darling, Annette and I are going to give you a wonderful wedding, wherever you want to have it, and once you have picked a date, you and Annette must start planning it. At once."

"Thank you, Marius, and you, too, Annette," Laurie responded, smiling at them. She was vastly relieved that Marius appeared to be happy about her engagement to his favorite, had obviously given them his stamp of approval. She had expected trouble, a big eruption on his part, but she had been wrong after all. Her glowing smile and sparking eyes reflected her happiness.

Malcolm said, "Thanks, both of you, and that's splendid of you, so very generous. We were thinking of the summer, obviously, perhaps late June, or July." He grinned. "There's the baby to consider. We wouldn't want to leave it much later than that."

Laughing softly, Laurie confided, "I wouldn't like to look too pregnant, you know."

"Of course not, darling. And you won't," Annette asserted. "And I think you should get married in July, when the weather's bound to be better. But you'll have to decide on a venue quickly, to make sure it's available. Listen, all of you, I want you to know that Jack Chalmers is sitting at the other side of the restaurant. I don't think he'll intrude on us, by coming over to say hello. By now I'm sure the entire restaurant knows we're having some kind of family celebration, but I just want you to be aware of his presence."

"He's a nice chap," Malcolm volunteered. "Lots of easy charm and always extremely pleasant."

Laurie was the only one who swiftly sneaked a look, and she said sotto voce, "I didn't believe you, Malcolm, when you said he was like the young Bill Holden, but you're right, he is."

"He's much younger than I expected," Marius added, after a quick glance across the room. "But that doesn't matter. He's a brilliant journalist and I'm glad I picked him. He'll do an excellent piece on you, Annette, I'm sure. Anyway, how have the interviews been going? You haven't said very much about them."

"They've been fine."

"Not grilling you too much, then?"

"No, Marius, no grilling at all. You were right about that," Annette answered, and changed the subject. She said to Laurie, "About the various venues . . . have you any idea about where you *would* like to be married? And what about you, Malcolm, what's your preference?"

It was Laurie who answered. "We've talked about a number of places, haven't we, darling?" She looked at Malcolm and added, "But I think we've . . . well, sort of changed our minds about a country wedding."

"Maybe, maybe not," Malcolm murmured. "And we must discuss the venues with you both at length. But first, I do think we ought to order dinner. Otherwise we'll be here all night."

Marius was sound asleep.

She could hear him breathing deeply, lost to the world. He had closed his eyes the moment his head had touched the pillow, had fallen into oblivion.

She wasn't surprised. He'd had quite a lot to drink over dinner at Harry's Bar . . . champagne, white wine, a good claret, followed by a large Napoleon brandy. And yet he hadn't been drunk, or at least he hadn't appeared to be inebriated. But then that was Marius. He could hold his liquor, never showed any signs of being done in by it, always in control of himself. And frequently of others.

She had no complaints about him tonight. He'd behaved perfectly with Laurie and Malcolm, had enthusiastically cheered them on, listening to the pros and cons of the various venues for weddings available in various parts of the country. He had discussed the number of guests they should have, menus, wines, flowers, and had even talked about Laurie's wedding gown. And finally he had advised them where to spend their honeymoon. He couldn't be faulted. Exemplary behavior.

She hadn't expected him to be otherwise. Once he had agreed to something, he stuck to it. Also, he knew her well enough to *truly* understand that if he in any way interfered with this marriage, she would fulfill her threat. Not to leave him; of course she couldn't leave him. He knew too much about her. But she could cut him off emotionally. And that he wouldn't be able to stand, or so she believed anyway.

Annette stared up at the ceiling, her eyes wide open in the dark. She wished she could fall asleep. But her mind churned with so many thoughts, almost all of them troubled, turbulent.

She wondered why he was *really* going to Barcelona again. When he had announced it, suddenly over dinner, explaining that he was leaving on Saturday for Spain, she had been taken aback, surprised that he had not brought it up before.

But then that was Marius, wasn't it? Making decisions at the last minute and going full steam ahead without ever consulting her. He just did what he wanted to do, blithely unaware of anyone else.

Malcolm had asked him if he was going to do research for his book on Picasso, and he had said he was. A week, he had then said to her, smiling, touching her arm lightly. Try and get some sun, she had murmured back to him, and wondered for the umpteenth time if there were other women in his life.

She had no idea about that. Probably not, but one never knew. He was a handsome man, full of charm and sophistication, and he had a special kind of elegance. Women found him attractive, of that she was aware. She also realized that if he did stray from time to time, and was unfaithful, she would never know. He would make certain of that. Because he did not want to give her any reason to leave him . . . as if he would ever let her.

What a fool she had been all those years ago. She herself had handed him the chain with which he bound her to him. She had confessed to him, told him what she had done, and he had taken control of her at once. And had never let go.

Sliding out of bed, Annette left the bedroom and went down the corridor to her office. Sitting down at her desk, she tried to do some work, but her mind was elsewhere. She was thinking of Jack Chalmers.

She had been conscious of him all evening, but had eventually begun to relax after the first hour. Harry's Bar was not such a big room, and narrow, and there were waiters milling around constantly, serving food and pouring wines.

Most of the time her view of him sitting against the opposite wall was obstructed. Nonetheless, she could not forget he was there. From time to time he caught her eye, half smiled, looked away, or turned to talk to the two men he was with. And when the three of them finally left, he had simply given her a half wave and slipped out of the dining room.

She had been relieved about this, but now, unexpectedly, she wondered why he had left without coming over to their table. Obviously he hadn't wanted to intrude, disturb them whilst they were eating. Or was it another reason? Would he have been uncomfortable? Nervous, perhaps? Did he feel the same way she did? No, that was not possible. He was, after all, much younger than her. . . .

Annette let these thoughts slide away, a feeling of tiredness enveloping her. Turning out the desk lamp, she got up, went over to the sofa in the alcove, and lay down, pulling the cashmere throw over her body. Closing her eyes, she tried to sort out the myriad thoughts filling her head.

She fell into a deep sleep.

The past became reality. Dreams of violence dominated. It was the same violence that had been her constant companion in that cold, dark house built in the shadow of the implacable windswept moors. . . .

"My name is Marie Antoinette and I am Queen of France. Won't you come and dance?"

"I am Empress Josephine, favorite of the French, and there's my husband Napoleon, sitting on the bench. Emperor of France. Won't you come and dance, dance, dance?"

Their tender, lilting voices echoed on the cool air, and their small shoes tapped against the bare wood floor as they danced in circles around the room, holding hands, laughter on their pretty faces. They were happy for a few moments, their hardship, fear, and loneliness forgotten, if only for a short time.

They did not see him lingering in the doorway, were not aware of his terrifying presence until he came rushing in, swooping up on Marie Antoinette and dragging her screaming out of the room. She cried out to Josephine, "Don't follow me! Stay there! Stay there!"

"She'd better stay there. Or I'll kill her," he hissed, and went on dragging her . . . across the hall and into her bedroom, where he ripped off her pink tutu. He pushed his contorted face against hers and whispered harshly, "I'll kill her! Kill her! Kill her! I'll make you watch while I torture her. You're a whoring bitch. A little bitch. I'll kill you when I've finished with you. I'll throw you away."

Terrified, she stood shivering against the wall, cowering in front of him. She begged, "Don't hurt her, please don't hurt her. I'll do it. I'll do anything you want, just don't hurt her."

"You bet you'll do anything." He leered at her as he tugged off his trousers, then, reaching out, pulling her to him, he picked her up, threw her onto the bed, and lay down next to her. Roughly, angrily, he took her breasts in his hands and squeezed and squeezed until she cried out in pain.

He laughed, enjoying hurting her. Her pain gave him pleasure. He began to slap her face, and then put his hands around her neck and tightened his grip, choking her. But suddenly he stopped, pushed his bunched fingers into her, harder and harder and with such force she began to scream. He rolled on top of her roughly, entered her with great force, then moved against her with violence. She screamed and screamed but he did not stop.

Unexpectedly, the bedroom door burst open with a crash. Her cousin Alison flew into the room in a fury. She was holding one of their grandfather's walking sticks, began to hit him across the shoulders with it. She was shouting, "Stop it, stop it, you bloody monster! Stop it or I'll kill you." She hit him on his head. Blood spurted and ran down his face and he screamed in pain. There was blood everywhere.

He lay on the bed holding his head, groaning, and the blood ran down onto his hands.

Alison took Marie Antoinette in her arms, comforted her, and then helped her off the bed, led her out of the bedroom into the corridor. "I am going to take you away," she whispered gently. "Out of this house forever. Go and wash." She opened the door of the bathroom in the corridor. "Wait for me here." She did as her cousin said.

Alison went back into the bedroom, pulled her brother upright, and stood over him, glowering. "Get out of this house now, before I do serious damage to you." Her furious voice held a threatening note he could not fail to miss. "Get going, you bastard. Now. Otherwise I'll finish what I started. But then you're not worth swinging for. You foul, sadistic pig."

He ran out of the room, down the stairs, across the hall, and out onto the moors, clutching his trousers and vowing to come back and kill them all, screaming the words at the top of his lungs.

Quietly, with great calm and purposefulness, Alison packed their suitcases, and then helped them to get dressed in their proper traveling clothes. And just before she closed the last of the cases, she folded the torn pink tutu and put it inside, promising to mend it for Marie Antoinette.

She took them on the train to London and they never went back to Ilkley again. Their mother was there to meet them at King's Cross railway station and they all three went with her to her flat in Islington, where there was a room for them. And a stepfather.

And forever after Marie Antoinette never forgot what Alison had said to her on the train to London. "You must protect Josephine. Always, always, Marie Antoinette. I rely on you to do this. You must promise me."

She made that promise. And she never broke it.

Annette awakened a few hours later, cold and shivering. Throwing back the cashmere shawl, she went to her bathroom and took a hot shower. As the water sluiced over her icy, trembling body, she whispered to herself, "I did protect my little Josephine. I kept her safe. And now she's even safer because she has Malcolm." And she began to cry, filled with relief that her baby sister would soon have a husband who would protect her as she had, would be there for her if she was no longer around. This knowledge brought her a sense of peace and was profoundly comforting.

Chapter Twenty-four

I'm beginning to understand how much you genuinely love art," Jack said, tearing his eyes away from Annette, glancing at the Degas sculpture on the coffee table in the yellow living room of her Eaton Square flat. "It really means a lot to you on a very *personal* level, doesn't it?" he asked, looking across the room at her again.

"Yes, it does," she replied, somewhat surprised by his astute observation.

"Look, I realize that someone who is a dealer, consultant, and art historian has to understand every aspect of art, be it a painting or a sculpture, and love it, as well. But somehow I feel your love goes very, very deep. More than might be . . . usual."

"Art has been my whole life, actually, and it's saved my life, if you want the truth," Annette confided, and wondered why she had said this. Because she trusted him?

Bringing his gaze back to meet hers, he said, "I do want the truth, yes, and since you brought it up, may I ask *how* it has saved your life?" He leaned forward slightly, glancing at the digital recorder, making sure it was working.

"In times of great sadness, when I've lost people. By that I mean family."

"You're referring to your father, aren't you?"

She nodded. "He died very young, when I was young myself. I took refuge in art, lost myself in it. He was an artist, you see, but took a job teaching art because he had to support a family. He taught me, of course, and encouraged me to study, especially the Impressionists, which were his favorites. After his death I went on doing what he'd taught me to do, because it made me feel closer to him. And it was an antidote to grief. It kept me calm, steady."

"I understand what you mean." Jack was aware of the sadness in her eyes, the whole change in her demeanor. After a moment's reflection, he went on quietly, "You said *people*. Who else did you lose?"

"I had a lovely cousin who I adored when I was a child. Her name was Alison. She didn't die, though. She went to live abroad, and I haven't seen her for years." Annette shook her head. "Her absence from my life was like death. She was gone. So I learned to bury myself in art, and in its beauty. It was a solace to me, and somehow I coped. It kept my sorrow at bay."

Jack decided to change the subject. "When you were talking to me about *that*," he said, nodding to the Degas sculpture, "I was utterly captivated, marveling at you, at your incredible knowledge, not only about the sculpture but Degas himself. Art is so . . . all-encompassing in your life. Well, actually it's part of . . . your soul, isn't it?"

Annette felt a shiver run through her. No one had ever said anything like that to her before, and it was true, art *was* part of her soul. How extraordinary that he had put his finger on this aspect of her character.

Clearing her throat, she said, "You're absolutely correct." She gave him a long, thoughtful look. "Nobody's ever said that to me before. No one. Not ever. How perceptive of you."

"I've been listening to you very carefully, you know," he responded, giving her the benefit of his engaging smile.

Leaning back against the sofa, she gazed at *The Little Fourteen-Year-Old Dancer* for a moment or two. "There's another one like this in the Louvre, and I often go to see it when I'm in Paris. It's always been a favorite of mine. Imagine my excitement when this one fell into my hands. I was ecstatic and I still am."

"I understand why. It's perfectly beautiful, and I don't

mind about the torn tutu, or that it's dirty." Giving her a very direct and penetrating stare, he asked, "And how much do you think it will bring at auction?"

"A lot!" she exclaimed, sitting up straighter. "I do know that, but I'd prefer not to put a price tag on it, or speculate, because . . ." She shrugged. "You never know what might happen. Things can go awry so easily. But I will tell you something, Jack, another little dancer like this was auctioned in about 1997, and it went for eleven million dollars. It was at Sotheby's in New York. They auctioned it, and did very well."

"Wow!" Jack looked impressed. "So I bet you're thinking you could double that, aren't you?"

She laughed. "I'm not going to put a price on it. You're not going to trap me."

"And the Giacometti standing over there?" He glanced across the room at the sculpture on a table in the corner. "How much do you think that will bring?"

"No, no, Jack, I won't speculate about that either."

"So be it. I won't pressure you. By the way, your sister is staggeringly beautiful. Tony Lund, the dark-haired guy with us last night, is a Hollywood producer, and he thought she was breathtaking, movie-star gorgeous. And my brother, Kyle, said the same, by the way."

"She is lovely, and, in fact, she always wanted to be an actress. Until she was in the car crash, and then it was impossible."

"How old was she when it happened?" he ventured, knowing he had her confidence. She trusted him, thank God. It made things easier.

"Fourteen. She was with a friend and the girl's mother, and they got sideswiped by a lorry that sent the car spinning out of control. It hit a wall, somersaulted. . . ." She let her voice trail off, shaking her head, then finished softly, "She's lucky to be alive. Her friend Janice and Janice's mother were killed outright."

"How tragic." Jack, looking sympathetic, had picked up on her sadness.

Annette continued, "But last night was a happy occasion for her, for all of us. Laurie became engaged to Malcolm Stevens. I think you've met him several times; anyway, he seems to think so. We were celebrating. They're going to get married this summer. Incidentally, don't you want to speak to her for the profile?"

"Yes, I do. I can do the interview on the phone, if she'd prefer, whatever she wants. I don't need very long. Just a few questions."

"I'll talk to her about it, and let you know."

"Thanks. Now, getting back to the upcoming auction in September, which paintings are going on the block along with the two sculptures?"

"Three that Christopher Delaware also owns. A Mary Cassatt, a Berthe Morisot, and a Degas."

"Impressionists. Correct? You must forgive me, I don't know a lot about art, Annette."

"You're right, though, and I picked these particular painters because they knew each other. Mary Cassatt and Degas were especially close. Platonic relationship, though. Berthe Morisot knew both of them and they were all part of the Impressionist movement at the same time. This seemed to suggest a theme, and also the women were the only two in the movement."

Jack was impressed. "My God, this is going to be some auction! I'd love to be there. I can come, can't I?"

"I'd like you to be there, Jack. I'll make sure you get an invitation."

He took her to lunch at Daphne's in Chelsea.

It happened to be a restaurant she liked because it was intimate and comfortable, and also she, who did not crave food, always enjoyed the Italian cuisine. She told him this. It made him happy. He wanted to please her.

They were seated at a small table in a corner, facing each other, and Jack was glad she looked more relaxed. In the cab coming over from Eaton Square, she had suddenly seemed tense, almost apprehensive, and he had not understood this sudden change in her demeanor. But he had kept his distance in the cab, had kept the conversation businesslike, still discussing art with her, and the art world in general.

Once they were settled, he asked, "Would you like a glass of wine? Champagne?"

"I don't usually drink at lunchtime," she murmured.

Jack laughed, glanced at his watch. "It's almost two, the interview went on a little longer than I expected. So, it's two o'clock on a Friday. Surely you're not planning to go back to your office, are you?"

"No, no, I'm not." Feeling suddenly awkward, she forced a laugh. "All right, I'll have a glass of white wine, please."

"Sounds good. So will I." Once Jack had ordered from the waiter, he said, "You're really amazing, you know, the way you rattle off all this information about art. How on earth do you remember such a lot of complex details? I mean, that incredible stuff about pieces of sculpture being scattered over three floors of Degas's studio after his death, and about Bartholomé, Degas's friend, being in charge of it all, and Hébrard, who made the reproductions at his foundry. You must have a computer in your head."

"I've got a really good memory, actually, Jack. But, of course, when you study a lot, are especially focused on one particular painter and his work, then the information seems to stick. It's something like learning a poem by heart. It just so happens that Laurie is even better than I am, at least when it comes to Degas. She's an expert on him, and has committed everything to memory."

"Yes, you said she was in the art business?"

"As I told you before, she wanted to be an actress when she was growing up, but after the accident that was impossible because of her disability, not being able to walk. Also, I think she lost her ambition, saw the whole idea of acting as extremely difficult. She'd never shown any interest in painting as I did when we were little, but she was exposed to art because of my father. We both knew she had to be occupied, have a career, if she was going to lead a halfway decent life, and she opted for art research. And she's been happy doing it, enjoys her work."

Jack nodded and picked up the glass of wine which had just appeared in front of him. Raising it, he said, "Here's to you, Annette, and the auction in September. May it be the best ever."

She clinked her glass against his. "And to you, Jack, for making being interviewed so painless. And enjoyable."

He smiled, looking pleased. After taking a sip of the wine, he leaned forward. "Have I really made it painless?"

"*Absolutely.* I'm not very good about doing interviews, and I was really worried, but, well, you've managed to make me feel relaxed, and, somehow, not at all threatened."

"Is that what you've felt in the past? *Threatened?*" He frowned, seemed puzzled.

"A bit, yes, but not with you, as I just said." She saw that he was looking intrigued, and also curious. Swiftly, she changed the subject. "Where do you live? Is it around here, Jack?"

"No. I live in Primrose Hill, actually." He suddenly began to chuckle. "Near my mother's old junk shop, oddly enough. Nice little flat, but it's just somewhere to hang my hat, or should I say park my computer? It's not my home, my real home, I mean. I have a villa on the Côte d'Azur."

"Do you really? I like the south of France. Whereabouts is your place?"

"In a little town you probably don't know, Beaulieu-sur-Mer, near Monte Carlo."

"But I know it very well! My favorite hotel's there."

"I bet you're referring to La Réserve?"

"I am, Jack. I love that hotel, and I always have. It's had a special place in my heart—" She cut herself off, annoyed that she was telling him so much. But it was true. She felt at ease with him, she might as well admit that, and also his general manner, the cozy way he had about him, encouraged confidences. Good asset, for a journalist. She wondered how much he cultivated this. Or was it his natural manner?

Jack said, "I started going to La Réserve when I was a little boy. So when did you stay there for the first time?"

"When I was eighteen, and it's such an amazing place . . . especially for a romantic interlude." As the words left her mouth, she could've bitten her tongue off, and as he sat there smiling at her knowingly, she felt the heat flooding her face.

"You're blushing," he said, still smiling in that amused, knowing way of his, and, reaching out, he took hold of her hand. "Don't be embarrassed, Annette. I hope it was a memorable weekend. Well, I guess it must have been, since you've obviously not forgotten it."

She nodded, swallowed. She was mortified. Unexpectedly, she began to shake inside because he was holding her hand. She removed it from his. Wanting to distract him, she murmured, "Perhaps we should order. I'm feeling a bit hungry." Picking up the menu, she studied it intently, glad to hide behind it.

"Yes, let's do that," he agreed.

He didn't know what to do, what to say. She had retreated into herself in the last ten minutes, saying nothing to him, simply picking at the food in front of her. She had ordered the same as him, thinly sliced prosciutto ham with slivers of melon, but she didn't appear to be enjoying the food.

He wondered if she had drawn back, become remote so suddenly, because he had taken hold of her hand. *Perhaps*. She might have found it too familiar of him. It had been a natural move on his part. Still, she had blushed in embarrassment and pulled away, maybe because she had confided in him when she hadn't meant to.

Surely that had to be it . . . the involuntary confidences which had just slipped out; she wasn't the kind of woman to give confidences very easily, of that he was convinced. Being with her this morning in a more relaxed environment had been an eye-opener. He had seen another side of her, and it had encouraged him to become a little more personal.

He couldn't help wondering if he had blown it. He must make amends immediately. He wanted to pursue this relationship, build it into something. He had never felt this way about a woman before, and he had known quite a few, some rather intimately.

Deciding that he must put her at ease, he said, "I want you to know that once the recorder is *off*, then anything you say to me is *off the record*. I would never use it."

When she simply gazed at him unblinkingly, saying nothing, he said swiftly, "I'm not the kind of journalist who plays tricks, you know. I'm very honorable."

There was a hint of indignation in his voice, and she exclaimed, "Oh, I do know that, Jack, and I do trust you, and thank you for telling me about the tape recorder."

"Just don't forget it, that's all," he admonished, sounding cross, still staring at her. "And what about the food, don't you like it?"

"I do, yes, it's delicious, but it is a rather large portion."

Jack laughed. "I was thinking the same thing, and we have the risotto primavera next. Can you believe I've ordered so much food? It's enough to feed the Seaforth Highlanders."

Annette began to laugh. "I've never heard *that* expression before."

"My father always used to say it. His father was in the Seaforth Highlanders in the First World War. I guess it was his version of saying there was enough to feed an army."

She was still laughing, and he was glad of that. Her demeanor had changed, was relaxed again, and he wanted to keep it that way, so he said, "Listen, Annette, thanks again for showing me the sculptures this morning, and for telling me so much about art and how you feel about it, what it means to you. It was very nice of you, and I know how busy you must be, planning the next auction."

"I am a bit, yes, but I've been happy to talk to you, Jack. . . . As I said before, you have made it easy, and enjoyable."

"I've enjoyed it, too, and I just wanted to ask—" He broke

off as the hovering waiter came forward and asked, "Have you finished, Mr. Chalmers? Was everything all right?"

It was a waiter he knew, and he said, "Yes, we have, and it was delicious, but you do serve very generous portions."

The waiter smiled, took their plates, and disappeared. Jack sat back, sipped his wine, and told her, "I don't usually eat much for lunch. When I'm in France it's a salad and a glass of water."

"I'm the same," Annette admitted. "Do you commute to Beaulieu and back? I mean, how do you manage it?"

"I'm here in London a lot when I have journalistic assignments. I write most of them here, if they're relatively short pieces. When I go to France I usually stay for about ten days to two weeks, but when I'm writing a book I spend several months there. Unless something special comes up, and then I hop over to London for a week, maybe a bit longer. It works out well. And I do love my little house by the sea."

"How did you find it?" she asked, her curiosity aroused.

"Oh, thereby hangs a long tale. . . . I'm not sure you need to hear it."

"Yes, I do," she insisted, wanting to know more about him and his life.

"Well, it was like this. When I was young, a woman fell in love with me, good-looking lad that I was, and decided to let me have the villa at the cheapest price anyone ever heard of. . . ." He began to laugh when he saw the odd look on her face. "No, no, it's not what you think. Let me tell you the real story. Madame Colette Arnaud owned the Villa Saint-Honoré and knew how much I loved the place. And this is what happened."

Annette listened to him attentively, relishing what she was hearing. He told a story well. But then he would, wouldn't he? He was a writer. Nonetheless, he embellished it in just the right places, and she found the story of the little boy and the old lady touching, and told him this when he had finished.

After this, lunch went very smoothly. They ate their risotto primavera, and Jack ordered two more glasses of white wine. And he kept her laughing for most of the next hour.

It was over coffee that he asked her if she could spare some time the following day. "I just need a couple of hours with you, Annette, to tie up a few loose ends. Also, I'd like to have a word with your sister on Sunday or Monday. I can do it on the phone if she prefers."

"I am sure she would be happy to see you in person, whichever you want. And I can see you tomorrow afternoon, or Sunday. Marius has to go to Barcelona tomorrow on business, so I'm free."

"How about tomorrow afternoon? At your apartment?"

"That will be fine," she agreed, and instantly regretted this. But she could not take the words back without looking foolish. If she was still nervous tomorrow, she could always cancel the appointment.

Chapter Twenty-five

The shrill ringing of the telephone brought Annette out of the shower, and she grabbed the receiver and said, "Hello?"

"Helloannetteit'schristopherandyou'vegottocomedown hereimmediatelyanywayassoonasyoucanI'vefoundsome thinginteresting—"

"Please slow down, Chris, I don't understand you, you're babbling. Start all over again, please."

"Okay. Sorry. I said, Hello, Annette, you've got to come down here immediately, anyway as soon as you can, I've found something interesting, and then you interrupted me."

"Because I couldn't understand, you were speaking in such a rush of words. So what have you found?"

"Some paintings." He sounded excited.

"Let me take this in my office, Christopher. I'll put you on hold for a moment."

"Okay."

Pulling on a terry-cloth robe and sliding her feet into a pair of matching slippers, she almost ran down the corridor to her office, excited by this news herself. Sitting down at the desk, she picked up the phone and said, "Well, no wonder you're babbling. I'd be babbling, too. Tell me all about it."

"Several weeks ago I decided to spruce up some of the rooms here, including my bedroom, and my uncle's upstairs den next to it—"

"I thought you didn't use the master bedroom because of . . . *the suicide incident*," she interrupted, appalled at the thought of him sleeping there.

"God no, of course I don't use it! I'm shuddering at the thought. I'm talking about another bedroom, which I've made my own, along the corridor. Anyway, I hired a contractor to do the work. He started last week, but only began renovation on my uncle's den yesterday. And guess what? One of the painters was scraping off the old paint when he leaned against a wall, and it caved in. He fell down three steps. Into a small room. A hidden room. There was a filing cabinet, and some paintings."

"Good paintings?" she asked, hardly daring to breathe.

"I'll say! *A Degas*, Annette, a Degas ballet dancer."

"Oh, my God! That's wonderful, fabulous. What else?"

"Two Manets, a Pissarro, and two Cézannes, and don't worry, there's no soot on the two Cézannes. In fact, the paintings all seem to be in pretty good condition, at least to me they are."

"I can't believe this, I just can't!" Annette was almost speechless, thrilled by his discovery.

"Believe it. So what time can you get here today? In time for lunch?"

"Yes, I'll do my best." She glanced at the clock. It was not quite eight-thirty. "I'll get ready at once. Oh, wait, I'll have to phone Jack Chalmers and cancel my appointment with him this afternoon. I hope he's going to agree. It's his last interview with me before writing the profile."

"Bring him with you, Annette. The more the merrier, I say. This is a fabulous discovery, and he could write about it, couldn't he? Bet he'll jump at the idea of coming with you."

"But I don't know that I should do that," she said, thinking out loud, hesitating. "I don't usually do my business with journalists sitting on the sidelines, listening to everything."

"But you're not really doing business, are you? Actually, you're coming to view some paintings . . . the paintings you believed were here *somewhere*, and you were right. As usual."

"I did think some art had gone missing, yes, because your uncle was reputed to have quite an extensive collection."

"Ask Jack to come, Annette. I liked him. He can finish his interview with you on the drive down."

Although she was still hesitant, reluctant to invite Jack to accompany her, Annette finally said, "Let me talk to him, and I'll play it by ear. But don't worry, *I* will be there today for lunch, Christopher. This is too important. Maybe Jack will interview me tomorrow."

"That's fine. Do what's best for you, Annette, but please call me back so I can tell Mrs. Joules how many will be having lunch here."

"Give me ten minutes," Annette answered, and hung up. She sat for a moment staring into space, her mind working rapidly. There was no question in her mind that she must go to Knowle Court today; this discovery was far too important to ignore. But the thought of bringing Jack along was worrisome, and for a variety of reasons. His presence disturbed her, because she reacted to him on an emotional level. His charming manner encouraged her to confide. Also she did not particularly want an audience when viewing the paintings.

A thought struck her, and she dialed Christopher's number. He answered on the second ring. "Chris, it's Annette," she said.

"That was quick. And I bet he said yes."

"I haven't phoned Jack yet. I just wanted to ask you a question. Is James Pollard with you this weekend?"

"Yes, he is. Why?"

"I think that's good. He can keep Jack company. If I decide to ask him, that is. Give me a couple of minutes." Again she hung up, found Jack's mobile number, and punched it in. It rang and rang. Voice mail did not pick up, and just as she was about to click off he answered.

"Jack Chalmers here."

"Good morning, Jack. It's Annette Remmington."

"Hi, Annette, nice to hear your voice. Oh God, you're not canceling, are you?"

"No, no, of course not. Something's just come up, though,

and I wondered if you could change our date. Can we meet tomorrow?"

"It's going to make it tough for me. I've got to start writing the profile tomorrow. It has to be in on Tuesday."

"But you said you're not going to interview Laurie until Sunday or Monday."

"That's right. However, I can write the profile of you tomorrow, and simply insert her quotes later on Monday. . . . I'd like to help you, just let me think a minute. . . . Now how can I work this out?"

Detecting a note of worry in his voice, she made a sudden swift decision. "Never mind. Let's not change our date for today. This is my problem, but maybe we can solve it together. Let me explain. I've just had a call from Christopher Delaware. He's found several paintings at Knowle Court. He wants me to go down to Kent to see them and have lunch. And I really should do that. However, when I explained I had a date with you, he suggested I bring you along. How do you feel about that, shall—"

"I feel great about it," he exclaimed, cutting her off. "I'd love to come with you."

"All right. Can you be here in an hour?"

"Of course. I'm ready now."

"But I'm not, I'm afraid. I'll order a car and driver, and you can do the interview on the way down."

"You don't have to order a car, Annette. Kyle left for Paris today with his producer, Tony Lund. He gave me the key to his Aston Martin DB24. So I can drive us down."

"But what about the interview?"

"I have a digital recorder, remember. All I have to do is turn it on. And you can hold it, can't you?"

She simply laughed.

"So that's okay, is it?"

"Yes. By the way, Knowle Court is quite close to Aldington."

"Oh, I know Aldington quite well, and I once went to Goldenhurst. But not when Noël Coward lived there. I went to a charity event."

* * *

Second-guessing him, Annette said, "I suppose you want to ask me about my mother, don't you?"

"Indeed I do," Jack said without looking at her, keeping his eyes on the road. "So you're ready to start, are you?"

"Whenever you want."

"Turn the recorder on, and then we can begin. Just a few questions, Annette."

"All right, let me deal with this." She checked the recorder as she spoke and added, "We can start."

"You never did tell me your father's name, by the way. What was it?" Jack asked.

"Arthur . . . Watson."

"And your mother's name?"

"Claire Watson."

"You told me that after your father died, you and Laurie went to live with your grandparents in Ilkley. And your mother, too, I presume?"

"Yes. After my mother died several years later, we went to live with our mother's sister. Our aunt lived in London. Her name was Sylvia Dalrymple. She was widowed and had no children. She was happy to take us in, actually. My aunt was very encouraging, liked my paintings, wanted me to have a career in art. It was she who sent me to the Royal College of Art, in fact. I thought I was very lucky."

"Going back to your mother for a moment, did she ever do anything? What I mean is, did she work, or was she solely a wife and mother?"

"A wife and mother mostly, but she did have aspirations about going on the stage, being an actress. At times, she even did do some amateur acting when we were small. But her career never really developed or came to much," Annette explained, reciting the revamp of her mother's life, which she had worked out earlier.

"Perhaps that's where Laurie's desire to be an actress came from, right?" He cast a quick look at her, then focused on the road ahead.

"Probably," Annette replied with a faint smile.

"How long have you been married to Marius?" Jack asked unexpectedly, changing the subject.

He had taken her by surprise. She said, "It will be twenty-one years this coming summer. I was nineteen."

"That long! My goodness, you have had a successful marriage, haven't you?" he murmured, and couldn't help wondering about their union and how much the length of time mattered.

"Yes," she said. "Aside from caring about me, Marius has been my mentor over the years, has taught me a lot about art, and he's always encouraged me, been my champion."

"But you do work separately from him now, don't you? Since you founded Annette Remmington Fine Art? Why did you go out on your own?"

Turning slightly in her seat, looking at him, hoping the questions would soon be over, she answered, "I suppose it's called *ambition*. I wanted to have my own company, under my own name, but I didn't want the responsibility and the high overhead of a gallery. That's why I started my consultancy business. I advise clients, find art for them, buy it, sell it for them, evaluate their collections, advise them about restoring their art, make decisions about whether the art *needs* restoration, and bring in other experts, if necessary. I provide a *service*, in other words. And I don't have to carry a huge inventory of paintings and sculpture, which can be extremely costly, as you can imagine."

"Thanks for explaining that last bit, and I understand now why you didn't go for your own gallery. Just a couple more questions, Annette, and then that'll be it, I think."

"I'm glad to answer," she said.

"Okay. What do you think drives you?"

"Gosh, that's a hard one. . . . I suppose I'm driven . . . because it's my nature. But I've always thought that in a way it's the desire to succeed, *the ambition*, that creates that drive. Am I making sense?"

"Yes, you are. And I believe those two things do go hand

in hand, plus an aptitude for a lot of hard work. You do work hard, I think, don't you?"

She nodded. "Laurie often accuses me of being a workaholic." She laughed. "Most people say that, actually. But I enjoy my work, and I love the sense of accomplishment I have when something's gone really well."

"I bet you felt this when you auctioned off that Rembrandt, didn't you?" He glanced at her again and grinned.

"I certainly did. And I don't mind admitting it was a wonderful feeling. The best. I can't wait to feel it again."

"That's a great last line for my piece. Thanks, Annette, for a fabulous sound bite."

"If you think of anything else, we can discuss it on the way back to London. And if the interview is really over, I'd like to ask you something."

"Go ahead, ask me anything."

"What did you think of Goldenhurst? And what was the charity event?"

"That's two questions," he teased. "I loved the house, it's such a beautiful old place, and as I walked around I couldn't help thinking about Noël Coward, who wrote some of his most marvelous plays and music there. Many years ago, of course. And the charity event was something my aunt Helen dragged me to. It was for a local hospice, and so worthwhile. I enjoyed the afternoon, in fact."

"You know its full name is Goldenhurst Farm, and it was Noël Coward's country home for thirty years. It's close to the White Cliffs of Dover, a song he sometimes sang at the piano. Vera Lynn also sang it, and made it famous in the Second World War," Annette volunteered.

"I happen to love the Romney Marsh, and in certain very flat parts of it the sea looks as if it's higher up, above the land and part of the sky. *Marvelous*."

"If I ever had a country house, I would like it to be in Kent," Annette confided, and again wondered why she told him things she had never mentioned to anyone, not even Laurie.

"It would be near the marshes, I'm certain of that," Jack said.

Annette merely smiled, and they went on talking about houses and art and country homes for the remainder of the trip to Aldington. Jack did not ask any questions about the paintings Christopher had found, nor did she volunteer anything.

But at one moment, she surprised herself when she suddenly asked, "Have you ever been married, Jack?" The words had just flown out of her mouth, and she regretted them.

He gave a quick glance and said, "No, never. But that doesn't mean I haven't thought about it. However, I don't think I've met the right woman yet."

"What kind of woman would be the right woman for you?"

"Someone like you." He cleared his throat, and wondered if he'd made a mistake.

"Oh," she said, swallowing, and then fell silent, her heart pounding. And panic took over again.

Chapter Twenty-six

They didn't say much after this, and toward the end of the journey they fell completely silent, lost in their own thoughts. Annette was suddenly focused on the questions Jack had asked, which hadn't been very many, and she couldn't help thinking he had insisted on keeping the date because he wanted to see her, to be with her. After all, he could have easily asked them over the phone.

She was well aware that she had invited him to come along, much against her better judgment, because she liked the idea of spending the day with him in Kent. But now she wondered if she had done the wrong thing. She did trust him, believed him to be honorable, but she was making him privy to her business. She had never done that before, did not even allow Marius to get involved, except on extremely rare occasions.

Well, so be it. Here she was, sitting next to him in the Aston Martin, and enjoying being with him. To her surprise she was no longer as nervous and agitated as she usually was when they were in close proximity. Was it because she had begun to realize that he was as attracted to her as she was to him?

Jack suddenly spoke, cutting into her thoughts. He asked, "How close are we now, Annette? In my estimate we must almost be there."

"We are," she answered, sitting up straighter in the car

seat. "In a couple of minutes we'll be in Aldington. You'll drive through the town, pass by Goldenhurst, and within a few seconds you'll see big iron gates. That's Knowle Court."

"I expect it's a grand house, isn't it?"

"Sort of. Actually it looks a bit like a small castle." An involuntary shiver ran through her.

Jack noticed this through the corner of his eye and said, "You don't like the place, do you?"

"No, I don't, and neither did Laurie when she was here a few weeks ago. It's sort of . . . creepy. We both felt that."

"Don't worry," he said, starting to laugh. "You've got me to protect you."

"I shall rely on you then." Swiveling slightly, focusing on him, she said, "Jack, there's something I want to say to you. Would you mind pulling over for a moment?"

"Of course not. What's the matter?" he asked, as he slowed down, stopped, and pulled on the brake. He turned in the car seat to look at her. "Is something wrong? You sound worried."

"No, nothing's wrong. It's just that I want to establish something with you. The other day you told me that when the recorder is off everything is off the record. That will be the same rule today, won't it?"

"Naturally. As far as I'm concerned, this is a social visit. I've finished the interview with you. Actually, I have a couple of other questions, not very important, and you can answer them on the way back." He paused for a moment, his eyes intently searching her face. Finally he said, "Put the recorder in your bag. . . . That'll make you feel secure, won't it?"

"Oh, Jack, don't look at me like that. I do trust you, don't be offended. It's just that I'm about to embark on some important business with a client—"

"I know, and I don't want to write about that," he cut in. "I promise you. As I told you, I'm not one of those sneaky journalists out to get somebody," he finished in a cold tone.

She looked slightly hurt; he leaned forward and took hold of her hand, wanting to please her. "I would never do anything to upset you, Annette." He stared into her blue eyes, and before he could stop himself, he leaned even closer and kissed her on the mouth. She returned the kiss, as passionate as he was, and then quickly pulled back, a stricken expression on her face.

"Oh, Jack . . . ," she began, and stopped, shaking her head.

"I'm sorry. I couldn't help it. I've wanted to do that since the first day I met you. You wanted it, too."

"Jack, I didn't! Honestly, we can't do—"

"Yes, you did want it! And I know we can't do anything about how we feel. But we can be good friends, can't we? And we can trust each other, and we *must*."

She nodded, handed him the recorder. "This is yours." Suddenly she smiled at him. "I just want you to know I'm very glad you came with me, drove me down here. It's lovely being with you."

"That's exactly how I feel. But we'd better get going if we're going to arrive in time for lunch." Turning on the ignition, he drove on down the main road, wondering how he was going to cope with this problematical situation. She was under his skin, and he wanted her. For himself. And he aimed to get her, no matter what. Inexplicably, he knew there was something amiss in her marriage.

Annette settled back against the seat and closed her eyes, thinking of Jack. She was playing with fire, she was fully aware of that. There was no question that this situation could become volatile. She must handle herself carefully, and with much more caution, not permit herself to become involved with Jack Chalmers. If she did, she would be ruined. Marius would see to that.

"My God, don't tell me there's a moat!" Jack exclaimed, an astonished look flickering across his face as he drove up to Knowle Court. "And a drawbridge. Well, there would be, wouldn't there?" As he braked and turned off the ignition, he glanced at her. "I see what you mean about it being a creepy-looking place."

"It's worse when the weather's bad. Today it's lovely and sunny, and therefore appears less forbidding."

"Here comes Christopher, and another fellow."

"That's a friend, James Pollard. He's really rather nice, you'll like him. Come on, let's brave it, shall we?"

Jack nodded, opened the door, and jumped out. He went around to help her alight. As he took hold of her arm, he bent toward her swiftly, kissed her cheek, and smiled inwardly as she slipped out of his grip and hurried over to greet her client.

He followed slowly, giving her time to embrace the two men, thinking how lovely she looked in a casual loose cream jacket and shirt, worn with brown slacks. He noticed she was wearing penny loafers, like his. He smiled to himself, and then increased his pace as she turned, beckoning to him to hurry.

After shaking Christopher's hand, he was introduced to James Pollard, and then they all moved into the house. He understood why Annette didn't like it as they went into the gargantuan entrance hall. There was a sinister feeling about it; it was oddly oppressive, and very gloomy.

Christopher hesitated in the hall, seemed fit to burst with excitement, looking at Annette pointedly.

Immediately, she seized the moment, instantly took charge. Glancing at Jack, she said, "Jim is going to give you the grand tour before lunch, while I do my business with Chris. All right?"

"Perfectly," he answered.

Jim said, "Would you like a cup of coffee or tea, Jack? There're various refreshments in the library."

"Thanks, Jim, I wouldn't mind a cup of coffee, actually."

"Come on then, let's go." Jim took his arm and ushered him across the hall and down a corridor, murmuring, "I'd like coffee myself."

Once they were alone, Annette said, "Where are the paintings, Chris? In the room where you're storing the others?"

"Exactly. I'm so chuffed about this I can hardly contain myself, and obviously I can't wait for you to see them." Taking hold of her hand, he exclaimed, "It's amazing, isn't it, when you think about it . . . the way the paintings unexpectedly came to light. You always believed there were some hidden away here. How did you know that?"

"I didn't really *know*, Chris," she answered, hurrying toward the storage room. "I just *assumed*. I felt there must be *some* concealed in a safe place. You see, it was quite a well-known fact in the art world that your uncle had a sizable collection, and that it was valuable. So, when you first showed me the gallery here, I was surprised there weren't more paintings hanging on the walls. However, it's not unusual for collectors to hide their favorite paintings, put them away. Some do it to view the art privately, others just to hoard certain paintings until the prices rise."

"I understand. And certainly I shall be eternally grateful to that chap yesterday who leaned on a particular wall in the den, and made the find of the century."

"Let's hope so."

She followed him into the room where he had been storing the other paintings, along with the ruined Cézanne. She was relieved to see that it was nowhere in sight. Hopefully he had destroyed it.

Hurrying across the room, she stood in front of a series of paintings she had not seen before. They were propped up against one of the walls. What caught her eye first was the Degas painting. It was of a ballet dancer; shades of blues and grays predominated. She stood in front of it for a long time, drawing closer, moving back, eyeing it from various angles, her focus very concentrated.

"Well, what do you think?" Christopher's anticipation and excitement had him on edge. He could hardly stand still.

"No comment, Chris, until I've viewed everything. Ah, here are the two Manets!"

Once more, Annette studied the paintings, her scrutiny fixed, penetrating, and then she moved on to view the Pissarro, and after that positioned herself in front of the two Cézannes, which held her attention the longest.

Christopher remained standing next to her, not daring to say a word. He was taut . . . expectant. And also afraid. Afraid of her verdict, her judgment.

Annette took a step forward, startling Christopher as she did, and began to lift the Degas.

"Here, let me do that." He went to help her. "Where do you want me to put it?"

"Over there on the table, near the window, where we had the Degas sculpture. The light is good."

She followed him across the room, asking, "Where are the papers you found? What authentication is there? How many of these paintings have provenance, Chris?"

Placing the Degas ballet dancer on the table, he swung to face her. "I couldn't find anything on this." He indicated the Degas ballet dancer. "And only one of the Manets had provenance. The painting of the bunch of violets."

"What about the Pissarro and the Cézanne paintings . . . their own versions of the same scene?"

"There is proper authentication, and very good provenance for both. No problems."

"And the other Cézanne? Anything?"

He shook his head. "No, but that doesn't mean much, because my uncle might have put papers elsewhere."

"Anything's possible," she muttered, wondering what else was hidden in this mysterious house.

Lifting the Degas off the table, Annette took it to the window and placed it upright in a chair, gazing at it for a long time. "There's something not quite right about it, Chris. It's wrong. . . . I hate to tell you this, but I think it's a forgery. And without provenance no one will buy it."

"But it looks so much like a Degas," Chris ventured, sounding nervous.

"I know, and whoever painted it has genuine brilliance. But I'm certain it's *wrong*. Just as I know the Cézanne is wrong. . . . I'm referring to the one with the red roofs and melting snow. Its actual name is *The Thaw in L'Estaque*. Now it's all coming back to me. It was in a private collection and then sold a few years ago at auction. To another collector. So there's no question it's a fake. It's known in the art world as *The Red Roofs*, by the way."

"So we don't have to bother looking for papers for that, do we?" he muttered.

"No, we don't. Nor do we have to bother looking for provenance for the Manet, because that is currently hanging in the Musée du Petit Palais in Geneva. I saw it recently, in fact."

"It's odd, I thought *that* was a fake," Chris told her. "But only because the face of the woman has smudges on it."

Annette gave him an odd look. "That real painting by Manet is entitled *Berthe Morisot with a Veil*. What you thought were smudges is actually the veil of her hat."

Christopher grimaced, gave her a hard stare. "So why did Uncle Alec put them in the hidden room, do you think?"

"Who knows. Possibly to protect them. The real ones certainly, and perhaps he was also protecting the fakes. Because he *knew* they were fakes? Maybe he did. He had great knowledge of art. But three paintings out of six is not bad. In fact, I'd go as far as to say it's a most wonderful discovery."

"Jim found two more paintings this morning."

"*What!*" Startled, she stared at him. "Why didn't you say so before?"

"I haven't had a chance. It was only about an hour ago. We were up in the hidden room, well, actually, in the den itself, and Jim was walking around, banging on the paneling, and suddenly he hit the end wall near the window. One of the panels just flew open, as if on a spring, and it was a cupboard. In it were two Graham Sutherlands. And a briefcase with some papers, including the bills for the Sutherland paintings from a Mayfair gallery. And provenance as well. Everything is upstairs, and the paintings, too."

"How fantastic! Christopher, don't look so down in the mouth. Several of these paintings are simply wonderful, special. And valuable." That should please you, she thought. If nothing else does. It was always the money with him.

"Will you put them in the September auction?" he asked.

"I don't know." She walked across the room. "Take me upstairs to see the Sutherlands, please, Christopher. I'd also like to see the priest hole."

"Priest hole?"

"Yes, that's what it's called . . . a place built for a priest to hide. During the Stuart period there was much religious strife, as I'm sure you know from your history lessons. Many aristocratic families were still Roman Catholics, and had their own family priests. But they had to hide their religion, be secretive, with Protestantism on the rise in England. The hidden rooms accommodated a priest when soldiers came to search the houses."

"How do you know so much?"

"It's part of my business." She gave him a long, thoughtful look, realizing that he continued to wear a sullen expression. It's disappointment. What else can it be? Disgruntlement? Was he put out because she had told him three paintings were forgeries? Most probably, she decided.

Annette remembered the small den the moment she walked into it. She had seen it the first time she had visited Knowle Court, when Christopher had given her a tour of the house many moons ago now. Today it was without its furniture; there were drop cloths on the floor and a tall stepladder in one corner, along with the painter's tools.

"That's it over there, the priest hole, as you call it," Christopher said, and indicated a small door, set in the paneled wall, which stood open.

Turning around to face her, he continued, "And this is the cupboard which Jim discovered this morning. Here are the two Graham Sutherlands." As he spoke, Christopher bent down, lifted out one of the medium-size paintings, and then another one. He leaned the two of them against the wall.

Staring at her, he asked, "What do you think?"

Annette peered at them for several minutes, eventually nodding and looking extremely pleased. "Wonderful! They're great examples of his best work. Let's take them downstairs with us, so I can examine them in a better light. Right now, I'd love to climb down into the priest hole. Just out of curiosity."

"Be my guest." Christopher laughed. "There's not much to see, and it's very poky."

"They always are," Annette murmured, hurrying across the room. She went down the three small steps without hesitation. She wrinkled her nose. It smelled musty, like an old church, and it was dark, but there were never any windows in priest holes. Just enough room for a man to stand, walk a few steps, and lie down.

Shivering, she wondered how many priests afraid for their lives had hidden here centuries ago. *A lot.* No doubt in her mind about that. Religious persecution had been rampant at different times in England.

Climbing up the three steps, she stepped into the den and said, "Please bring the paintings, Chris, would you, and I'll carry the briefcase."

"No problem," he answered, and handed it to her. He picked up the two Graham Sutherland paintings, and together they went downstairs.

"Let's go to the room where you're storing the other paintings. The light is excellent in there," Annette said. "Also, I'd appreciate it if you could give me the papers you found in the filing cabinet in the priest hole."

"There was quite a lot stored in it, and I had two of the workmen bring it downstairs yesterday. It's in the room with the paintings."

"Incidentally, I didn't notice the ruined Cézanne in there. Did you destroy it after all?"

He shook his head. "No, but I've locked it in a cupboard."

This did not please her, but she made no comment; they walked along the corridor in silence, heading for the sitting room.

The moment they were inside, Annette put the briefcase and her shoulder bag on a chair and took one of the Sutherlands from Christopher. She carried it over to the window, and again a smile flitted onto her face as she examined it in the good light. It was a great example of the artist's work.

Christopher hurried across to her with the other one,

exclaiming, "I can tell you're pleased, Annette, and look at this one. Jim thought it was also a beauty."

After a few more minutes studying both paintings together, Annette nodded. "These are a great discovery, Chris. You must thank Jim for having the foresight to bang on the walls. Why do you think he did it?"

Christopher shrugged. "On a whim? No one was more surprised than he was when that cupboard door flew open."

"And nobody ever told you about the priest hole?"

"There was no one to tell me. My father was dead, and anyway, I'm sure he didn't know. Because if he had, he would have told my mother, and certainly she would have told me, especially when I was named the heir in my uncle's will. And I wasn't close to my uncle, as you know. I'd only met him a few times when I was a young boy, and he never got in touch with us."

"I understand, and I suppose a man who is a recluse doesn't do that. But what about the staff, Chris? Didn't they know anything?"

"I'm sure not. *Why* would they know? If my uncle didn't tell his only sibling, my father, or *me* later, then why would he confide in any of the staff here?"

"But I thought some of them had worked here forever, or almost that."

"Yes, Harold, the handyman has been here since my father was a boy. My mother actually remembers him. And Mrs. Joules, of course. She started here as a parlor maid and worked herself up to being the housekeeper. I can ask my mother exactly how long she's been working at Knowle Court, but it must be over thirty-odd years, maybe longer."

"How did she react when the workman found the priest hole yesterday?"

"She was surprised. *Why?*" He raised a brow, then frowned, staring at her intently.

"What exactly did she say?"

"She said, 'Well, I never, Mr. Delaware. Wonders never cease.' Some cliché like that, but she was surprised, I can tell you that." Christopher appeared puzzled at Annette's reaction, and asked, "Why are you focusing on Mrs. Joules? What troubles you about her?"

Annette lifted her shoulders, shook her head. "No reason really, except that it seems odd that someone who has worked here for years didn't know about the priest hole, that's all. The help often know a lot more about a place, and its secrets, than family members, you know."

Christopher grimaced. "You've hit the nail on the head there, Annette, but I don't believe my uncle told *anyone* about the hidden room. He was very secretive, as I understand it, and weird, at the end of his life. Let's not forget that he went a bit odd after *the incident*, as it's known around here."

"*Incident*," Annette repeated. "What a strange thing to call that dreadful suicide." She shivered involuntarily. Taking hold of herself, she focused on business. "I'll glance at the various provenances you found in the briefcase and the filing cabinet, Chris, and I do mean glance. I would prefer to study them, and all the other papers, at my office. So I'll take all of the papers with me when I leave later. I'm sure that's all right, isn't it?"

"Yes, of course," he agreed.

James Pollard and Jack Chalmers stood talking to each other in front of the fire in the library when Christopher and Annette walked in to join them for drinks before lunch.

Both men turned around at once, and Jim exclaimed, "Ah, there you both are! So, what do you think about the discoveries, Annette? They're major, aren't they?"

Before she could answer him, Christopher announced, angrily, "Fakes! We've got some bloody forgeries."

His words dropped like a bomb into the middle of the room.

There was a deathly silence. No one uttered a word.

Jack, totally focused on Annette from the moment she stepped into the library, now witnessed her shocked reaction, saw the ice enter those beautiful blue eyes. He wanted to go to her but didn't dare. She remained perfectly still. At

that moment she was caught in a shaft of sunlight streaming in through the window; it highlighted her blondness, her
beauty. And her terrible pallor. Her face had gone white,
looked oddly drained.

Finally, she spoke. She said quietly, in a voice of steel,
"You spoke incorrectly, Christopher."

Without looking at him, she moved forward into the room,
and came over to the fireplace. Focusing on Jim, she said in a
cool, precise voice, "The paintings which were found yesterday are worth millions. . . . A Manet, a Cézanne, and a Pissarro are totally genuine. Three others have a question mark
hanging over them. For the moment. And the Graham Sutherland paintings are another wonderful find. So yes, Jim, the
discovery is indeed *major.*"

"What wonderful news!" Jim responded, smiling at her,
endeavoring to hide his irritation with Christopher.

"Yes, it is," Annette said. "And as I told Chris, he owes
you a big thank-you for banging on the paneling in the den.
If you hadn't been inspired to do that, the Graham Sutherland paintings would still be hidden away in that concealed
cupboard."

"I don't know why I was suddenly prompted to do such a
thing," Jim answered, shaking his head. "It was sort of idiotic in a way, don't you think? But I had heard of hidden
rooms, concealed cupboards behind paneled walls and book-
shelves."

"Not so idiotic," Christopher ventured, hoping to ease the
tension in the room, realizing he had made a terrible faux
pas. And that he had upset Annette. Clearing his throat, he
continued, "And Annette is right, I do owe you a very big
thank-you, Jim. Now, how about a glass of the old champers
to celebrate?"

"That would be great," Jack said, moving closer to Annette. Looking at her anxiously, he asked, "Would you like a
glass of champagne?"

"Thanks, Jack, I think I will have one."

Jim and Christopher both walked across to the drinks table, where Jim began to open the bottle of champagne. Chris-

topher stood watching him, obviously still self-conscious and ill at ease.

Jack took hold of Annette's arm, and in a low voice he said, "Not the brightest bulb in the chandelier, is he?"

"Correct," Annette murmured. "He doesn't mean any harm. I'll explain later. In the meantime, he is now in possession of some genuine masterpieces worth millions of pounds. So he shouldn't focus on those that might be wrong. Did Jim say anything? About how they were unexpectedly found?"

"No, he didn't. He wouldn't, would he? He seems like a first-class guy. I like him. Anyway, he didn't tell me one solitary thing, nor did I ask him any questions. I know you'll tell me about this discovery if you want me to know."

"I will, and I know you won't write anything about it until I say that you can."

"You mean I *can* write about it? Later?" He squeezed her arm. "Maybe for the New York piece I'll be doing?"

"I think so. I should have all my ducks in a row by the end of next week."

"What do you mean?"

"I must talk to Carlton Fraser on Monday, and ask him to clean the paintings I'm certain about. I also need him to examine the others. Here comes Chris with two glasses of champagne."

As he approached her almost tentatively, Annette thought that Christopher looked chagrined for once, and a trifle pale.

He handed her the glass of champagne, and apologized. "I'm so very sorry, Annette. Please forgive me for speaking out of turn." He then handed the other flute to Jack, who murmured his thanks.

Annette said, "You're forgiven, Chris, and please try to remember I prefer to speak about business privately. It doesn't matter who we're with. I don't want to discuss it in front of them. I must always speak to you alone. Do try to remember."

"I will," he said, and went to get a glass of the champagne for himself.

Jack said, "Very gracious, Annette. You've made him feel better."

"I don't want an atmosphere over lunch, and I know him well enough now to understand that he just says what comes into his head at times, and without thinking. Besides, it's marvelous that these paintings have come to light at last, and certainly they are worth celebrating."

"I know I shouldn't ask, because I'm sure you don't want to discuss them, but what happened? How were the paintings found?" Jack gave her a puzzled look.

"Let me explain," Annette said, and sat down on the sofa near the fireplace.

Jack joined her and listened most attentively as she told him about the priest hole, and what had been discovered there yesterday, and how that had happened in the first place.

"What a story!" Jack exclaimed when she had finished. "Remarkable, actually. How fortunate that Chris decided to renovate his uncle's den. If he hadn't, the paintings could have gone undiscovered for years."

She touched her glass to his. "Here's to you, Jack."

"And to you," he said, then asked in a low voice, "Any chance of my seeing the paintings? I'd be thrilled if I could."

"I don't see why not. I'll show them to you before we leave after lunch."

Chapter Twenty-seven

Annette had no real reason to be suspicious of Mrs. Joules, and yet, much to her astonishment, she realized she was. The housekeeper had a certain air about her, appeared to be possessive about the house and also about Christopher Delaware, and this grated on Annette.

Throughout lunch in the octagonal dining room, Annette had continued to wonder why this rather stern-looking woman behaved in such a manner, acted as if she owned this ancient pile and everything in it. She wasn't exactly arrogant, but almost, Annette thought.

Christopher broke into her thoughts when he said, "So you *do* want to take the paintings back to London with you after all, Annette?"

Turning, glancing at him, she said, "I do, yes, Chris, I want to get them to Carlton as quickly as possible. I'd like his opinion, and also I want him to clean those paintings which need it."

"Well, if you don't mind doing that, it would certainly be a help, since it saves me a trip to London on Monday. I'd made a date with my contractor, and I really do want to keep it if I can."

"Jack says he can get all of the paintings in the Aston Martin, and with ease. Carlton—" She broke off when the kitchen door swung open yet again, and Mrs. Joules once more sallied forth, this time with dessert. She was accompanied by her satellite, the young maid Brenda.

Looking at the housekeeper, smiling, Christopher asked, "So, what's the surprise, Mrs. Joules? You *did* say the pudding was really going to please me."

"It's your favorite, Mr. Delaware."

"I've got a few favorites," he murmured, continuing to smile at her.

"It's your *first* favorite. An English trifle."

"Oh, goody goody! You're a wonder, Mrs. Joules, that you most certainly are. And very spoiling."

"Thank you. Now Brenda, come along, put the bowl of trifle over there on the sideboard and I will serve it."

As the housekeeper spooned trifle onto the plate and Brenda passed the plates around, Jack began to tell a story about how he had taught a friend in France to make an English trifle, and a friend who was a well-known chef at that. He was a marvelous raconteur and told the tale with a great deal of gusto, humor, and self-deprecation. Instantly he had them all laughing at his hilarious yarn.

Annette couldn't help thinking what a lot of charm Jack had; and it was a natural kind of charm that put everyone else at ease. He was undoubtedly one of the most relaxed people she had ever met in her life; she imagined he must be very popular with his family and friends, Mr. Congeniality.

When they had been served, Christopher said, "Thank you, Mrs. Joules. I know we're all going to enjoy it."

Mrs. Joules merely smiled, nodded, and hurried out of the dining room, bustling Brenda along in front of her.

He caters to her, Annette decided as she picked up her spoon and dipped it into the trifle. And *she's* a peculiar mixture. Overbearing, yet somehow obsequious as well. And extremely self-satisfied. Very sure of herself. Certain she'll never be fired. I wonder why? Because she knows too much?

Mrs. Joules reminded her of someone. *Who?* She racked her brains for a moment and suddenly it hit her. *Mrs. Danvers.* As played by Judith Anderson in the film of *Rebecca*. It was one of her favorite old movies, starring two actors she had always loved: George Sanders and Laurence Olivier, who played Maxim de Winter in the film of Daphne du Maurier's book. Yes, Mrs. Danvers indeed . . . that was Mrs. Joules to a T. Very proprietary, self-important, and a terrible snob. Thinks she's better than all of us.

Annette swallowed a knowing smile, glanced across the table at Jack, and immediately saw that he was gazing at her intently. She smiled at him.

He smiled back, and seemed as if he was about to burst into laughter. But he didn't. Instead, he said, "What a delicious lunch, Christopher. My compliments to the chef."

"That would be Mrs. Joules," Christopher answered. "She does everything around here. I don't know what I'd do without her, actually. She runs a very tight ship and runs it brilliantly. I rely on her completely."

Jack nodded. "She's a splendid cook. Makes the best trifle. Now, since everyone's finished, I wonder if Annette and I can be excused, Chris? She did say she would show me the paintings before we left for London."

"But of course. Jim and I will go into the library. Mrs. Joules always serves coffee and tea there. We'll wait for you."

They all pushed back their chairs, rose, left the dining room, and walked across the main hall.

Annette stepped closer to Jack, explaining, "The paintings are in one of the sitting rooms, along that corridor there. Come on, let's go." To Chris she called, "See you in a minute or two. We won't be long."

"Take your time," Christopher answered, following Jim into the library.

"Thank goodness you spoke up when you did," Annette said to Jack once they were alone. "The lunch seemed to be interminable."

"It did. But I must admit I was fascinated." Lowering his voice, Jack went on, "I was fascinated by the dynamics at play. Between employee and employer."

"Don't tell me! I was, too. I just can't make out what that relationship is all about."

Leaning even closer, Jack murmured sotto voce, "Mrs. Joules acts as if she owns the place. And owns him."

"That's true. But she's also somewhat obsequious, don't you think?"

"Uriah Heep. Well, Mrs. Uriah Heep. A bit unctuous, wouldn't you say?"

"Yes. But then Dickens always did create unique characters, didn't he? Anyway, to me she's a replica of Mrs. Danvers. If you know who she was."

"Of course I know. *Rebecca* is one of my favorites. And so is good old George Sanders, who was in it. I loved him in *All About Eve*."

"I enjoy him, too." She eyed Jack with curiosity and asked, "So you like old movies, do you?"

"I have a mountainous collection." He grinned at her and teased, "You must come up and see my old movies sometime."

"I will," she replied, sounding suddenly distracted. "Here's the sitting room where Chris stores the paintings at the moment."

Jack's eyes roamed around the room as he followed Annette in; she was heading toward the bay window at the far end. He noted the Aubusson carpet on the floor, several antiques, plus a comfortable sofa and chairs in front of the fireplace. There was a mirror on one wall, but no paintings were hanging in here.

Coming to a stop in front of a pair of chairs, Annette said, "I want you to look at these two paintings. One is by Cézanne and the other by Pissarro, and they are genuine. The real thing, Jack. And both have the proper provenance."

He went and stood next to her, stared at the paintings. Each one was balanced in an armchair, where they were shown off to advantage in the best natural light from the window. After studying them for a moment, he said, "But haven't they each painted the same scene?" He sounded puzzled.

"Yes, they have."

"But why?"

"Cézanne and Pissarro were friends and associates, and they worked together. You see, they wanted to learn from each other. . . . They painted together side by side for about ten years." Annette indicated first the Pissarro then the Cézanne, and said, "You can see they each have very distinctive styles. And, you know, they really admired each other's work, enjoyed collaborating in this way, and they endeavored to help each other when they could."

"I can see the difference," Jack told her. "The Pissarro rendition of the scene is paler, everything is much lighter. The Cézanne is somewhat darker, the brushstrokes stronger. How very interesting. And how much are they worth?" Jack swung his head, stared at her, a blond brow raised questioningly.

"Each one is worth millions. However, if they are auctioned as a pair, I might be able to get much more at auction. Instead of selling them individually, I mean. This is something unique . . . having the two paintings available together."

"Alec Delaware knew a lot about art?"

"*I* believe so," Annette answered. "He bought some really good paintings, like these two Graham Sutherland paintings over there. And of course this Cézanne and this Pissarro are fabulous. They need cleaning, there's grime on them, but otherwise they look as if they are in perfect condition."

"And the Sutherlands?" Jack asked.

"They're over here, prime examples of his work. Two of his religious watercolors, painted in the mid-nineteen-fifties. Incidentally, he designed the tapestry *Christ in Glory* for Coventry Cathedral in 1962. Anyway, his paintings are much sought after today. He died around 1980 and his prices have increased." She took Jack over to look at them.

"And these were found in the priest hole?" he asked, after studying them for a few seconds.

"No, in the hidden cupboard that Jim accidentally discovered. The Cézanne and the Pissarro were in the priest hole, along with a Manet, over there."

Annette now walked across the room, followed by Jack. She stood in front of another painting propped in an armchair. "That's the Manet. . . . It's very simple but I love it."

"A bunch of violets," Jack murmured. "And this is also genuine?"

"Oh yes, and one of the reasons I like it so much is because it refers to Berthe Morisot, the Impressionist painter who was a friend of Manet's. If you look hard, you'll see part of her name on the white sheet of paper propped against the red fan."

Jack leaned closer, peered at the painting, and nodded. "Now I see the name. And is this also worth millions?"

"I can't really put a price on it at the moment. It might go for much less. On the other hand, a collector of Manet might grab it."

"And which are the fakes? I'd like to see them."

"This Cézanne, known as *The Red Roofs*, is probably not real." She drew him toward the painting propped against a wall.

"But how do you know that, Annette? How can you tell?"

"It doesn't look right to me, therefore it's *wrong*, and incidentally that's the word always used by dealers and people in the art business to describe a forgery."

"And which is the other fake?"

"There are two actually, Jack. A Manet, supposedly of Berthe Morisot, and a Degas ballet dancer which really looks terribly wrong to me. Let's go and look at them, and then I'll take you to see the priest hole. After that I think we must leave for London."

Chapter Twenty-eight

J ack was filled with a mixture of feelings as he drove
back to London. In the next seat was a woman he had
fallen heavily for. . . . He was enamored, full of admiration, and exceedingly impressed by her. And just a little
in awe.

They had only gone a few yards down the main road
when she told him she needed to think hard about the paintings they were taking to Carlton, and did he mind if she
settled back in the seat, closed her eyes, and concentrated?

He said he didn't, and for the last hour he had been driving along, preoccupied with his · own thoughts . . . about
himself, about her, and about the two of them together. He
realized he was besotted with her.

What you *saw* when you met a woman for the first time,
what she looked like, was what initially attracted you, drew
you to her. And certainly he had felt the strong pull of her
pale blond beauty, the shining hair, the crystal-blue eyes,
and the peaches-and-cream skin. And the lovely figure, of
course, and those ever-so-long legs. He found her sexually
desirable, exceedingly exciting. He wanted her fiercely. But
the physical pull aside, he was captivated by her reticent
manner, her shyness, and her refinement that spelled class to
him. She was a complex mixture. Fire and ice.

And then there was her brain. Her knowledge of art history, of artists and paintings, was so extraordinary it blew

his mind, and she became articulate and even loquacious when she spoke about art, and those brilliant and talented people who created it.

Jack found it both fascinating and baffling that she could study a painting and think it didn't look the way it should, didn't look right, and then analyze why. And then deem it a probable forgery. Her skills and expertise were incredible, as was the computer in her brain. That prodigious memory of hers was astonishing.

He had rather liked the Degas ballet dancer, and was absolutely gobsmacked when she told him it was *wrong*. It certainly looked right to him. But then what did he know? Not too much about art, certainly. But the Degas style he *was* familiar with, especially the ballet dancer paintings. Many were made into popular prints, were seen everywhere.

Now they were on their way to meet with Carlton Fraser in Hampstead. When Annette had phoned him just before lunch at Knowle Court and told him what had happened, Carlton had insisted they bring the paintings when they got back to London that afternoon or early evening. He had told Annette he would reward them with a wonderful cocktail or a *coupe de champagne*.

Jack wondered how he could ensnare her for dinner tonight. He knew her husband had gone to Barcelona early that morning. She was alone for the coming week. He wanted to be with her, didn't want her out of his sight. Not ever.

He sighed under his breath. Being with her filled him with total joy. It was also a special kind of torture. He longed to kiss her, touch her, wrap his arms around her, make love to her passionately. He wanted to possess this woman, become one with her. He wanted her for himself for the rest of his life. But was that possible? *She was married.* Until now he had stayed away from women with husbands.

There were moments when he was near her that he felt a rush of sexual feelings and erotic emotions, and knew he was about to get an erection. Somehow he managed to control himself. But, nevertheless, he felt at times like an adolescent boy when he was around her. Utter torture to be so near her and yet not near at all. For the moment.

He put her out of his mind, focused on the road ahead. He drove on steadily, thinking how curious life was. Some people thought things happened for a reason, were meant to be, were even preordained somehow. Others actually believed completely in the randomness of life. . . . You threw a pebble in a pool and the ripples spread out . . . growing wider and wider and ever wider.

Look how all this had actually begun.

A young man sits next to a beautiful blond art historian at a dinner party. . . . Some months later he becomes heir to a well-known art collection, seeks out the art historian, and asks her to sell a Rembrandt for him, a lost Rembrandt that hadn't been seen in public for years. And she does so. And in the process becomes famous and a star in her world, and the press laps it up. Her husband selects a young journalist to interview her. And the journalist falls in love with her and she with him. A *coup de foudre*, as the French so aptly called it . . . struck by lightning, love at first sight.

Suddenly, quite unexpectedly, Annette sat up and said, "Gosh, I fell asleep! Where are we, Jack?"

Startled, he glanced at her out of the corner of his eye. Then he immediately focused on the road again, and said, "About an hour away from Hampstead, not doing so bad, are we?"

"No, *you're* not." She turned to look at him and continued, "So tell me something, Jack. What did you think of Knowle Court?"

"It's awful. You called it creepy, forbidding, but I think it's worse than that. There's something about it that's . . ." He shook his head. "I actually think it's malevolent."

"What a strange thing to say." Annette frowned.

"I know it is, but that's what I feel. I've always thought houses have an atmosphere about them, are filled with the past lives that lived there. I know whenever I go to Carlton's house I have a sense of spirituality, of purity, and I believe that comes from Marguerite and Carlton, who are truly good people. I sensed it was a great place to be when I was much younger, just a kid. Other houses have less peaceful feelings, are filled with remnants of unhappy lives, while some are downright cold, eerie, unwelcoming. I've often thought that rotten things which happened there and strange people who lived there have somehow left their imprint on a house. Left their violence behind."

"You mean wickedness has seeped into the walls? Is that it?"

"Good way of putting it, that's exactly what I do mean. Brutal doings. Bad deeds. Evils acts. Rows, quarrels, and fistfights, goodness knows what else."

"*Malevolent* is not such a strange word for you to use, when I think about it. I know a house that had the same kind of dreadful atmosphere. It was malevolent and oppressive, and frightening, in fact."

"Really. What house was that?"

"Where we grew up. Or at least we lived there for a few years when we were little. In Ilkley. And—" Annette suddenly stopped, very abruptly, and compressed her mouth. It was as if she regretted her words.

"Tell me what you were going to say," Jack pressed.

"Oh, it's not important, I prefer not to discuss it."

"I see." Jack slowed the car, came to a standstill. He pulled on the brake and turned in his seat. "Why did you stop talking about the house in Ilkley?"

She shook her head, shrugged, did not answer.

Jack said, "I think you were going to confide something about your childhood, and then changed your mind. Because you don't trust me. That's it, isn't it?"

"No, it's not that, Jack. Honestly." Her voice quavered.

He slipped his hand into his jacket pocket and took out his recorder, handed it to her. "I want you to keep this in your bag, and then you will certainly know I'm not taping everything you say."

"Please, Jack, don't be silly. I don't think that. And I *do* trust you." She wouldn't take the recorder.

"Okay, I believe you, but I want you to have this in your possession anyway." He dropped the small recorder into her lap. "Keep it safe for me till the end of the evening."

Turning on the ignition and releasing the brake, he drove the Aston Martin out onto the road, his eyes focused ahead, his jaw set in a stern line.

She didn't speak for a while, knowing that she had offended him. And she regretted this. He had proved to her that he was sincere, that he was not out to write a bad piece about her, and that he was trustworthy. But she had so much to hide, so many terrible secrets, she was afraid of blurting something out unintentionally.

After a moment, she put the recorder in her bag and swiveled slightly in her seat. "It was a frightening house because it was so large, dark. The rooms were big and empty of furniture. We lived there with our grandfather, after our grandmother died, and Laurie was always scared. Actually, so was I."

"Where was your mother?"

"Oh, she was there, but sometimes she went out with friends, or was doing the shopping, always busy with her life, acting, that sort of thing."

"And when she died you went to live with your aunt."

"That's right, yes, first in Twickenham, later we moved to St. John's Wood. We loved that house. It was smaller but cozy, comfortable. *Welcoming*, that's the right word."

"Knowle Court must date back to the Tudor or Stuart periods, doesn't it?" Jack asked.

"Stuart, according to Christopher. The Delawares have lived there for centuries, and the house is entailed, can't be sold. Has to be passed on to the next in line."

"So Sir Alec Delaware had no alternative. He had to leave the house to his nephew. Mind you, it's more like a castle, in my opinion." He shook his head. "My mother had a funny expression. She would often make the remark, 'If only walls could talk.' And she was right. What stories walls *could* tell. Murder most foul and all that stuff. By the way, Jim made a comment about Sir Alec's *tragedy* to me. What did he mean?"

"Oh, God, I wonder why he'd bring that up? It was a terrible act, just awful. Sir Alec's fiancée, Clarissa Normandy, committed suicide a few days before their wedding. She hanged herself in the master bedroom. Wearing her wedding gown."

"Oh, Jesus!" Jack exclaimed, sounding horrified. "I chose the right word, didn't I, when I called the house *malevolent*!"

"Yes, you did, and who knows what went on in it before? Hundreds of years ago."

"And perhaps more recently. I suppose it was after the suicide that Alec Delaware became a recluse?"

"I think so, from what Christopher says. Mind you, he doesn't really know much about the family history. Certainly he didn't know about the priest hole."

"So I gather. I wonder, though, if Mrs. Joules did?"

"I wondered that, too. But surely she would have told Christopher when he inherited the estate if she'd been aware of it."

"Who knows. She's certainly well embedded there, and she rules the roost in my opinion. When did the suicide occur?"

"About fifteen years ago, I think."

"And Mrs. Joules was looking after Sir Alec, tending to his needs . . . perhaps *all* his needs? Many a housekeeper has turned out to be a keeper of the house and the owner, don't you know?" He started to laugh. "There I go, writing Victorian fiction in my head again."

"Are you implying that Mrs. Joules and Sir Alec might have been lovers?" she asked, sounding surprised.

"It's not unlikely. Housekeepers have always had a knack of worming their way in, and after he got over the shock of his fiancée's suicide he might have needed a bit of tender loving care and comfort. And after all, it was right there on his doorstep. Or rather, in his kitchen. Perhaps I should say his bedroom."

Annette couldn't help laughing. "You certainly know how

to spin a good yarn, as I learned at lunch today. But you could be right. If she *was* involved with Sir Alec, and for years, it would give her a sense of entitlement. It might explain her *cock of the roost* attitude."

"How old do you think she is?"

"I don't know," Annette replied. "Fiftyish? She started working there as a parlor maid at about fifteen, and was upwardly mobile. Eventually became the housekeeper. She's been there over thirty years, I would think, perhaps longer."

"She seems older than fifty, but maybe it's her overbearing manner, the pulled-back hairdo. But she's not a bad-looking woman, Annette, and she does have beautiful eyes."

"You noticed a lot in a short time."

"Of course I did. It's my job to be observant. And you'll be forty soon, won't you? In June?"

This remark took her by surprise. She glanced at him surreptitiously. "My birthday's on the third of June. And how old are you, Jack?" This last question just slipped out.

"Twenty-nine," he answered. "I'll be thirty in May. On the nineteenth."

"I see." She leaned back in the car seat, thinking, *He's ten years younger than me*, and this suddenly troubled her. She fell silent.

Jack said, "Listen, would you do me a really big favor, Annette?"

"If I can."

"Would you rescue me tonight?"

"What do you mean?"

"Once we've seen Carlton, and he's looked at the paintings, told you what he thinks, I have to go home to an empty place, with no food. Therefore, you could come to my rescue and do a good deed at the same time. If you came to dinner with me."

"Well, I'll have to think about it."

"Why?"

"Because."

"Oh, come on, don't be daft. Have dinner with a lonely old bachelor."

"Not so old, and I'm sure not so lonely either. But yes, I'll take pity on you, and have dinner with you. After all, you will need all of your strength tomorrow. To write your piece about me?"

"Only too true," he responded, smiling to himself, enjoying their unexpected repartee.

Chapter Twenty-nine

❊

I f this is a forgery, then whoever painted it is bloody clever!" Carlton exclaimed. He stood in front of the easel in his studio, staring at the painting of a ballet dancer, supposedly by Degas.

All the strong lights blazed in the vast area. Two high-powered standing lamps were focused on the painting, so that every inch of it could be properly seen, and studied for any faults.

"I agree with you," Annette said. "Obviously a talented artist did this. Whoever it was. And look, perhaps *I'm* wrong about it being *wrong*. Nobody's infallible, least of all me. The unfortunate thing is, there's no provenance. Well, as of this moment there isn't."

"You said you had two shopping bags full of papers from Knowle Court in the car. Might it not be amongst them?"

"It might. Sir Alec was so careless, and Christopher's not much better. On the other hand, he did find the papers for the Cézanne and the Pissarro, which the two of them painted at Louveciennes, and also for the Manet violets. At least he now knows how to isolate bills from dealers, letters and bills from galleries, and also reports from art experts. And he now recognizes what provenance is. At least he's learning."

"Has he learned enough to destroy the soot-damaged Cézanne?"

"I don't think so."

"So where is it?" Carlton asked, suddenly looking worried, shaking his head in obvious dismay.

"He told me it was locked in a cupboard. That's all I know."

"I see." Carlton shrugged, compressed his lips, and muttered, "It does belong to him, so I suppose he can do what he wants with it." Glancing at Annette, he went on, "Take me through it. . . . Tell me what you don't like about the Degas here." He pointed to it. "You said it doesn't look right to you, so it must be *wrong*."

"A few things seem rather pronounced to me, Carlton. I know that when you first look at it you see a Degas ballet dancer. But that's at first glance. Look at it for longer and you'll notice that the dancer's stance is very ugly. I think it's extremely awkward. Then the brushstrokes are not exactly right . . . almost, but not quite. I also find the woman's body somehow too top-heavy, just *wrong*." She gestured to the shoulders and added, "They're not right to me either."

"I do see now, yes. However, Degas did not always paint dancers who were elegant and beautiful. Sometimes they were, well, odd-looking, to be honest. Granted, he tended to paint groups of dancers, or pairs, and this dancer is standing alone at the barre."

He blew out air, shook his head. "There's not even the shadow of another dancer in *this* painting here." He walked away, turned around, and stared at the painting again from a distance. "Aha! It looks unfinished, Annette!"

"You're correct, that's it. Now you've pinpointed it. And don't you think it looks a bit . . . *rough* in some ways? However, I will search for the Degas papers in the two shopping bags. Also, if you don't mind, I will have Laurie come up to see it on Monday. As you know, she's truly *the* expert on Degas."

"I could take it to her if you want," Carlton offered.

"No, no. First of all, these lights are important for proper viewing, and you know she likes to be independent. So I know she'd prefer to come here. She hates to be treated like an invalid."

"I understand." As he spoke he lifted the Degas off the easel and leaned it against the wall. He picked up the smaller painting of a woman in a veiled hat, which was attributed to Manet.

After studying the picture for a few minutes, Carlton turned around, frowning, and asked Annette, "Why do you think this is a fake? Actually, it looks as if it's covered in soot to me. Like the Cézanne was."

"That's what Christopher said, but it's *not* soot. Manet painted it that way, smudges and all. It's called *Berthe Morisot with a Veil*, and was done in 1872. She was married to his brother Eugène, and she painted with Manet at different times."

"Yes, I did know that. So, no provenance to prove its authenticity, eh?"

"No, and how could there be? The provenance is with the directors of the Musèe du Petit Palais in Geneva, where the real Manet actually hangs. I saw it with my own eyes quite recently."

"Then this is a copy, but it's a bloody good one, Annette."

"Not just good, brilliant, Carlton. Another very talented artist painted this woman with a veil," Annette agreed.

Taking down the painting, Carlton now reached for the second Manet, a painting of a bunch of violets resting against a red fan. He placed this on the easel. "And this one?"

"Oh, that's real all right! There are loads of papers on it, and it has proper provenance. All is in order. It's a small painting, I know, but it'll probably go for a lot because it was once owned by Berthe Morisot. Manet gave it to her to show his appreciation to her for being his model from time to time."

"That's an interesting detail," Carlton exclaimed, then laughed. "You'll know how to milk *that* in order to promote the painting, push up the price. Nobody's been better at that than you, love, as far as I'm concerned. So, Annette, this painting of the violets by Manet, the Pissarro, and the Cézanne country scenes are genuine. And I believe they're extremely valuable. The forgeries are the Manet of the woman with a veil, the Cézanne known in the business as *The Red Roofs*, and possibly the Degas ballet dancer?"

"That's right. I have just one question, Carlton. I know the genuine paintings do need cleaning. But do they require a lot of restoration?"

"No. They look as if they're in pretty good condition to me. There's obviously grime on them, but that's relatively easy to remove."

"And you do have the time to work on them for me?"

"I certainly do, my darling girl. Would I ever turn you away?" He shook his head. "Never, ever, Annette." He stared, giving her an intent look. "Why is Jack with you? Why did he drive you to Knowle Court?"

"Because he was supposed to finish the last part of his interview with me today. When Chris called me early this morning, to tell me he'd found some paintings in a hidden room, he urged me to go down to Kent. Immediately. I felt I had no alternative. He is, after all, an important client. When I explained I had a prior engagement with Jack, Chris suggested I bring Jack with me. He thought Jack might like to see Knowle Court, that it could be useful background material for the piece he's writing for the American paper."

"So you invited him to go with you, and no doubt he saw the paintings."

Aware of an odd note in Carlton's voice, Annette answered swiftly, "You sound funny. Do you think he shouldn't have seen them? Because of the forgeries? Don't you trust him?"

"I'd trust Jack with my life. He's sincere, ethical, and true-blue. Don't forget, I've known him since he was a lad. He won't write about the fakes, or talk about them, or any of the real paintings either, not unless he has your permission. But knowing you, how smart you are, I'm sure you've extracted a promise from him to keep everything to himself."

"I have. I happen to trust him, too. I agree he has integrity. Anyway, he doesn't need to use any of the new stuff he gathered today to complete his profile of me. He's got plenty of material."

A warm look crossed Carlton's face. "Jack and Kyle were great kids. They've turned out to be winners. Peter brought them up very well. I always liked him. He was a good man."

"And Jack's mother? What was she like?" Annette probed, riddled with curiosity about Jack.

"A nice woman, and good to Kyle, her stepson. But to be honest it was Peter who had the most influence on the boys, and it shows. They've made a success of their lives." Carlton lifted the Degas from against the wall as he spoke, and over his shoulder he said, "Now let's take a dekko at the Graham Sutherland watercolors. And then we'll go and join Marguerite and Jack, and have that special cocktail of mine."

"I'm wondering something," Marguerite announced all of a sudden, about half an hour later. She looked straight at Annette and asked, "Why didn't Sir Alec tell anyone about the hidden room? Or leave a letter to be opened after his death? Or put something in his will about it? After all, he'd stored valuable paintings in that priest hole."

"I've been wondering that myself," Annette replied. "The only thing I can come up with is that he didn't expect to die when he did. Apparently he was in good health when he had the heart attack, which in the end proved to be fatal. He was only about sixty-nine, seventy at the most, and that's not old today."

"No, it's not." Marguerite took a sip of her drink. "Nevertheless, he could have put something in his will as a protection, in my opinion. It seems a bit irresponsible that he didn't."

"That's true. Except a lot of people don't want to face their own mortality, or can't. They just want to avoid thinking about dying," Annette pointed out.

Carlton exclaimed, "But in this instance there were those priceless paintings to consider! Why on earth didn't he think of them?"

"I'm not sure he was thinking, at least not *rationally*," Annette murmured. After taking a sip of her cosmopolitan, Carlton's famous cocktail, she continued, "From what I've heard about Sir Alec, he'd grown rather strange by then. Even a little weird perhaps. That might account for his carelessness in regard to the provenance of a painting. As well as bills, receipts, that kind of thing."

She stared at the famous restorer, a man she trusted and who had been her good friend for many years. "For all I know, the Degas could be real. Because *I'm* troubled by it doesn't mean it *is* a fake. I could be totally mistaken. Only provenance speaks the truth. Alec Delaware knew that. Yet he left a mess behind him, and that's not like the businessman he once was. Somehow it's out of character. To me it is, anyway."

Jack looked across at Annette. "I would love to know what Mrs. Joules knows, wouldn't you?"

Annette nodded.

Marguerite asked, "Who's Mrs. Joules?"

"The housekeeper at Knowle Court," Jack replied. "An odd woman, actually. Both Annette and I thought she was the Mrs. Danvers type."

"Do you mean the Mrs. Danvers from *Rebecca*?" Marguerite threw him a quizzical look.

"I do indeed."

"Why do you think she knows something?" Carlton interjected.

"I made a simple deduction," Jack said. "When you've worked for a man for many years, lived in the same house, you know everything there is to know about the man, the family, and the house. Mrs. Joules started as a parlor maid, climbed the domestic ladder to become the housekeeper. She's got to be stuffed with information."

Annette said, "I find it hard to believe she didn't know about the priest hole."

"If she did know, why wouldn't she have told Christopher?" Jack had a puzzled look on his face.

"Maybe she *knew* there were some fakes hidden in there. Perhaps she didn't want that to become known." Annette paused for a moment, looking reflective, then said, "There's a lot of loyalty involved. I think Mrs. Joules is the kind of woman who would want to protect Sir Alec's reputation."

"Buying a fake doesn't reflect on a person's character, does it?" Carlton ventured, then, as an afterthought, added, "I guess it reflects on his judgment, though."

"I suppose that's true," Annette agreed. "But this is all speculation. Anyway, it doesn't really matter anymore, since the priest hole was discovered and everything is now out in the open."

"Only too true," Jack said. Turning to Carlton, he picked up his drink. "Here's to you, Carlton. This is the best cosmo I've ever had."

"What's your secret?" Annette asked.

"Shaken not stirred." Carlton winked at her.

"I'm glad you're both staying to dinner." Marguerite looked from Jack to Annette. "I've made *blanquette de veau*, and even though I say it myself, it's delicious. I've never had one better anywhere in the world."

Jack stared at Annette, frowning.

Annette ignored the look he gave her. She said, "*Oh*. I hadn't realized you were inviting us to dinner as well as drinks, Carlton."

"Oh, yes. Didn't I make myself clear?"

Annette shook her head, now threw Jack a baffled glance.

Marguerite stood up. "I'd better go and check the veal stew." She hurried out of the living room.

Carlton said, "The two of you can't leave, you know. She's made enough food for ten. And anyway, she'll be hurt if you go."

"Of course we'll stay for dinner," Jack reassured him, aware of the worry in the older man's eyes, the disappointed expression on his face. "And since we're staying for dinner, I think it's safe to have another cosmo. If I may, please."

Carlton sprang to his feet, hurried across to the drinks table. "My pleasure, Jack, coming right up. And how about you, my darling girl?"

"I'd love one, even though I do think it's a very lethal drink." Out of the corner of her eye she saw that Jack was smiling at her. There was a wicked glint in his eyes. He's lethal, too, she thought. The most dangerous man I've ever met. Sudden panic invaded her. She was afraid of him, afraid of being alone with him later. Afraid of herself and what might happen between them. She was now fully aware of how he felt about her; danger lurked between them.

She shivered when she eventually looked across the room at him, caught a glimpse of the expression on his face. It was full of yearning. For her. Alarmed, she averted her face. And the panic took hold again.

Chapter Thirty

✣

"I want to say something." Annette peered at Jack in the darkness of the car. "Explain something to you."

"What is it? You sound worried. And go ahead, I'm listening." He swiveled in the car seat so that he was looking at her. They were sitting in the Aston Martin parked outside Carlton's house and Jack was about to drive her home.

There was a short silence before Annette said, "There mustn't be any kind of leak about the fakes Chris found yesterday. This must be kept quiet. I've got another auction coming up. I can't have any hint of forgeries in the Delaware collection. It would be ruinous for the auction and for me and my business."

"I understand that," Jack answered. "And you must understand you don't have to worry about me. Not a word will pass my lips. I would never do anything to cause you trouble, Annette, surely you know this."

"Yes, I do. I just couldn't help saying it, even though I trust you. I'm afraid the art world is a tricky place. It breeds greed, overweening ambition, cunning, betrayal, double-dealing, rotten, often vicious gossip, and a lot of competitiveness. It's not a world you know, Jack, and I just wanted you to be aware that the slightest hint of forgery would spread like wildfire."

"Please don't give it another thought. I'm like a grave-yard, and anyway, I don't really know anybody in the art business, except for Margaret Mellor, and she's your friend. So whom would I tell? However, what about Christopher Delaware? I've only met him a couple of times, but he seems awfully young and inexperienced. And he shoots from the hip."

"I'm well aware of his shortcomings. Before we left, after lunch, I warned him not to discuss anything with anybody. And as far as Jim is concerned, he knows to keep his mouth shut. Also, he's a good influence on Master Delaware."

"I couldn't believe it when Chris came into the library with you and blurted out that he'd found what amounted to a lot of fakes. I don't blame you for being furious with him."

"He won't do that again, I can assure you."

"You made it very plain to him that he'd been foolish, thank God."

"I've also made him understand that if he talks out of turn he'll lose money. That's my big stick."

Jack looked surprised. "He's hardly broke. Quite the contrary, in fact, after the sale of the Rembrandt."

"True. But he loves money. Anyway, I'm sure he'll keep his trap shut. He'd better."

Jack laughed.

She said, "What is it?"

"You sounded very tough for a split second."

"I have to be tough with some of my clients. And believe me, a few of them can be extremely tough with me. I'm in a big-money business."

Jack turned on the ignition and the car slid forward. As he drove down the street, he said, "Do you mind if I stop for a moment at my father's house? I promised Kyle I'd drop in every day whilst he's away, to make sure everything's all right."

"No, that's fine."

A few seconds later he came to a standstill in front of the big old house he had grown up in, and braked. Turning off the ignition, he put the key in his pocket and got out. He walked around to her side of the car and opened the door. "Come on."

Annette seemed startled, and exclaimed, "I'll wait here for you, Jack. I don't mind, really."

"No, no, please come inside. It's better. I have to check a couple of things, and Kyle thinks I should turn off the boiler in the basement. I prefer you to wait inside." He helped her out, and as they went up the short path he said, with a laugh, "You'll like the atmosphere here. It's totally the opposite of Knowle Court."

She did not respond. Panic had flared inside her again.

Jack let go of her arm to open the door. When they stepped inside together, he turned on the hall light, closed the door behind them, and led her into the middle of the floor. Looking at her and smiling, he said, "Can you feel it? The warm, loving atmosphere? It still lingers here, don't you think? The happy feeling my parents created. Well, at least I feel it." When she did not respond, he peered at her. "Don't you?"

"I do," she said at last, and forced a smile.

"I'll only be a moment. I've just got to run down to the basement and deal with the boiler." He strode off, and she walked through the arched doorway into the living room. Tall French doors opened onto the garden, and the room was bathed in moonlight. She stepped up to the French doors and looked out, saw the huge full moon, radiant in the ink-black sky. It was a beautiful night, and even though it was still only the middle of April, it was mild.

Moving away from the glass doors, she walked into the center of the room, glancing around. She realized that the antiques were really good. Two lovely old chests, a secretary against one wall, and a pair of chairs with carved wooden backs were all of excellent quality. So much for his mother's old junk shop; it probably wasn't that at all. Perhaps he had been teasing her.

She heard his step in the hall, and suddenly he was walking into the living room, coming toward her. Slowly Annette turned around.

Their eyes met and held, and she took several steps in his direction and then stopped in her tracks. Her heart was racing.

He came to a standstill at last, stood staring at her, his light-gray eyes searching her face, his expression questioning. She wanted to look away, found she could not. It seemed to her that she was mesmerized by him.

They moved closer to each other at exactly the same moment, came into each other's arms. Jack held her close, stroked her hair, his heart clattering against hers.

They clung to each other for a long moment, and then he bent his head, found her mouth with his. They kissed as passionately as they had in the car earlier that day. But now they went on kissing and she did not pull away. She felt weak at the knees, and in need of his arms to support her.

Finally they drew apart, stared at each other, looking slightly shell-shocked. He said quietly, "You see, it is the same for you as it is for me. Don't deny it."

"I won't. . . . It's true."

Jack moved closer once more, put his arms around her, and held her as tightly as before. Against her hair, he said, "Come upstairs with me . . . to my old room. I want you so much, I want to make love with you."

"I can't! Oh, Jack, I can't. I have to go home. Please try to understand," she whispered back, the panic spiraling out of control, engulfing her. She was shaking inside.

A deep sigh escaped him. Without releasing his hold on her, he went on whispering, "Yes, I know that, but let me hold you just a moment or two longer. *Please*. I can't let you go just yet."

They lingered there together, standing in the middle of the room in the moonlight, clinging to each other almost desperately, and then she broke away from him finally. He did not prevent her; he simply took her hand in his, walked with her into the hall without speaking. Turning off the hall lights, he led her outside.

When they were in the car, he drove off.

Neither of them spoke.

It was not until they were well away from Hampstead Heath and heading in the direction of Belgravia that Jack finally broke the silence.

He said, "Listen, if I finish my profile of you tomorrow, will you have supper with me?"

"I don't know."

"But you promised to have dinner with me tonight, and somehow it got sabotaged. So you owe me one, you know."

She couldn't help smiling. He sounded so woebegone.

"All right," she agreed. "I'll have supper with you. Just call me tomorrow to let me know what time." She was surprised that her voice sounded so normal, considering how disturbed she was.

"I will," he answered, his voice as level as hers even though he was flustered, his emotions in a turmoil.

They talked only intermittently as he headed toward Eaton Square. Once they arrived there, he insisted on helping her with her two shopping bags of documents from Knowle Court. He carried them into her building, accompanied her in the lift, entered the front hall of her flat, and deposited them.

"See you," he muttered, squeezing her arm, and left.

After closing the front door of the flat behind him, Annette sat down in one of the hall chairs, leaned back, and closed her eyes. She was shaking inside, still panic-stricken.

Jack had the most extraordinary effect on her. She trembled when he touched her, was overwhelmed with desire when he kissed her, and she was totally amazed at herself for responding the way she did. Passion had almost always eluded her; she had never felt like this before. Well, only once, long ago.

Suddenly she wondered how she had managed to keep her hands off him at Carlton's house earlier. Sheer willpower, she decided. She knew he had faced the same dilemma.

Every time Marguerite and Carlton went to the kitchen together to check on the food, Jack had leapt up, rushed over to her to kiss her cheek, touch her shoulder, or simply stare at her, his longing for her etched on his face. He was in love with her, she realized that.

Eventually she roused herself, got up, took the two shopping bags, and carried them into the dining room. Later she would spread the papers out on the table, hoping to make sense of them. Perhaps she would even find the missing provenance for the Degas ballet dancer. She somehow doubted that.

She went from the dining room to her office, turned on the desk lamp, and looked at the answering machine. Nothing. Groping around in her shoulder bag for her mobile, she flipped it open to check her messages. There were none. The only two people who would call her were Marius and Laurie. Neither had.

Her next destination was the dressing room, where she took off her clothes, put on a nightgown and silk robe, then hurried into the adjoining bedroom, turning on the lights as she did. After placing her mobile on the bedside table, she lay down, endeavoring to relax.

Jack Chalmers was truly in her life now. And she wanted him there. But she was frightened of what might happen between them. And the consequences of a liaison with him. No, there couldn't be any kind of relationship. That wasn't possible. She mustn't let him get any closer. She mustn't sleep with him. If she did she would be lost. His forever.

There was no future for them. Marius would never let her go. And if she left him, if she ran away with Jack, he would pursue her, punish her, and betray her secrets. She had always understood Marius could be a very dangerous adversary.

Annette's mother had once told her that a secret was only a secret as long as only one person knew it. When a second person had knowledge of it, then it was no longer a secret at all.

Her mother. The lovely Claire. But not so lovely when she died. An alcoholic and a drug addict. Annette shivered involuntarily, and she pulled the robe tighter around her.

Timothy Findas sprang into her head, and she shivered again at the thought of him. He had been her mother's true downfall, her supplier of drugs and booze. . . .

The landline shrilling next to her on the bedside table cut into her thoughts, and she picked it up. "Hello?"

"It's me, darling," Marius said. "I hope I'm not waking you up?"

"No, no, it's fine, I wasn't asleep. How was the flight? Did you have a good trip?"

"Perfect, and I couldn't phone before. I was tied up with a client. I got your earlier message about the find at Knowle Court in the newly discovered priest hole. Tell me what happened. What's the good news?"

"Three genuine paintings, Marius! But sadly also three fakes. Well, two for sure, and one very suspect Degas."

Marius remained silent. After a moment, he said in a low voice, "Explain about the ones that are right and not *wrong* first."

"A Cézanne and a Pissarro, from the time they were painting side by side. . . . The scene is of Louveciennes. It's a country scene, very distinctive styles, of course. As a pair I believe they are a priceless item. Worth millions of pounds."

"They are indeed. And the third?"

"It's a Manet of a bunch of violets and a red fan, and Manet gave it to Berthe Morisot, to show his appreciation that she modeled for him sometimes. It's small, but lovely."

"Then you're in clover, my darling girl. Three more Impressionists! You could make the auction in September very important indeed. Bigger than the Rembrandt auction."

"I had thought of that, Marius. On Monday I shall start revamping the theme for the auction."

"Good idea. And what were the forgeries?"

"A Manet actually. It's a copy of a painting that is currently hanging in the Musée du Petit Palais in Geneva. I saw it recently."

"Somebody's not very bright," he muttered in an odd tone. "And the others?"

"A Cézanne of—"

"Not with soot all over it?"

"No. But it's *The Red Roofs*, as it's known in the business, and I was present at the auction when it was sold. It's in a private collection. There's no chance it's authentic, although it looks it."

"Perhaps that's why Sir Alec bought it?"

"I should think so. It's damn good. The last painting is of a Degas ballet dancer, and I really feel funny about it. Gut instinct tells me it's wrong."

"Why don't you show them to Carlton Fraser? He can make tests on the canvases and the paint, as he did with the other Cézanne."

"Actually, Marius, I took them to Carlton this evening." She swallowed, and wondered whether to tell him Jack had been with her. He could so easily find out from Carlton. No, Carlton hardly ever saw Marius. Swiftly, she added, "I took them from Knowle Court immediately. I think I need to have the information as soon as possible."

"I agree. What did Carlton think?"

"Obviously the only painting he needs to truly scrutinize is the Degas. We know that three are genuine and two are fakes because *I* can *trace* the fakes, even though they don't have papers. It's just lucky I know where the real ones are hanging."

"I understand. I'm sure he'll get to work immediately. And tell me, Annette, what about the provenance on the paintings that are real?"

"Christopher did manage to find them. There was a filing cabinet in the priest hole, and his friend James Pollard found a hidden cupboard in the same room. There were two Graham Sutherland watercolors in it, plus a briefcase."

"My God, quite a discovery indeed! And the Sutherlands are okay?" He sounded suddenly excited.

"Oh, yes, very genuine. *No question*. I also now have a lot of papers I can sift through, Marius. I'm going to spend tomorrow doing that. I think they might well tell me a great deal." She glanced at the clock and saw that it was eleven-thirty. Twelve-thirty in Spain. "So you've had dinner, darling, have you?"

"I have, yes. Just got back to the hotel."

"It's late there. I'll say good night, Marius."

"Sweet dreams, darling," he replied, and hung up.

Annette replaced the receiver and lay back against the pile of pillows, wondering if she should have told Marius about Jack Chalmers accompanying her to Knowle Court. Had she made an error? She wasn't sure. It was too late now. And she couldn't very well call him back. It would look awkward, perhaps even guilty. Let it go, let it go, she told herself.

Sliding out of bed, she went to the kitchen and took a bottle of sparkling water out of the refrigerator, poured herself a glass, and carried it back to the bedroom. A short while later she turned out the light and tried to go to sleep. But sleep eluded her and she turned restlessly for a long time.

Suddenly she sat bolt upright on the bed and snapped open her eyes. What was the statute of limitations on murder? There wasn't a statute. She knew that only too well; a murder case that has not been solved was always open, a cold case. So she could still be tried for murder. . . . Marius knew that. . . . She should never have told him all those years ago, never confided her secrets in him.

Chapter Thirty-one

❊

Elizabeth Lang, wrapped in a colorful kimono, sat cross-legged in the middle of the bed, her gaze focused on her lover. He stood near the desk, speaking on his mobile, occasionally glancing out the window toward the port. He moved again, twisting slightly, staring at the far wall, very concentrated, listening so attentively he was unaware of her fixed scrutiny.

She studied his profile. He had a noble head, a Roman nose, and a thick crest of hair. His profile reminded her of some great Caesar embossed on an ancient coin.

Her name for him was Toro, because he was her big raging bull. Tall, broad of chest, and well built in every way, he was a commanding man, very handsome, and outstanding on many levels. They had been lovers for fifteen years, and the relationship suited them both. He was a married man who did not want to divorce; and since she did not want to be married, they were ideally suited. She had been married once, years ago, and it had been a total disaster.

Being the mistress of this unique, talented, and successful man was enough for her. It was, in fact, quite a thrill. And most especially when they were in bed. He was sleek, inventive, passionate, and demanding, and she gave him what he wanted, met all of his sexual needs with a great deal of enthusiasm and enjoyment.

He had called them a good pair right from the beginning,

and they were. Good for each other, with each other. Neither of them had any intention of breaking off the relationship, which was satisfying on every level and gave them much pleasure.

There was one thing which troubled him these days and this was a slight slowing in his sexual drive. She was fifteen years younger than he was, and full of energy, and occasionally now he could not keep up with her. It constantly worried him.

However, earlier tonight he had been like his old self, the raging bull, her Toro. Forceful, passionate, more demanding than ever, and remarkable in his staying power, better than ever.

He had been thrilled that his strength and vigor had suddenly returned, and she had praised him, stroked his ego, and he was loving and tender after their four-hour marathon in this bed.

She had resorted to a trick to work this magic, but thankfully she had succeeded, and she would continue to use it again and again. If that proved necessary. It was simple enough. A crushed Viagra in his Bellini, which contained more peach juice than champagne. But he must never know this about the little pill. It would infuriate him if he did.

Elizabeth glanced at the empty flute by the bed and instantly got up, took the glass to the kitchen, rinsed it thoroughly, and put it away.

He caught hold of her when she returned to the bedroom, pressed her close to him as he ended his phone call. She was as tall as he was, and they were eyeball to eyeball as they looked at each other. She smiled slightly, and so did he, and she untied his silk dressing gown, opened her kimono, and stepped into his arms. She rubbed her body against his, and he reached for one of her breasts, stroked it lovingly, cupped it in his hand. He had always been excited by her voluptuousness, her mane of red hair, and her honey-colored eyes. "Golden eyes," he called them.

"We must stop this," he suddenly said, stepping back, shaking his head, holding her away from him. "Rafael is waiting for us at the restaurant. We must go. *Now.*"

She stared at him, understood that he meant it, and nodded. "Five minutes to put on makeup and clothes."

"No makeup. *You* don't need it. Throw on a skirt and blouse and let's get going. He's already ordering the wine, if I know him."

Within minutes she was dressed in a navy cotton skirt, a white shirt, and high-wedge espadrilles. After brushing her hair and spraying on perfume, she mingled two pashminas together, one lime green and one red, flung them around her shoulders, and grabbed her purse.

"I'm ready, Toro," she said and stood waiting at the bedroom door as he slipped on a navy-blue blazer over a white T-shirt and white pants.

"We're the best team," he announced, and took hold of her arm and guided her through the front hall of the flat and down three flights of stairs to the street.

Elizabeth loved living close to water, and she was glad she had chosen this flat overlooking the port. He, too, enjoyed being near the sea, and they were also in walking distance of all manner of restaurants situated around the harbor.

It was a nice evening, mild, with only a light breeze blowing off the sea. Elizabeth clung to his arm as they walked toward the port, enjoying the fresh air. At one moment she looked up and gasped. The full moon was as bright as the sun almost, a gigantic silver orb in the star-filled sky.

"What a night!" she exclaimed, glancing at him.

He leaned into her and kissed her cheek. "What a night indeed," he agreed. "I hate to be boastful, but I've never been better, have I?"

"No, you haven't. You're my raging bull more than ever, Toro. But I wasn't so bad either, was I? Certainly I met all your demands, and with immense enthusiasm, I might add."

"You did! You always do. With you I'm always at my macho best, Elizabeth, you're just incredible in bed."

"Do I satisfy you, do I please you? Do I, Toro?"

"You know you do." He glanced at her, frowning.

"More than your wife?"

"Come on, let's not go there. You've always known I don't have a great sex life at home."

"And my sister? Am I better than she was?"

For a moment he was struck dumb, and stopped abruptly, turned to look at her, the frown in place again. "Let's not go there either. But the answer is *yes*. Okay?"

She simply smiled at him and linked her arm in his again, and then walked on in silence until they came to the seafood restaurant which was their favorite.

Within a few seconds they were being shown to the table where Rafael Lopez was sitting. He rose when he saw them approaching, beaming at his partner and that beautiful mistress of his who was so ripe, voluptuous, and sexy. Rafael's mouth watered every time he set eyes on her.

"Elizabeth!" Rafael exclaimed. "More beautiful than ever. It is good to see you again."

"And you, Rafael," Elizabeth replied, sitting down in one of the chairs.

Rafael grinned at his partner and friend of twenty-five years, and the two men embraced, showing their affection for each other, then sat down on chairs on each side of Elizabeth.

"I've ordered a good red, your favorite, Marius," Rafael said. "And we've much to celebrate tonight. I have sold the Picasso which we have been so carefully treasuring for the last few years. I closed the transaction verbally this afternoon."

Marius Remmington was completely taken aback, stunned, in fact, and he literally gaped at the Spanish art dealer who mostly operated out of Madrid. Finally, he asked, "But why didn't you tell me on the phone?"

"Because I wanted to see the surprise on your face when I made the announcement. Are you not happy, Marius?"

"Ecstatic. Give me all the details, won't you?"

In answer to this request, Rafael took an envelope out of his pocket and handed it to Marius, who opened it, glanced at it, then put it away in his pocket. "Well done, my friend.

Very well done indeed. Did we break a record with this amazing price? I suspect we did."

"That is correct."

Elizabeth looked at Marius, asked, "How much did it go for?"

"Sixty-five million," Marius answered.

"*Pounds?*" She sounded incredulous, her face registering shock.

"No, no, dollars," Rafael answered before Marius could. "It was sold to an American. We dealt in dollars. Which he preferred. If I had pushed harder, possibly I could have perhaps got him up. However, I realized he was growing edgy. I did not wish to lose the sale. And I do prefer the private sale, so much easier in many different ways."

"That it is," Marius agreed. He picked up his glass, which had just been filled with red wine. "Here's to you, Rafael. You never cease to amaze and surprise me, and usually in the very best way."

The two men touched glasses, and then Elizabeth's, who said, "Cheers! And congratulations, chaps. This is definitely going to be a celebratory dinner."

"We'd better order," Marius said, and glanced at his watch. It was already one-thirty in the morning, and he realized, suddenly, that he was starving.

"I have ordered already," Rafael announced, and winked at Marius. "It occurred to me you must have been rather preoccupied with other matters since your arrival from London."

"Very true, and I am hungry. I suppose you've ordered the usual?"

"Fresh mussels steamed in white wine, a large grilled whitefish, and fresh vegetables. Antonio assured me the mussels will come in a moment or two."

Marius nodded and leaned back in the chair, letting the news of Rafael's sale sink in. He was still somewhat startled that his partner had pulled off this truly big deal, but then Picasso had become popular again, and lately his paintings were suddenly going for huge sums of money. He and Rafael had acquired the Picasso almost seven years ago, and had stored it in Madrid until prices went up. It had only been on offer in the last year.

The Picasso had impeccable lineage and a watertight provenance. It had been acquired by Paul Rosenberg, the famous New York dealer, from Picasso himself in 1936. Rosenberg, one of the finest dealers in the world, had kept it for years, then later sold it to a couple in Pasadena, who thirty years later had given it to their daughter. It was this woman's daughter who had sold it to them. They believed it to be one of the artist's best works, executed by Picasso during one of the high points in his extraordinary career.

The last time Marius had been in Barcelona, doing research for his book on Picasso, Rafael had flown in from Madrid so that Marius could introduce him to Jimmy Musgrave, a new American client. Later on, Musgrave had sent his brother-in-law to see Rafael once he had returned to Madrid. It was through this man that Thomas Wilmott had been offered the Picasso some nine months ago. He had turned it down, but today Wilmott's business partner had bought it for the exact price they had hoped to get.

Marius and Rafael had worked well together for twenty-five years, had never quarreled or had a cross word between them, something unheard of, to his way of thinking.

His thoughts went to London . . . and to Annette.

These new fakes showing up yesterday in the Delaware collection truly alarmed him, although he had endeavored not to reveal his worry about this when speaking to her earlier. He couldn't help wondering exactly where they were coming from.

Rafael said, "How long are you staying in Barcelona, Marius?"

"Four or five days, and then we're going to Provence, primarily to Vallauris and then onto Aix-en-Provence. I want to visit some of Picasso's favorite haunts in the south of France, where he lived in the fifties and sixties. Until the end of his life, in actuality."

"He died in 1973," Rafael said. "And several homes have become . . . shrines."

Elizabeth exclaimed, "I didn't know I was coming with you to France! I'm not sure that I can."

"Of course you can. I won't take no for an answer," Marius said in a sharp voice. "I need you with me."

Elizabeth nodded, made no further comment.

She knew better than to argue with him when he had made up his mind, most especially in front of Rafael, who worshiped at the feet of the great Marius Remmington.

So did she in her own way, although at times she regretted that she had succumbed to his various charms. He was the bossiest man she had ever met. Not only that, he was manipulative and controlling, and these traits in him genuinely annoyed her. She was an independent kind of woman who could think for herself, had never liked a man telling her what to do.

"You've grown very quiet," Marius suddenly said, staring hard at her, frowning, looking displeased.

She stared back. "I was just trying to rearrange my schedule in my head," she improvised. "So that I can come with you to Provence."

He conveyed his pleasure by taking her hand in his and kissing it. "You're going to be glad you made that decision," he told her. "You wait and see."

Chapter Thirty-two

❋

To cut to the chase, Annette, you know for sure that two more paintings in the Delaware collection are fakes," Malcolm Stevens said.

Staring at her across the lunch table at the Ritz Hotel, he went on, "The Manet with the veiled hat and the Cézanne with the red roofs. Too bad, very disappointing, and also something we must all keep buried deep. You can't afford to have doubt cast on the overall collection. Otherwise you'll be in serious trouble."

"I know," Annette responded. "I'm aware of all the pitfalls."

"You said you also have doubts about the authenticity of the Degas ballet dancer," he murmured, his expression glum, his eyes worried.

"Yes, I do, Malcolm."

He was silent, just shook his head.

"When will you know for certain?" Laurie asked.

"Hopefully early next week." Leaning closer to her sister, Annette continued, "Carlton has the painting, as I told you on the phone. He'll see you any time you want to go there tomorrow. Once you have studied the Degas ballet dancer, he will make tests of the canvas and the paint, to see what they reveal about their age. We just have to be patient."

"I understand," Laurie replied. "But *you* don't think the Degas is right, do you? You feel it's wrong. Why is that, Annette?"

Her sister shook her head. "I don't want to set you up, influence you in any way. I want you to go and look at it cold, without any input from me. I trust your judgment, Laurie darling, but Carlton will have the last say. Remember, we can't argue with paint and canvas, no one can. That's the true test."

"It's unbelievable, the tricks forgers get up to," Malcolm volunteered, taking a sip of the white wine he had ordered for their Sunday lunch in the dining room at the lovely old hotel overlooking Green Park. "Rubbing dirt into canvases, or soaking them in coffee and strong tea, buying old nondescript Victorian and Edwardian paintings and cleaning the canvases, then using them on which to paint forgeries of great art."

"And reusing old *frames* from nondescript paintings," Laurie pointed out. "It's amazing the effects that can be created, how simple it is to make a fake. It was a bit foolish, though, for someone to copy a Cézanne auctioned in the last two years, and a Manet that's hanging in a museum."

"But perhaps the forger didn't know this, didn't have that information," Annette suggested. "Also, these forgeries Christopher just found in the collection might be old, could date back twenty years or even longer. Carlton did say he thought the other Cézanne with the soot on it had been painted about eighteen years ago."

"That's true, he did," Laurie murmured, and cut into a piece of roast lamb.

"I still wonder if that particular Cézanne was done by John Myatt." Malcolm gave Annette a hard stare. "And these others might have been painted by him as well. He was, and is, a brilliant painter."

"That's possible."

Malcolm chuckled, breaking the serious mood of the lunch. "Just imagine, Myatt's still painting, but now marks his paintings *Genuine Fakes* with an indelible inscription. I remember going to his first show. I think it was in 2000, after he'd served four months of his year's sentence in jail, and was out for good behavior. That show was an extraordinary success. He sold about fifty-five paintings, something like that, anyway. He was suddenly famous rather than infamous as a forger of great art."

"He and John Drewe were incredible together," Laurie said. "Don't you remember, when we read about it we marveled at the way they had fooled so many art dealers and their clients."

"Drewe was the brilliant schemer, and he also managed to forge provenances," Malcolm pointed out. "And he even conned the Tate Gallery. What a success they had whilst they lasted. A gallery owner once told me that now when a customer asks Myatt *not* to put the *Genuine Fakes* inscription on a painting he won't agree. He explains he's now legitimate."

"Whatever *happened* to John Drewe?" Laurie asked, looking across the table at Malcolm, a brow lifting.

"He's around, I suppose, but not often seen. He did serve about four years of his six-year sentence, as I recall. One thing I do know, forgeries are on the rise. I just recently read that the British market loses about two hundred million pounds a year because of fakes."

"Oh, my God, that's a lot of money!" Laurie cried, aghast.

"I remember reading about Drewe and Myatt," Annette said. "The press called their scam the greatest art fraud of the twentieth century. But there was also Elmyr de Hory, a Hungarian, who was also known as the greatest art forger of the twentieth century. He must have forged hundreds and hundreds of canvases in the fifties and sixties. He was another extremely talented painter who copied and was as brilliant as Myatt. Elmyr de Hory specialized in Picassos and Renoirs, as well as Matisses, Vlamincks, and Dufys. He had a career that lasted a very long time. Apparently, it was hard to tell the fake from the real thing. Even art experts were totally fooled."

"Sir Alec Delaware was fooled," Malcolm said. "He bought a number of forgeries, without realizing what they were, of course. I feel certain of that."

"A lot of art collectors do get fooled." Annette gave Malcolm a knowing look. "That's why it's so important for collectors to use an expert art historian. But not all do, and there are a lot of fakes hanging on walls in the homes of the rich, who have been cleverly conned into buying forgeries." She sighed. "Christopher Delaware is more upset about the fakes than happy about the real paintings. I pointed out to him that he is now the owner of a Cézanne, a Pissarro, and a Manet which are genuine, and which he didn't know he had, and that he should be happy, joyful, about it."

"Yes, he should," Laurie agreed. "I don't know if you know this, Annette, but Degas asked his dealer Paul Durand-Ruel to bid on some of Manet's works after his death. Degas bought the painting *Berthe Morisot with a Veil*, which was painted in 1872."

"Good heavens, that's the beginning of some provenance!" Malcolm exclaimed. "That's something I didn't know."

"And it's with the real painting in the Musée du Petit Palais in Geneva," Annette was quick to point out in a pithy tone.

Malcolm and Laurie laughed.

Annette went on, "Enough of all this stuff about fakes and forgeries. Let's get to your wedding. What about the different venues you were considering? Did the brochures tell you anything? Have you found a venue you like yet?"

"No, to all your questions," Laurie answered. "And we might have everything in London, after all. The wedding and the reception."

Malcolm nodded. "We haven't picked a date as of this moment, but we're thinking of July and—"

"Because I want to wear a beautiful wedding dress," Laurie interjected. "I don't want to look *too* pregnant."

"I don't blame you," her sister said, giving her a warm smile, glad to see the genuine happiness on Laurie's face.

"And neither do I," Malcolm added, his eyes filled with total love and adoration for Laurie. "In fact, I insist on a fabulous gown."

Laurie exclaimed, "Gosh, I forgot to tell you! What with all this talk of fakes it went out of my head, Annette. Jack Chalmers called me this morning. To ask a few questions."

Annette stiffened in the chair and stared at her sister. "What did he ask you?"

"Fairly mundane questions, actually. What were your own paintings like? What were Daddy's paintings like? Did I think our father's paintings influenced you? And a few questions about *our* relationship, yours and mine. It was easy, and he was very nice, charming, and the whole thing lasted about twenty minutes."

Annette merely nodded, and sat back in her chair, filled with relief that Jack had finally spoken to Laurie.

All of the interviews were now finished, and he had mentioned last night that he thought he had enough material for the New York piece. Even so, she knew he would want to continue seeing her. He was in her life, and she didn't know how to get him out. And did she want to?

Picking up her glass, she sipped the white wine, and went on talking about the wedding, and their marriage plans in general, pushing thoughts of Jack to the back of her mind. He spelled trouble.

Later that afternoon, Annette stood looking down at the pieces of paper placed on the dining room table, filled with frustration. She had laid everything out that morning, before going to lunch at the Ritz, and had spent an hour going over them before leaving.

There was nothing. *Nothing at all.* Bills, yes, but not for paintings; letters from galleries with nothing definitive about paintings; no provenances, and certainly not much pertaining to the art collection.

The briefcase and the two filing cabinets had not produced one thing which was of value to her. She continued to marvel at the mess left behind by Sir Alec, the business tycoon. It seemed so out of character. Unexpectedly, she wondered if someone had rifled through the papers before her. Mrs. Joules? If so, why? And why was she so suspicious of the housekeeper? Annette had no idea. What motive could the housekeeper possibly have? None that Annette could think of, but suspicion of Mrs. Joules lingered. The woman worried her.

Tired, she turned away from the table laden with paper, went into her dressing room, took off her trouser suit, and slipped into a robe. She then went to rest on the bed. Drowsiness soon overwhelmed her. It's the wine, she thought, as she began to doze, thoughts of Jack Chalmers floating around in her head as she fell asleep.

"Where are you taking me to supper?" Annette asked, turning her head to observe him, thinking how handsome he looked in the black sweater and jeans and a red scarf around his neck. *And young.*

She buried the thought of their age difference, settled back in the car seat, emptying her head of all her troubling thoughts.

"It's a surprise," he answered, glancing at her quickly, a faint smile on his mouth. "And also a . . . *celebration.*"

"*Oh.* Of what?"

"I've finished the profile of you, and I think you'll like it. Actually, I'm sure you will. I'll be surprised if you don't. So I want to celebrate."

"Then we shall. When is the piece appearing?" Annette asked, although she didn't want to read it. What if she didn't like it? Then what?

"This coming Sunday," he answered.

"So quickly! Gosh, I didn't realize. And now I know why you were so anxious to get it finished."

He merely smiled, then said, "By the way, I spoke to your sister earlier, but no doubt she told you that."

"Yes, she did. Her fiancé took us to lunch at the Ritz, and she mentioned it in passing."

"She's going to see Carlton tomorrow, isn't she? To look at the Degas ballet dancer," Jack asserted.

"That's right, and no matter what her opinion is, Carlton is going to test the canvas, because there is no provenance for the painting. Her opinion and mine, and *his* actually, really don't count. It's the age of the canvas and the paint that are important."

"I understand. But I'll tell you something, Annette, I never realized that a forged painting could be so good. I was really startled by that. I've been wondering if there might not be a good magazine piece on art and crime, fakes, that kind of thing."

"Possibly. If you want to write about forgery, I can point you in the right direction, send you to see the people who could be of help, who know a lot more than I do."

"What about Scotland Yard? Are there any special kinds of . . . well, police divisions that deal with crimes like that?"

"As a matter of fact, there is one division. It's called the Art and Antiques Squad, and they investigate forged paintings, fakes, the people involved with the forgeries. They helped to bring down John Drewe, who was eventually prosecuted and sent to jail."

"Tell me something about him, will you?" he asked as he drove on, heading in the direction of Hampstead and hoping she might not notice this if she was involved in a complicated conversation.

Annette began to tell him the story of John Drewe, an eccentric, even talented, man who had masterminded a scheme to have an artist forge paintings by great painters for him to sell to unsuspecting galleries. Jack listened attentively, letting her speak at length without stopping the flow of her words by asking her questions.

By the time Annette had finished telling him everything she knew about John Drewe, she realized they were heading away from the West End, and that they were, in fact, driving in the direction of Hampstead Heath.

Swiveling in the seat, staring at him, she exclaimed, "Are we going to check your father's house before going to supper? Are we eating in that area, Jack?"

"As a matter of fact, we are," he replied, his voice and manner genial. "But I must check on the boiler, see that all is okay before we have dinner."

"But I thought you turned the boiler off," she responded, a frown on her face.

"Yes, yes, I did. I have to check out things in general, you know," he lied, hoping she bought this story but not really caring, since once they arrived and she went into the house she would be captivated.

He stifled a yawn, promptly sat up straighter at the wheel. He had been up most of the night, writing the profile about her. He had slept for several hours, then made a large fried-egg sandwich and also a bacon butty for breakfast. Replenished by food, he had gone shopping, then driven up to the house in Hampstead, made his preparations, and left.

Once back at his flat in Primrose Hill, Jack had slept again, later showered and shaved, then reread his story about her. He had finally dressed in a pair of jeans and sweater, thrown a scarf around his neck, and gone to fetch her a short while ago.

Sneaking a quick look at her, he said, "You were so strange when I spoke to you on the phone this afternoon. I thought you'd turn me down, get out of our date."

"*Strange?* If I was, I didn't mean to be. . . . I'm not sure I know what you're getting at," Annette said, sounding puzzled.

"When I said, 'I'm coming to get you,' you caught your breath and didn't answer. I had to repeat myself."

"I was a little taken aback I guess. You said it so forcefully. . . . I'M COMING TO GET YOU. . . . It was like Genghis Khan telling me he was coming down from the hills, to capture me and take me back to his lair."

Jack threw back his head and laughed gleefully. "Genghis Khan indeed!"

"You sounded very macho, that's all," she murmured, and wondered what he had planned for the evening. Something special, she decided. A shiver ran through her, and she pushed the panic down inside her. It seemed to her there was no going back now. They were set on a course that somehow was inevitable . . . and dangerous.

Chapter Thirty-three

✳

Annette stood on the top step of his father's house, where Jack had instructed her to wait, and she couldn't help wondering what this was all about. She turned the knob, but the door had automatically locked behind him when he had gone inside.

A split second later the front door suddenly opened and Jack came out. He took hold of her hand and led her into the house without saying a word. He walked her through the hall and into the living room, and after kissing her lightly on the cheek, he said, "I'll be back in a minute," and disappeared. She heard his footsteps retreating down the corridor in the direction of the kitchen.

Slowly she turned, her eyes roaming around the room; she found herself marveling at its transformation. Candlelight and flames from the fire mingled to create a rosy glow. Logs crackled in the hearth behind a firescreen, votives in small glass pots were lined up along the mantel shelf, and tall crystal candlesticks, holding long white tapers, stood on the antique chests supposedly from his mother's junk shop. On each chest a vase of pink roses had been placed between the candlesticks, and there were pink roses in a bowl on the glass coffee table in front of a sofa. The latter, which had miraculously appeared from somewhere overnight, had been filled with plump cushions.

Annette looked across the room, where a small table and

two chairs were standing near the French doors leading into the garden. She noticed that the table was covered in a white cloth, and had been set for dinner for two. Along with the table silverware there was a single pink rose in a bud vase, and also a candle in a silver stick as yet unlit. The living room, half empty and somewhat desolate-looking before, had been given new life and a special kind of beauty.

He had done all this at some point during his busy day of writing. And it was for her. She was so touched her eyes filled with tears; then she understood, at this precise moment, that he was in deadly earnest about her, and she was afraid.

She was already emotionally involved with him, even though nothing had yet happened between them, other than a kiss. To become further enmeshed would be dangerous, had to be avoided at all cost. Could she avoid it? Did she really want to walk away?

A cold chill swept over her as she realized how terrible the repercussions would be if Marius found out about them. She fully understood that her life would change drastically. It would be the end of everything for her. *She must leave this house now.* Whilst there was still time. She must flee at once.

She took a step forward, found her legs would hardly move; she was almost but not quite rooted to the spot. Turned to stone. Or a pillar of salt.

Taking a deep breath, Annette forced herself to walk toward the arched entrance leading into the hall, where Jack suddenly appeared before her. He was carrying a bottle of champagne and two crystal flutes, that wide, endearing smile flashing on his face.

"Could you take these?" he asked, thrusting the glasses at her. She simply nodded, accepted them from him, and followed him back into the living room.

After placing the bottle of champagne on the coffee table, Jack said, "Can I have the flutes, Annette, please?"

"Yes, of course," she answered, her voice suddenly husky.

After putting the glasses in front of him on the coffee table, she sat down on the sofa, not knowing what else to do, understanding that she was lost. And she couldn't help wondering if one night with him was worth the inevitable chaos that was bound to erupt. . . .

"Why are you looking so troubled?" he asked as he poured the champagne into the crystal flutes.

"I didn't know I was," she answered swiftly, and took the glass of champagne he was offering her.

After pouring one for himself, he joined her on the sofa, touched his glass to hers, and said, "Welcome again to my family home. I do hope you can feel the love here. . . . It still lingers, at least so I believe. It seeps into the walls, you know. . . . There's a loving atmosphere. It was always a happy house."

She smiled at him, staring into those clear, very candid gray eyes, and finally accepted that she had fallen in love with him, just as he had with her. There was no going back, was there? She had to see this through, be with him here. She could not flee. . . . She knew she would regret it if she did. At least I can have tonight, she thought. This one night. And then it will have to end. It must end. Marius will never let me go. And if I leave him he will punish me. He will ruin my life, that is one thing I am certain of, know to be the absolute truth.

After taking a sip of the champagne, Annette finally answered Jack. "Yes, I *can* feel the love here, and the warmth and the happiness." She looked deeply into his eyes, and said softly, "Thank you for this—" She broke off and looked around. "For making the room so beautiful . . . the flowers, the candles, the fire, everything. I'm very touched, Jack."

"I'm glad about that. You see, I wanted to be alone with you, close to you, and I suddenly decided we should have a picnic here, and we will later. I have dinner for us, you know."

She smiled at him. "Jack, you're such a romantic, aren't you?"

He just laughed, looking pleased and happy, and took a swallow of the champagne.

Annette said, "It must have been wonderful growing up

here. It's such a beautiful old place. One day I think I'd rather like to have a house . . . one just like this."

His eyes narrowed slightly, as he asked, "Would you really? Would you like to own this one? I can easily buy my brother out; and you and I could live here happily ever after. How does that sound?"

If only, she thought, but said, "Oh, Jack, what a lovely thing to say, but you know that's not possible. Not possible at all."

"Anything's possible if you want it enough," he replied, and placed the flute of champagne on the coffee table. After a moment he said, "There's something I need to tell you, Annette."

He sounded so serious she was startled. "What is it? Is there something wrong?"

"No, no, not at all. I just want you to know that for the past year, on and off, I've been involved with a woman. Her name is Lucy Jameson and she lives in an old farmhouse in the hills above Beaulieu. In fact, she's the chef I mentioned, the one I taught to make an English trifle."

"Jack, please, I don't need to know about this—"

"Yes, you do," he interrupted. "Listen, since I've been in London I've been preoccupied with work, as you well know. So much so, I haven't been in touch with her very much. In any case, I've always been somewhat ambivalent about her, about us together, as she has been about me. Now I know the reason why."

"And what is that reason?"

"I'm not in love with her, and I never was. And there's no way I can have a permanent relationship with a woman I'm not in love with. So I'm going to break it off with her. I must. It would not be fair otherwise."

"So what kind of a relationship was it?" she asked, as usual filled with curiosity about him and his life. And suddenly filling with unexpected jealousy about this unknown woman, Lucy. She was aghast at herself, and sipped the champagne quickly, wishing she hadn't asked him such a stupid question. She felt like a fool.

Jack said, "It was a friendship mostly, also companionship, and I liked her. Actually, I still like her. That hasn't changed."

"Did you sleep with her? That's obviously a silly question, you must have."

He glanced at her quickly, and nodded. "Yes, of course I did. But that's not enough, sex, I mean. There's got to be a lot more in a relationship if it's going to work. . . . I just didn't love her. And now I know that. Because I'm in love with you, and my feelings are overwhelming. Having the comparison makes for the truth."

"Jack, please don't talk like this. You hardly know me, or anything about me really. And there's one other important thing. An enormous impediment. I'm married."

"That I'm only too well aware of . . . Look, I want you to understand something, and it's this. I've never poached another man's woman before. I just fell in love with you the first moment I met you, and I can't help the way I feel. Also, I believe you share my feelings. Please don't say you don't, because you do."

She was silent, sat staring at him helplessly, mesmerized by him once again. He leaned into her, took her glass away. Moving closer to her, he put his arm around her shoulders, bent into her, and kissed her fully on the mouth.

She wanted to push him away, escape while it was still safe. But she found she could not. Instead she kissed him back, responding to his desire for her with the same passion and ardor he was showing. After a while they drew apart and looked at each other, and he touched her cheek with one finger and then kissed her gently on the forehead.

Jack rose, pulled her to her feet. Against her hair, he murmured, "Please come with me . . . to my old room."

"Jack, no! We can't! We mustn't do this! It can only lead to heartache. Trouble."

"Please, Annette. *Please*."

She did not answer. She just stood there staring at him, frozen in front of him, so terribly frightened she could not move.

* * *

The light was dim.

She stood there in the middle of the room, perfectly still, filled with dread. How had she gotten here? Jack had led her upstairs, of course, slowly, gently, coaxing her, persuading her, guiding her up the staircase as if she were a fragile thing about to break, his arm around her waist.

And so here she was. Finally. Standing in the room where he had grown up. Familiar to him but not to her. But he himself was familiar after the time they'd spent together.

She trusted him. There was something about him that made her feel safe. And yet she was frightened . . . not only of the future but of what was going to happen next. Between the two of them. She endeavored to push the dread away, keep panic at bay, but was not very successful.

"It's better with the curtains open," he said, startling her, making her jump nervously. She had been so concentrated on her own thoughts and her apprehension that she had been in a kind of trance. Momentarily.

"What do you mean?" she asked, her voice taut, sounding huskier than ever. It was her nervousness; she was aware of that.

"With the curtains open you can see the tops of the trees in the garden, and the sky above. The stars and the moon. When I was a little boy I used to lie in bed, staring at the sky sometimes. . . ." His voice trailed off, and he opened the draperies covering the third and last window in the room.

He swung around, staring at her for a split second, and then he walked over to her, took her hand in his, and drew her over to the windows.

"It's a beautiful night, darling, isn't it?" he said. "A night for us to be together at last."

She ignored his comment, but she had no option but to look out the window, and when she saw that he was right about the view, she said, "It is, yes."

Unexpectedly she felt awkward, and was surprised at herself. Until this moment she had been so at ease with him, as if she knew him, had known him for years. There was an odd feeling of familiarity about him at times, and especially tonight. In the way he said something, or moved his hands when speaking, walked alongside her, and something about his gait stirred a memory in her head and was immediately gone.

He took hold of her shoulders, drew her closer, kissed her lightly on the mouth, and began to open the buttons on her white silk shirt. She stood there and let him do it, didn't move an inch. But she cringed when he slipped it over her shoulders, took it off. She gaped at him, her eyes riveted on his face.

Jack gave her a soft smile, and brought her into his arms. "You seem so afraid, Annette. Please don't be. I'm not going to hurt you."

"I didn't think you were," she whispered, and didn't say another word as he unzipped her skirt. It fell around her feet. She stepped over it and moved away from him then, turned around, waiting for him to join her near the bed.

In a moment he was by her side. He held her close once again, touching her shoulders, sliding his hand down her back, opening the fastening on her bra. And before she could even blink, he was pulling off his sweater, sliding out of his jeans.

A moment later they were both naked, lying on the bed together. She closed her eyes and did not move, shaking inside. She knew she was rigid next to him, but she couldn't help it, and there was nothing she could do about it.

Jack was fully aware how taut Annette was beside him, and he suspected she had never had an enjoyable sex life. He was not in possession of any knowledge about her marriage, or her life before that, but he did know women. And he was certain she had been damaged somewhere along the way. He wondered quite suddenly if she had been abused as a child, and then let the thought go. It was up to him to make her feel secure, to treat her tenderly, to give her pleasure, to love her as she deserved.

Leaning over her, he kissed her nose, her eyelids, her

forehead; then he began to stroke her shoulders and her arms, let his hands wander down onto her legs.

She moved slightly, and he realized she was beginning to relax. Kissing her on the mouth once more, he touched her face and her hair tenderly, and in between his kisses, he whispered to her. "It's all right, darling, we'll go slowly, we'll take it one step at a time. . . . No hurry . . . Just let your body go limp, relaxed. Annette, let me help you."

She opened her eyes suddenly and stared up at him, and he felt his heart tighten. Her eyes were so blue at this moment he was truly startled, felt as though he were drowning in their blueness.

She lifted her hand, touched his mouth, and then brought his face down to hers. They kissed for a long time, the kisses growing in passion. There was a moment of true intimacy when his tongue grazed hers, and she kissed him back in the same way, allowed her tongue to rest next to his.

Annette realized her taut body had begun to respond to his caresses. She became aware of a lovely lassitude in her limbs, and slowly her entire body grew soft, open, and welcoming.

Jack felt her flinch when his hand touched her inner thigh, but he ignored this, began to caress her intimately yet tenderly. He increased the pressure until she spasmed, moaning. Before he could stop himself he took possession of her; he lay on top of her, his arms around her, and she accepted him willingly and they found their rhythm instantly. "You're wonderful," he said against her breast, and she murmured, "So are you."

After that they grew silent, concentrating on each other, caught up in their mutual desire. Repressed for days, they were finding release at last, thrilled by the way they had so quickly become lovers tonight.

Annette was amazed at herself, at her joyous and willing responses to Jack and everything he was doing to her, and at her awareness of her own pleasure. He had rapidly brought her to a climax just by touching her; now as they moved together furiously, invading each other's bodies, devouring, taking, giving, she accepted that she had entered a different world. It was an extraordinary world of sexual fulfillment, one she had never previously known before. She had never felt like this. Nor had she ever been loved like Jack was loving her now.

Unexpectedly, he tightened his arms around her, lifting her slightly, and they soared together, higher and higher, reaching a plane of pure ecstasy. As they came together he said her name over and over. She called out his, which she had never done before with anyone. Always, she had been mute.

Jack held her in his arms for a long time, not moving, lying on top of her, breathing against her neck. At last he said, "Am I too heavy?"

"No, no," she murmured quietly, stroking his back.

Eventually he rolled off her, then pushed himself up on one elbow, looked down into her face. "Are you all right?" he asked in the gentlest of voices, searching her face for signs of displeasure.

She did not answer, just stared up at him. Tears began to seep out of her eyes, rolled down her cheeks.

Alarmed, he came closer to her, flicked the tears away with a fingertip. "Whatever is it? What's wrong?"

"Nothing." She gave him a weak smile. "I've never made love like that before, never had this kind of pleasure."

"You won't believe this, I know, but this was a rather unique experience for me, too. It's never been quite like it was with you tonight." He kissed her cheek, and that endearing smile flickered. "I think it's called being in love. Not that I'm diminishing the extraordinary power of sexual attraction. That works, too, but when there is boundless emotion involved it's . . . just different, that's all. Infinitely better."

He insisted on serving her dinner, refusing her help.

Once they were dressed and downstairs again, they drank a glass of champagne before Jack escorted her to the small table near the French doors.

After lighting the lone candle on the table, he touched her shoulder lightly. "The first course is—"

"You mean there's more than one?" she interrupted, laughing.

"Naturally. What do you think I am? A cheap date? I have smoked salmon, but if that's not to your taste, I can offer you caviar, madame."

"Smoked salmon's fine, thank you."

"Don't go away. I'll be back in a jiffy."

And he was. He returned with a bottle of chilled Pouilly-Fumé, filled their glasses with the white wine, put the cold bottle on the table, and departed.

Within seconds he was back with two plates of smoked salmon, decorated with wedges of lemon.

After putting the plates on the table, he sat down opposite her and said, "This is much better than going out to a restaurant, isn't it?"

Annette nodded, picked up her fork. For once in her life, she felt hungry, and began to eat the smoked salmon after squeezing the lemon on it. "This is good," she said, and looked across at him. "How did you manage to do all this, Jack? I'm absolutely amazed."

He grinned. "Speedy Gonzales, that's me!" He shrugged, lifting his glass of chilled white wine. "Here's to you, my darling Annette."

She touched her glass to his. "And to you, Jack." After taking a sip, she held his gaze. "Come on then, tell me how you managed to revamp this room and give it such a lovely look. And make dinner as well."

"All right, I will. First I went to Harrods and bought everything. The wine, the champagne, the food, the candles, the flowers. Then I came up here, and did my decorating. After that, I set the fire, made the next course we're going to have, and tidied up my bedroom. It took me about three hours, but it was worth it, wasn't it?"

"Yes. I was very touched you'd gone to so much trouble for me."

"My pleasure. I enjoyed doing it."

After finishing the smoked salmon, Annette sat back in her chair, regarding him quietly, thinking what a genuinely nice person he was, quite aside from his good looks and his talent as a writer.

"You're staring at me," he murmured after a moment or two, his head on one side as he studied her in return.

Not wanting to reveal what she was thinking, she said instead, "Where did the sofa come from? That's the one thing that genuinely puzzles me."

"It's always been in the room next door, my father's den. I had a devil of a job dragging it in here, I can tell you, but I managed somehow."

"And what about all this? The lovely china and silverware, the vases, and the sheets on the bed upstairs?"

"There's still a lot of small stuff like that in the house," he explained. "Aunt Helen, my mother's sister, is coming to pack everything and take it away, when she gets back from Canada next week. She's been visiting her son and his family. Kyle and I want her to have it."

"With all this shopping and decorating and what have you, when on earth did you find the time to write?"

"During the night," he replied. "I'd outlined the profile of you already, so that helped. I just sat down and wrote and wrote, until I finished early this morning. I had a few hours' sleep and then I went into action." He rose, picked up their empty plates. "Next course coming up. It's salad Niçoise. I'm sorry it's another cold dish, but I didn't know what else I could make, under the circumstances."

"Can I come and help?" she called after him.

"No way! I told you I'm serving you dinner."

She watched him go, and then turned in her chair, sat staring out of the window. There was a huge full moon again, and the lawn was bathed in its cool silver light as it had been yesterday. It was another beautiful night, with hundreds of stars in the sky, a light breeze rustling the trees, and a garden of great beauty that looked ethereal, magical.

Annette sighed, relaxing in the chair. She was truly at ease with Jack now. All of the tension and anxiety had dissolved, gone away. She was filled with a strange kind of joy which she had never experienced before. It was sexual fulfillment, and the giddy feeling of being in love, she was certain.

Time stood still. At least for tonight. They were encapsulated in their own little bubble. She knew it would burst. That was inevitable. Tomorrow, she thought. I'll deal with the problems tomorrow.

Chapter Thirty-four

✤

W hatever spa you went to this weekend, I want its name!" Esther exclaimed, staring at Annette. "I'm going to go there myself as fast as I can."

Annette started laughing. "I haven't been to a spa," she said. "I've been working most of the weekend, actually."

"You look pretty fantastic, whatever you've been doing," Esther responded, eyeing her appraisingly. "Your skin is beautiful, and so are you."

"Thanks for the lovely compliments, Esther." Leaning across the desk, Annette fixed her cool blue gaze on her assistant. "We've got a problem to contend with."

"What is it, boss? You sound worried."

"I am a bit. There's a new situation with the Delaware collection, and I don't want any leaks about it."

"How could there be leaks? And what about? Oh, God, you're concerned about Christopher Delaware, aren't you? I don't blame you. He's a loose cannon, in my opinion."

"You've pinpointed it as usual, Esther. He *is* a loose cannon, although he doesn't mean to be anything of the kind. He just has a bad habit of blurting things out. Without thinking."

"So what can he blurt out?" Esther sat back in the chair on the other side of Annette's desk and stared at her. "What's the new development?"

"There are two, possibly three, paintings in the collection which are forgeries, and we must absolutely keep this under wraps. We can't have leaks, which would be detrimental to my business. You know how gossipy the art world is, and the mere mention of the word *fake* in connection to the Delaware collection and Annette Remmington Fine Art would be disastrous. Even though I have nothing at all to do with the forgeries showing up, I'd somehow get smeared. You know how it is. People make assumptions, even invent things."

Esther grimaced. "I certainly do know. But do you mean there are two more forgeries plus the Cézanne with the soot covering parts of it, or has a new one popped up?"

"There are three more that were found, yes. Let me tell you about the weekend, and what happened."

Annette leaned back in her chair, carefully explained, in great detail, the events of Saturday and the discovery of the priest hole and its treasures as well as the fakes. She also told her about the Graham Sutherland watercolors.

When Annette had finished, Esther exclaimed, "How marvelous! It's a fantastic windfall. You can now revamp the next auction, can't you? Do what you really wanted to do originally."

"You're right. I can have an auction of the six Impressionist paintings, and one sculpture, Degas's *The Little Fourteen-Year-Old Dancer.* I will probably hold back the Giacometti, auction that later in the year, along with the Graham Sutherland paintings, which fit together better since they're all modern. But this collection of Impressionists is unique, now guarantees an important auction."

"Christopher must be over the moon about this," Esther said.

"I've discovered that Christopher's cup is always half empty, never half full. He's got a negative personality. . . . Nothing is ever right, there's always *something* wrong. He's a whiner and he's focusing on the fakes, not the windfall, as you call it."

"But surely you can caution him, warn him, insist he doesn't talk about the forgeries, which his uncle obviously bought. Can you explain how dangerous that would be?"

"I have already, and I believe he understands, especially

since I brought the word *money* into our discussion. However, I can't keep him under lock and key, or have him permanently by my side, and therefore there is always that risk, that he might say the wrong thing to somebody."

"I understand." Esther frowned, then stopped speaking as the office secretary opened the door, having just knocked on it, and said, "Mr. Jack Chalmers is in reception. He says he doesn't have an appointment with you, Annette, but that it's urgent he sees you."

"Thanks, Marilyn," Annette replied. "Tell him I'll see him in a moment."

The secretary nodded and closed the door.

Annette said, "It must be something to do with the profile he's writing."

Esther wondered why he hadn't simply phoned, but refrained from saying this. "I'd better go and get him, bring him in," she murmured, and stood up.

"I was supposed to see him Saturday to finish the interview," Annette volunteered. "And when the situation developed with the discovery in Kent, I asked Jack to come with me. We were able to do the balance of the interview on the way down, and on the drive back to London. In fact, he was very kind and transported the paintings in his car, which we took to Carlton."

"Oh, I see," Esther murmured, and hurried over to the door so that Annette wouldn't see the sudden expression of glee on her face. Now she understood why Annette looked so different. She had been with Jack Chalmers, who most definitely had designs on her. Esther was so pleased she was positively beaming when she walked into reception to greet the good-looking journalist.

A moment later Esther returned with Jack at her side, showed him into Annette's office, and closed the door behind her.

Smiling, Jack leaned against the door and beckoned for Annette to come to him. She hesitated only momentarily, and then walked across the room. "What's so urgent, Jack?" she asked in a low voice. "Why are you here?"

"I have a solution to your problem," he murmured softly, and pulled her into his arms, kissed her lightly on the mouth, nuzzled her neck. He whispered, "God, I've missed you so much, darling. All night, in fact."

Still clinging to him, her heart pounding, Annette whispered, "Why on earth are we leaning against this door?"

"To prevent anyone from opening it," he whispered back, and kissed her again. Then, eager to tell her why he was there, he let her go, and they walked across the room together. He took the chair Esther had just vacated, and she sat behind her desk.

Annette looked at him for a long moment, and finally asked, "Which problem do you have a solution for?" She finally smiled at him, her eyes loving. "I have so many."

"I know how worried you are about Christopher Delaware blabbing about the forgeries. Oh, by the way, any news from Laurie?"

"No, but she'll be calling me shortly. She went to see Carlton early this morning. I'm expecting to hear from her any moment."

"Good." Leaning forward, his strong gaze fixed on her face, he began to talk, the words rushing out of him. "You've got to get the jump on Christopher. You've led me to believe that the merest mention of forgeries could be damaging to you, that just being linked to them could be a black mark against you. And since you worry he might . . . let's say inadvertently talk about them, *you've* got to take control. Immediately."

"What do you mean get a jump on him? Take control? I'm not following you."

"You've got to make an announcement tomorrow or Wednesday. You must tell the world about the amazing discovery in a long-forgotten priest hole at Knowle Court. Reveal what's been discovered. Three fabulous Impressionist paintings, worth millions and millions, by Cézanne, Pissarro, and Manet. Play up those by Cézanne and Pissarro, the two different views of Louveciennes by these great artists working side by side. Talk about the Graham Sutherland paintings, also discovered in the room. Play them all up. Make no mention of any forgeries. If there are any questions about whether other paintings were found, be dismissive, fluff it off, just say that there were a couple of nondescript unimportant canvases by unknown artists. Making the announcement will do the trick. Christopher will immediately get caught up in the ballyhoo that will occur, because you know how to do that. And even he will see how idiotic it would be to talk about forgeries, when these valuable paintings are in play and the press is writing about his fantastic collection."

"It's brilliant, Jack! And you're brilliant. But it sounds as if you're suggesting I give a press conference. Are you?"

"I was, yes. That was the idea I had this morning as I was shaving, then dressing, getting ready to come and have lunch with you."

"Are we having lunch?"

"You betcha!"

"I don't think I want to have a press conference. Couldn't you write the story, Jack? After all, you went to Knowle Court with me. You were sort of, well, in on it, in a sense part of it. That would make the story better, wouldn't it?"

"Yes, it would, and I thought of that myself when I was in the cab coming here. But I didn't know how you'd feel. I certainly didn't want you to think that I'm trying to push myself into your world. Or worse, make money on you, even manipulate you. After all, you get enough of that, and—" He broke off, realizing what he had just said in the excitement of the moment.

He looked at her carefully. Her face had paled slightly, and there was an expression of surprise in her blue eyes. Or was it hurt? He cursed himself under his breath, and said gently, "Sorry about that, Annette."

"You must have been asking some very probing questions about me before writing the profile. And about Marius."

"No, I haven't," he protested. "I promise you. It's the truth, darling, and there must always be truth between us, no matter what. I did talk to a few people in the art world, said

I was writing a profile of you for *The Sunday Times*. Several of those people I spoke to mentioned that Marius was a bit of a Svengali, manipulative, controlling. I found this rather strange, since you're such a strong and independent woman."

She nodded, relaxed her taut body, believing him. After a moment, she said, with a light laugh, "Marius does think he knows what's best. For everyone, not just me."

"I understand. Look, I left my laptop outside in reception with my raincoat. Let me get it. You can read the profile on it if you want, although I did send it electronically to my editor at the paper before I left the flat."

"I trust you, Jack, honestly I do. And I *would* actually prefer you to write the story. But won't that interfere with your profile, since that hasn't appeared yet?"

"No, I don't think so. I could wait a week to write the news story, but I think it's better that it appears as fast as possible. Just in case our Chris gets a bit too chatty." Jack rose, walked over to the window, looked down into Bond Street, stood there thinking for a few moments.

Annette was focused on him, watching him, realizing what a wonderful profile he had. Suddenly it was there again, that flicker of a fleeting memory that was gone in an instant.

Walking back to the chair and sitting down, he said, "I'm going to phone the editor who edits my stuff for *The Sunday Times* a bit later. I want to tell him about what happened on Saturday. I think he'll suggest I write it for *The Times*, our daily paper. It can run before Sunday. With it they can reference my profile of you, coming up on Sunday. How does that sound?"

"Good to me, but you're the journalist. Just one question. If you do write the story for *The Times*, and they run it this week, will I have to speak to a lot of other journalists on the phone? I mean the rest of the press will hound me, won't they?"

"You might get some calls, yes, because every paper wants its own quote, wants to ask questions. But you can handle that, I'm sure. However, I'll make my story very comprehensive, cover everything I can think of, so there won't be too much fresh material for anyone else to probe for, okay?"

"All right then, let's go for it. When are you going to write the story, Jack?"

"Right now, if there's a spare desk somewhere here. After that I'll take you to lunch."

"And where will that be?"

"I thought about Le Caprice. It's in walking distance, and they make great fish cakes."

"It's such a public place," she said worriedly.

"I promise I'll behave myself."

"But we'll be seen together."

"What's wrong with that? I'm writing about you, I'm writing about your upcoming auction. A good cover. When is it, by the way?"

"In September. Sotheby's agreed to the date. I thought I'd told you."

"Yes, I think you did." He stood up. "Where can I sit for an hour or two, darling?"

"I'll take you to the little conference room. It's nice and quiet. And, Jack, please don't call me darling in front of anyone here, will you? *Please*."

"Of course not. Do you think I'm daft, or what?" He grinned at her, pulled her to him, and kissed her on the mouth.

Annette extricated herself quickly, and shook her head when he made a glum face. "You're quite the actor, aren't you?"

"This is not an act. I hate it when you push me away."

"I'll make it up to you," she murmured.

"You can be certain I'll hold you to *that*," he said, and allowed himself to be propelled across the floor and out into the reception area.

Esther listened to Annette and then took charge of Jack, explaining that the conference room was a perfect place to write. As they walked off together down the corridor, she glanced at him surreptitiously, couldn't help thinking he looked like the cat that had swallowed the canary. Very well pleased. She smiled inwardly, hoping he and Annette would have a long friendship. But then that depended on Annette. The thought of Marius Remmington wiped the happy expression off Esther's face, filled her with unexpected worry.

Annette returned to her office and sat down, staring into space, thinking about Jack. He had come up with a clever idea; still, deep down she dreaded the thought of the press on her back. She was afraid they would dig into her past. So far they hadn't done so, but she still fretted about this.

Her private line began to ring, and she picked it up at once. "Hello?"

"It's me," her sister said. "I'm here with Carlton."

"What's the verdict?"

"I'm ninety percent sure the Degas dancer is a fake. In fact, I thought so at once. It has a certain crudeness about it, a roughness. It's not a copy of any Degas dancer I know of, though. I think somebody just tried to paint in his style, but did their own thing."

"You see it the same way I do, Laurie. At first glance you think, Oh, great, a Degas, and when you look again you're not certain. I assume Carlton is going to test the paint and canvas."

"Yes, of course. He needs to speak to you. Here he is."

"Hello, my darling girl," Carlton said. "Laurie spotted it straightaway, confirms what you thought originally. Look, to be absolutely sure, I would like to bring in Ted Underwood to examine it with me. Is this all right?"

"Absolutely. Do what you have to. Test everything, including the frame. I thought it looked like a bit of old molding, to be honest."

"I have a question for you, Annette, but I don't believe you can answer it."

"What is it?"

"What is Christopher going to do with these new forgeries? There are now three more showing up in the famous Delaware collection. Well, three if the Degas dancer is a bust. Don't you think they ought to be destroyed?"

"I do, but he hasn't destroyed the earlier Cézanne yet, at least not to my knowledge. I'll speak to him again."

"Very good. I'll be in touch within the next few days."

Laurie came back on the line and said, "Unless you need me for anything else, I'll go back home."

"Do that, darling, and we'll speak later."

"Big kiss," Laurie said, and hung up.

Annette sat for a long time, staring into space. Who had created these forgeries? Why had Sir Alec Delaware bought them? Had he been truly out of it when he did? Dementia? Everyone seemed to think he had become weird after his fiancée had committed suicide. Had *she* advised him, earlier on in their relationship? Annette compressed her mouth. It beggared belief that a man like Delaware had been duped.

On a sudden impulse, Annette buzzed Esther on the intercom and said, "Could you look up an artist in the various British painters reference books? Modern painters. By modern I actually mean contemporary."

"Yes. What name?" Esther asked.

"Clarissa Normandy," Annette answered. "The woman who was engaged to Sir Alec, then later killed herself."

"Give me two minutes," Esther said, and put down the phone.

Ten minutes later Esther hurried into Annette's office, explaining, "Sorry, it took longer than I thought it would. She's only listed in one, and then there's not much, only a few lines. She attended the Royal College of Art, showed great promise, but never made it as a famed artist before her so-called untimely death. Here, I made a couple of notes." Esther handed her the piece of paper.

Annette glanced at it and shrugged. She read aloud: "Born in Gloucestershire. Maiden name Lang. Oh, Normandy must have been her married name. Obviously divorced or a widow, since she became engaged to Sir Alec. You're absolutely correct, though; there's nothing to help us."

"Why did you think she could?"

"It occurred to me that she might have advised Sir Alec. I mean, why on earth did he spend good money on forgeries?"

"I guess because he didn't know they were."

"Only too true," Annette said, and then asked, "Are the Estrins scheduled to come in later this week?"

Esther nodded. "Yes. I put the appointment in your book. They're currently in Paris, but they'll be flying to London tomorrow."

"Very good, and thanks, Esther."

Two hours later, around one o'clock, Jack came into Annette's office, and beckoned to her. "Can you come to the conference room, where I'm set up, please?"

Annette rose, walked across the floor, asking, "Have you finished the story?"

"Yes, more or less. I had a few calls to make as well. I've got an okay on doing this piece for *The Times*. I don't usually do this, show my stories to anyone except my editors, but I'd like you to look it over. If the basics are correct, as far as you're concerned, and as I remember everything, then we're fine. I'll polish it first thing in the morning and send it electronically tomorrow, for Wednesday's paper."

"Are you usually this quick?" Annette asked, as they went to the conference room.

"Sometimes. I was writing from memory, not constantly checking notes, so it went pretty fast. Remember, this is a news story, and it's just the facts, ma'am."

Annette frowned. Those words rang a bell. Someone else had once said them to her. But who was it?

"Why the puzzled look?" Jack asked, staring at her.

"Those words seemed so familiar to me. *Just the facts, ma'am*, I mean."

"Oh, you're remembering the actor Jack Webb saying them. He played a detective called Joe Friday in an American television show called *Dragnet*, and he used to say, 'My name's Friday. I'm a cop. Just the facts, ma'am.'"

"I guess you're right," she agreed, and walked on with him. But she wasn't so sure he was right. But what did it matter? Her main concern was her secret past. She had buried it deep, prayed it would stay there. She shivered involuntarily. Fear was a strange thing. It came and grabbed you by the throat unexpectedly.

In the conference room, she sat down in front of his laptop and slowly read the story he had written about the events of last Saturday. It was good clean copy, no folderols, and everything was correct. "It's perfect, Jack. And what a good memory you have."

"Thank you." He stepped to the door, closed it, and came back to her, pulled her to her feet and took her in his arms. "Do you really want to go to Le Caprice? Shall we go to my flat and have a picnic?"

"Don't you want to be seen in public with me?" she shot back.

He laughed. "Damn right I do. Who wouldn't want you on his arm? Tonight I'll cook dinner for you in Primrose Hill."

"But, Jack, we can't—"

"No buts," he cut in, smiling at her.

Later that afternoon, when Jack arrived home, he went straight to his desk and dialed Lucy's number. The machine was on, and he left his name, asked her to call him, and hung up.

He had made up his mind days ago to be honest with her, play it straight. She deserved that. She was a decent woman and she had always been nice with him, and a phone call, nothing less, was the only way to handle the situation. To ignore her or send an e-mail would be shoddy behavior.

Opening his laptop, he was ready to start polishing the story about Annette and the newly found Impressionists when his landline rang. He grabbed the receiver. "It's Jack Chalmers."

"Hello, Jack, it's me, Lucy. How're you?"

"Pretty good, and you?"

"Busy with work, as I'm sure you are."

"I am, Luce, and I'm sorry I haven't called you. But I've had my hands full."

"When are you coming back to Beaulieu? Any time soon?"

"I'm not sure. I'm going to be stuck here for a bit longer, I think. Listen, Lucy, I've been thinking a lot about us lately, and, frankly, I don't believe we're going anyplace fast. Do you?"

There was a sudden silence at the other end.

He said, "I like you a lot, very much, and we've always been good together on certain levels. But I can't string you along. I think honesty is the best policy in life, especially between us, because we are good friends. And—"

"Are you breaking up with me, Jack? Is that what you're trying to say?" Lucy asked.

"Well, yes, I am."

She laughed and said at last, "I'm sorry, I'm not laughing at you, Jack, but at myself. I've been trying to get my courage up to speak to you about our relationship. Now you've done it, and set the record straight, and I don't have to do it after all."

"Are you telling me you were going to break up with me?"

"Yes, I am."

"Wow! Another man, is there?"

"No, there isn't."

"But you wanted to break up with me anyway?"

"Yes, that's right."

"But why?"

"Because I know that deep down you're still very ambivalent about us being together, Jack, in spite of the last time you were here at the farm, the things you said and did, our very romantic night in each other's arms."

He remained totally silent.

She suddenly exclaimed in a sharp tone, "Jack, you have to find yourself! Find out who you really are as a man. I don't think you will ever be able to truly love a woman until you do."

"I'm sorry, Lucy, truly sorry it's ending like this."

It was Lucy's turn to be silent; she said nothing.

"Can't we still be friends, though?" Jack asked quietly.

"I don't know. Maybe, maybe not. But frankly, I don't think so. Goodbye. Thanks for calling."

She had hung up on him before he could utter another word, and he immediately understood that she was furious with him. Also very hurt. He regretted hurting her, but he'd had no choice. He was in love with another woman.

Chapter Thirty-five

✴

Annette sat at her desk in her Bond Street office, making notes for the Estrins, the clients she would be seeing later, when her private line rang. As usual she picked it up on the second ring, and said, "Hello?"

"Hello, darling girl," Carlton Fraser answered in a low voice. "I'm afraid I have bad news for you."

"It's a fake, isn't it?" she asserted, having been convinced all along that there was something peculiar about the Degas ballet dancer.

"Yes, that's correct. Ted and I tested the paint yesterday, and it's definitely new paint, Annette. And a relatively new canvas, possibly eighteen years old, like the soot-covered Cézanne is."

"I wonder if the Degas was painted by the same artist? What do you think, Carlton? And Ted? What did he have to say?"

"Ted and I are not certain that the same person painted the Degas dancer and the first Cézanne landscape. The Cézanne is much truer to the real thing, and, let's face it, you were deceived by it, and frankly so was I. Ted and I believe it was a more experienced artist who executed the first Cézanne, the one ruined by the soot."

"And we've no way of knowing who, have we?"

"No. Unless it was the person who did the Manet of the woman in a veil, and the Cézanne called *The Red Roofs*. I tend to think it might be, mainly because the painter was so much better. Anyway, it could well be two forgers at work, you know."

"But eighteen years ago, right?"

"Approximately."

"Well, at least we know the truth now."

"When are you going to tell Christopher?"

"Not today, Carlton. He's enjoying all the glory at the moment, basking in the wonderful publicity about the Delaware collection, which is now *his*. I think we've managed to shut his mouth when it comes to idle and dangerous chatter."

"Oh, I'm certain of that! In the meantime, I really hope he's going to destroy the fakes he owns. You never know what can happen in life. For example, what if they were stolen, and then sold as the real thing? It's so risky keeping fakes around. Very dangerous in the long run."

"I know. I'll tackle him about it later, and insist they are slashed or burned. And by the way, thanks so much for letting us come up to the studio yesterday, and allowing the *Times* photographer to do the shoot there. Jack was very grateful, as was I."

"I was happy to oblige. And Jack wrote an excellent story. You're going to have a very big auction on your hands in September."

"I hope so, Carlton. And thanks again for doing the tests so quickly."

"I wanted you to have the information as fast as possible. Talk to you later." He hung up before she had a chance to say goodbye.

Annette immediately dialed Laurie and gave her the news, and then phoned Jack to fill him in. Her third call was to Malcolm Stevens. She wanted him to know about the Degas. After these phone calls she went to see Esther in her office across the corridor.

Knocking on the door, poking her head around it, Annette said, "I'm afraid it's a dud, Esther dear. Another forgery. Unfortunately."

"Damn and blast!" Esther exclaimed. "I was so hoping that this one was going to be genuine."

Annette heard the private phone ringing in her office, and ran to answer it. "Hello?" she said, sounding a little breathless as she grabbed the receiver.

"Have you gone mad?" Marius bellowed at the other end of the line. "Releasing this story *now* about the discovery of the three Impressionists is absolutely ridiculous! Fucking insane, if you ask me."

Annette was so startled by his angry tone and bad language, she was speechless for a moment. Taking a deep breath, she finally answered him. She said in a steady voice, "What's got into *you* this morning? You sound like a raging bull, screaming down the phone in this manner. And it is *not* ridiculous. It makes perfect sense. It's good advance publicity for the auction and—"

"It's only April, for God's sake! And why didn't you tell me you were going to do it? You always keep me informed, use me as a sounding board. You should have spoken to me, tapped into my experience."

"Actually, I didn't need a sounding board in this instance, Marius," she answered in an icy voice, annoyed by his aggressive verbal attack on her. "I knew I had to prevent Christopher Delaware from blabbing, which he has a tendency to do. By playing up the three newly discovered Impressionist paintings, two of them extremely important and valuable, I diverted his attention away from the fakes. He's basking in the attention and publicity, enjoying every minute of it, and he'll not spoil this by admitting there are fakes in his collection. That might cast doubts about these three."

"Do you have the provenances?" Marius demanded.

"Of course I do. I thought I told you that on Saturday."

Ignoring this comment, he shouted, "And why did you take Jack Chalmers with you? That was bloody ridiculous, if nothing else was. And now he's gone and betrayed you, written about it."

"First you're accusing me, and now Jack. I *asked* him to write about it, because that suited my plan."

"Why didn't you tell me he went with you to Kent?" he pressed, still angry, and also sounding irritated.

"I forgot. I was so excited about the real Impressionists, and anyway, you phoned when it was late on Saturday and I was half asleep."

"You should have phoned me back the next day."

"That's a laugh! You know you don't like me to phone you when you're away. And I never have. Ever. In all the years we've been married. Besides, it hadn't occurred to me that it was important that Jack went with me."

"And why did he, might I ask?" he snarled.

"Because he needed to finish his interview with me, and I had to go to Kent unexpectedly. After all, Christopher is an important client. I thought it was the best way to kill two birds with one stone. He interviewed me on the way down and on the drive back to London."

"I see." He sounded petulant, but he wasn't shouting anymore.

Annette said, "Whatever you think, this is great publicity for the auction. The *Times* story was excellent. Don't you agree Jack did a good job?"

"It was okay, and that's all it was."

"The profile will appear this coming Sunday," she went on coldly. "Will you still be in Spain?"

"I think so. Anyway, I have to be on my way now. I'm late for an appointment."

"Goodbye." Annette hung up. He was obviously in a foul mood. Suddenly she hoped that he wasn't reading something more into Jack's trip to Kent with her on Saturday. Did he know about them? Don't be stupid, she chastised herself. How could he know? He'd been in Barcelona for almost a week doing research for his book on Picasso.

An hour later Annette was greeting her clients, the Estrins, who were on a trip to Europe looking at art. She had had dealings with them in the past, and they were two of her preferred clients. They were both charming as well as knowledgeable, and she enjoyed working with them on their art collection. They had recently moved from Bethesda to live in Palm Beach.

Annette led them over to the seating arrangement near the long credenza, and as they sat down Melvyn Estrin said, "Congratulations. That was quite an impressive story in *The Times* this morning, and I'm sure you'll have an extraordinary auction in the fall."

"I hope so," Annette answered, then asked, "Can I offer you any refreshments?" She smiled at Melvyn's wife, Suellen, and added, "Tea, coffee, water? Anything you want."

"No, thank you," Suellen replied in her soft Southern voice, and her husband also declined.

"I hope you'll come to the auction in September," Annette went on. "I know you are more interested in contemporary artists of the last fifty years than in Impressionists, but I do think this auction will be unique. There'll be a lot of excitement, and because of your love of art you're bound to enjoy it. It'll be an experience, anyway."

"We'd love to come," Suellen replied. "As a matter of fact, I was hoping you might be able to show us some modern English Impressionist paintings. I've taken a liking to the work of Dame Laura Knight." She looked at her husband and added, "And Melvyn has become very interested in sculpture."

"In particular Henry Moore and Barbara Hepworth," Melvyn explained. "But I do realize their work is hard to come by."

"It is, yes, and actually so is Dame Laura Knight's," Annette said. "She's become rather popular lately, and there's not much of her work available. However, I do know that an associate of mine has two at his gallery. I'd planned to take you there later anyway, so we'll walk over shortly. I'm afraid I've nothing here to show you, since I didn't know exactly what you had in mind and were looking for."

Melvyn nodded. "I see your walls are empty, as usual. But I thought you might be bringing something out to tempt us as you have in the past."

Annette laughed. "I've nothing hidden away, unfortunately. But Malcolm Stevens does have some interesting contemporary paintings by Lucian Freud and Francis Bacon. However, I have a feeling you'd prefer to look at a couple of Ben Nicholson paintings he has, since I know how much you like abstract art. Nicholson's work is formidable, in my opinion."

"We like to see everything," Suellen murmured, "because we love art in general. That's one of our pleasures when we come to Europe. Visiting galleries and discovering new artists is a passion of ours."

"Let's walk over to see Malcolm Stevens. His gallery is not far away," Annette suggested. "I told him we'd be coming over around eleven, and he is waiting to meet you both. He's very knowledgeable, and I know you'll like him."

Malcolm, always friendly, welcomed them in his usual genial manner when they arrived at the Remmington Gallery ten minutes later.

Once everyone had been introduced, Annette said to Malcolm, "Melvyn and Suellen are mostly interested in contemporary painters, as I told you the other day. But they are adventurous and open-minded when it comes to art, and would like to look at those Ben Nicholsons you have, and also the Dame Laura Knights."

"That's great. Let's go down to the other end of the gallery, to the room where we display contemporary art," Malcolm said. Turning to the Estrins, he continued, "I think you'd like to talk to my assistant, David Loudon, who's an expert on British artists of the last seventy years, and in particular Nicholson. He's also extremely well versed, full of information, about those artists from the Newlyn School, who lived and painted at the artists' colony at Newlyn in Cornwall, such as Lamorna Birch, Alfred Munnings, and, of course, Dame Laura Knight."

"We'd be happy to meet him," Melvyn said.

Malcolm walked ahead with the Estrins, now explaining

about various painters. He'd taken an immediate liking to them, was obviously enjoying their company, as they were his.

Annette loitered slightly behind, checking her mobile phone for messages and worrying about Marius. Suddenly he was in the forefront of her mind. She had not liked his nasty manner on the phone a short while ago, was alarmed that he had adopted a distinct attitude because Jack went with her to Kent. She felt panic rising inside, but managed to push it away. There was no way he could possibly know about her involvement with Jack. No one knew. And that was the way she aimed to keep it. And as Jack had said, they had a good cover, since he was writing about her.

Taking a deep breath, she hurried forward and caught up with Malcolm and the Estrins, who were a nice couple. Melvyn, a successful businessman and a Broadway producer, was as handsome as he was charming, while Suellen, a former model, was lovely. Tall, elegant, with bluish green eyes and auburn hair, she reminded Annette of Laurie a little.

She thought of her sister, and remembered she was supposed to call her back. Punching in the number quickly, she said when Laurie answered, "Sorry, darling. I got delayed. I'm here with Malcolm, and that American couple you liked so much last year. The Estrins."

"Oh, yes, they're nice. And I guessed you were caught up. Shame about the Degas being wrong, but look, you're still coming out the winner. I thought the Impressionists were beautiful when I saw them at Carlton's, especially the Louveciennes landscapes. That pair will go for millions."

"I know. How much do you think, Laurie?"

"Maybe thirty to forty million pounds *each*."

"We're on the same page then. They are rare, and it's a fluke finding them *both*. It adds to the value enormously because of their history."

"I agree."

"I'd better go and catch up with Malcolm. He's showing the Estrins into the Contemporary Art Room, introducing them to David. Talk to you later."

"You haven't forgotten about tonight, have you?" Laurie asked swiftly, just before Annette hung up.

"*Tonight?* Are we doing something? Oh, gosh, yes! Malcolm's taking us to dinner at the Ivy. Sorry, darling, it had slipped my mind. . . ."

There was a silence and Laurie said, "Annette, are you there?"

"Yes, I'm just thinking. I'd told Jack I would have supper with him. To celebrate his story appearing today. But I can cancel it."

"No, don't do that. It's not nice. Bring him along. I'd really like to meet him properly; I've only seen him across the room in Harry's Bar, and spoken to him on the phone. It'll be nice to be with him in person. Malcolm's booked a table for seven-thirty. See you there."

"All right, Laurie." Annette cut off her phone and instantly wondered if she had made a terrible mistake. Jack's feelings were constantly written on his face. She would have to warn him to be scrupulously careful, or otherwise Malcolm and Laurie would certainly suspect there was something between them.

Chapter Thirty-six

❋

Laurie and Malcolm listened to Annette attentively as she told them about the phone call she had received from Marius that morning. When she had finished, she added, "And that's the reason I told Jack to come at eight. I wanted to talk to you both before he got here."

Malcolm shook his head, let out a long sigh. "You know very well a man can't even glance at you without Marius getting mad. He's very jealous, Annette, and he always has been. At least about you at any rate."

"Marius is extremely possessive of you," Laurie interjected. "Look how silly he was about Christopher Delaware, insisting Chris had a crush on you."

Annette stared at her sister and raised a brow. "You teased me about Chris as well, don't forget. And there was no crush at all. Certainly we now know where his real interest lies. He and James Pollard are inseparable, and I for one am glad about that. Because Chris has a stable, more mature person in his life, one who can give him sound advice and guidance. But getting back to Marius, I found his anger a bit out of place, actually, and also he's totally *wrong* about my breaking the story too early. It is the right time."

"I agree." Malcolm took a sip of his red wine, a reflective expression settling on his face. After a moment, he gave Annette a knowing look when he said, "Marius flared up because Jack Chalmers went with you. That's what the phone call was about."

"How silly he is!" Annette exclaimed, shaking her head. "He's the one who selected Jack to do the interview with me in the first place. Actually, he forced the interview, and Jack, on me. I was reluctant all along about getting chummy with the press."

"And are you?" Malcolm asked, his eyes not leaving her face.

Annette, far too astute to get trapped, said in a level voice, "Of course I'm not *chummy* with Jack, which is what you're getting at. I like him, he's been very nice. But we'll see how nice he really is, and whether I still like him, after the profile appears on Sunday."

Leaning back against the chair, she lifted her glass of sparkling water and stared Malcolm down without flinching. Nor did she blush, which she was prone to do sometimes.

"I don't think you should pay much attention to Marius's outburst. He's undoubtedly working hard on his research, missing you and feeling lonely without you," Laurie remarked, squeezing Annette's arm.

"Perhaps," Annette conceded.

Malcolm said, "I've got your back as always, Annette, but I think you should be careful. Tread cautiously."

"I know you've got my back, Malcolm, and for that I'm grateful. But why do you say I should be careful?"

"There's a bit of gossip in the air, a few Chinese whispers."

"About me?" she exclaimed, shocked.

Malcolm nodded. "*And Jack*. Someone told me yesterday that your boyfriend had gone down with you to Kent, and that together, you'd unearthed lost Impressionists worth millions of pounds."

"My God, the things people conjure up!" Laurie cried, sounding angry. "And how did the person who told you *know* about Jack going to Knowle Court with my sister?"

"I've no idea, but somebody said something to someone, and it got passed along. Also, Fenella Anderson told me herself that she'd seen you at Le Caprice having lunch with a very dishy man, and that the two of you seemed extremely cozy."

"We weren't at all cozy!" Annette shot back, speaking the truth. She and Jack had been very discreet when they'd lunched together at the popular restaurant near the Ritz. She'd insisted on that, and he'd agreed, just as he had agreed to be well behaved tonight. "Not a flicker of an eyelash in my direction," she had warned him, and he had solemnly promised to act with the utmost decorum.

Laurie leaned across the table and said to Malcolm, "Is there any way Marius could have heard the Chinese whispers, darling?"

"But he's in Barcelona," Annette muttered, staring at Laurie.

"I don't think he could have heard anything," Malcolm said. "But how can I know for sure?" Turning to Annette, he took her hand, held it in his, and said in a quiet voice, "But just do as I say, *be careful*."

"But there isn't anything between us," she protested.

"I believe you, but anything can be misinterpreted, and things do get blown out of proportion all the time."

"Here's Jack now," Laurie exclaimed, and beamed at him as he walked toward their table.

Malcolm immediately stood up and shook Jack's outstretched hand; after greetings had been exchanged by all, the two men sat down next to each other. Jack looked across at Annette, who was facing him, and smiled. "I hope you had a successful day with your American clients."

"I did indeed, thank you," she answered. "They thought your story was great, and now they want to come to the auction in September."

Malcolm announced, "Actually, Jack's story broke at exactly the right time, in my opinion. You have four months, more or less, Annette, in which to promote it. Actually a bit less time than you had for the Rembrandt." Motioning to the waiter hovering nearby, Malcolm turned to Jack and asked, "What would you like to drink?"

"I think I'll have a glass of red wine, the same as you. Thank you, Malcolm."

Once the order had been given, Laurie said, "I can't wait to read the profile of Annette on Sunday. I'm a big fan of yours, Jack."

He smiled at her warmly, realizing once again how beautiful she was, and how glamorous. Suddenly growing aware that he was staring at her, he said quickly, "I was rather taken with that Degas dancer, and believed it to be the real thing. Just goes to show what I know about art."

"I think a lot of people would have been deceived," Laurie told him. "The average person doesn't go around thinking a painting is a fake, and not the real thing. They don't suspect anything."

"I understand that." Jack turned and said to Malcolm, "Annette has been telling me about various forgers, the great ones, I mean, and I'm formulating an idea about writing a piece on fakes and forgers, and how it's done, drawing on Elmyr de Hory and the John Drewe–John Myatt collaboration. She said you'd be able to help me."

"I'll try," Malcolm replied. "I know a few people who have been stung in the past."

Jack's red wine arrived, and he lifted his glass to toast Laurie and Malcolm. "To the two of you. Congratulations on your engagement. And to you as well, Annette, and your next auction. May it be the greatest ever."

The dinner went smoothly, much to Annette's relief. Malcolm and Jack hit it off immediately, and spent a lot of time talking about fakes, forgers, and crime in the art world. It was obvious he wanted to write about it. Both she and Laurie interjected occasionally, especially about the way John Drewe had so successfully penetrated the archives of the Tate. It was an act of such daring it defied belief.

When the men went on to focus on sport, expressing their views about football, footballers, and their extraordinary antics with women when off the field, Annette and Laurie plunged into a long discussion about Laurie's upcoming marriage. Veering from the venues for the reception to wedding dresses and which churches Laurie preferred, they then touched on the date. Finally they settled for the first Saturday in July. Laurie explained that she and Malcolm preferred this month, and Annette agreed it was the perfect time to have a wedding.

Once the food had been served, they began to chat together as a group. Annette discovered that Jack shared quite a few of their interests, and this pleased her, as did his lovely sense of humor. He was irreverent and very funny in his comments about the famous, be it folk from the world of entertainment to politicians. He kept them laughing all through dinner.

Toward the end of the evening, Jack suddenly said, "I'll give you a lift, Annette, I have a car waiting. And what about you and Laurie, Malcolm? I can drop you off as well."

"Thanks, Jack," Malcolm answered. "But I have a car and driver tonight, since there's really nowhere to park down here."

Once they were outside, Jack got on his mobile, calling his driver; Annette said goodnight to Malcolm and thanked him, then hugged her sister. Jack did the same, promised to phone Malcolm to make a lunch date, and helped her into the car when it arrived.

Once they were pulling away from the Ivy, Jack took hold of her hand and said, "I need to talk to you. Shall we go for a drink? How about Annabel's? The Dorchester?"

Annette hesitated, and shook her head. "I think we'd better go somewhere private where we won't be seen."

Jack stared at her intently in the dim light of the car, but made no comment. He gave the driver his address in Primrose Hill. Moving closer to her, he asked quietly, "Is something wrong?"

Speaking in a low voice, she told him about Malcolm's conversation earlier, the comments made to him about her taking her boyfriend to Knowle Court, and the report of their cozy behavior in Le Caprice.

Jack was astonished. "But we've been so scrupulous! Not only at Knowle Court, but most definitely in the restaurant. God, people are terrible, the way they invent, embroider, and gossip."

"I agree. However, I think it's wiser to heed Malcolm's advice to be careful."

"He doesn't know about us, does he?"

"Of course not. Neither does Laurie. No one knows, actually, Jack. Those who spoke to Malcolm, passed on rumors, are making assumptions. He calls it Chinese whispers."

"Do you think Christopher's said something to someone, about me coming with you to his house?"

"No, I don't, even though he is a bit of a chatterbox. He wouldn't do anything like that. Also, he was the one who suggested I bring you down to Kent with me. In fact he insisted on it. I've no idea who's spreading stuff. But why take any chances?"

"You're right."

"What do you want to talk to me about? You sounded very serious."

"Several things, but let's wait until we get to my flat."

Annette leaned against him, and murmured, "It was a good story in the paper today, Jack, very well written and intriguing, and great promotion for the auction. So thank you again."

"My pleasure." He lifted her face and kissed her lightly on the mouth, and for the rest of the way they were silent, their arms wrapped around each other, lost in their thoughts.

When they arrived at his flat in Primrose Hill, Jack asked the driver to wait and escorted her into the building. "That's a bit extravagant," Annette said, peering at him. "Keeping the car."

"I realize that. But I know you won't stay the night, and I do have to get you home safely. Sometimes taxis are hard to find around here."

Once they were inside his flat, Jack pulled her into his arms and kissed her, and she responded to him ardently. As they drew apart, he said, "That was a bit tough, being so formal with you earlier, but you were pretty good, you set the perfect tone."

Annette gave him a faint smile. "I think we're both good actors, don't you? We've missed our calling."

Jack laughed and led her into the living room, explaining, "Let's sit here. Down at the other end I have my work area." He guided her to the sofa, walked over to a drinks table, and asked, "Would you like a glass of wine? Anything?"

"Nothing right now, thank you."

Jack poured himself a small cognac and went back to join her on the sofa. Immediately he plunged in and said, "I'm afraid I have to go away this weekend, and I want you to come with me."

Taken aback, Annette gaped at him. "Jack, you know I can't go anywhere with you. I couldn't even go to Clapham Common with you, if it meant being away from Eaton Square overnight. Anyway, where are you going all of a sudden?"

"I have to go to Beaulieu. I got a call at four o'clock to-day. Amaury, my caretaker, had a bad fall down the cellar steps at the villa," Jack explained. "He's broken his left arm and left leg. Hortense, his wife, is a bit overwhelmed, and I think I must get down there to organize them. I need to find someone to do his work until he's better. Also, Hortense seems to be so upset that I must hire a young woman to take over some of her chores." Jack took a swallow of the brandy and continued, "I thought it would be nice if you joined me for a few days, and I do want you to see the villa."

"Jack, you know it's an impossibility." Taking a deep breath, she said, "Marius was very nasty on the phone this morning."

Looking at her, frowning, Jack said, "What do you mean?"

Annette filled him in, repeating Marius's comments to her, and explaining about his angry attitude, the way he had shouted at her.

Jack sat back and closed his eyes for a moment, think-ing. After a few seconds he sat up straight on the sofa, swiveled to face her, clasped her hand in his. "I want you to leave him. The sooner the better. I want us to live together until you're divorced and then I want us to get married, Annette."

"Oh, Jack, you know that's not possible."

"But I love you, and you love me. You do, don't you?"

When she remained silent, he said, "You know you love me, so say it. Please, Annette." He was suddenly tense, anxious, and the strain echoed in his voice.

"Yes, I'm in love with you, Jack. I've never been in love with anyone before you. . . ." She stopped, tears glistening in her bright blue eyes.

"Not Marius? When you first got married?"

"I loved him, yes. And I grew to love him even more as he looked after me, cherished me. And I love him now. But I wasn't *in love*, not in this way. Never before, and that's the truth."

"What about that man? The man who took you on your romantic trip to La Réserve all those years ago. Weren't you in love with him?"

"Very infatuated, very captivated, dizzy with emotions, but now that I look back, I don't believe I was *in love* with him. Mind you, I thought I was then. We had such a short time together, it was so very brief."

Leaning forward, Jack drew her toward him, gazed into her face. "Our feelings for each other are overwhelming, and very genuine, Annette, and I want to spend the rest of my life with you. I'll be honest, I've been engaged twice before and broken it off. Because I knew I wasn't in love, just as I wasn't in love with Lucy, and I've told *her* that now. I phoned her the other day. But I know that I'm in love with you, and I will be for the rest of my life. You are my life now."

"Oh, Jack, darling . . . he'll never give me a divorce, and—"

"I don't care about that," he swiftly cut in. "We can live together. We don't need a piece of paper to make our love *true*. Anyway, those kinds of conventions don't seem to matter these days. People live together, have children, make a family, without the benefit of a piece of paper. Why not us?"

"I'm too old for you, Jack. I'll be forty in June, and you will want children one day."

"You're not too old! And if we don't have children, I don't care. It's you I want, not children I don't even know at this moment in time. You must ask him for a divorce when he gets back from Barcelona. At once, you mustn't wait."

"Jack, please believe me, he'll never let me go. He'll be vindictive, make trouble for me, and for you." Tears spilled, trickled down her cheeks.

"Oh, darling, don't, please don't," Jack said gently, wiping her tears with his fingertips. "We *can* be together, I promise you. I love you so much, my life won't be worth living without you. . . . I know that sounds dramatic, but I mean it. We're soul mates, we're meant to be together. We fit in every way. I love you so very much."

Annette gazed back at him, knowing he meant every word. She also knew that Marius would hound them for as long as he lived. She didn't really care what he did to her, but she couldn't permit him to persecute and punish Jack. "Oh, darling, I love you in the same way. But it just can't be."

"Yes, it can." He put his hand into his pocket, brought out a small, rather worn red leather box, and handed it to her. "This is for you."

She opened it and gaped when she saw the diamond ring nestled on the black velvet. "Jack, I can't take this! I can't get engaged to you, and you know that. But I'm very moved, and I thank you for offering this to me. . . ."

Jack took the box she was offering, slipped out the diamond ring, grasped her right hand, and slipped the ring on her third finger. "There. It's done. One day you'll wear it on your engagement finger."

"I can't take this, Jack, and I—"

"It's not an engagement ring," he interrupted peremptorily. "It's a *friendship ring* for the moment. It belonged to my mother, and I've never given it to any woman. Ever. It was my biological father who gave it to my mother, and when she married Peter she took it off and never wore it again. She gave it to me instead, and said this: 'It was given to me in true love, Jack, and you must only give it to the woman you know you truly love.' And that's you, my darling."

Annette was immeasurably touched, moved to tears again. She did not want to fight him about the ring, or force him to take it back. Not at this highly charged moment. She would put it away and give it to him when he was able to accept it calmly.

"Look how beautiful it is on your finger," Jack murmured, suddenly smiling. Leaning over her, he began to kiss her passionately, and after a moment, he said against her neck, "Come on, let's go and find a bed and seal our bargain with each other."

For the next three days they were inseparable, lived in what Annette called "their bubble of love."

On Thursday and Friday morning Annette went to the office, did some work, and then left around eleven. Each day she told Esther she was going on a shopping expedition, looking for a dress for herself for Laurie's wedding, and also trying to create a trousseau for Laurie. She explained she wanted to put together a suitable selection of clothes for her honeymoon with Malcolm in Italy.

Whether Esther believed this or not, Annette did not know. Her assistant seemed to accept it, and if there was anything pressing she would phone Annette on her mobile.

Once she had left her office, she took a taxi to Jack's apartment in Primrose Hill, where they talked, made love, ate, dozed, and made love again.

Twice they went to his father's house in Hampstead, so that he could check that everything was in order. Inevitably they always ended up in the room he had occupied as a boy, making passionate love on that narrow bed, besotted with each other.

There were moments of quietude between them, and as they lay side by side, Annette marveled at herself. She, who had never enjoyed sex, could not get enough of Jack, had become insatiable, was enraptured by him and transported by her desire, and her newly discovered sensuality.

He had invaded her, taken possession of her completely—her body, her heart, her soul, and her mind. She belonged to him. And she knew she always would. There were moments when she stopped to think about him, and remembered what he had said once about the power of sex, and how it could transform people. He was right. She had been transformed. By him.

Suddenly it was Sunday and he was gone. As he was flying to Nice to take care of the problems with Amaury and Hortense, she was reading the profile of her in *The Sunday Times*, and smiling to herself.

He had mostly written about her life as it was now, had hardly mentioned her childhood or what little he knew of her past. It was all about the sale of the Rembrandt . . . and her intelligence, her cleverness, her prodigious memory, her skill, her extraordinary knowledge of art. But he had also made her sound human, caring and warm. And beautiful. It was, in its own way, a love letter to her. And she accepted this, and was pleased.

Later that morning Malcolm and Laurie called her, as did Margaret Mellor, and Christopher and Jim. They each said the same thing . . . that Jack had written a wonderful piece and she should be happy, because it was great coverage.

But she wasn't happy, in that she was already missing him. Jack Chalmers. Her lover. The man she loved. She now understood that she must break up with him. If she didn't leave Jack, but instead left Marius, she would ruin Jack's life. She was convinced that Marius would undoubtedly wreak revenge on him. And on her. He most likely would turn her in to the police, making a cold case a closed case. She could easily spend the rest of her life in jail.

Chapter Thirty-seven

✳

"I am all right, Monsieur Jacques. It was not necessary for you to come. I am managing," Hortense exclaimed, once Jack had stopped hugging her. "And next week, my niece Albane is coming from Marseilles to help me in the house."

The two of them were standing in the middle of the entrance hall at the Villa Saint-Honoré, where he had just put down his two small bags. Jack said, "That's good. I'm sure you've enough to do looking after Amaury, so you can't be attending to the house as well."

"Amaury is better today, Monsieur Jacques. He was not good yesterday. It was the shock."

Hortense and Jack walked through the kitchen and the back hallway into the apartment facing the vegetable garden. It was here that Hortense and Amaury had lived for forty years.

When they entered the living room, a wide smile flashed across Amaury's weather-beaten face, and as Jack came forward, he exclaimed, "I'm sorry, Monsieur Jacques, I cannot get up."

"Don't even try," Jack replied warmly, bending over the older man, shaking his hand, patting his shoulder. "And I'm sorry this happened to you. I hope you're not in a lot of pain."

"It is not bad. Difficult to move around." Woefully, he looked at his arm and then down at his leg, both in plaster casts and bandages. He made a face. "A stupid thing, Monsieur Jacques. I was in a hurry. For no reason. I am very sorry."

"It was an accident, Amaury, these things happen. And the cellar steps are steep. You'll be fine in a few weeks."

"The garden . . . who will tend it, Monsieur? I worry."

"Just take care of yourself and get better, Amaury. I will call my friend Madame Claudine Villiers. I'm sure she can be of help. She knows everyone in the area. Perhaps she can recommend someone."

"*Oui,* Monsieur Jacques. *Merci.*"

Back in the front hall Jack picked up his laptop and small overnight bag and hurried upstairs. In his office he put the laptop and the bag down, glanced around. Everything was in place and exactly as it should be.

The windows were open, and the scent of flowers wafted in on the light breeze. It was a beautiful day, sunny with a cloudless blue sky. He wished Annette were here with him. He had already spoken to her twice today. Once from Heathrow, later when he had landed in Nice. He was glad she was happy with the piece he had written about her, but he had known she would like it.

Taking off his jacket, draping it around the chair back, he sat down at his desk and dialed Claudine. The machine came on at once, and he left a message, asking her to phone him as soon as she could, adding that it was fairly urgent.

Within minutes the landline was ringing, and he picked it up at once. "Hello?"

"Hello, Jack. It's Claudine. You called me?"

"Claudine, hello! Yes, I did. I've got a problem here, and I'm wondering if you can help me."

"If I can. What is it?" Claudine asked.

He told her about Amaury's fall down the cellar steps, his broken bones, and asked if she knew a gardener who could work at the villa for a couple of months. She promised to get back to him within an hour.

Jack remained at his desk for a while, feeling lost and bereft without Annette. The long hours he had spent with her in the last few days had spoiled him. He wanted her beside him, now and always. He sighed. He was fully aware that it was going to be tough for both of them, especially when Marius returned to London.

Marius Remmington. He knew Annette was afraid of him, but he did not understand why. Her husband was manipulative and controlling, that he knew from the gossip about Marius, yet something more than this seemed to scare her. She kept saying that Marius would never let her go, never divorce her. But she could just walk out, couldn't she?

He pondered for a long time. In a sense, the man was as mysterious as Annette was. And she was certainly wary, cautious about revealing her earlier years to him. What could she possibly have to hide? Nothing, surely.

Within the hour Claudine called him. "I have found a gardener for you, Jack. His name is Antoine. Shall I tell him to come to see you around three tomorrow?"

"Absolutely, that's a good time for me."

"And will you come to dinner on Tuesday?"

"That'll be great, Claudine. By the way, how is Lucy?"

"She's away, Jack. In Italy on business. See you on Tuesday."

A moment later Hortense appeared and said, "Ah, there you are, Monsieur Jacques. Will you have lunch now?"

"*Merci,* Hortense," he murmured, and went downstairs to the terrace where the table had been set for one.

Annette had not called him back all day and this troubled him, but he decided to wait until much later in the evening to call her again.

She saved him the trouble. Much to his delight, she phoned around nine in London, ten o'clock his time.

"I'm sorry I didn't get back to you before, Jack," she said, her voice subdued. "But I went to supper with Laurie and Malcolm, and just got home. They loved the piece."

"Thanks, darling. Listen, I'll be back sooner than I thought."

He told her about Amaury's injuries, the imminent arrival of Hortense's niece, and Claudine's success in finding a gardener, and added, "But I'll stay longer if you'll come and join me."

"If only I could, but you know I can't. And Jack, we do have to . . . play it cool, you know," Annette warned.

"I understand," he said, deciding to go along with her. "When is Marius coming back, actually?" he asked gently, not wanting to irritate her.

"I don't know. But toward the end of this coming week, I suppose. He never knows how long the research is going to take."

"I understand. Did he like the profile?"

"I didn't hear from him today."

Jack was startled. After all, it was Marius who had selected him to write about her. He said, "Maybe he hasn't seen it yet, since he's in Spain."

"That's right."

They talked for a short while longer, and he refrained from pushing her about leaving Marius. It would only rile her. All he knew after he hung up was that he was relieved she had finally returned his call. Now he could go to sleep a happy man.

But he did not sleep well. He tossed and turned for several hours. When he finally did drop off he was assailed by terrible dreams . . . nightmares.

He was on a battlefield piled high with the bodies of the dead, searching for his father, calling out his name, turning bodies to look at faces. There was blood and death everywhere, but where was he? What country was he in? And then he saw his father coming forward, carrying a body. Jack ran toward him, stumbling over the dead, rushing to help. And when he got to his father he saw blood all over his face, dripping down off his chin onto the girl he was carrying. She was crumpled and lifeless, wearing a wedding dress. The white had turned to crimson from her blood. Jack shuddered when he saw her empty eyes, her drooping head. She was dead.

His father said through his tears that it was Hilda, his dear friend Hilda. He wanted to find a doctor to help her. Jack walked on with his father, afraid to say the girl was gone. And soon they found a Red Cross nurse kneeling in the mud and blood, her pristine uniform mud-splashed and stained red from the dead. It was Aunt Helen and she was holding a stethoscope. She reached for the girl, her arms wide.

Jack left them. He began to move through the field of mud. But it was hard. His mother was waving, urging him forward, but he kept sinking into the mud. It was like treacle, pulling and sucking at his feet, hindering him. Suddenly he could not move. He heard his brother Kyle shouting, calling his name. He shouted back, and saw his stepfather, Peter, and Kyle, and they came and pulled his arms, dragged him out of the mud, saving him.

In the distance he could see an ambulance. The driver was waving. The three of them struggled on, trudging through the mud. Everyone had inexplicably disappeared. The three of them were alone, except for the dead, the only ones left alive on the killing field. When they came to the ambulance it was his father Nigel who was waiting, his biological father. He said, "Find Hilda Crump. She's out there somewhere, alive."

Jack went on down the road, leaving the three of them behind. In the distance he could see Annette. She was pushing the wheelchair. When he got to her he saw that tears were rolling down her face. She kept saying over and over again that she had lost Laurie, and didn't know where she was.

They walked together down the road. Gunfire started again. The sound of bombs exploding was shattering. Annette let go of the wheelchair and began to run away from him. He ran after her but he couldn't catch up. "Annette, wait! Annette, wait for me," he shouted, but his words were blown away by the wind, drowned out by the gunfire. . . .

The light of dawn, trickling in through the slatted wooden shutters, awakened him and he sat up with a start. He was bathed in sweat.

Jack struggled out of bed, taking off his damp pajamas as he crossed his bedroom. He had a severe headache, which was unusual for him. He went into the bathroom, stepped into the shower, turned on the taps, let the water sluice down over his sweaty body.

After drying himself and combing his hair, he went back to his bedroom. Glancing at the clock, he saw that it was only six. Putting on shorts and a pair of Moroccan flat mules, he went downstairs to the kitchen, where he made himself a cup of coffee and took it outside to the terrace.

The fresh air was cool, soothing. He sipped the coffee, remembered his nightmare, and shuddered. He shook his head and swallowed more of the coffee, hoping his blinding headache would subside.

Hilda Crump.

He wondered what had really happened to her. Certainly the private investigator he'd hired hadn't been able to find a trace of her. She had seemingly disappeared into oblivion. *Maybe she was dead.* So he had told the PI to drop the matter.

He only knew her name from his mother, who had called her his father's girlfriend. That was all he had to go on. And the fact that his mother had once told him Hilda Crump had worked at the Remmington Art Gallery.

Seemingly she hadn't, according to the PI. At the gallery no one had ever heard of her, and she wasn't on their books or in their computerized records. The PI had drawn a blank.

Oh, well, what does it matter now, Jack thought, and walked back into the kitchen to get another cup of coffee. As he filled his mug, he reminded himself that he had been looking for Hilda Crump because he wanted to know more about his biological father. He had believed she would be able to enlighten him, tell him something important, more than he already knew.

He had so wanted to know if his father had been a decent guy as well as a womanizer. But how would that really help *him*? Make him feel *better*, if his father had been one of the good guys? He didn't know and suddenly he didn't care. He, Jack Chalmers, was exactly who he was, and now that he thought about it, he liked himself. He had always been ambivalent about the women he had been involved with because he hadn't been in love with them. He understood that now. Not the way he wanted to be in love, the way it was with Annette.

It was that simple. He'd played around because he hadn't found true love. He would accept who he was, and what he was as a man, because he knew he could live with himself. He was sincere, honorable, had ethics and integrity. That was enough for him. He had his father's genes, and his mother's, too, but a good man had brought him up, and Jack believed Peter Chalmers had done his job well.

And that was all he needed to know.

Part Four

AN ACCIDENTAL
INFORMANT

Knowledge is power.
Francis Bacon, *Meditationes Sacrae* (1597)

How dreadful knowledge of the truth can be.
Sophocles, *Oedipus Rex* (c. 429 B.C.)

Chapter Thirty-eight

✳

In many ways, Jack was a creature of habit, and whenever he came back to the Villa Saint-Honoré he made a point of going to La Réserve for breakfast, lunch, or dinner.

On this lovely Tuesday morning, bright with sunlight, the air filled with the many fragrances of spring flowers and foliage in bloom everywhere, he set out for the lovely old hotel he had been visiting since childhood.

There was a jauntiness in his step as he left the villa at eight-thirty, the perfect time for him to have breakfast on the terrace of the hotel overlooking the Mediterranean.

He felt more like himself today; he had slept well, and there were no memories of bad dreams to haunt him. The headache which had dogged him most of yesterday had gone, and he felt refreshed and ready to tackle anything.

He had worked hard on the manuscript until late last night, pleased with the fine-tuning done by his editor, who had been insightful, precise, and careful, and the quality of her superior work showed. He'd already sent her an e-mail, telling her what a superlative job she had done and thanking her. He was relieved that there was nothing to cut or add, and no rewrites, only line editing. He would be able to finish reading it by this afternoon, add his own edits, and get back to his publisher well before the given date.

This thought made him happy, because he was a true professional. He never missed deadlines and rarely objected to editing unless it was heavy-handed, which so far his editor had always avoided. He was also happy because he had received two phone calls from Annette yesterday, and of her own volition.

The first was to tell him she had been inundated with phone calls about his profile, and that people were already clamoring for information about the next auction, wanting to be on the invitation list. The second call was to confide that she had had three huge offers for Degas's *The Little Fourteen-Year-Old Dancer.*

"All from good clients, old clients with big bucks to spend. But I turned them all down," she had explained late last night. "I simply don't want to sell it in that way . . . accept a preemptive offer. My gut instinct tells me it *must* be in the auction. It's a masterpiece, and something unique, and the publicity it will generate is of incalculable value, and I know I'll get a huge price if it's in the auction. And Sotheby's also does a superb job."

He had agreed with her, told her how brilliant she was, and they had gone on to chat for half an hour about a variety of things, barely touching on their relationship. Instinctively, Jack had known she did not want to go that route late at night, and so he had refrained from bringing up their future together. They had finished their phone call in a very loving way, and without a fight about breaking up.

Jack walked steadily along Boulevard Maréchal Leclerc, and waited for the traffic to slow before crossing the busy main road to the hotel. He paused for a moment at the gates, thinking how beautiful it looked set against the blameless blue sky and the backdrop of the deep-blue sea.

Strolling leisurely down the path, he spoke to the doorman and then to the concierge in the small lobby, who both welcomed him back.

He ran down the few steps into the long bar, and walked along its terra-cotta-tiled floor, heading for the restaurant and the terrace beyond.

The shrill sound of loud blaring music on a mobile phone caused him to pause and look around, but he was the only

person in the bar. When the phone went on blaring relent-
lessly he glanced to his right, looking through the French
doors to the garden where breakfast was also served.

Instantly he caught his breath, and automatically stepped
back into the shadowy part of the room, closer to the actual
bar, resting his hand on the back of a tall bar stool.

He couldn't believe what he was witnessing. Nor could he
tear his eyes away. A tall, voluptuous young woman with
flaming red hair had her arms wrapped around a tall, silver-
haired man, and they were kissing passionately, ignoring the
constant ringing of the mobile. And there was no mistaking
who the man was. The Silver Fox himself. None other than
Marius Remmington.

Jack couldn't believe his eyes. He was stunned. There
was no other word for it, and he discovered he was rooted to
the spot, watching them closely. Finally, they drew apart,
and the woman reached into her large snakeskin bag on the
chair, finally took out the phone, and spoke on it. Marius
slipped out of his dark blazer, hung it on the back of a chair,
and sat down. Once she was off the phone, the young woman
seated herself next to Marius. They had their heads together
at once, talking intimately, and kissing each other in between. Marius couldn't keep his hands off her.

Jack would have remained there much longer, fascinated
and horrified, but a waiter came out of the restaurant, heading in his direction. It wasn't a waiter he knew but he turned
around and swiftly left the bar; he hurried up the steps and
entered the lobby.

The concierge seemed surprised to see him so soon, and
Jack felt the need to explain. He said, "I'll be back shortly. I
forgot to get my newspapers."

"I can send a boy, Monsieur Chalmers," the concierge
said. "If you tell me which newspapers you want. It's no
trouble."

"I'm not sure, so I'll go and get them myself, but thanks
anyway, Marcel." With a nod and a wide smile, Jack walked
across the lobby to the front door.

He stood on the step for a moment, and when the young

doorman suddenly appeared, pushing a luggage cart, Jack strolled over to him and said, "I think I just caught sight of an old friend of mine, Magda Rollins, a very well-known English actress."

The doorman shook his head. "There's no one in the hotel of that name, Monsieur."

"But I just saw her," Jack protested. "She is with a tall silver-haired Englishman. They're sitting in the garden outside the bar."

"Oh, that's Madame Elizabeth Lang. She's not an actress, Monsieur Chalmers. She is an artist."

"Do you mean a painter?"

"*Oui, oui*," the young doorman answered, and smirked, raised a brow, and threw Jack a knowing look.

Jack laughed, then said, "Well, she certainly has someone who looks just like her living in London."

At this moment a sleek burgundy car came rolling down the short driveway and stopped just short of the front door of the hotel. The driver got out and walked over to the doorman.

Jack stepped to one side, but did not leave, and discreetly listened to their conversation. The driver of the car was explaining that he had come to collect Monsieur Remmington, but that he was too early. Could he park where he was?

Giving the doorman a salute, Jack walked up the short drive heading for the gate. As he passed the car he noticed that it was a collector's item, a costly Bentley Continental Drophead Coupe, probably twenty years old but in beautiful condition. He also noticed that the license plate on the back was from Geneva.

Jack was still flabbergasted by what he had just seen, and he couldn't get it out of his mind. The woman was so flamboyant in her looks she was almost vulgar, and yet she *was* quite beautiful. Everything about her was big. Her height, her hair, and her bust. She was definitely a big girl, and yet she wasn't overweight. She was also well dressed in white trousers, a white shirt, and a white sweater thrown around her shoulders.

She wore a lot of gold jewelry and had a large yellow diamond ring on her engagement finger. What a striking couple they made, tall, good-looking, and well dressed. And he's a bastard, Jack added under his breath.

Walking through the open gate of the hotel, Jack headed along the boulevard, making for the flight of steps leading down into the little port of Beaulieu, where yachts, sailboats, and motorboats were docked. Within minutes he was entering one of his favorite cafés. After sitting down he ordered café au lait and a croissant, and then sat back, still feeling utterly gobsmacked, reeling, in fact, not yet capable of absorbing that scene.

Never in a million years would he have expected to see Marius Remmington with another woman. Or behaving in that intimate manner in a public place. On the other hand, it was early in the morning and there was no one in the garden. But still, they had been really at each other, apparently oblivious to their surroundings.

Jack closed his eyes.

He didn't know what to think or what to do. He needed to talk to somebody, but there was no one he dared talk to. Kyle? Forget that. His brother was very preoccupied with his new movie, and he had a feeling that a relationship was developing between Kyle and his assistant, Carole. And besides, Kyle didn't know the players, couldn't make a judgment.

He couldn't talk to Laurie. Or Malcolm Stevens. And certainly he was not going to reveal what he had seen to Annette. He didn't want to hurt or upset her, and at this moment there was no need for her to know. "A still tongue and a wise head," his mother used to say to him, and never had this old saying been more appropriate than now. He reminded himself that knowledge was power.

Eventually Jack calmed down and relaxed slightly, sat drinking his coffee and eating the croissant, wondering what to do. But there was nothing he could do, was there? He thought about Remmington and the redhead. . . . Had they been staying at the hotel for the weekend? Or dropped in for breakfast, as he had? Was that Remmington's Bentley? Or the woman's? Were they staying on at La Réserve or were they leaving today?

It didn't really matter, although he would have to stay away from the hotel until he knew for sure. He didn't want to run into Remmington and the woman.

Much later, walking back to the villa, Jack couldn't help thinking what a stinker Marius Remmington was, controlling Annette's life, manipulating her, making all the rules in their marriage, whilst two-timing her.

There was nothing new about a successful man having a mistress; many of them did. Even unsuccessful men had mistresses. It was the way men were. And women, too. It was not possible to tango alone.

What should I do about what I now know? Jack asked himself later, as he sat in his office, pondering the situation. He had no answers for himself. Because there weren't any. He had no one to use as a sounding board. And he could not tell Annette. Not yet. But he might have to eventually.

Jack left early for dinner with Claudine at the farm. He drove into Beaulieu, went to the best flower shop and bought a beautiful white orchid for her, wrote a card, and paid. Outside in the car he took out his mobile, dialed the hotel, adopted an American accent, and asked if Mr. Marius Remmington was available. The hotel operator told him immediately that Mr. Marius Remmington had checked out that morning. This was good to know. At least he could now come and go to the hotel whenever he wished, but couldn't help wondering where those two lovebirds had gone off in the beautiful Bentley.

It took Jack about forty minutes to drive up into the hills to La Ferme des Iris, the old farm high above Monte Carlo. He drove slowly, thinking about the new situation in Annette's life. Maybe it wasn't new. How long had Marius had a mistress? All manner of possibilities swirled around in his head. The woman he loved, and who loved him in return, was stuck in a marriage she was certain she could never leave, insisting her husband would not divorce her.

And the husband was a shit. He was having an affair with another woman, and touting that woman around on his arm, or in his arms, in public. Didn't her husband's adultery give her grounds for divorce? Or since she was doing the same thing, the husband could divorce her, couldn't he? Except that the husband didn't want a divorce . . . he wanted his cake and he wanted to eat it.

But the knowledge I have is a bargaining chip, Jack suddenly thought. He tucked this thought away at the back of his mind for use later, when he needed it. And as he drove on toward the farm he cheered up. Somehow, he felt better about everything. He chuckled to himself. If the truth be known, he had Marius Remmington by the short hairs.

Claudine Villiers was waiting for him on the doorstep of her charming new villa when he pulled into the large square yard which separated the two houses facing each other.

After Jack had climbed out of the car and hugged her, he reached inside, brought out the orchid, and gave it to her.

"Ah, Jack, my lovely Jack. Always so gallant," Claudine murmured, accepting the orchid from him. "*Merci beaucoup*," she added, and tucked her arm through his, explaining, "We are going to have the dinner in my new house. I thought it better. . . . I didn't want the twins to get excited, seeing you again. You know how they are. . . . So they are in bed, with Marie watching over them. I will sleep at the farm tonight, as I do when Lucy is away."

"I understand. Anyway, I want to see your new villa, now that it's finally finished. You worked so hard on it, I know that, and I'm sure it's perfection."

"I think it's very cozy and charming. I will show you around later. First we must go to my kitchen, and have an aperitif. We must catch up, *n'est pas*?"

Claudine led him proudly into the kitchen, which he had seen before when it was still being finished, and immediately he exclaimed about it. It was obviously well planned and colorful, with blue-and-white tiles everywhere, shining copper pots, stone planters filled with flowers, a big stone fireplace, and ceiling beams from which hung many different bunches of dried herbs and lavender, dried sausages, and more copper pots and pans.

"I think you've done a wonderful job," Jack said, meaning this, walking around, taking everything in. "And I love the wine storage behind the glass door. Very clever. Chic, if I can use that word about a kitchen."

Beaming, her eyes warm as she opened a bottle of red wine, Claudine murmured, with a little smile, "I copied the wine cupboard from a restaurant in New York. I fell in love with it when I saw it." She looked very gleeful when she added, "And now my friends are copying this one."

Jack laughed with her, accepting the large glass of red wine, and cautioning himself to sip it very slowly. He had to drive down that mountain later.

Claudine touched her glass to his, and said, "*Santé*," and Jack did the same. Taking his arm, she led him over to the huge window at the far end of the kitchen, where the view of Monte Carlo far below was spectacular. "Let's sit here, Jack," Claudine murmured, and indicated one of the big armchairs facing the window.

Once they were both settled comfortably, Claudine said, "I am only going to say this once, Jack, and I want you to know I do mean it. Most sincerely . . ." She paused and stared at him, her dark eyes warm.

He looked back at her, nodded. "It's about Lucy, isn't it?"

"It is. I want you to know how much I . . . well, approved of your relationship. I did have great hopes . . . that it would flower into marriage. It was not to be. I am so sorry, Jack. I admit I have . . . warm feelings for you. I wish you well. . . . You're a special man."

"Oh, Claudine, what a lovely thing to say, and I'm regretful, too. I do care about Lucy. A lot, and you know I adore the girls. But . . ." He shrugged and gave her a direct look. "I loved her, still love her, she's a wonderful woman. But, you see, Claudine, I wasn't *in love* with Lucy. And I don't think she was in love with me either."

"Perhaps not . . . Ah, well, *c'est la vie*." She smiled; it was soft, but knowing.

"She is all right, isn't she?"

Claudine nodded. "She is involved with her work, the cooking school. She is ambitious, and wants to make a mark in life. And I trust her. . . . She will succeed. And you, Jack, what about you? Something unusual, even world-shaking, must have happened to you. Lucy did tell me you called her to bring your love affair to an end." A dark brow lifted and Claudine gave him a smile that was loving, very tender.

"I did meet somebody, you are correct. It was a *coup de foudre*. We experienced that strange and frightening thing. . . . I call it the shock of recognition, Claudine. I'm sure you know what I mean with your experience of life."

The Frenchwoman nodded and sipped her wine. After a moment she said, "But you sound so sad, Jack. Is it not going the way it should? Are there . . . *problems*?"

Later Jack would never know why he said it, but now he blurted out, "She's married." He could have bitten his tongue off.

"*Mon Dieu!*" She shook her head. "That is the most terrible trap in life. I know only too well. I have been there, Jack." She sighed, reached out, touched his arm. "Cannot she get a divorce?"

Jack shook his head. He took a long swallow of the wine. "I don't think her husband will give her a divorce. . . . It's tricky, complex."

"Ah yes, it always is."

Looking across at Claudine Villiers, remembering her kindness to him over the past few years, and recalling her intrinsic wisdom, Jack made a sudden decision. He was going to tell her what he had seen today without mentioning names.

Taking a deep breath, he plunged in. "Claudine, what I'm going to tell is confidential, and—"

"Jack. Oh Jack, do not say any more. I am not a woman

who wishes to play God. I do not repeat anything. Please, unburden yourself to me. It might help. And what is an old lady for, except to listen to the love tribulations of the young."

"You're not old. And thank you for your reassurances. I do trust you, Claudine." He told her a little about the marriage of the woman he loved, and her manipulating, controlling husband. And then he confided what had happened at La Réserve that morning. What he had seen occurring in the garden.

For a moment or two Claudine sat thinking. "And what are you going to do about this, Jack?" she asked at last. "You now have some genuine ammunition . . . a loaded gun, perhaps? To point at his head?"

"I don't know what to do. I'm certainly not going to tell *her*. The woman I'm in love with."

"No, no, you must not, Jack. You will look . . ." She lifted her hands in Gallic fashion, murmured softly, "*Shoddy*. Which is not what you are as a person."

"It's ironic, isn't it? My lover believes her husband will never set her free, and I discover he is having an affair."

Claudine shook her head and murmured gently, "They are both playing the same game, are they not?"

Jack was silent, merely inclined his head. After a moment's silence he said, "I just don't know what to do, Claudine."

"There's nothing you can do at this moment."

"She's trying to break off with me, because she believes her husband will ruin me if he finds out about us. I can't give her up. It's an . . . impasse, between us, I mean."

"I think you should return to London. Can you leave?"

"I can, yes, thanks to you. I met with Antoine yesterday and he will start work tomorrow. Amaury met him as well and seems to like him. Hortense is bringing her niece Albane from Marseilles, and she can stay as long as she's needed. I think the household will run well, will be fine."

Claudine said, "When you return to London, talk to your friend, tell her to be brave, to have the courage. She must ask her husband for the divorce."

"I hope she will do that," Jack said, remembering the fear

in Annette's eyes when she spoke about Marius ruining him, and her as well.

"It might be that the husband wishes the divorce. He might welcome knowing that his wife wants to end the marriage."

"You're right!" Jack exclaimed. "I didn't think of that."

"If there is a lot of money involved, the husband might not merely welcome the idea of his wife leaving him. *He might be overjoyed.*"

"I do have some good ammunition, don't I?"

Claudine laughed, suddenly stood up. "Let us go and eat, my dear friend." She walked with him across the kitchen to a small dining corner near the window overlooking the yard. "I have made a fish stew. I remember how much you have enjoyed it in the past. I hope you're hungry."

"I am now. You've made me feel so much better. It's always good to have a sounding board."

"A what?" she asked.

"Someone to talk to who will give you the right advice. Someone who is wise."

Chapter Thirty-nine

After dinner Claudine took Jack on a tour of her house. Leaving the kitchen, they crossed a small hallway with a polished terra-cotta floor and went into the living room.

The last time Jack had seen it, the room had been bare except for a large sofa and several chairs all upholstered in a soft bluish gray fabric. Whilst the room itself was architecturally beautiful, with a fireplace and an array of windows which offered a spectacular view of the towns below, the furnishings had seemed mediocre. Tonight the room looked superb.

It was the paintings which brought it totally to life, adding color and movement, whilst carefully chosen accessories and large table lamps added the finishing touches.

"I call this the Matisse room," Claudine explained, as she glanced around. "And you can see why. Isn't that extraordinary?" She directed Jack's gaze to a large painting, a still life, over the fireplace. "I enjoy his use of color, don't you?"

"Absolutely, and this is a fabulous painting," Jack said, gazing up at it.

"Ah, yes, one of my favorites, too." Claudine swung around and said, "That smaller Matisse over there is actually the one I like the best, and also the Braque landscape on the side wall. They sit well together in the same room, those two paintings. You may not know this, but they painted alongside each other when they were in their Fauvist period. Let us continue the little tour."

Jack followed Claudine out into the hall and into the dining room opposite. Again it was simply furnished, with a round antique wood table, eight wood chairs with rush seats, and a small carved wood chest under the side window.

"*A voilà!*" Claudine exclaimed, and pointed to the Modigliani over the fireplace. "The woman is a classic Modigliani model. I have always admired his elongation of figures and use of bright color. He was a great figurative painter, and Vincent collected him, as well as Cézanne."

Jack's ears pricked up at the mention of Cézanne, and he said, "And do you have any of Cézanne's paintings?"

"I do. In the library. Let us go and see them. I didn't know you cared about art, Jack."

"I like certain painters, mostly Impressionists, which I understand. Some painters are too obscure for me, especially the contemporary abstract artists."

"*Ah, oui.* I know what you mean."

"So Vincent collected art, did he?" Jack asked, glancing at her.

"Most of his life. In fact, all of the paintings in this house were Vincent's. He left them to me in his will, as well as his villa in Villefranche." She smiled at Jack. "Which is where Antoine still works. Vincent employed him as a gardener for years."

The moment they walked into the library Jack spotted the two Cézanne paintings at once. They were distinctive and filled with strong color, especially dark greens and the more somber hues. He liked them, and went over to look at the landscapes more closely. It was then that his eye caught sight of the Degas dancer hanging on a side wall, and he stepped over, stared at it. He couldn't help thinking how much it resembled the Degas fake which had been found at Knowle Court. Obviously this was the real one. Swinging around, he said to Claudine, "I've seen a similar painting to this. . . . I like Degas. I understand his work."

"So do I. This was one of Vincent's early purchases, when

he first started collecting seriously. Shall we go upstairs? There are a couple of paintings I would like you to see, a Vlaminck and a Braque."

"I enjoyed that," Jack said once he and Claudine had returned to the kitchen. "Thank you for showing me the art collection." He sat down in the armchair in the seating area of the kitchen and picked up his glass of red wine, taking a sip.

Claudine joined him and said, "Perhaps you would prefer something else, Jack." She laughed. "You have been nursing the same glass of wine all night."

"Another coffee, please, Claudine. I do have to drive down that mountain, you know."

Claudine said, "You shall have your coffee immediately, Jack, and I fancy a Napoleon. I enjoy a cognac after dinner, a habit I acquired from Vincent."

As she rose and went to the drinks table to pour the cognac, Jack's gaze followed her. She was a striking woman, very handsome, and she did not look her age. Her hair was still jet-black and luxuriant, and she moved around with ease and energy. There was a certain vivacity about her that he admired.

He said, "So Vincent was an art collector. You've never told me that before."

"Did I not? Perhaps I assumed you knew. From Lucy." She came back to the seating area, handed him a fresh cup of coffee, and sat down next to him.

"I had the paintings in storage. After I sold Vincent's villa in Villefranche, I wanted to live here at the farm. To be close to Lucy and the girls. The villa was too large for me alone. And that is when I had the idea of building this little place for myself. It serves two purposes. . . . I am close to my family and I can display Vincent's art. He loved it. And it gave him great pleasure."

"It's quite a collection. It must be very valuable," Jack said. "Worth a fortune."

Claudine merely nodded. Unexpectedly she volunteered, "Vincent and I could not marry. He had a wife, you see, Jack. We had been together for forty years when she suddenly died. We decided not to bother making our relationship . . . *legal.*" She began to chuckle. "*Why?* I asked him, and he agreed. He had no children or relatives left, and so he made me his sole heir."

"As long as you were happy together, that's all that really counts," Jack said. "Which is what I keep telling my friend."

Claudine sighed, then offered him a small smile, but made no comment. She sipped her cognac, feeling great sympathy for Jack. *Toujours l'amour* . . . always love. Always pain.

Jack leaned forward and said urgently, "Listen, Claudine, I hope you have an alarm system here. I didn't notice one when I came in, and you must be protected. My God, all this valuable art! It must be worth hundreds of millions of euros."

Claudine gazed at him, her black eyes full of sudden merriment. She said, "I do have an alarm system, Jack."

Laughter overcame her for a few seconds, and when she had calmed herself, she said, sotto voce, "I have a secret, Jack. I shall tell you. However, you must swear to keep it. No one can ever know."

Intrigued, Jack nodded. "It seems to be our night of sharing confidences, doesn't it?" He smiled at her. "Whatever you tell me, I shall bury it deep. I will never betray you."

"The paintings are not real."

Jack gaped at her. "*Forgeries?*" He was momentarily stunned, so startled he went on staring at her, gobsmacked. "I can't believe it," he muttered.

"I know you can't. When Vincent first bought most of them, thirty years ago now, he truly thought they were genuine. But the prices were so low, he eventually questioned the owner of the gallery. This fellow was an old friend. . . . They went to school together. Pierre finally admitted they were fakes. He begged Vincent to keep his secret, he even offered to buy the paintings back from Vincent at a loss, because of their long friendship. Vincent refused. He loved them. It amused him. To own fakes which everyone thought were real made him chuckle. So he kept them hanging on his walls. When people admired his masterpieces he would merely smile. And he never betrayed Pierre, whom he had known at school."

"He was the gallery owner?"

Claudine nodded, picked up her brandy balloon, and took a sip.

"Was the gallery in Nice or Monte Carlo?"

"It was in Paris. The Pegasus Gallery."

"Did the owner ever get caught?" Jack asked, his curiosity as a journalist kicking in. But he was also thinking of the forgeries which had turned up at Knowle Court. He seemed to be stumbling over fakes these days.

"No, fortunately for him. And his partners. They were lucky. But I believe they did become nervous, and the Englishman also. So Pierre finally closed the gallery, and retired."

"*Englishman*? Do you know who he was?"

"I cannot remember his last name, Jack. His first name was most unusual. *Marius*. He had a gallery in London. And he had a special friend. *Mon dieu!* What was *his* name?" Claudine closed her eyes. "Let me think. *Ah, oui* . . . the friend of this Marius was a journalist. English also. Famous. Nigel! That was his name."

Jack sat up straighter, his face tightening. He asked swiftly, "Was his last name Clayton?"

"I am not sure. But he was a boulevardier. I heard he liked *les femmes* . . . the women."

"Boulevardier . . . a man about town," Jack said. "Is that all you know?"

"Yes. Why are you so curious, Jack? This all happened long before your time." She gave him an odd look, raised a brow.

"Not quite. I was a baby, though." He forced a smile. "So nobody knows you own forgeries, Claudine?"

"That is correct. And no one must. Fakes must be destroyed in France. It's the law." Her face became serious. "I trust you, Jack."

"What about Lucy?" he asked, giving her a penetrating stare.

"She does know. I had to tell her. She is my heir. But she will keep the secret. She knows she cannot sell the art."

"Do the paintings have provenances?"

"No! No! *C'est pas possible!* A provenance is hard to fake." She threw him a questioning look. "What do you think of my art collection, is it not good? You were fooled, I know."

"It is good, and yes, I was fooled, you're right about that, Claudine. Now, would it be possible to have another cup of coffee, please, before I head on down that dangerous mountain?"

Jack was relieved when he pulled into the garage at the Villa Saint-Honoré. He let himself into the house, went straight upstairs to his office, and called Annette on her mobile. She did not answer and he left a message, asking her to phone him. Then he sat back in the chair, his mind in a turmoil.

Marius Remmington was a crook.

He had been involved in selling forgeries through a gallery in Paris thirty years ago. So was he behind the forgeries which were suddenly being discovered now? He did not know. Maybe this was just a coincidence? And was the man Claudine remembered as Marius's friend, a man called Nigel, his own father? Had Nigel Clayton and Remmington been in cahoots? Had his father also been dealing in forged art through the Pegasus Gallery in Paris?

He did not know. But he aimed to find out. Only the truth would do. But how could he find out anything? His mother and father were dead, as was his stepfather. He could hardly go and question Marius Remmington. Who else might know something? My God, his aunt! *Of course.*

Aunt Helen was still alive, and had just returned from Canada. He must go and see her immediatcly, question her.

He was, after all, a damned good journalist, had once even been an investigative reporter. *He would get the facts, no matter what.* Aunt Helen was the key to the past, wasn't she? Because Helen and her sister, his mother, Eleanor, had been like two peas in a pod. Fast friends, intimates, and extremely close until the day his mother died.

The Louis Vuitton trunk.

Jack remembered it and zeroed in on what he had seen in it. All those notebooks and diaries. He had merely flipped through them, and briefly, had hardly paid any attention to them. There were photographs as well. The trunk held a lot of information. And secrets? And answers to more secrets? He hoped so. He sighed to himself. He hadn't been paying attention to the trunk because of Annette and his sudden obsessive fascination with her.

His thoughts settled on Annette. He wondered if there was any way she could have been involved. He doubted it, knowing her as well as he did. She was as honest as he was.

Claudine had said it all happened thirty years ago, before his time. *1977.* Annette would have been only ten years old. She couldn't possibly have had anything to do with it.

Two shocks in one day, Jack thought, and both involved Marius Remmington. *How about that.* He was determined to get to the bottom of everything, no matter what it took, and he was certainly going to tell Annette about the fakes in France. She would have to promise to keep his confidence. But he knew, and without a shadow of a doubt, that she could be trusted.

Annette had to know about Claudine's collection of art and where it came from, because she had to understand that her husband was a crook. And also an adulterer.

Despite what Claudine had said, the way she had cautioned him to keep quiet, Jack was going to tell Annette about the scene he had witnessed at La Réserve. She was an adult. She had to know. And she could handle it.

Standing up, Jack went and retrieved his manuscript from the other desk, put all the rubber bands around it, and went to find his small overnight bag in the bedroom. He packed the manuscript in it, then did a quick survey of the office, found all of the small things he had brought with him. These he placed next to his laptop, including his extra mobile.

He was going to fly to London tomorrow. He had no other choice. He must do his investigation so that he would discover the truth about everything. And everyone.

Chapter Forty

Organization was one of Jack's strong suits, and on Thursday morning, back in his flat in Primrose Hill, he took everything out of the Louis Vuitton trunk, carefully laid it out on his freshly made bed. Then he began sorting the photographs, the trivia, the notebooks, and the diaries into separate piles.

He spent most of his time going through the diaries and the notebooks. They confirmed a lot. Much to his chagrin, he did discover that his father had indeed been a close friend of Marius Remmington's, and there were mentions of trips to Paris, the Pegasus Gallery, and paintings by Braque, Pissarro, Sisley, Cézanne, and Matisse.

And yet there was nothing incriminating to do with either his father or Remmington. No mention of paintings sold, bought, or exchanged. Nothing about deals being made at the Pegasus Gallery, paintings being sold or delivered. And not one word about forgeries or forgers. *Zilch.*

Yet the Pegasus Gallery had obviously been a part of his father's life; he seemingly had known a great deal about art. According to what he had written, he loved paintings and painters, liked to socialize with them, was at ease in the bohemian world.

At one moment, Jack went and sat down in a chair, and closed his eyes, thinking. Naturally there would not be one thing that was incriminating on paper. His father had undoubtedly been too smart for that.

What had been the connection between his father and Remmington? Were they simply mates? Two chaps who liked each other, liked to carouse and womanize together? He just didn't know. Whilst the notebooks told him a lot about his father, there was not one word in them which connected his father and Remmington to any criminal act.

So his father was out of the picture in a sense.

Remmington was still very much in it. Jack could not deny facts. Claudine had indicated that Remmington was a partner in the Pegasus Gallery. She had told him Pierre, Vincent's friend, wanted out, as had the Englishman, i.e., Marius. Later, he had established that the gallery had closed in about 1979. He was facing a brick wall.

What was he actually looking for? Information which he could use to bring Marius Remmington down. Unfortunately, to Jack's annoyance, it just wasn't there. And yet he could not dispel the feeling that the fakes from thirty years ago had something to do with the forgeries so recently found at Knowle Court. If anyone asked him why he felt this, he wouldn't be able to explain. And yet the suspicion lingered that Marius Remmington was somehow involved.

Getting up out of the chair, Jack did some push-ups and stretches, and then sat at the desk and dialed Annette's mobile. It was turned off. Glancing at his watch, he saw that it was just ten o'clock. He rang her office, and was relieved when Esther answered.

"It's Jack Chalmers. Good morning, Esther."

"Hello, Jack," she answered in a bland voice.

"Could I speak to Annette, please?"

"I'm afraid she's not here. She won't be in today. Is there anything I can do?"

"Er, er, not really. I had a few questions for her, regarding the piece for *The New York Times*."

"Why don't you e-mail them to me, and I'll get them answered," Esther suggested.

"I prefer to do this directly with her." Jack paused for a moment, then asked, "Can I get her at home?"

"She's not there. She's out and about, on business. But I will pass on your message when I hear from her."

"Thanks, Esther. I wonder if you can tell her something else."

"Of course, I'll tell her anything you want."

"Would you tell her I need to speak to her about the paintings recently found at Knowle Court? The fakes. And tell her it's urgent."

"I will, Jack. Bye."

"So long, Esther," he murmured, and hung up.

Jack sat staring at the phone. He had not spoken to Annette since Monday. He had left countless messages on her mobile and her private line at the office, and on the office answering machine. Esther knew all this, at least about the calls to the office, yet she hadn't referred to them. He might as well admit it, a wall had gone up between himself and Annette, and she had erected it. Because Marius was due to come home soon; perhaps he was already home. She was frightened of her husband, and Jack was fully aware she was not able to handle their love affair because of this. She was terrified they would be found out.

He thought back to some of the things she had said lately. . . . *We must cool it.* . . . *We have to break up.* . . . *I can't continue seeing you.* And on and on. And when she grew really scared, she warned him that Marius would ruin him. And also her.

But how? By bad-mouthing him? Or them? By putting her out of business somehow? Did Marius have something on her? Was there some kind of blackmailing going on here?

Certainly there was nothing Remmington could have on him, because he was squeaky clean. Could Remmington reveal something terrible about his father? Even if he could, what did that matter today? His father had died years ago. Yes, he had been a famous journalist, but who remembered him nowadays?

Suddenly, none of this made sense, and all Jack knew

was that he was frustrated on every level. Furthermore, he genuinely needed a sounding board, somebody to talk to about Annette, Marius, and the forgeries. Whom could he trust? Whom could he unburden himself to here in London? Who knew the players to be able to make a proper judgment?

Margaret Mellor. No way. She seemed trustworthy enough, but they weren't exactly close friends and she was a journalist. He dare not expose Annette's life to her. *Laurie.* A possibility. But he would have to be cautious. *Malcolm Stevens.* Maybe Malcolm would be the best person to talk to. He would call him. And right now to make that date for lunch.

The two men met the next day for lunch at Wiltons in Jermyn Street. Malcolm had suggested it and Jack was happy to eat there. It was one of his favorite restaurants in the world, and he was always tickled by the line which went under the name: *Noted since 1742 for the finest Oysters, Fish & Game.*

Malcolm was already waiting for him in a quiet corner when he arrived, and as Jack sat down he realized again how much he had liked Malcolm the night they had dinner together at the Ivy. He was a straight shooter.

Jack declined a glass of wine, asking instead for sparkling water. He explained, "I'm working on the piece about Annette for *The New York Times Magazine.* So I'm sort of on the wagon."

"I understand, and I rarely drink at lunchtime. Anyway, I'm delighted you phoned, Jack. It was really odd. . . . I was just about to get in touch with you, actually."

"Great minds think alike," Jack said, and swiftly went on, "How's Laurie?"

"Extremely well, and fussing about the wedding." Malcolm smiled indulgently. "You know what women are like when it comes to that particular occasion."

Jack nodded, and jumping in with both feet, he said, "And how's Annette? I haven't spoken to her for a few days."

"As far as I know, she's fine, and I think rather pleased about the reaction to your story last Sunday."

"She told me all about that, and the marvelous fuss being made over *The Little Fourteen-Year-Old Dancer*." After a sip of the water, Jack went on, "You've known her a long time, haven't you?"

"About fifteen years, or thereabouts. I know it was before I bought the Remmington, and that's ten years ago already. You know, I can hardly believe it. My father lent me the money, and he thought he'd never get it back. But he was wrong."

"I understand you've made it into a bigger success than it was when Marius owned it."

Malcolm grinned. "It's true, but don't let him hear you say that, it gets his goat. On the other hand, I think in many ways he's glad to be rid of it. He has his freedom, and that allows him to do so many other things."

"I can well imagine," Jack said pithily.

Malcolm looked at him alertly, and laughed. "You don't really like him, do you?"

"I don't really know him," Jack shot back diplomatically.

"He's a bit of a blowhard at times, and he's boastful, so he's not the most popular chap in town. But he's basically okay."

"You're one of his protégés, a favorite, so I'm told."

"I was a protégé years ago, and Annette has always said I'm the favorite, but I don't really know if that's true. Actually, nobody knows how or where they stand with Marius. He's a clever fellow at hiding his feelings and dissimulating."

Jack was startled by Malcolm's forthrightness, and the candid manner in which he was speaking about Marius; he wondered if a message was being sent.

Deciding to test the water, Jack went on, as he picked up the menu, "There's been gossip about Annette and me, I know that, Malcolm. Do you think Marius has heard it?"

"Yes, I do."

Further taken aback, Jack said, "And why do you believe that? Has he said something to you, talked about us?"

"No, I haven't seen him. He's been in Barcelona. He just

returned on Tuesday night. And we haven't spoken on the phone either."

"So how do you know he's heard the gossip?"

"Marius has always had his ear to the ground, and lots of people sort of . . . well, report in to him. And then there's the cadre of young men who have worked for him, or still do, and they carry lots of tales. They want to curry favor with him." Glancing at the menu himself, Malcolm looked at Jack and asked, "Do you know what you want?"

"I do. Shall we order?"

Almost immediately a waiter came over, and Jack said he would like Colchester oysters, grilled English sole, and chips.

Malcolm laughed and said, "I'm not an adventurous eater, so I'll have the same as you."

Once they were alone, Malcolm decided to open up to Jack. "I know you're wondering if you can trust me, and I want to assure you that you can. My loyalty lies with Annette, Jack, and it always has. So you may feel free to speak, as candidly as you wish. It will go no further. I believe you've got a lot to get off your chest."

"I do, yes, how did you guess?" Jack asked, giving Malcolm a penetrating look.

"We did have dinner together, remember, and whilst you both were extraordinarily discreet, I picked up on the undercurrent between you. And incidentally, so did Laurie. Who's exceptionally bright, by the way."

"I'd rather gathered that. And yes, I do feel in need of someone to talk to. Also, it goes without saying that I trust you, Malcolm. Otherwise I wouldn't have called about our having lunch together."

"I'm glad you did. I think you might need a friend. . . ."

"So you know all about us, Malcolm, is that what you're trying to say?"

"No, not trying. I'm saying it. And frankly, I'm glad. It's about time she has some sort of personal happiness. God knows, she needs it."

"And before me there was never another man?"

"Not to my knowledge."

"Listen, there's something I want to tell you now. It's imperative that I have your promise not to reveal to anyone what I'm about to say."

"I thought we'd agreed on total confidentiality at the outset of this conversation."

"We did. But what I'm about to tell you could cause the most terrible trouble for someone, an older person I care about."

"I understand. So, please, go ahead."

At this moment the waiter arrived with their plates of oysters, and once they had been served, Jack continued his story.

He said, in a low voice, "I know for a fact, from a most reliable and impeccable source, that our friend was involved with an art gallery in Paris, as well as owning the one you now own. It was called the Pegasus, and the owners dealt in fakes. Fabulous forgeries that were so brilliant everyone believed they were genuine." Lowering his voice even more, he finished, "Marius was apparently a partner in that gallery, until they all got nervous and closed it down in 1979."

Malcolm was so astonished he was speechless. Then he shook his head. "It's very hard to believe he would do anything like that. It's criminal. They could have all gone to jail. But I trust your source. If you say it's impeccable, then it must be. The law is very tough in France when it comes to fakes, forgery, you know."

"I do. I'd like to change the subject for a moment. Will he give Annette a divorce?"

"No."

Jack nodded. A faint smile flickered. "He has a mistress."

"I'm not surprised," Malcolm answered, threw Jack a pointed look. "A lot of men do."

"Annette could divorce him. Citing this woman."

"How would she ever know who it was?" Malcolm's brow shot up quizzically.

"I would tell her. You see, quite by accident, I know who the woman is. In fact, I saw them together on Tuesday of this week. At La Réserve in Beaulieu. I might say caught them red-handed. Well, almost."

"I'll be buggered!" Malcolm exclaimed, astonishment on his face. "How on earth did that come about?"

Jack filled him in, adding, "I want to see Annette, Malcolm, but only to talk. I must tell her everything I've told you. The problem is, I can't get to her. She won't return my calls."

Malcolm nodded. "I'm sure she's running scared. And I do mean scared. Sometimes she seems to be quite frightened of him."

"Don't tell me. I've picked up on that. I've some more checking to do, a little more investigating, but when I'm ready to see Annette, will you arrange it for me?"

"Of course I will," Malcolm responded, and then paused as the plates were removed. After a moment, he went on, "I want to point out something. Marius is a powerful man, devious at times, and perhaps even dangerous. Are you sure you want to take him on?"

"You can bet your bloody life I do!" Jack exclaimed.

Chapter Forty-one

✳

Annette knew she had to stay away from Jack to protect him. As long as she didn't see him, had no contact whatsoever, he would be safe. He could live his life normally and it would be intact. One move toward him and he would be ruined. Marius would see to that. She knew how vengeful her husband could be.

She sighed heavily as she walked across Eaton Square in the direction of Chesham Place. It was Saturday, and she was going to lunch with Laurie, as she usually did at the end of the week, and looking forward to it. And to being out of the flat.

Marius had returned earlier this week and he was in a foul mood. Bad tempered, snappish, critical, and in general out of sorts. If she didn't know better, she would have said he was ill. But he was as strong as a bull and in remarkable health. Only last month he had seen his physician for a checkup, and had come through with flying colors.

No, it was not ill health that was troubling him. He was angry because he was back home. In the past, when he returned from a trip, he was always in a good mood, caring, loving, and aiming to please. But not this week. Aside from his anger and moodiness, he talked incessantly about the virtues of Barcelona, and she noticed he had made countless phone calls to Spain in the past few days. Speaking in Spanish.

Why this was she didn't know. Business? Another woman? She couldn't be bothered to fathom it out. She didn't care.

Annette felt a wave of tiredness sweep over her as she walked toward her sister's building. For the last few days she had been exhausted. She had barely slept, had lain awake most nights thinking about Jack, worrying about him, aching to see him, to be with him. She was in love with him, but he was lost to her. It broke her heart knowing they would never be together. Yet she would willingly spend her life apart from him, if this meant he would be safe. That was how much she loved him. He came first. She must protect him.

Endeavoring to shake off her tiredness, and pushing a bright smile onto her face, she went into Laurie's building, heading for her flat. Instead of using her key, Annette rang the bell, something she had been doing lately since Laurie had become engaged. She never wanted to intrude on her sister and Malcolm, infringe on their privacy.

It was Angie, Laurie's caregiver, who let her in, smiling cheerfully, wishing her good morning.

"Laurie's in the den, Annette," Angie said, and disappeared in the direction of the kitchen.

Annette's heart lifted when she saw how lovely Laurie looked today, her happiness a palpable thing.

"I'm so glad you're free for lunch," Laurie said after they embraced. "I know it's been such a crazy week for you, with the huge fuss about the next auction and the Degas sculpture. You must be feeling good about it, though."

"I am," Annette replied, sitting down opposite Laurie. "There's a lot of work to do, but it's encouraging to know how much anticipation there is, rather exciting, actually."

"I'll help you as much as I can," Laurie reassured her.

Annette smiled at her indulgently. "*You've* enough to do! What with a wedding and a baby on the horizon. You are feeling all right, aren't you? Healthy?"

"Yes, I am, and I go for weekly checkups to the doctor. I'm very good. And so is Malcolm. There's nobody like him, Annette, he's so thoughtful and loving, I'm very lucky."

"Yes, you are. He's one in a million, and he'll be a good husband to you."

"I know. And talking of husbands, how's Marius?"

"Not nice. In fact, he's being beastly, quite nasty."

"Could he have heard that silly gossip about Jack?" Laurie looked worried suddenly.

"I don't know, and I really don't care."

"Did he like the profile Jack wrote?"

"Do you know, he's never even mentioned it to me. Nor has he asked any questions about the general reaction to the two stories in the papers. Or the follow-ups in other newspapers which have been running. He seems totally without interest. But that's fine by me. I've never wanted him messing around in my business."

Laurie sat back in her wheelchair, a reflective look settling in her eyes. After a moment, she said, "You might not agree with me, but I think Marius is jealous. I don't mean about Jack, but about your success. First there was the fabulous Rembrandt auction, and now the enormous excitement about the upcoming auction, and the discovery of *The Little Fourteen-Year-Old Dancer.* You've been in the newspapers all this week, and you're getting enormous publicity. I think he's . . . ticked off about it. You've stolen his thunder, don't you think? You're the star these days, not him."

Preoccupied with Jack and their affair, Annette had not thought much about anything else for the past week. She had automatically done her work, with her usual professionalism, but she certainly hadn't given a thought to the continuing publicity. And now she knew that Laurie had just pinpointed something important . . . possibly the truth.

"You may be right, darling," Annette said, and went on, "So where shall I take you for lunch? We might as well go out and celebrate my . . . newfound fame! Even though I think of fame as being totally useless and ephemeral. And not all that important."

"I asked Angie to make lunch for us. Do you mind if we eat here? She went to Harrods this morning and bought all sorts of goodies. Smoked salmon, a roast chicken, oysters, chocolate mousse, beetroot salad, and strawberry ice cream."

Annette stared at her sister and laughed for the first time in days. "Which are you going to start with? Talk about a special menu for a pregnant woman! Are you craving things?"

"Well, you like most of those things, Annette, you know you do. I ordered for both of us, not just myself."

"I'm teasing you, and of course we can stay here. I prefer it, actually."

Over lunch the sisters talked about Laurie's upcoming wedding in July. She and Annette decided that a save-the-date card should be mailed as soon as possible, and Laurie promised to get the invitations ordered immediately.

As they discussed the venue, the menu, the flowers, and the guest list, Laurie unexpectedly said, "I wish we knew where Alison was. I'd love her to be at my wedding."

"And so would I, darling, but I've no idea how to find her. As you so well know, she's rarely been in touch over the years. Sadly."

"The few cards we've had were postmarked France, and I know that's where she would choose to live. She was a genuine dyed-in-the-wool Francophile, wasn't she?"

Annette nodded, and suddenly smiled, remembering their lovely cousin. It was Alison who had given them the names Marie Antoinette and Josephine, and written the song for them, which was called "The Rainbow Queens."

Almost as if she read her mind, Laurie suddenly began to sing. " 'My name is Empress Josephine and I am Queen of France, won't you come and dance?' " She paused and looked across at Annette, and exclaimed, "Oh, you're crying! Have I upset you? Have I brought back bad memories of those awful days? I'm so sorry."

"No, good memories," Annette answered, wiping her tears away with her fingers. "I was thinking of Alison, and

with much love in my heart for her. . . . She saved our lives."
Annette took control of herself, and smiled at her sister.

"In more ways than one, don't you think?" Laurie said.
"First she saved you from *him*. And she saved our sanity
when she took us out to play in the fields, and out to tea. And
when she finally removed us from Craggs End, and went
with us to London, to our mother. It took courage on her part,
to defy our grandfather. As if he cared whether we were
there in Ilkley with him or not."

"I don't think he did, but I've realized over the years that
he was simply a tired, defeated old man with no strength left."

"He didn't protect you from Gregory when he came home
from school," Laurie pointed out.

"No, but Alison did, and then paid for it in so many ways."

There was a small silence, and finally Laurie murmured in a
low voice, "The wisest thing you ever did was go to Dr. Stepha-
nie Lomax. She really helped you to cope with your childhood
abuse and rape, didn't she? Helped you to get better."

"Yes, and we also talked a lot about the abuse I suffered
when I was older. I learned how to deal with everything
eventually. But it did take years. Because abuse is so very
damaging."

Annette started to cry and took a tissue out of her jacket
pocket, wiped her eyes. "I'm so sorry, Laurie. We shouldn't
be talking about the past in this way, not today. We're supposed to be planning your wedding, settling on the details.
So let's do that, shall we? Let's be happy today."

Laurie merely nodded, and ate a little of the smoked
salmon, endeavoring to push away the past, bury it deep. It
took a few moments, as it usually did; she knew she would
never be free of those memories of what Annette had gone
through to protect her when they were little. And she would
never forget Annette's screams when Timothy Findas had
beaten her. Their mother had not been able to help. She was
always drunk.

* * *

Later, when Annette returned to the flat in Eaton Square, she found a note from Marius. He had gone to Gloucester-shire to see a client, and would not be back in time for dinner. He'd added that he might stay over.

This news filled her with relief. She took off her clothes, put on a robe, and went to lie down on the bed. Exhaustion swamped her, and she tried to sleep but found she could not. Her mind was whirling with thoughts of Jack. She loved him, needed him, wanted him, but it could not be. The tears started again. Her heart was broken and she cried for a long time. But she found some release as she wept, and eventually, worn out, she fell into a deep sleep. And for once it was dreamless.

On the other side of London, Jack Chalmers was visiting his aunt, who lived in a comfortable flat in St. John's Wood.

Helen North was delighted to see her nephew, and as she poured the tea, she said, "It was lovely of you to bring these things of your mother's, Jack. I shall treasure them, especially the dressing table set. She loved those silver brushes and the mirror."

"I'm glad I picked the right things, Aunt Helen," Jack answered. "I know she valued them enormously. And listen, there is a lot more stuff at the house in Hampstead. I'll go up there with you tomorrow, if you can make it, and you can look around."

"That's so nice of you." Helen glanced at him and asked, "Don't you want the silver and china? And what about Kyle?"

"Neither of us want it, Aunt Helen. So you can pick and choose, and I'll bring it back here for you. I'm using Kyle's car while he's away, and we can make a couple of trips if necessary."

"I'm sure you've better things to do than ferry your aunt around on a Sunday," Helen said.

"It's fine, honestly, I'm happy to do it. The house is for

sale, and Kyle and I are anxious to get everything out as soon as possible."

"All right then, we have a date."

"Good. I'll pick you up about ten, is that all right?"

"Perfect." She indicated the plate of small tea sandwiches and asked, "Aren't you hungry?"

"No, not really, but thanks." He sipped the tea, put the cup down, and said, "Aunt Helen, I'm wondering if you could help me with something . . . something about the past."

"If I can I will, Jack, what is it you want to know?"

"A few things about my father. I mean my biological father, of course. Nigel Clayton."

Helen frowned. "Good Lord, Jack, whatever can I tell you about Nigel that you don't already know?" She seemed surprised.

"Quite a lot, I think. You see, I never really knew him, and my mother always bad-mouthed him. Peter, God bless him, never uttered an unkind word about anybody, and chose not to discuss Nigel with me, when I asked questions as I grew older."

"But what is it you want to know?" She frowned, peered at him. "And why now?"

"Because I'm writing about something that happened in the nineteen-seventies, and I think he might have been friends with one of the men featured in my piece," he improvised.

"Oh, I see, all right then. Ask away, my dear."

"It's a story about art, actually, Aunt Helen, and I was told that my father used to be a friend of a man called Marius Remmington. Is that true?"

Helen was silent for a moment, and then she nodded. "They were more than just friends, Jack, they were best friends. At one time they were virtually inseparable, as I remember it. That would have been thirty years ago, in 1977. Before Marius had opened the Remmington Gallery in Cork Street. He had a much smaller one called the Glade Gallery, I think."

"Do you know if my father was ever involved in business with him? In the art business?"

"I don't know. . . . I don't think so. Why?"

"I just wondered, that's all. So was Marius married in those days?"

"Oh, no, he was single, and quite the gay blade, the man about town. So was your father, well, a little bit. . . . Nigel was a flirt, and it was all harmless fun, as far as he was concerned. But I know your mother used to get angry with him." Helen shook her head. "She just didn't like Marius. She thought he was a bad influence on your father, leading him astray."

"You say that as if you don't believe it." Jack scrutinized his aunt, wondering about those years long ago, very curious now.

"I never thought your father betrayed your mother, not in the early days. They were married when they were both twenty-eight, and in love. Then you came along two years later. Nigel was all right, a nice chap, as I said."

"And Marius? Tell me more about him."

"He was good-looking. Very handsome, and the silver hair was unique, especially with that young face of his. He played around a lot, but he *was* single at the time. Then he became entangled with some young artist. I can't remember what she was called, it was an odd name, but she was beautiful, and they were an item for a long time. It might have been that the friendship with your father cooled a bit around that time."

"So they quarreled? Is that what you're saying?"

Helen sat thinking, and then murmured, "No, I don't think they fell out, nothing like that. But Marius was really involved with the girl. For several years at least, and I guess she took up a lot of his time. And I think your father was . . . well, left out."

"I know what you mean, two's company, three's a crowd. Anyway, were Marius and my father still friends when Nigel was killed?"

Helen sat up in the chair with a slight jerk and stared at him. "*Killed*? What do you mean by that?"

"Nigel was killed in battle. He stepped on a land mine on

some battlefield in some far-flung corner of the world, according to my mother."

"Your mother told you *that*?" Helen's eyes narrowed, and she kept shaking her head over and over, looking baffled and a bit put out.

Jack said, "My father was a war correspondent, wasn't he?"

"No, he wasn't."

"But he *was* a journalist?"

"Yes, and right in the beginning, when he was in his twenties, he did a short stint as a war correspondent. After he married your mother, Eleanor made him give it up. You see, she was afraid he would be killed. And after that he was based in London. He soon made a name for himself with a very clever column, which was so well written it won him countless accolades and major prizes all the time. He became famous."

Jack sat back, gaping at his aunt, shocked by her words. Why was nothing ever the way it seemed? he wondered, and let out a long sigh. Then he asked, "Why on earth would my mother fabricate that whole story about him being addicted to war? Forever chasing danger, being blown up on a battlefield? It doesn't make sense."

"I'm afraid it doesn't, Jack, and I don't know why she told you a pack of lies. Nor do I know why she bad-mouthed him to you." There was a pause, then she continued, "Perhaps she felt let down by him. About twenty-five years ago, Marius broke up with the artist, and he and your father were back being best mates. If I remember correctly, that's when your mother was growing disenchanted with your father. Perhaps after his death, when you were old enough to ask questions, she wanted to glamorize him, and so she said he was a war correspondent who died in action. A hero perhaps? I just don't know."

"I cannot believe she'd do that. . . . She lied to me. And over and over again. Why did she want me to hate him? Because she did?" Jack was suddenly angry, as well as shaken up.

Helen North shook her head, as baffled and upset as her nephew was. Rising, she went and sat down next to him on the sofa, took hold of his hand. "I have no explanation for her behavior, Jack, and I know how upsetting it is to hear that she didn't tell you the truth. But I am telling you how it really was."

"Oh, Aunt Helen, I know that. I'm just bloody astonished and shocked. Anyway, how *did* my father die?"

"He fell down some steps and hit his head. It was a bad injury."

"Where did this happen, Aunt Helen?"

"In his house in Notting Hill. You might not remember it, but you lived there as a child."

"No, I don't remember the house. So what happened? I mean, was he dead and someone found him? Or what?"

"Actually your mother and I found him, Jack."

"Oh, my God! That's terrible. It must have been some shock for you both." He threw her a sympathetic look, squeezed her hand.

"It was. Let me explain. Your mother and father had separated. He loved the house, your mother didn't, so she was happy to let him keep it. She moved into a flat near me. Anyway, one evening she decided we must go over to see him. She wanted to pick up certain things. She still had a key. We went in and found him on the hall floor. Bleeding. There was a lot of blood, Jack."

"Oh, my God." He shuddered. "So you called an ambulance, is that it?"

"Yes, we did. . . ." Helen paused, bit her lip. "It was a shock for your mother, and for me . . . finding him like that."

"Was he actually dead when you arrived? Or did he die in hospital?" Jack wanted to know everything.

"In the ambulance," Helen murmured, her voice low and sad.

"Well, at least I know the whole truth now," Jack asserted quietly.

Helen sat back on the sofa, remembering that night so well. It was as if it had happened only yesterday, so vivid was it in her mind. And she also remembered something else. She wanted to tell Jack about what she had seen, but hesitated, not sure that she ought to do so. All this had happened so long ago.

Jack, as always astute, said, "Are you holding something back, Aunt Helen? Is there something you're not telling me? You do know you can tell me anything, don't you? After all, we're family. In fact, except for Kyle, you're the only family I have left."

"I know. . . . I was remembering that night. It came back to me with such vividness I feel a little shaken, to tell you the truth." She turned to him, looked into his eyes, and said slowly, in a voice so quiet it was almost inaudible, "I saw something when we were going into the house. . . ."

"What was it?" he asked tensely, his gaze riveted on her.

"I saw *someone*, Jack, and I thought at once that the person must have just left Nigel's house. . . ." She stopped and took a deep breath, obviously not wanting to go on. "I do remember thinking exactly that."

"But whom did you see?" Jack pressed, anxious to know everything.

"Marius Remmington," she said at last. "Just a few yards down the street, getting into a taxi. It was April, and there was a full moon, and I recognized his profile, and especially the silver hair."

"And what did my mother say?"

"She didn't see him. She was looking in her bag for the key, getting it in the door, then going into the house. I was behind her on the step, and happened to look down the street. And I saw him. I heard your mother scream, and I ran into the house, and I forgot about seeing Marius in the street. But much later, I did think about it again, and worried about it."

"Why?"

"Because the doctor at the hospital made a remark about not being sure if your father had died because of the fall. Or because he had been hit by an object which had caused blunt force trauma. Words to that effect."

"You mean somebody might have hit Nigel on the head?"

"Perhaps. Of course there's no way of knowing, and perhaps I shouldn't have told you. I don't want you to think I'm accusing Marius Remmington of anything, because I'm not. I *think* it was him in the street that night, but obviously I can't swear to it."

"But why would Marius Remmington want to kill my father?"

"There was no reason. They were best friends," Helen said, wishing she had kept quiet.

"Perhaps Marius arrived, found Nigel before you got there, discovered he was dead, and just left," Jack ventured.

"But would he leave his best friend in that condition? Wouldn't he have called an ambulance? Like your mother and I did."

"Yes, he would. And I don't think Marius would have been that callous. Nigel might have fallen after Marius left."

"So many doubts . . . Am I not correct, Jack?"

"Yes, you are. Was there an inquest?"

"There was. The verdict was accidental death."

"So the blunt force trauma was never proved."

"No, it wasn't. . . . There was always doubt there."

Jack stood up, walked over to the window, and looked out, his thoughts racing. Finally he turned to face his aunt. "You've told me a lot more than I expected to hear today, Aunt Helen, but I'm glad you did. It helps to know the truth, at least most of it."

Helen gave Jack a penetrating glance. "I hope you won't use that bit about Marius, because I'm not really sure it was him in the street, you know."

"Of course I won't use it. He's still alive and I don't want to get sued for libel or defamation of character or some such thing. I'm afraid I've got to leave now, but I'll pick you up tomorrow at ten."

"That'll be lovely, Jack," Helen said, and walked with him to the door.

After hugging her he left and went down in the lift, his thoughts still racing. *Marius Remmington*. The man was more paramount in his mind than ever. Malcolm had said he was dangerous. Was he a murderer? Jack aimed to find out.

Chapter Forty-two

❊

Malcolm Stevens is in reception, Annette," Esther said from the doorway. "I know you're about to leave for a meeting at Sotheby's, but he absolutely *insists* on talking to you. He says it's an emergency."

"Oh, my God! I hope Laurie's all right. Please show him in, Esther." Annette stood up and walked around her desk.

"What's wrong, Malcolm?" Annette asked as he came into her office a moment later. She saw how worried he looked and knew something serious had happened. She went over to him and he hugged her.

"It's nothing to do with Laurie," Malcolm then reassured her. "It's about Marius."

"Marius?" She looked puzzled. "What about him?"

"He's in hospital, Annette. St. Thomas's. We must go to see him immediately. I have a car waiting."

Annette grabbed her handbag, and as they hurried out she stopped at Esther's office, quickly explained where they were going and why, adding, "Please cancel my appointments for today. I'll be in touch."

Once they were in the street and Malcolm had called the car on his mobile, she said, "What happened to Marius? Was he in some kind of accident? What's wrong with him?"

"I'm not exactly sure, but we'll know as soon as we get there. I received a phone call about twenty minutes ago, from a woman called Elizabeth Grayson. She said she had a breakfast meeting arranged with Marius. It was about buying a painting. She was waiting for him in the lobby of the Dorchester. As he came in, he saw her, waved, and came walking over, then suddenly collapsed in the middle of the lobby. She ran to him, as did several of the hotel staff. An ambulance was called, and as they were waiting for it to arrive, Marius gave her my number, asked her to call me. Which she did."

"But why did he collapse? What's wrong with him? Didn't she say anything else?"

"No. Just that Marius wanted her to phone me. She did explain that the ambulance men didn't want her to go to the hospital with him. That's all I know."

At this moment the car arrived. Malcolm helped her in, went around to the other side, and got in next to her. "Try not to worry. I'm sure he's going to be all right," he said, squeezing her arm.

"He just had a checkup, Malcolm. The doctor said he was very fit." After a moment, Annette added, "Elizabeth Grayson must be a new client. I've never heard of her, have you?"

"No, I haven't."

"I wonder why Marius told her to call you, not me?"

Malcolm was silent.

Annette looked at him, and said in a quiet tone, "I don't actually know where exactly he was this weekend. He went to Gloucestershire to see a client."

Turning, Malcolm stared at her. Frowning, he asked, "Didn't he phone you over the last couple of days?"

"No. He'd left me a note. I found it after I came back from lunch with Laurie. He'd written that he might stay over. I didn't give it another thought. He's always been like that, sort of . . . well, evasive, vague, hard to pin down, to find. Not that I ever try to do such a thing now. Once when I did he was furious."

"He's always been a bit of a loner in a certain sense."

"Yes." She looked out of the window, wondering what was wrong with Marius. Thinking out loud, she said, "Could he have had a stroke? A heart attack? What do you think?"

"I don't want to play guessing games," Malcolm murmured. "Let's wait until we get the proper opinions from doctors."

The traffic was moving quickly and the car was soon traveling at a good speed down Westminster Bridge Road, heading in the direction of St. Thomas's. A few minutes before they reached the hospital, Malcolm's mobile rang. He flipped it open, said his name, and listened. "Thank you, Maeve. So we're to ask for Dr. James Ellwood," he said, and thanked her again.

After closing the phone, Malcolm said, "I had my secretary call a surgeon I know at St. Thomas's. Luckily he was able to locate someone to meet us. Better than going there cold."

Malcolm asked for Dr. James Ellwood at the reception desk in the lobby of the hospital, and a few minutes later a tall, fair-haired man was walking over to them.

"I'm Dr. Ellwood, Mr. Stevens," he said. "Your friend Dr. Latimer asked me to meet you, since he's operating at the moment."

The two men shook hands, and Malcolm said, "This is Mrs. Annette Remmington, Dr. Ellwood. Her husband collapsed this morning in the lobby of the Dorchester Hotel, and was brought here by ambulance."

He shook hands with Annette, and gave her a friendly smile. "I heard that from Dr. Latimer. Your husband's on the cardiovascular floor, Mrs. Remmington. I'll take you up there."

"Has my husband had a heart attack, Dr. Ellwood?" Annette asked as she walked with the doctor and Malcolm to the elevator.

"Not exactly. But that is not my area of expertise, so I'll refrain from answering. I don't want to mislead you. They'll tell you everything you need to know."

"I understand," Annette answered as they went into the elevator. Within seconds they were stepping out on the cardiovascular floor, being introduced to Dr. Martin Chambers. He explained he was in charge of the case of Mr. Remmington, who was now his patient.

"What has happened to my husband?" Annette asked at once, sounding anxious and looking pale, worried.

"He is suffering from aortic dissection. This is a potentially life-threatening condition, Mrs. Remmington," Dr. Chambers said, then went on to explain. "It is a condition in which there is bleeding into and along the wall of the aorta, the major artery leaving the heart. And quite obviously it is serious."

"What causes it?" Annette now asked.

"A number of things, but usually aortic dissection occurs because of a tear or damage of some kind to the inner wall of the aorta. It usually happens in the chest portion of the artery, but can also occur in the abdominal portion," Dr. Chambers told them.

Annette nodded. "I understand, or at least I think I do. What you're saying is that my husband has a tear in his aorta, the main artery from the heart. Am I correct?"

"Yes, you are. Mr. Remmington has an eight-and-a-half-inch tear, rather a bad one I'm afraid. It is a diagonal tear."

"How is this treated?" Malcolm asked.

"First of all, we have to prevent complications, and that's why immediate hospitalization is required. A Type A aortic dissection requires surgery to repair the aorta, but a Type B aortic dissection can be treated with medication. That's what we are doing, Mrs. Remmington, treating your husband with medication."

"So it's Type B?" she asserted.

"Yes, it is."

"What caused it, do you know?" Malcolm interjected.

"High blood pressure, in my opinion. Mr. Remmington told me his physician had prescribed pills some time ago, but that he often forgot to take them. In the last hour his blood pressure had been going up and down like a yo-yo. We have to control that, and are doing so."

"Is he in pain?" Annette asked.

"He was earlier. What caused him to collapse were severe stabbing pains in his chest and then under his shoulder blades and on his back. But he's on strong painkillers, and, as I said, drugs that lower blood pressure are being given. He's more comfortable now."

"May we see him?" Annette looked at the doctor hopefully.

"He is in intensive care, but you can look in on him for a moment. If you'll both come with me."

Annette and Malcolm followed the doctor, and when they were shown into the IC unit Annette was immediately struck by Marius's pallor. He was asleep and he looked very ill to her, and she turned to the doctor. "Could he die?" she asked.

"We're not going to let such a thing happen, Mrs. Remmington. We're always very hopeful here."

"When should we come back?" Malcolm said. "Later this afternoon or tonight?"

"I think you should come back at six o'clock. He needs to stay quiet for the rest of the day. I think it's best to let him sleep at the moment. And he's in good hands here."

"Thank you very much, Dr. Chambers," Annette said, and Malcolm repeated her words.

"What do you think, Malcolm? Is he going to get better or not?"

"I think so. He's always been strong, very healthy. Did you know he had high blood pressure?"

"No, he never told me, and if I had known I would have made him take those pills."

"I know you would."

As they walked out of the hospital and got into the car, Malcolm said, "Listen, Annette, I need to talk to you about something. Can we go somewhere for a cup of coffee?"

"What's the matter? Is there something wrong?"

"I think I should say something has been wrong for a very long time, but I will let you be the judge of that when I've spoken to you at length."

"You sound very serious, Malcolm. Is it anything to do with Laurie? Or you and Laurie? Or your business?"

"None of those things."

"So it's about me then, is that it?" She gave him a pointed look, then frowned, looked down at her hands, thinking.

"It's not exactly about you, or I should say it's partially about you, but it's mostly about Marius."

"About his health?"

"No, not at all."

"Is it about that woman Elizabeth Grayson?"

Malcolm glanced at her swiftly, thinking how astute she was. She was already wondering how true the story was about a breakfast meeting to discuss a painting, just as he had done.

"No, it's not about her. Not at the moment anyway."

"I am now completely mystified, and also intrigued. Come on, explain. *Please.*"

"It's about a lot of things Jack has stumbled upon, that's the best way of putting it. Let me absolutely assure you he wasn't out looking for information."

"But he found some disreputable things about Marius, is that what you're trying to say?"

"That's only part of it."

"I trust Jack implicitly, Malcolm. I know he's a perfectly good man. And he would never intentionally hurt me, or anyone. So where shall we go for our chat? Obviously not to my apartment because Elaine's there. I prefer not to go to Laurie's because she's there. And Esther is in my office and Maeve in yours." She grimaced. "I know you want us to be very private, so that no one hears a thing except me. And Jack. That is what you want me to do, isn't it? You want me to go with you to Jack's flat."

"If you would, yes. It was my idea, not his, and we were actually planning to talk to you today, before Marius collapsed." He gave Jack's address to the driver, thinking how damned clever Annette was.

She nodded her agreement and looked out the window, her mind turning. This was not going to be good, she knew that instinctively. Jack had found out something by accident and needed her to know. She couldn't help wondering what he had found out about her.

Malcolm had phoned Jack from the car, and he was waiting for them when they arrived at the flat in Primrose Hill.

He greeted them with his usual geniality, but Annette noticed at once how tired he looked, with dark rings under his eyes.

"I know Marius is in hospital, Annette," Jack said immediately. "What's wrong with him?"

"He has an aortic dissection," she replied. "It's a tear in the major artery leaving the heart, and it's very serious, life-threatening."

"My God!" Jack exclaimed. "That's bad."

"It is, yes," she agreed, and went on. "I know you have stumbled on something about Marius and it's obviously important. Would you please tell me, Jack. I really do want to know. *Everything.*"

"I wasn't looking for dirt," Jack said quickly, "I really wasn't. You must believe that."

"I do." She went and sat down in a chair, and so did Malcolm.

Jack remained standing for a few moments, and explained. "Last week, when I was in France, I went up to have dinner with Lucy's aunt, Claudine Villiers, at her new villa on the grounds of Lucy's farm above Beaulieu. I'd never seen her art collection because it was in storage while she was building the villa. She had inherited it from her partner of forty years, after he died. But this fabulous collection, including works by Cézanne, Matisse, and Modigliani, all turned out to be forgeries."

Sitting down, he told her the entire story, leaving out nothing. When he had finished Annette simply nodded and sat back in the chair, looking profoundly sad.

Malcolm asked, "*Did* Marius own part of the Pegasus Gallery, or don't you know, Annette?"

"I think he did. I vaguely remember the name coming up once or twice."

"Jack discovered something else, Annette, but he is some-what reluctant to tell you. However, I do believe you must know the truth. Only by knowing everything will you ever be able to straighten your life out and move on."

"I understand, and you're right. Is it about me, Jack? Or Marius?"

"Not you, no. Last Tuesday morning I went over to La Réserve for breakfast. I was going through the bar and I heard a loud mobile ringing. I looked out at the garden on my right, and I saw Marius with a red-headed woman in a very intimate embrace." He stopped, staring at her, worried about her, worried how she would take it.

She understood this without him saying a word, and mur-mured, "Tell me the rest, Jack. It's really all right, I'm not upset."

"That's it, actually. I quickly left the bar. But I did man-age to find out that the woman's name was Elizabeth Lang, and also that they had checked out that morning after break-fast."

"I see. Lang rings a bell. I researched Clarissa Normandy the other day, and discovered that her maiden name was Lang. And that she came from Gloucestershire. What an odd coincidence that is, don't you think?"

Jack exclaimed, "The doorman at La Réserve told me that Elizabeth Lang was a painter. Wait a minute." Jack jumped up and went over to his landline. He dialed his aunt, and when she answered, he said, "Hello, Aunt Helen. Listen, something just struck me. The artist who was Marius's girl-friend, the one you mentioned yesterday. Was she called Clarissa Normandy?"

"Why yes, Jack, she was," his aunt replied. "However did you come up with this name?" His aunt sounded delighted that he had called her with this news.

"Something just clicked in my head. You wouldn't know if she had a sister by any chance, would you?"

"I believe she did. I remember Marius once complaining

that they had been lumbered with her over the weekend. She was younger than Clarissa, and he resented having to play babysitter. He was also angry with the girls' aunt, Glenda Joules. He told us this at a dinner your mother gave later that week. You certainly sparked my memory. I suddenly recall that both those girls had bright red hair. Goodness, Jack, you're taking me back years and years, to my lovely youth."

"Thanks, Aunt Helen. Got to go. Talk to you later."

Once he had hung up Jack repeated Helen's conversation, and then added, "Elizabeth Lang is a redhead. And now the circle begins to join up, doesn't it? Just imagine, Glenda Joules is their aunt. Glenda Joules of Knowle Court, I've no doubt at all."

"Neither have I," Annette said. "I always knew there was something suspicious about that housekeeper. She knows more than she's telling."

Jack sat down again. "If Marius was selling forgeries in the seventies, he could still be selling them now. It occurred to me that Clarissa might have worked for him then, and later when she was engaged to Sir Alec. Perhaps Elizabeth Lang is painting for him these days."

Malcolm said, "That makes sense, but would he have been selling them lately? I mean, why? He's rich."

"If he did sell forgeries, whether it was then or now, it's a criminal act," Annette said, her voice subdued. "He could go to jail."

"But only if someone tells the police, and who's going to do that?" Jack asked, looking at both of them.

"None of us," Malcolm answered.

"There's one other thing I need to tell you, Annette. I discovered through Claudine that my father was a friend of Marius's in those days. In the seventies. He was a well-known journalist. I'm talking about my biological father. His name was Nigel Clayton and—"

"Oh, my God!" Annette exclaimed, aghast, staring at Jack. "Your father was *Nigel Clayton*?" She sounded disbelieving and afraid.

"Yes, why?" He was looking at her intently, startled by

her tone, her sudden shrillness, and saw at once that she had turned deathly white. He also noticed that she had begun to shake so badly she was clutching the arms of the chair.

"Annette, Annette, whatever is it? What's wrong? Why are you reacting like this? *Tell me*." Jack got up, went to her. "You're so terribly upset, whatever is it?"

"Your father . . . he was the man who took me to La Réserve, he was my romantic interlude . . ."

Jack knelt down, just stared at her, dumbfounded.

Annette closed her eyes, unable to look at him. *Jack was Nigel Clayton's son.* The only other man she had ever loved. Or thought she had loved all those years ago . . . when she was eighteen. Oh, my God!

The decades fell away.

The horror of that awful night held her in its grip. She was there in the bedroom of the house in Notting Hill with Nigel, quarreling with him, struggling with him as he tried to force her to the bed.

"Nigel, let me go, I don't want this. I don't want to stay the night!" she cried, endeavoring to pull away. He tightened his grip, his hands like a vise on her arm. And as she looked into his face she was afraid. His eyes blazed with anger, and his mouth was contorted. She knew he'd been drinking before she arrived; drink made him cruel, and sometimes violent.

Grasping the arm of a chair, she pulled away from him, and as he continued to hold her she kicked his ankle, and he yelled and let go of her.

Fleeing the bedroom, she ran down the corridor and made it to the landing before he caught up to her, grabbed hold of her once more. Shouting that she was ungrateful, he slapped her across the face with some force.

Crying out in pain, and trembling with fear, she tried to punch him in the arm, but the blow hit the air. Her fear spiraled, and with every ounce of her strength she struggled, fought him, suddenly freed herself.

As she moved toward the staircase he lunged at her, lost

*his balance, and fell down the stairs, landing with a thud at
the bottom in the middle of the marble-floored hall.*

Her screams echoed in the silence of the house.

*She ran down the staircase to the hallway, where he lay,
not moving at all. There was blood close to his head, and in
his light-brown hair. Kneeling down, she took hold of his
hand, found his pulse. It was extremely faint, hardly a pulse
at all. And he was very still.*

*She knelt there for a few minutes, tears in her eyes, and
she was certain he was going to die any minute. Standing
up, she looked around, not knowing what to do. She was
suddenly terrified, filled with panic. She would be blamed
for his death. She knew she would be. She began to shake
uncontrollably, sobbing. . . .*

She opened her eyes and looked at Jack.

Malcolm went to the drinks tray in the kitchen and poured
a brandy, brought it back to her. She was still shaking and
looked as if she was about to pass out. But she wouldn't accept the drink, and muttered, "Oh, God. Oh, God."

Annette continued to stare at Jack, tears rolling down her
face. "I killed him," she said. "I didn't mean to kill him. We
had a fight, he fell down the stairs. It was an accident. Oh,
Jack—"

Without saying a word, Jack jumped up, grabbed hold of
her, and pulled her to her feet. He wrapped his arms around
her and held her close. "No, you didn't kill him, Annette.
You didn't. I believe I know what happened, I really do. It
wasn't you. Please believe me, darling, it wasn't you. You
didn't kill my father."

She began to sob and he held her until she became
calmer, and then he led her to the sofa, sat with her, still endeavoring to calm her.

Malcolm said, "I don't know about you, Jack, but I need
a cup of coffee." He rose, went into the kitchen, and filled a
mug, his head reeling.

When he came out of the kitchen, Annette had stopped
sobbing, and he said to her, "You told Marius, didn't you?

That's what he's had over you all these years, isn't it? You thought you'd killed Nigel, and you told him, because you'd nowhere else to turn. He was the only person who could protect you, and he did, I'll say that for him. But it *was* a form of blackmail, Annette, you must understand that."

"We quarreled, and Nigel hit me, and I saw red. Because I'd been abused by men throughout my childhood. I struggled with him and he slipped, fell down the stairs."

"And then what happened?" Jack asked quietly, holding her hand.

"I ran down the stairs. There was only a faint pulse. I was terrified. I was going to call for an ambulance, but I phoned Marius first. He told me to leave the house. He said that he would call the ambulance. And so I left."

"And the next day he told you Nigel was dead, didn't he?" Jack said.

Annette nodded. "Yes, he did."

"Let me tell you something I just heard this weekend. My aunt told me that she and my mother had gone to the Notting Hill house to get some of her possessions. They were the ones who found Nigel and called the ambulance. But my aunt confided something else to me on Saturday. And it's this. As she stood waiting for my mother to open the front door, she glanced down the street. She saw Marius getting into a cab. She recognized his silver hair, his profile, knew it was him."

"What are you saying, Jack?" Annette said, much calmer now.

"That when you left, Marius arrived. But he didn't call an ambulance. He more than likely hit my father on his head and killed him. My aunt said one of the doctors mentioned blunt force trauma really being the cause of death."

"Wasn't there an inquest?" Malcolm said.

"My aunt told me the jury brought in a verdict of accidental death."

Annette appeared to be truly shocked. "But Marius always let me believe I'd killed Nigel." She leaned back against the sofa and closed her eyes wearily, her face as white as bleached bone.

"My aunt will verify this, darling," Jack murmured, taking hold of her hand again.

"Whatever are we going to do?" Malcolm said, staring at Jack, a worried expression on his face.

"I hope nothing," Jack responded. "Marius is in the hospital with a life-threatening condition and could easily die. So what else is there to do but nothing?"

The three of them sat drinking coffee for a while. Annette and Malcolm were endeavoring to absorb the shock of Marius's collapse and wondering about the outcome, and Annette was also trying to come to terms with the revelation about Nigel being Jack's father.

Jack was sifting through his prior knowledge of the past, which had come to him from his mother, until he had talked with his aunt the other day. Now the story was almost complete.

He glanced across at Annette, and realizing she was much calmer, more collected, he said, "Did you know a young woman in those days called Hilda Crump?"

Annette was silent for a moment or two, and then nodded slowly. She cleared her throat and said, "I am Hilda Crump, Jack. That's my real name."

Jack gaped at Annette and so did Malcolm. The two men exchanged glances, but neither of them said a word. Malcolm drank some of his coffee, and Jack stood up, walked across the room, stood looking out the window for a few minutes, needing to absorb everything she had said.

It hardly seemed credible that this superbly elegant and beautiful woman who sat behind him on the sofa was Hilda Crump, whom his mother had described as a trollop or, conversely, a ragamuffin. But then he could not give credence to his mother any longer. His aunt had proved her to be a liar.

"Now I understand," Jack said, turning around, looking at her.

"What do you mean?" Annette whispered, sounding exhausted.

"My mother blamed Hilda Crump for the breakup of her marriage. Is that the truth?"

"No, it's not!" she exclaimed, sitting up on the sofa, a flicker of sudden anger in her eyes. "They were already separated, she had started divorce proceedings when I met him with Marius. I worked for Marius at the Remmington Gallery, and Nigel was always hanging around. Nigel . . . well, he sort of went after me. I fell for him, Jack. Then when he asked me to go to Beaulieu with him, to La Réserve, I couldn't resist. I thought I was in love with him. But I soon discovered that he became a bully, a bit nasty when he was drunk. I couldn't accept that. . . . I was abused when I was a child, and I always reacted if a man treated me badly."

She paused for a moment, as if remembering it all, her face taut, full of pain. She finished slowly, "That night when he died he'd been drinking earlier, and had become nasty. . . . I fought him off. You know the rest."

"I do." Jack looked off into the distance, as if seeing something unique, visible only to himself. And in a sense he was. He was envisioning Annette rushing to Marius for protection, a Marius most probably in love with her also, and full of jealousy. . . . Perhaps he saw a chance to rid himself of a rival? For a moment Jack thought he was being far-fetched, overly imaginative, and then he changed his mind. People did terrible things in the name of love, even resorted to murder.

Malcolm, who had done most of the listening, said to Annette softly, "Why did you change your name?"

"Because I didn't like it. I always wanted to be called Marie Antoinette. . . . Marius said it was too long, a mouthful, so I chose to be Annette . . . Watson. Laurie and I used our mother's maiden name." She shrugged lightly. "That's all there was to it. Nothing very complicated."

The three of them went on talking, mulling things over, unable to do much but wait things out until Marius recovered. It was Annette who finally stood up and said she wanted to leave, to go home and rest before visiting the hospital later.

Jack wanted to take her home, but she shook her head. "Malcolm has the car downstairs. I'll go with him. But thank you, Jack."

When she got home she told the housekeeper what had happened, and then retreated to her bedroom. After phoning Esther and filling her in about Marius, she stripped off her clothes and got in the shower. As the water ran down her she leaned against the tiled wall and wept. She cried until there were no tears left in her, and then she wrapped herself in a toweling robe and lay down on the bed.

The tears came once again, and the sorrow and the anger. She asked herself over and over again how Marius could have led her to believe for all these years that she had killed Nigel Clayton. He had been cruel, unconscionable.

She had always believed he was her savior, and that his protection of her was a form of love. Perhaps it was in his eyes, but she had been his captive and he had ruled her life. It was only because of her own willpower and strength of purpose that she had been able to break free. Partially. Quite suddenly, unexpectedly, she realized that for the first time in almost twenty-two years she *was* free. Because she knew the truth. Marius no longer had any hold on her.

Later that day Annette went to St. Thomas's Hospital with Malcolm and Laurie. They went straight up to the cardiovascular floor, and Dr. Chambers came out to see them.

Annette knew from the doctor's face that something was not right, and she asked swiftly, "Is my husband any better?"

"A little, but not as much as I expected, Mrs. Remmington." There was a slight pause, then he said, "His blood pressure has been rising dramatically and falling dramatically all day. But I think we finally have him stabilized."

"Can we see him?"

"Yes. He's suffering from confusion, disorientation, but that's not unusual with aortic dissection."

The doctor allowed Laurie to come with them in her wheelchair, but she remained in the doorway when Annette and Malcolm went in to see him.

Marius lay very still and his pallor was extreme. He opened his eyes, but when he saw them there was not a flicker of recognition, and he said nothing.

Annette bent over him, spoke to him, but he was totally mute, did not respond in any way. Malcolm followed suit, and again there was no reaction. They might not have been there.

They left the IC unit within minutes, and Dr. Chambers told them that Marius was behaving in much the same way with the nursing staff, although he had partially responded to some questions.

When they left the hospital Annette knew the prognosis was bad, and so did Malcolm and Laurie. They did not need a doctor to tell them that.

Several hours later Marius Remmington died. It was May 1 . . . May Day, as it was called.

Chapter Forty-three

That night, and for many nights after, Annette stayed with Laurie at her flat in Chesham Place. Quite simply, she did not want to be alone in her own flat in Eaton Square. There were too many memories there, and she felt Marius's presence most acutely even though he was dead.

One night, a few weeks after the funeral, Annette and Laurie talked long into the night, sifting through everything that had happened, analyzing things constantly, as they were prone to do. At one moment Annette exclaimed, "I just can't understand how he could be so cruel. To allow me to think I'd killed Nigel was reprehensible, unforgivable." She sounded angry again.

"Yes, it was. I agree with everything you say. But you can't dwell on it anymore, Annette. You must now let the past go. . . . You must live in the present, pick up the pieces, and start a new life. You must look to the future."

Annette stared at her sister. "I don't think I can let the past go. . . . There's so much pain inside me, and hurt and anger, so many emotions and feelings. A lot of damage has been done to me."

"You can let it go, and you will," Laurie insisted. "You're a survivor, Annette, and I know that extremely well. Remember, I know what you survived as a child."

Suddenly Annette sat up in the chair, a look of understanding settling on her face. Her voice was stronger, more positive, when she said, "If I could survive abuse and rape, poverty and deprivation, and so many losses over the years, then, yes, I can survive. I *can* put the past behind me. And let go of all of my bad thoughts about Marius! I can release all my anger. All I have to do is just let it go."

For the first time in weeks she smiled at Laurie. "I can start my life all over again. Because I am a survivor. . . . I've proved that already. If I can survive my terrible childhood, I can survive anything."

"Yes, you can!" Laurie agreed, filling with relief to see her sister's fighting spirit coming back.

"I will be reborn," Annette said. "I shall begin again."

And that is what she did.

The next few months were hard, but Annette persevered, managing to do her business and cope with her riotous emotions. Many feelings of anger, despair, hurt, and anguish invaded her, took over at times. Nonetheless, she had come through the storm, a little scathed yet still upright, facing the world with strength and confidence, standing tall.

She was well aware she had a number of people in her life she could not do without, and was grateful for; her sister and her friends who were loyal, supportive, and went beyond the call of duty every day. Laurie, Malcolm, and Jack were her rocks, her loving support system, and Esther was part of the team. There was Carlton Fraser and Marguerite, Jack's aunt Helen, and his brother, Kyle. They were her family now . . . the family she and Laurie never had. And she loved them all, and relied on them.

It was Malcolm and Jack who helped her to find out the truth about Marius's business. His assistant of thirty-five years, Agnes Dunne, was the only source of information. But she was willing to help them unravel everything because she needed them on her side. It was obvious to Annette that she knew so much about Marius's business that she was at risk, and did not want to be accused of helping him to sell fakes. Which, as it turned out, he had done, although mostly in the past. Apparently not so many had been put on the market in the last few years. His sources, several talented painters, had dried up.

Agnes led them to a couple in Gloucestershire who lived in two huge barns near Cirencester. Madeleine Tellier, the owner of the property, was married to a gifted artist, Raymond Tellier, originally from Grasse, in the south of France. It was he who had been supplying Marius for many, many years, along with Clarissa Normandy, and for a while, her sister, Elizabeth Lang.

According to Madeleine Tellier, her husband's paintings had been bought by museums, as well as by wealthy collectors, and everyone had been fooled by the fakes. He was that good, she had told them. Madeleine Tellier explained that Clarissa had specialized in Cézannes and Manets, and Elizabeth had proved masterful when painting in the style of Matisse, Braque, and Modigliani. But Elizabeth was no longer available and Clarissa, as they all knew, was dead.

On the day in late May when they visited Cirencester, Annette asked to meet Raymond Tellier. His wife took them into the barn where they lived, and introduced them to her husband. They all knew at once he would never paint again. He had been felled by a stroke eight years ago, and was now almost incapable of moving. He spent his life in a wheelchair. On that day Annette asked to see the forgeries which were left, but according to Madeleine there were none. They had all been sold, she said, and was adamant about this.

Since Agnes Dunne confirmed her story, Annette, Malcolm, and Jack had to accept it. The three of them hoped that somebody who had bought a Cézanne, a Manet, or a Picasso from Marius didn't suddenly discover that they had paid millions for a fake.

As for Christopher Delaware, Annette forced him to destroy the forgeries, which were still part of the Delaware collection. He finally agreed that she herself could do so when she threatened to resign as his art representative. James Pollard had made him agree to her proposal, she was convinced of that. She went down to Knowle Court with Malcolm and took a box cutter to the fake canvases, slashing them to pieces.

That same day, Annette also questioned Mrs. Joules, who admitted being the aunt of the two Lang girls, but denied she knew about any wrongdoing. Annette did not really believe her and told her that her nieces had painted forgeries for Marius Remmington.

Glenda Joules protested at first, but soon caved in under pressure.

"Come on, Mrs. Joules, I know you're lying," Annette exclaimed, her voice sharp. "If you don't tell me everything you know, I will go after Elizabeth Lang. I know where she lives in Barcelona, and everything about her, thanks to the excellent security and investigative firm I use in my art business. I'm also aware she was my husband's mistress, as indeed was Clarissa Normandy before her, and before he and I were married."

Recognizing that there was no point in lying any further, Glenda Joules said: "It's true, they did paint some of his fakes. But it was years ago, and it had nothing to do with me. I had no influence with them. I was angry about it."

"Tell me about Clarissa Normandy."

"She was beautiful, and a talented painter. I was furious that she wasted her talent and time painting those fakes for Marius. She wouldn't listen to me. She was besotted with him, and under his influence."

"Who was her husband?" Annette asked.

"She was never married."

"Where did the name Normandy come from?"

"She liked it. Chose to use it, that's all. Instead of Lang."

"Did she paint the Cézanne which was covered in soot? The one I've just destroyed?" Annette demanded.

"Yes. And when Sir Alec found out it was a fake, he threw the soot on it. He wanted to damage it so it could never be sold. After that things between them deteriorated, and he broke off his engagement to her." Glenda Joules shook her head, looked sorrowful when she added, "That's why Clarissa committed suicide, at least I think that's the reason. It was because Sir Alec dumped her, just as Marius had several years before."

Annette sighed, then asked, "Did she paint other Cézannes for Marius, which he then sold to Sir Alec?"

"Yes, that's true. She was clever, I told you that."

"Why didn't Sir Alec do anything about those fakes? Accuse Marius Remmington? Sue him to get his money back?"

"I don't know, but Sir Alec was already an eccentric, strange in so many ways. He was reclusive even when Clarissa was still alive. However, I believe he thought those new Cézannes were the real thing. Marius could be very convincing, and you know that."

"Did you know about the priest hole?" Annette gave her a hard stare. "Surely you did. You've worked here for years."

"I swear I didn't, Mrs. Remmington. But I did know Sir Alec took some paintings down from the gallery walls, stored them somewhere. I just wasn't sure where they were."

"You say that Sir Alec was odd before Clarissa's death. Did he really get worse, or is that part an invention?"

"It's the truth. He did become much worse, more reclusive than ever, extremely weird, and even a little demented. I thought Clarissa's suicide had really driven him round the bend. I looked after him as best I could."

Annette nodded, knowing that Glenda Joules had told her the truth. "I think this conversation should remain confidential, Mrs. Joules," Annette now said quietly. "I am not going to say anything to Mr. Delaware about Marius Remmington and the fakes. I shall let that remain a mystery. Nor shall I tell him that your nieces painted fakes for Marius. How does that sound to you?"

A look of relief settled on her face, and she exclaimed, "Thank you, Mrs. Remmington! I'm very grateful for your consideration. I wouldn't want to leave Knowle Court, I've lived here most of my life, and I like young Mr. Delaware. But what will you say about the Cézanne covered in soot? And won't he ask questions about our conversation?"

"I shall tell the truth about the soot-covered Cézanne,

and say that Clarissa sold it to Sir Alec. And later, when he
discovered it was a forgery, he ruined it himself. However, I
am not going to say anything about the other fakes. What
does it all matter now? Sir Alec is dead, as is Clarissa. And,
as you no doubt know, Mr. Remmington died in hospital
recently. And actually there's no proof that he sold paintings
to Sir Alec. It's all finished, as far as I'm concerned. Remember, by not going into any more details you are out of
the picture, exonerated, Mrs. Joules. Not that you did anything wrong—you just didn't tell Mr. Delaware what you
know."

"I see the sense in everything you're saying, Mrs. Remmington. And I thank you. This conversation is between us.
I shall never repeat it."

Annette nodded, left the kitchen, and went back to the
library, where Christopher, Jim Pollard, and Malcolm were
waiting for her. She repeated Mrs. Joules's story about the
ruined Cézanne, and how Sir Alec had damaged it to prevent it from ever being sold. She then explained that he had
been angry with Clarissa for bringing him a fake, and had
broken off the engagement. And this was the reason she
had killed herself. She did not mention that Clarissa was
Mrs. Joules's niece.

They had accepted the story, and for once Christopher
Delaware had very little to say.

On the drive back to London, Annette suddenly exclaimed
at one moment, "I just can't believe that Marius, of all people,
would deal in forgeries, Malcolm. He who so revered art
and the great painters. It's just unbelievable to me. What a
terrible hypocrite he was."

Malcolm, who was driving, was silent for a while, and
then he said, "I thought I knew Marius so well, and yet now I
realize I never knew him at all. He has become the biggest
mystery in the world to me. He taught me so much about art,
and taught you, too, Annette, and he was brilliant, dedicated,

and so knowledgeable. But he was a crook, wasn't he?"

"I'm afraid so," Annette responded. "Among other things."

That evening, alone in the flat in Eaton Square, Annette sat for a long time thinking, her mind focused on Marius and his criminal activities, which is what they were. His behavior was incomprehensible to her; she just couldn't get her mind around it.

He had loved art, just as much as she did, and yet he had denigrated himself and the great painters he so admired by having others paint forgeries of their work. *Why?*

Could it have been for the money? That was the only reason she could think of; lots of money would permit him to maintain a mistress. Or mistresses? Elizabeth Lang couldn't have been the only one. There must have been others before her.

It suddenly struck Annette that Marius had betrayed himself and everything he was, betrayed her, in the sense that he had instilled in her the importance of art and the great masters, and had then gone and sold *fakes*. Marius had no integrity, no ethics, and he had been a hypocrite, as she had told Malcolm earlier in the day. *He had been a thief.* He had stolen the talent of those great master painters, had shown them nothing but disdain.

This thought chilled her to the bone, and she suddenly understood why she had been unable to mourn him. . . . She had lost respect for him, and whatever love she had had for him was gone. The terrible truth about him had shattered the image she had of him, and of who she believed him to be.

She felt nothing but contempt for him now, and she knew this would never change.

The following few weeks were busy for Annette as she and Malcolm endeavored to understand Marius's art business, and close it down. Fortunately, Marius had done legitimate business, and Annette was relieved to discover that it was in

the black. However, there was not much money in the bank
account of Remmington Art Ltd. Nor were there any papers
about forged paintings. On the other hand, she had not expected to find any. Marius was too smart to leave incriminating evidence floating around.

Agnes Dunne was as helpful as she could be, and Annette
began to realize that this woman, who had devoted herself to
Marius for over thirty years, did not have much understanding of what had really been going on. Marius, duplicitous as
usual, had kept her in the dark most of the time, had only allowed her to know about things which were relatively innocuous. Seemingly, Agnes was aware that a few fakes had been
sold in the past, but had no idea of the scale of it. And she did
not know about the Pegasus Gallery in Paris.

Both Annette and Malcolm were relieved that Agnes was
not so well informed, since they did not want anything to
leak out. Only a few people who were unlikely to talk knew
about the forgeries which were sold by Marius . . . plus
themselves, Laurie, and Jack. Not even Carlton Fraser, who
was a close friend and colleague, had any idea about the real
situation and Marius's culpability.

"It's best to keep everything under wraps," Malcolm said
to her one afternoon, when they were having a meeting at
Annette's office. "All we need is someone going to the Art
and Antiques Squad at Scotland Yard and chattering about
Marius Remmington and fakes. Besides, we only know about
the few Christopher Delaware had in his possession. The
others are floating around in oblivion, according to Madeleine Tellier, and she's not going to talk since her husband
was the forger. Everyone else is dead. End of story."

"Yes, thank God," Annette murmured, and then lowering
her voice, she said, "I haven't found the manuscript of the
Picasso book, nor has Agnes. Since it's not at the flat and not
at his office, then where is it, Malcolm?"

"God only knows. . . . Maybe there is no book. Maybe he
was lying about it, using it as a ruse to keep flying around
the world to the Picasso Museum in Barcelona, to Provence,
where Picasso lived for such a long time, and God knows

where else. Announcing that he was researching Picasso's life was a wonderful front, wasn't it? Perhaps it was a cover for him . . . to see Elizabeth Lang."

"Or to visit his secret Spanish partner, Rafael Lopez, who I just recently found out about through the security firm I use. Kroll Associates are the best. Marius and Rafael had been in business for years, apparently, but I never knew it, nor did I ever meet Rafael Lopez. He usually does business out of an art gallery in Madrid, but I discovered he also has an office in Barcelona."

"Are you planning to go and see him?"

Annette shook her head. "No, I don't want to know any more than I already do. Who knows what those two got up to? It seems the relationship was an old one. They'd been partners for years. I'm better off if I stay far away."

Malcolm agreed with her and she never mentioned Lopez again.

By the middle of June, Annette knew she finally had things under control as far as Marius's art business was concerned. She breathed a sigh of relief. Then almost before she could blink, it was the day of the wedding, the happiest event for them all in recent months.

Laurie and Malcolm were married at Malcolm's family home, where his parents, Andrew and Alicia Stevens, were the hosts. Laverly Court was a lovely Georgian manor house in Suffolk, with beautiful gardens and an ornamental lake. The local vicar came to officiate at the old manor, which was a local stately home full of mellow antiques and a collection of superb art.

On this July Saturday the house brimmed with urns of roses and other cut flowers, their varied scents filling the air with their mingled fragrances.

Later, whenever Annette thought of their marriage on that glorious summer's day, she smiled with genuine happiness for her sister and Malcolm, knowing they were true soul mates.

Laurie's face was full of radiance, and she had never looked so lovely. She was wearing a cream satin wedding gown with a headband of orange blossoms in her red hair; Malcolm was a handsome bridegroom in his morning suit, with a gray silk tie, and a white rose pinned on his lapel.

Malcolm had asked Jack to be his best man, and it was Annette who gave her sister away. Walking next to Laurie in her wheelchair, Annette accompanied her through the living room, where their guests were seated, and down to the fireplace. It was here that the Reverend Sturges stood with the bridegroom and best man. Annette felt her heart clench when she stepped aside for Malcolm, who reached for Laurie's hand and held it tightly in his, a loving smile on his face.

All of their mutual friends had come to the wedding. Jack's brother, Kyle, with his assistant, Carole, to whom he had just become engaged. Jack's aunt Helen, Carlton and Marguerite, and Ted Underwood, that other great restorer. Annette's assistant, Esther, and Laurie's caregiver, Angie, were also present, along with Mrs. Groome, Laurie's housekeeper. Margaret Mellor from *ART* magazine mingled with Christopher Delaware, James Pollard, and countless others from the art world.

On this day, when she saw Laurie married to a most honorable and devoted man, Annette understood that this was the fulfillment of a childhood dream for her. Her little sister was truly safe at last and would be always.

After their honeymoon in Italy, the newlyweds came back to settle in Malcolm's handsome flat in Cadogan Square, to await the birth of a baby. They already knew it was going to be a girl, and it was the most anticipated event, with everyone's excitement running high for weeks.

Annette and Malcolm were on tenterhooks until after the delivery early in November. The child was born by Caesarean section, and she was absolutely perfect, and Laurie was not only well, but ecstatic.

"We're going to call her Josephine," Laurie told Annette a few days after the birth, smiling at her sister. "Actually, her full name is Josephine Annette Alicia Stevens. Alicia in honor of Malcolm's mother."

Annette, overflowing with gratitude and happiness, instantly choked up, unable to say a word as she hugged her sister tightly in her arms.

But she made up for this on the day of the christening later in November, at the reception afterward. This was held at the Dorchester Hotel in Mayfair. Asking Laurie and Malcolm if she could hold the baby, she walked around the Orchid Room, showing her happily gurgling niece to everyone. She was as proud as if the child were her own.

"Look at her little puff of red hair," she said to Carlton and Marguerite. "And her eyes are exactly the same color as Laurie's," she pointed out to Kyle. "But she has Malcolm's mouth and broad brow, don't you think?" she murmured to Malcolm's mother, and everyone agreed with her.

Jack, who stood watching her on the other side of the room, was thrilled that Annette was so outgoing on this happy afternoon, more like herself at last. It was as if she had finally managed to put the difficult months behind her. She looked especially beautiful in a delphinium-blue silk suit, a string of large South Sea pearls lustrous against her creamy skin.

Striding over to join her, putting his arm around her, he said, "Everybody's thrilled to see you looking so happy today. And most especially me."

"I am happy, Jack," she responded as they slowly walked toward Laurie and Malcolm seated across the room.

Once she had handed the baby back to her doting father, Jack led Annette over to a quiet corner. He took two flutes of Dom Pérignon from a passing waiter and handed her one. Touching his glass to hers, he said, "Your pain is finally fading, isn't it?"

"Yes," she murmured, and took a sip of the champagne. "But sometimes I get an unexpected little jolt and remember all those years. I don't know why he was so cruel, holding me captive with such a wicked lie."

"That was the past, and the past is behind you," Jack said.

"It's gone." He looked into her heart-stopping blue eyes, now filling with tears, and shook his head. "Hey," he whispered gently. "No tears today." Taking hold of her arm, he turned her slightly. "Look over there at your little niece. She's a brand-new person on this planet. She has no past, only a future."

Annette nodded. "And she has her whole life ahead of her."

"And so do you, Annette," Jack answered. "A wonderful life, a life you never even dreamed was possible."

Epilogue

✳

LONDON, DECEMBER 2007

❋

Annette Remmington stood in front of the long mirror in her dressing room, considering her dress, not certain if it worked for her.

It was made of black velvet and was a short, straight sheath with a V neckline and long sleeves. Very severe, she thought, perhaps too somber. No, she suddenly decided, it's exactly right for tonight. Proper but chic. She reached for the pearl earrings with a small diamond drop and put them on. They were exactly right.

She wore no other jewelry except for an antique Cartier watch. Her hands were ringless. She had discarded her wedding ring long ago, had simply dropped it down a drain on Bond Street one day, in a moment of anger and disgust.

Stepping back, she regarded herself full length, liking the sheer, dusty-black hose and the high-heeled black silk pumps.

I'll do, she muttered under her breath, and went into the drawing room. She still lived in the same flat in Eaton Square, although it looked different now. She had changed everything, removed all traces of Marius. It was hers and reflected her taste in colors and in the art on the walls.

She glanced around, thinking how tranquil the drawing room was with its mixture of creams and whites, touches of deep pink and green in the cream-and-black Savonnerie carpet and the cushions on the sofas. The paintings were shown to perfection on the cream-silk-covered walls. Pink silk shades on the porcelain lamps and a fire burning brightly in the hearth added a lovely roseate glow.

Standing in front of the fire, Annette marveled that this day had actually arrived. In May she had asked Sotheby's to postpone her auction of Impressionist paintings and *The Little Fourteen-Year-Old Dancer* from the Delaware collection. The company was understanding of her many problems and agreed to hold it in December. It was now December 4, and in a short while the auction would begin. Expectations were high.

Tonight she was facing the world . . . the art world in particular. The publicity about the auction had been extraordinary, and she prayed that everything would go well. She could not afford to fail.

The ringing of the doorbell told her it was almost time to leave, and she hurried to open it, a smile already on her face.

Jack was standing there, looking impossibly handsome, smiling broadly. "Don't you look smashing!" he said, smiling at her, kissing her lightly on the cheek.

They walked into the drawing room, and he glanced around, spotted the pink roses on a table, and nodded to himself. She noticed this, and said, "Thank you again, Jack. The flowers are lovely."

"To wish you luck," he said. "Although *you* don't need it."

"Don't say that, I'm superstitious!"

He merely smiled and walked over to the drinks table, where a bottle of red wine had been opened. "Is this for me?"

"Just for you. I'm not having anything to drink before the auction," she said.

"Just a sip," he said. "I want to toast you."

"Oh, all right then."

Jack and she clinked glasses. "May this be the greatest auction ever." He grinned at her. "Until the next one."

Annette put her glass down and went over to the desk, took an old leather box out of a drawer, and came back to the fireplace where Jack was standing. She showed the box to him, opened the lid. "I'm ready to wear this now, Jack. If you still want me to, that is."

He took the box from her and looked at the diamond engagement ring, shook his head. "No, I don't."

Taken aback, she stared at him. "Oh," was all she said, her smile slipping.

Jack placed the old box on the coffee table, put his hand in his pocket, brought out a much newer red leather box. He opened it and took out a ring. "I would prefer you to wear this, Annette," he said quietly. "My mother's marriage didn't last, and maybe her ring is unlucky. For us. Because of its history. Please wear mine. And be mine, will you?"

Annette nodded, swallowing her tears. She found it hard to speak for a moment and simply put out her left hand. Jack took hold of it, slipped the ring on her third finger, and said, "This is your color, darling. I hope you like it."

She looked down at her hand and saw a square-cut aquamarine surrounded by diamonds glittering on her engagement finger. "Oh, Jack, it's beautiful. Thank you, thank you."

"It's the exact color of your eyes," he said, and kissed her cheek. "So put that other ring away, and keep it for another girl, a little girl who might come along one day, and who will grow up to treasure her grandmother's ring, perhaps."

"Oh, Jack, darling," was all she could say, touched by these words.

He took her arm, walked across the room with her. When they reached the door, he released her, took a velvet shawl from a chair, put it around her shoulders, and handed her the black evening bag.

"It's your big night, darling," he said. "Are you ready to go to the auction?"

"Yes, I am."

"Excited?"

"Yes."

"Afraid?"

"No, I'm not, Jack."

He smiled at her. "That's my girl," he said with pride.

She looked back at him and thought: Yes, that's me. *I am his girl*. And I always will be.

Author's Note

The long-lost Rembrandt, a portrait of a woman, which is featured in this novel does not exist in reality. I took literary license and invented it for the dramatic purpose of the story. In the novel, Annette Remmington, on behalf of the owner, consigns the painting to Sotheby's in London to be auctioned. It fetches $33.2 million.

This is by no means an exaggerated price and is based on my research on prices reached for great art between the years 2000 and 2010. Here are some of the most recent prices paid for masterpieces.

In December 2009, a similar painting by Rembrandt *did* sell for $33.2 million at an auction held by Christie's in London. In February 2010, Sotheby's in London auctioned a Giacometti sculpture which went for the staggering price of $104.3 million. A few months later, in May 2010, Christie's in New York sold a Picasso for $106.5 million, making it one of the most expensive artworks ever sold at a public auction. Not long after this huge sale, in June 2010, a Manet auctioned by Sotheby's in London brought $33 million.

Most art experts believe that art by the great master painters of the seventeenth, eighteenth, nineteenth, and twentieth centuries are the most tangible of assets, even when there are dramatic shifts in the economy. But of course the works of art must be by the great masters if they are to reach these enormous prices.

Bibliography

Gordon, Dillian. *100 Great Paintings: Duccio to Picasso.* London: National Gallery, 1981.

Gordon, Robert, and Andrew Forge. *Monet.* New York: Harry Abrams Inc., 1983.

Huffington, Arianna Stassinopoulos. *Picasso: Creator and Destroyer.* New York: Simon and Schuster, 1988.

Irving, Clifford. *Fake! The Story of Elmyr de Hory: The Greatest Art Forger of Our Time.* New York: McGraw-Hill, 1969.

Lévy, Lorraine. *Picasso.* Introduction by Pierre Daix. Translation from the French by Barbara Beaumont. New York: Henry Holt, 1991.

O'Neill, John, editor in chief. *Degas: Catalogue of the Degas Retrospective at the Metropolitan Museum of Art, New York.* New York: The Metropolitan Museum of Art, 1989.

Pach, Walter. *Renoir.* London: Thames and Hudson, 1984.

Rewald, John. *Cézanne.* New York: Harry Abrams Inc., 1986.

———. *The History of Impressionism.* New York: The Museum of Modern Art, 1973.

Richardson, John. *A Life of Picasso.* Volume 1: New York: Random House, 1991. Volumes 2 and 3: New York: Alfred A. Knopf, 1996, 2007.

Salisbury, Laney, and Sujo Aly. *Provence: How a Con Man*

and a Forger Rewrote the History of Modern Art. New York: Penguin, 2009.

White, Barbara Ehrlich, editor. *Impressionism in Perspective.* Englewood Cliffs, N.J.: Prentice-Hall, Inc., 1978.

———. *Impressionists Side by Side: Their Friendships, Rivalries and Artistic Exchanges.* New York: Alfred A. Knopf, 1996.

———. *Renoir: His Life, Art and Letters.* New York: Abradale Press, Harry Abrams Inc., 1988.